The Napoleon
Of Egypt

A.R. Duckworth

THE NAPOLEON OF EGYPT

)

The King and Her Children

Hatshepsut, the Pharaoh's daughter, finds and adopts an abandoned infant when she is still a child herself, and does not understand the enormity of her action.

By rescuing this boy, Hatshepsut finds love in an otherwise loveless existence. He becomes the core of her life and watching him grow into a man of extraordinary ability makes her audacious.

Her ambition for him drives her to seize the throne, becoming the king Egypt needs, so she can raise him to rule the proudest Empire on earth.

But who is this man, and does he have an identity better known beyond the borders of Egypt?

Hatshepsut and Senenmut are well known figures in Egyptian history, and while it has fallen to me to paint the story of their lives where it has been lost, these are people who once lived and breathed.

A Dedication

For all the friends who have helped me, and all the readers who love this
fascinating history,
as I do.

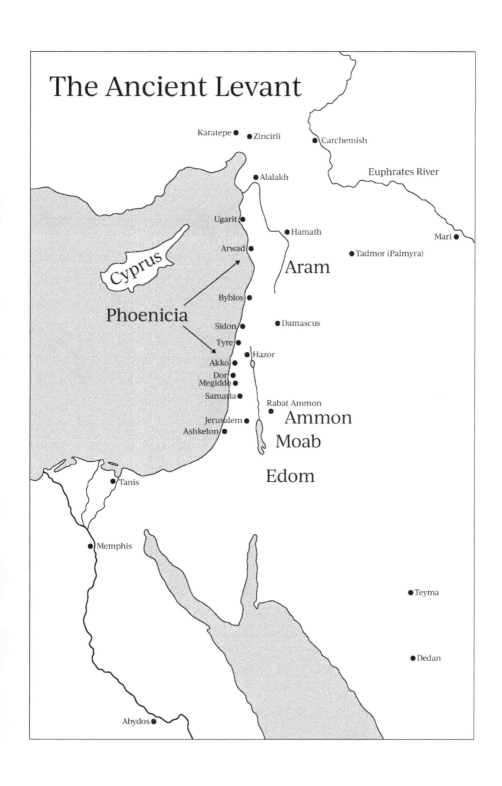

The Ancient Levant

Karatepe ● ●Zincirli

●Carchemish

Euphrates River

●Alalakh

Ugarit ●

●Hamath

Mari ●

Arwad ●

Cyprus

Aram

●Tadmor (Palmyra)

Byblos ●

Phoenicia

Sidon ●   ●Damascus

Tyre ●

●Hazor

Akko ●

Dor ●

Megiddo ●

Samaria ●

Rabat Ammon
●

Ammon

Jerusalem ●

Ashkelon ●

Moab

Edom

●Tanis

●Memphis

●Teyma

●Dedan

Abydos ●

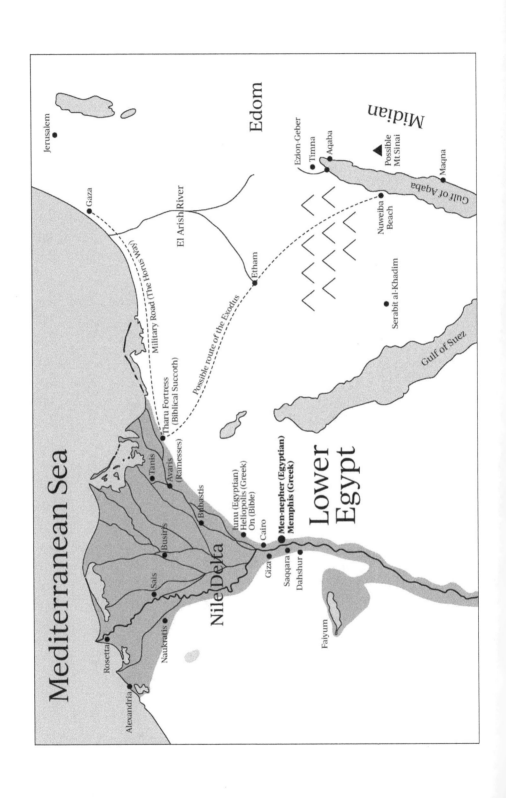

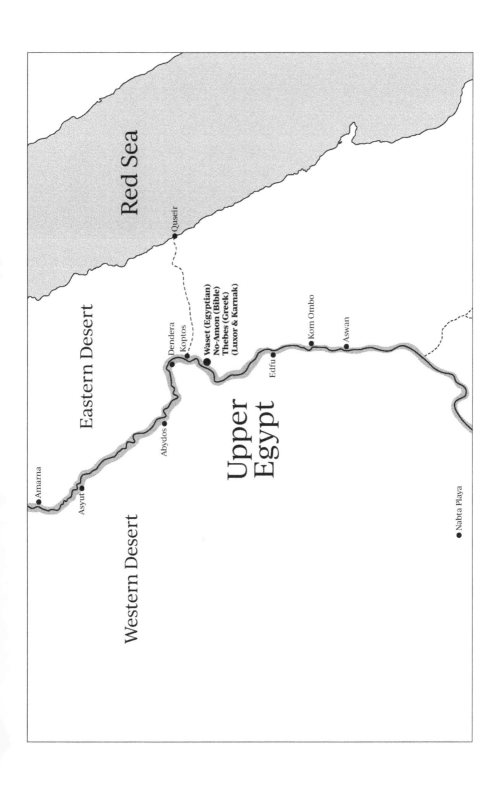

CHAPTER 1

PHARAOH TUTMOSE III; 1481 BC

THE AIR WAS COOL IN the stillness of the predawn. The young Pharaoh surveyed the track stretching ahead of him in the half light as a momentary panic filled his mind. He must practice. He must practice and practice again. The rumours reaching him from Canaan had proved true. With the death of his stepmother, the Pharaoh Hatshepsut, rebellion was afoot in the city of Megiddo where both the Canaanites and their northern allies were gathering. War was upon him! Time to show himself worthy to bear the name and title of his grandfather, the first Tutmose. Egypt's greatest warrior. He must lead his army to war and for that, his skill as a charioteer was paramount.

He had built this track years ago, in his feeble youth when he held no power, in the heyday of Hatshepsut who had shared his throne for the past 22 years and taken to herself the running of the whole country.

The light was growing, and he looked out across the practice ground as fear seized him again. He was alone! Egypt's sole Pharaoh! And he alone must lead the army against the enemies massing in the north.

Tutmose understood the craft of war. He understood strategy. He had been trained, although physically he was not a natural soldier. But now the whole weight of his family dynasty, the future of Egypt rested on his young shoulders. At 25 years old, just 10 years since his coming of age, he was Egypt's sole ruler. He could no longer rely on the courage and resourcefulness of Hatshepsut. He would rise or fall by the decisions he made, and he must make them alone.

The track stretched away from him, away from the palace, away into the pale light, and in the distance cut an arc as it curved back on the long return to complete the circuit. He must work. Behind him, blocking access to the thoroughfare of the river lay the palace itself, which had been expanded by his family since they came to power 50 years ago. To his right rose the high perimeter wall of the great Temple of Amun. Here he would be unobserved. He must train. No day was free of it. He turned to his bodyguard.

"I will drive. Wait here."

The man stepped down from the chariot. Tutmose grasped the reins and moved the horses forward as thoughts continued to circulate in his mind. Mounting a chariot always reminded him of the man who had trained him, and against his will his thoughts turned to Senenmut his half-brother, the man who had made a soldier of him. The man who also had a claim to his throne. The man he had idolised. The man he now hated!

It had always been known that Senenmut was not Hatshepsut's natural child. At 15 she was married to her brother, the second Tutmose, becoming his Great Royal Wife. But she had adopted Senenmut long before, when she was little more than a child herself, living in the harem at Men-nepher[1]. It was assumed that the child was born of a royal liaison in the harem, and no one cared to enquire as to the details. Hatshepsut had adopted him and fiercely maintained that he was now her child, but it mattered little. Senenmut should be no threat to the Pharaonic line. The Pharaoh would have a son and the line would pass from the Pharaoh to his son. But the second Tutmose died after a reign of only 12 years leaving his wife Hatshepsut with a single daughter. However, the Pharaoh did have a son. In the last years of his life, he had sired a boy with a harem woman, and this child, he himself, the third Tutmose was made Pharaoh. He needed a Regent, and Hatshepsut was the obvious choice. As a royal heiress herself, she was best placed to maintain the interests of the royal house, and the young Pharaoh would have the benefit of her wisdom and protection throughout his minority. And so it proved, but for one important and unexpected change.

The sound of the chariot wheels cutting the sand of the track broke into his reverie. Tutmose loved that sound. The sound that had challenged him in his feeble youth. The sound that had spurred him on, forcing his body to work until he could control the machine beneath his feet and the highly-strung stallions fighting him at every turn. Driving always freed his mind as if he became two persons. As if the control of his body could become separated from his mind, leaving it free.

All of Egypt was taken by surprise when, with the support of the High Priest of Amun, Hatshepsut took the extraordinary step of making herself Pharaoh. She did not depose her nephew. That was not necessary. It was a common practice to have two Pharaohs reigning together when an elderly Pharaoh wished to secure his choice of heir by creating a joint reign. That was normal. But to create a Senior Pharaoh over a child who was already reigning, was not. A Regency period normally sufficed. But of course, reasons were given for this action. The child was not strong and may not live, then with a Senior Pharaoh in place, Ma'at[2] would be maintained and the country kept stable. But as time passed it became clear that Hatshepsut had another reason for taking the throne.

Tutmose breathed deeply of the clean morning air, as his gaze moved beyond the level ground before him, out to the line of the eastern horizon. How strange life was. How strange the turn of events that had brought him to this point. Despite his sickly childhood[3], despite the covert schemes to remove him as Pharaoh, he had survived.

Hatshepsut had been limited to the role of Great Royal Wife of the King, until his death. But with his death, she was free to make her move. And she was a wealthy woman, inheriting a large income from her mother. Money talks, and the High Priest of Amun was pleased to support a plan that would bring wealth and prestige to his Temple.

By the time Hatshepsut took the throne, Senenmut, her adopted son was 16 years old, and had grown into a remarkable young man. Hatshepsut had seen first-hand a successful Pharaoh in her father, and an unsuccessful Pharaoh in her husband/brother[4] and knew what it took to rule Egypt. Maybe she saw in the child Tutmose a worrying lack of potential. Or was her decision more calculating? Either way, as time passed, with the support of the High Priest of Amun, the child known as her adopted son was groomed for the throne. Indeed, he was the only royal child for the first 13 years of his life, before Hatshepsut's own daughter was born, and it was not until he was 16 that this new Pharaoh, this third Tutmose was born in the harem at Men-nepher. Before that time, the fact that Senenmut was the only heir, posed no threat to anyone. It was only when the child Tutmose was born that Senenmut realised his mother's loyalty was now divided. She did not want her husband's child to usurp her adopted son. With her husband's death, although the infant was crowned, she made her move. As Regent she could not pass the throne to Senenmut, but as Pharaoh she could! And this was her plan.

Tutmose could see it all so clearly now. From the time of her husband's death, Hatshepsut had worked to put Senenmut on the throne. But Senenmut himself refused![5] He refused to be party to a plan that required the killing of a child. And from that point on refused to be known as Hatshepsut's son, an astonishing move, with the result that Tutmose was neither deposed nor murdered. So why did Tutmose carry this deep hatred for his brother?

The young king watched the sky lighten along the line of the horizon. He would drive this first leg of the track before the sun broke through, then turn his back on Ra's piercing rays as they woke the new day. Driving always cleared his mind and helped him think. But his thoughts turned again to Senenmut and immediately his mind was torn. Senenmut was the man who could have taken his throne, but instead had befriended him! And if love was something that gave of itself, then certainly Senenmut had loved him. Tough love, training him to be a man. Training him to lead the army. But Tutmose flung the thought away as fear entered his heart. And maybe his hatred of Senenmut was in fact fear. For no one had ever dreamed that Senenmut was of slave blood! How could a royal princess adopt a slave child? And worse. An Habiri[6] slave, the most feared of them all! The Habiri's origins were in Retanu[7], the homeland of the Hyksos[8], the very same people who had invaded Egypt. If Senenmut had gained power in Egypt, would the Hyksos return? Egypt would be destroyed! But Senenmut was finally unmasked and his loyalty to the slaves ran deep. There was clear evidence. He had killed an Egyptian to save a Habiri slave. It spoke for itself. He was forced to flee Egypt. No, Senenmut could not be trusted.

Tutmose's thoughts returned to the present with relief. At least that danger was past. Senenmut was gone and he himself was now sole Pharaoh. The undisputed Pharaoh. But where was Senenmut now? Hatshepsut with whom he had shared the throne all through his childhood and youth, was dead and buried. She could no longer support Senenmut's claim. His mind ran over the facts as he waited for dawn to break. He did not hate her, as his High Priest would like to persuade him. But he had feared her. Yes, and he feared her Ka[9] still. But she had failed in her quest to put Senenmut on the throne. The gods had made their choice, and now he alone was ruler of Egypt.

Tutmose drove the chariot with all his strength the length of the track. He would soon make the turn. The sky in the east had turned to gold and the light was growing with each passing moment. Soon Ra would break forth to greet him. The great Sun god, rising to greet the young Pharaoh, himself a god. The track curved beneath his wheels, turning the chariot, and at that moment, the brilliance of Ra struck the pinnacles of the Temple obelisks to his right with a blaze of blinding light. The hymn of the Lector Priest[10] rang out in the silence of the dawn, welcoming the great god back to the world of men. Ra, the powerful, the visible god, greeting Amun, the 'Hidden One' in their temple at Karnak.

But as he watched, another thought invaded the king's mind, scattering his elation and pride, for he knew in his heart that he was lacking the ultimate thing required for kingship, 'Solar blood'. The blood of the royal line descending from Ra himself, which he did not carry. True Kings of Egypt were the descendants of the gods. But neither his father nor his grandfather and certainly not his mother, none of them carried the 'Solar blood'. Hatshepsut had carried it, from her mother, and passed it to his half-sister, but not he.

Suddenly he did not want to see the dawn, to see Ra rise in all his splendour. He would drive no more today. He would return to his apartments and set his mind to plan the military expedition into Canaan. He did not want to be reminded of his deficiency.

The palace felt dreary as he returned. Too many old servants from his stepmother's reign. He would remove them. He would make changes inside the Palace as well. But a sudden weariness enveloped him, and he wandered back to his apartment and found his couch. His body still had moments of the weakness he had known in childhood. He lay down and closed his eyes. His body may be weary, but his mind was clear.

There was a way, he remembered, to right the deficiencies of his birth. Now that his stepmother was dead, she could no longer prevent his marriage to his half-sister Nepherure. He had always wanted Nepherure. She inhabited that secret place in his mind when all other thoughts had run their course. And she was truly Royal. She would give him a son of the Solar blood. And with her as his consort, as his Great Royal Wife, her Solar blood would confirm his Kingship and make up all that was lacking in himself. It was some months now since his young wife Satiah had died soon after their marriage, leaving him one son, his heir. But she was not royal. Now he could take Nepherure as his Great Royal Wife, then not even his own heart would question his right to the throne.

Tutmose rang the silver bell beside his couch to summon a servant.

"Bring wine and bread," he said, "I am hungry." The man moved swiftly to carry out the King's orders. Tutmose lay back. The feeling of general malaise had left him, he would be well again when he had eaten. Then he would send for his Generals. He was especially interested to hear General Djehuty's[11] opinion. Of all his generals Djehuty was the man whose opinion mattered. He understood strategy. He would give good advice. And they must respond swiftly to the rebellion in Canaan. Who could know if Senenmut was not aiding the rebellion? He had been known and revered both inside and outside Egypt as Hatshepsut's adopted son. With his help Hatshepsut had kept Egypt's subject nations, Kush to the south and Canaan to the north-east under control. Now Canaan was rebelling, and the spies reported that Egypt's greatest enemy, Naharin[12] itself, was supporting the rebellion. Reports were still arriving, but if Megiddo could outwit Egypt, rebellion would spread like wildfire. Other Canaanite cities would cast off the yoke of their overlord, and Egypt would lose the rich revenues that came to her from Canaan.

---

[1] Memphis

[2] Ma'at; the correct order of the universe; justice

[3] There are strong arguments to suggest that Tutmose lll was a sickly child.

[4] Hatshepsut had married her half-brother Tutmose ll as was normal in the royal family.

[5] The Book of Hebrews 11 v 24 in the Bible states that 'when he came of age, Moses refused to be called the son of Pharaoh's daughter.'

[6] Habiri is another name used for the Hebrews

[7] Ancient Syria

[8] The invaders of Egypt expelled by the New Kingdom Pharaohs

[9] The Ka was the spirit of a person that survived death

[10] The Lector priest recited spells and hymns during temple rituals.

[11] Djehuty is an historical character.

[12] Naharin was Egypt's great enemy in the time of Tutmose lll. It was more than a city state. It ruled a large area in eastern Syria straddling the Euphrates. Egyptologists often use the name, 'Mittani', for this state instead, but in Egyptian records the same name is used as in the Bible, Naharin. It is mentioned in the NIV Bible in Genesis 24 v 10.

CHAPTER 2

SENENMUT ESCAPES EGYPT

AGAINST ALL THE ODDS, SENENMUT escaped. His knowledge of Egypt carried him safely to the border. His understanding of men held open the last trap from closing around him. He was free. Free of Egypt. But to what end? Behind him lay his home, his identity, his standing, his purpose! And as his horses' hooves pounded the ground beneath him, every moment carrying him further out into the night, a scream started raging in his mind.

'Turn back! Return and fight! Stand up to your betrayers! Better die fighting than live a fugitive!'

Never had Senenmut imagined Tutmose's duplicity. Others may want to be rid of him, but surely not his brother. Why, when he had long since removed himself as a rival for the throne? He could never have taken the throne at the cost of destroying Tutmose. He would have served the lad well, steering Egypt through Tutmose's reign, just as he had served Hatshepsut. But while Senenmut did not look for treachery, his enemies acted. The old High Priest of Amun had done his work well. As soon as it was known that Senenmut was Habiri by birth, Menkheperraseneb[13] knew he had the weapon to destroy him, because all Egypt lived in dread of her Habiri slaves.

Menkheperraseneb had long ago decided that he did not want Senenmut ruling Egypt. He would bring change, and Menkheperraseneb did not want change. He knew he could not steer Senenmut as he could steer the young Tutmose. Second to the Pharaoh, Menkheperraseneb was the most powerful man in Egypt, and he wanted to keep control in his own hands.

As the pounding hooves continued to carry him out into the darkness, Senenmut knew he could not turn back. It was clear to him now. And his destruction had been so easy! All the High Priest had to do was to put doubt in the minds of Senenmut's supporters, first among them, the young Tutmose himself. Make them doubt that he could be trusted. To whom would he give his first allegiance after Hatshepsut's death? To the Habiri slaves or to Egypt? And placing doubt in every mind had been so simple.

It was a setup of course, because Menkheperraseneb knew Senenmut was loyal! Time and time again he had seen it. But setting the trap had been easy. No decent man could watch an old slave beaten to death by a slave driver and do nothing. Senenmut was sure to act. And if angry enough he would kill the slave driver. An Egyptian killed to save an Habiri! There it was. Stark proof. Who would trust Senenmut now!

As he fled the fort of Tharu[14], Senenmut rode out into the unknown. But now he must think only of escape. Safety lay out there in the darkness, away from his past, away from all he had ever known. His horse was fresh, and he rode quickly until looking back he could see the fort diminishing against the last glow of the western sky. The blackness of the night ahead diffused, and a pale moon gave him vision of a sort, as he remembered. There were two roads that divided as they left Tharu and he must find the lesser one. Not the northern road, the military road that he knew so well which ran east along the coast of the Great Sea.[15] That would mean certain capture, punctuated as it was with forts and soldiers along its length to the border with Canaan at the Arish River.[16] No, he must find the southern road, the camel trail, the trader's route which ran east across the scrubland of the Mafkat[17], visiting isolated settlements where he would find water. He remembered the first of these settlements, Etham, positioned as it was on one of the tributaries of the Arish River. South of the town rose huge mountains, carved with deep wadis which ran to the Sea near Aqaba. He had been through those wadis once before. Only once but it was seared on his memory. The terrified nomads pursued by Egyptian soldiers charged with eliminating them. Their animals crushed under chariot wheels. That was his first experience of army life when he was 16, accompanying the troops sent to wipe out the Shasu[18] brigands. Now he was the fugitive.

It was a three-day journey, he remembered, to Etham, so this would be his first brief contact with human society. He would travel at night, with the track and stars to guide him east, and would find shade to rest in the heat of the day. At Etham he could get water and supplies, then move on. The moon was new and growing. He should be safely over the border into Edom before it was full. Just into Edom on the coast was the port city of Ezion-Geber. It should be easy to blend in, in a bustling city. This must be his first goal. From there he might travel south to Midian and visit its towns on the east coast of the Sea, the Sea of Edom[19] called by some the Red Sea. The one friend he had made outside Egypt lived in Midian. Perhaps this backwater would hide him. But could he reach it? He had two good horses. One would always be fresh giving him the speed to escape if pursued. He looked at the blackness overhead. There was the Pole star in the northern sky. Keeping it there to his left would guide him east.

The first night passed without incident. The track ran before him clearly marked by the passage of many feet. As dawn broke ahead, he searched the horizon for some shade to rest. He was tired and the initial relief at making his escape, was turning to blankness, as he contemplated what sort of life he must now lead. He found an outcrop of Acacia trees which together gave a dappled shelter from the unflinching sun that would pass over him through the course of the day. He watered the horses and hobbled them, allowing them to find what pickings they could among the thorn bushes, and closed his eyes. He refused to be afraid. He must sleep. And if danger came, the horses should warn him. There were few flies to disturb his sleep in that isolated place, and only the sound of the horses broke the silence. Even the hard ground did not disturb his rest and he slept soundly until woken by the black stallion nudging him to ask for water. It was late afternoon and Ra was sinking towards the west. Time to eat and move on.

Senenmut reached Etham on the third day as he hoped, vaguely aware of his own surprise as the scant settlement rose out of the scrub land ahead of him. So he had managed to follow the track even at night. The moon had cast sufficient light, and the stars had confirmed his direction. He crossed the stream that ran through the settlement from the mountains to the southeast which was swollen with seasonal rain. It would continue north to join other rivulets forming the Arish river and run on to the coast. He entered the settlement early and found supplies, then moved quickly on. He did not want to arouse curious thoughts more than he must. Leaving the town behind he moved off, not stopping as the day advanced. He must be sure he was not followed. But as the sun rose higher and hotter, he searched for a place to rest.

---

[13] The High Priest of Amun at Karnak

[14] The most westerly of the Military fortresses along the north coast of the Sinai peninsular

[15] The Mediterranean Sea

[16] The Arish river is still the border between Egypt and Canaan.

[17] The Mafkat was the ancient word for the Sinai peninsular which from time immemorial has belonged to Egypt.

[18] Nomadic tribes of the Sinai.

[19] Some suggest that this is how the Red Sea got its name. It was in the territory of Edom and Edom means 'Red'

CHAPTER 3

THE PRINCESS NEPHERURE, DAUGHTER OF PHARAOH HATSHEPSUT

IN THE DAYS FOLLOWING HATSHEPSUT'S death, Nepherure was carried along by the demands of protocol. She could not think, and it was better that she did not. She was numb and followed obediently the dictates of the priests. The 70 days of embalming of her mother's body would be followed by burial in the Valley of the Kings. The strong voices of the chanting priests accompanied the Pharaoh's sarcophagus to its resting place, but as the entourage crossed the river, the Princess was aware of other family members with her among the priests. Tutmose was there of course. As Hatshepsut's heir he must perform the ceremony of the 'Opening of the Mouth'[20]. But others were there, whose presence only added to the burden she must carry. She longed to be alone, but foremost among the mourners was her half-sister Meryet[21], who as a semi royal had acquired a place for herself among the mourners and watched the Princess's every move. Hatshepsut had chosen Meryet as a childhood companion for her daughter. They had spent many hours together at the palace, but it was from Meryet, that Nepherure was to experience her first betrayal. Nepherure's instincts told her of jealousy in her sister which had only grown with time. Meryet was now a singer in the Temple but must be content with the modest allowance she received, while Nepherure had inherited a large income from her mother's estate.

The burial was over, and now Nepherure felt the true horror of her position. She had lost all who were dear to her. Her mother was dead and Senenmut, the man she loved, was gone from Egypt. To lose her mother was like losing the rudder of her life. Hatshepsut's presence had been all encompassing. But at least she had witnessed her mother's passing. She had accompanied the priests to the tomb. She had been there for the ceremonies of death, the 'Opening of the Mouth', and the sealing of the tomb. There was a rightness to it. Part of life. The great Pharaoh had completed her time on earth and had entered eternity.

But the loss of Senenmut had no such resolution. He was gone with no farewell. Gone like Ra into the blackness of night, and there would be no dawn to follow. He had been her sun, the light of her life, but he was gone, while she must remain. She felt utterly bewildered, but one thought came to her in her agony. One thing offered the hope that she might find a guide. She would go to Hathor[22]'s temple. Perhaps Hathor would be a mother to her. She would prostrate herself there. She would beg for understanding at the shrine of the mother goddess in the Temple of her earthy mother at Djeser Djesere[23].

The barge carried the Princess across the river from the land of the living to the land of the dead, but in her soul, the girl had already made that journey and entered a sort of death. A living death. This life without the man she loved. The long avenue of sphinxes stretched ahead, flanked by graceful trees, up to the first ramp of the Temple. But the sight of her mother's Temple only added to her pain. This great edifice was the work of Senenmut. She had shared it with him, and it brought back his memory, but not himself. She entered Hathor's shrine and the darkness engulphed her. She knew this shrine well, and the familiarity brought a kind of comfort. Here was a world beyond her own. The world of the gods. Where mysteries were no mystery. Where all was calm. Where the tide of human sorrow never left its mark. She was alone in the stillness and fell to her knees seeking out the dark eyes of Hathor which shone in her golden body by the dim light of the sanctuary lamps. Nepherure wept a little, knowing that she did not need to form words with her lips. The goddess could read them there in her heart. Her tears poured forth their own eloquence, and finally the weight of anguish in her soul formed itself into words.

"Tell me mother, how I am to live?" she pleaded as in the silence her thoughts rushed on.

"Am I to pass into the shadows of the Harem and spend my days in mourning? My heart contains only sorrow. No joy beckons me to remain at

Court. I cannot bring myself to marry my brother[24] Tutmose as all expect of me. This brother whom I do not love, when the man I love may still live!" She closed her eyes as sobbing shook her frame, hearing nothing but her own weeping.

Suddenly, in the empty space, a voice spoke.

"The man Senenmut is no more."

The voice was that of an old woman. Nepherure stared at the idol ahead of her as again the voice came, drifting towards her as if on a breeze, but the air was still, in the darkened shrine.

"Do you seek to know your destiny?—You will be the mother of kings.

Your life – long. —At its end your eyes will see your heart's desire."

The girl seized the words—but they were not the words she longed to hear. Except the last, which seemed to speak the impossible. But still she seized them.

"Mother how will I see my heart's desire if Senenmut is dead?"

But the sanctuary was now silent.

'Help me mother, help me. I have no other hope.' Whether the girl spoke the words or just felt them, she knew not. The Idol of Hathor was silent. The goddess would speak no more and had no words of comfort for the broken girl.

Nepherure lay prostrate before the idol as day faded to night. She was past tears, past feeling. She lay in a stupor seeking nothing but forgetfulness. The hours passed. Priestesses came like shadows and raising her in their arms - a slip of a girl – wrapped and carried her to a chamber where she slept like the dead. She woke at dawn with a raging thirst and drank deeply, then slept again, oblivious of all around her.

But news travels. It is simply a matter of servants talking. The network formed between the great houses, the Palaces and Temples, carried the news of every great happening, by many small steps, across the length and breadth of Egypt. Even the Nubian girl, Princess Jala[25], in her isolated palace in Waset, heard of the death of the great Pharaoh and the exile of her son. But then news for her ears only arrived from her homeland. Her brother Thaldi[26] was dead. There would be no more gold for herself and her household. The jewels he had sent, over the course of the last year must now supply all her needs. Her sense of loss and isolation was overwhelming. In her desperation she knew she must visit the shrine of Hathor and beg for wisdom.

Jala entered the great Temple of Djeser Djesere, turning her steps to the shrine of Hathor. She had visited before when loneliness overwhelmed her, but today was different. Fear and shock are etched on every face. Priests and priestesses alike show the alarm they feel for the Royal princess who seems to be dying right here in Hathor's shrine. Jala is ignored and as such is free to go into the shrine alone. She resolves to find Nepherure, who had briefly befriended her, and share her sorrow. She finds the girl staring blankly with unseeing eyes. She speaks to her of Senenmut and of her mother. Jala takes her in her arms and weeps over her, and the raw emotion finds a chord in the silent girl. The floodgates open, and her tears flow. The healing has begun.

"My Lady do not despair of life. You are greatly loved. And who can know that Senenmut is dead?"

Nepherure listens. To have another with whom to share her loss; with whom to speak the name she loves, brings her back from the edge of oblivion. Together the girls take up residence in Hathor's shrine. The priestesses attend them, and in each other they find comfort.

"But what is my life to be now?" asked Nepherure, when after days in mourning they start to think of the future.

"If my companionship can serve you, my Lady, I will gladly be your companion. I also am alone in the world."

"Then we shall share our loneliness and comfort each other," said Nepherure.

The days pass and Nepherure can face returning to the Palace with Jala as her companion. Quietly they take up residence in Hatshepsut's apartments, as ghosts in a world of living servants.

"Lady Nepherure, the Pharaoh wishes to attend you and see you restored to health," said the steward one day, some weeks after their return. Nepherure stared at the man without a word, but Jala replies,

"It will be good for the Princess to see her brother", she says.

Tutmose enters. He is a different man from the man Jala remembers. Indeed, he now is a man, not a stunted boy. He is self-assured. He is kind. And he is clearly fascinated by his royal sister. Their meeting is short and formal.

Nepherure raises her eyes to his face only once, but it is enough. Her innocence and beauty enchant him. She is the Royal heiress - of the Solar Blood. He resolves he must have her, and Jala reads in his face the resolve that Nepherure does not see.

"My Lady, I have seen today, a future for you, written in the face of the King. He wants you! Accept him! Bear a child. Build a future for yourself, and I shall be your companion."

---

[20] A ceremony before burial to allow the spirit of the dead man to re-enter his body.

[21] Meryetre-Hatshepsut was her full name. I have reduced it to Meryet. She is an historical figure, previously thought to be the second daughter of Hatshepsut, but now believed to be the daughter of a royal nurse Huy. I have assumed she was royal, probably another daughter of Tutmose 1 as she was married to Tutmose lll and named as his Great Royal Wife, an honour rarely given to non-royal women.

[22] Hathor was a mother goddess among other things, represented in the form of a cow.

[23] Djeser Djesere was the Mortuary Temple of Hatshepsut now known as Deir el Bahri.

[24] Brother / sister marriages were normal in the royal house.

[25] The beginning of Jala's story was told in the first book in the series. She is a Nubian princess whose story continues into the next book as a figure of history.

[26] Thaldi featured in the first book. He was the brother of Jala and king of Nubia for a time.

CHAPTER 4

TUTMOSE CONFERS WITH HIGH PRIEST OF AMUN
MENKHEPERRASENEB REGNAL YEAR 22

THE DAY HAD WORN AWAY while the young king had been confined with his generals. They would soon leave for the north and must prepare for war. The harvest was being gathered from fields up and down the land and soon Shemu, the season of harvest and low water would be past. The time when kings go to war.

The river had indeed fallen, nearly to its lowest ebb, but would suffice to carry the king and his generals north, to join the army in Avaris. But before leaving, Tutmose must confer with his old tutor, now the High Priest of Amun. Menkheperraseneb was the man who had ruled his childhood, and who now held the highest position in the land, after his Pharaoh, causing him to lend little more than lip service to the belief that Tutmose, now the Pharaoh, was by that fact, divine.

Tutmose did not enjoy the company of the old priest. He knew or at least suspected that Menkheperraseneb had been responsible for the sudden demise of Hatshepsut. He feared to confront him, but his feeling of distaste had caused him to avoid the old man since her burial. His own conscience was clear. He knew that as Hatshepsut's heir he had done his duty by his aunt. He had buried her body with honour and made ample provision for her afterlife. Her Ka, on leaving the world of men had become united with her father Ra to sail the heavens for eternity. But now he must speak with the old priest before he left for the north and wished to draw a line under the past. As he crossed the Great Court of the Temple and entered the chambers of the High Priest, the old man was waiting for him. Tutmose felt the need to state again that he had done his duty. He needed the support of his god, the powerful Amun, as he went to war but did not wish to waste words with this priest.

"I must leave for the north shortly my lord," he said. "I have fulfilled all that is required of me as Hatshepsut's heir. I pray that she and the gods are satisfied." But he was unprepared for the old priest's response.

"Majesty, if I may advise you, it would be wise, I think, to let the memory of the usurper die with her," said the High Priest.

The young king turned to face his old tutor, with anger in his eyes.

"My stepmother was of the Royal house, yet you and your minions presumed to murder her! You, not I, will bear the guilt of her death before the gods my lord priest!"

But the High Priest was unmoved. Only his smile changed from a show of respect to a grimace of contempt. But Tutmose was more than angry. Fear also consumed him.

"She was a great Pharaoh! You will not deny it. And I will be loyal to the memory of one who could have destroyed me!"

But the High Priest did not ask pardon for his words. Worse, he laughed quietly as he continued.

"Sire, she held your throne, and would certainly have destroyed you and given it to that slave she had adopted, had not he prevented it." He paused, eyeing his pupil, wondering how much more he could say. But his anger would not allow him to keep silent.

"It is a great pity, Majesty, that the woman was buried in her father's tomb[27]. The tomb of such a great Pharaoh as the first Tutmose, your grandfather, should not have been demeaned in this way. And it gives her too great an honour. Maybe in time it can be changed," he added and would have continued, but Tutmose would hear no more.

"Pharaoh Hatshepsut was buried with her father as was her wish, and my sister's wish. The Lady Nepherure's loss is almost too great for her to bear, and any small comfort I can offer I will gladly give her." He paused but knew that he must summon the courage to speak his mind now, or he would never speak it.

"You forget yourself my Lord. You are speaking of my family!" He paused, and for a brief moment his old affection for his brother Senenmut surged back and almost prevented him continuing on the path he had chosen. But with an act of will he regained control of himself.

"You must know that all affection I had for my stepbrother is dead and buried. Now we know the truth of his birth he cannot be trusted. The trap you laid for him proves that he is a friend of the slaves and a danger to Egypt. I pray the gods your spies have found him."

They were brave words, but the High Priest sensed that he must tread carefully. Tutmose had loved his brother and may yet waver in his decision to destroy him. The young king had known little of love. Few had loved him and Senenmut had acted against his own interest in befriending the lad. But he hoped that Tutmose's fear of the slaves, and his fear of Senenmut befriending Egypt's enemies, would bring about the necessary change of heart. An uneasy silence hung between the two men. The day was drawing to its close, when the sound of soldiers approaching was carried to them from the courtyard outside. Tutmose remained where he was as a troop of men entered the chamber. Their clothes and weapons were soiled and dishevelled. They had clearly travelled some distance and approached the High Priest with a sense of urgency, but seeing the Pharaoh, prostrated themselves before him. Tutmose observed them, disquiet registering in his young face.

"Rise," he said. "Who are you, and what causes you to come here in such haste?"

The men hesitated, looking first at Tutmose, then at the High Priest.

"We beg pardon Majesty, but we have returned with a report for the High Priest of Amun."

"What message do you have for the High Priest which is so urgent?" asked the Pharaoh regarding the soldiers, but his mind was unsettled. Were these the assassins Menkheperraseneb had sent to hunt his brother? Had they overtaken him? Was he dead?

"Give your message. I will listen," he said.

The commander of the troop was keen to discharge his report and turned to the High Priest.

"My lord you sent us to find the traitor." He glanced at Tutmose and hesitated.

"Continue man", said the High Priest with menace in his voice.

"For almost a year we followed the fugitive. We crossed the Mafkat[28] and beyond, my Lord, and know that he went north." Again, he hesitated, watching the harsh expression of the priest.

"We searched all the major cities of Canaan where a man such as he may find refuge, but the trail went cold, my lord. He has passed beyond our reach Sire. He has reached Naharin[29] or beyond by now Sire. The lands to the northeast must be his destination. We searched Moab and Edom but not to the south into Midian. A man of learning would not bury himself among shepherds in desert wastes such as Midian."

But a sudden outburst from the High Priest frightened the men.

"Fools!" he shouted. "How is it that a troop of armed soldiers cannot find a lone fugitive travelling in hostile territory? So, you have let him escape. Now we shall never be free of him!"

The men were terrified by the High Priest's response, fearing what punishment would be metered out. Tutmose too, was alarmed but wished to speak to Menkheperraseneb alone.

"Dismiss your men my lord priest. They are weary from their journey and cannot think clearly to answer questions at this hour, but we must talk."

The men left the High Priest's apartment while Tutmose and the priest remained together in silence.

Finally the King spoke. More than anything he wanted to convince himself that Senenmut was no longer a threat.

"If my brother has fled to Asshur[30] or Sumer[31] as your men believe, he is too far distant to be a danger to us. We are free of him."

"But if he is in Canaan majesty, where he is well known as the most powerful man of Hatshepsut's court, he could raise an army and invade Egypt as the Hyksos did before him. And the slaves here would welcome him and rise against us!" Menkheperraseneb said.

These were the very thoughts that Tutmose himself had wrestled with earlier. He knew this priest hated his brother. But he was not exaggerating. The threat was real, but he longed to convince himself otherwise.

"If Senenmut is hiding in Canaan despite your men searching for him, he could be a threat. But he himself built Egypt's army. He knows that we are well defended. And why would he raise an army to come and destroy me when he refused to destroy me and seize the throne when he was here?"

But Menkheperraseneb could not let the matter rest. He wanted certainty.

"Bitterness will change a man, my Lord," said the priest. "And his mother gave him the notion of being Pharaoh."

Now Tutmose's mind was divided.

"So was it foolish to drive him away? Have we made him dangerous!"

"No my lord. If we had allowed him to remain in Egypt, he would have championed the cause of the slaves."

Menkheperraseneb was set on the course to destroy his enemy. They must find another way.

"Majesty, if this first search has failed, it would be wise to send men to Canaan in another guise. Send educated men in a diplomatic capacity to the city states of Canaan. Such men would discover him."

Despite his feelings, Tutmose knew this was wise. They could not rest until Senenmut was discovered and destroyed. Nothing short of his death would remove the threat. But he had more to add.

"I will be taking the army to subdue Megiddo and her allies. I will be punishing these cities for their rebellion. In this way they will be weakened, and any threat removed. But for double measure we will place our spies there in Canaan also.

---

[27] Hatshepsut was originally buried in the tomb of her father Tutmose 1
[28] The old Egyptian name for the Sinai Peninsula.
[29] 'Naharin' is the name used by Egypt and in the Bible for the people otherwise called 'Mittani' who ruled ancient Syria at this time.
[30] The name for early Assyria.
[31] Ancient Babylon

CHAPTER 5

SENENMUT REACHES SEIR

SENENMUT WOKE WITH A START, the cold sweat standing on his forehead. The same nightmare woke him every night since that last terrible day in the Mafkat. Delayed fear not felt during the attack itself, but returning to haunt his dreams, even here where he had found safety of a sort in the company of other men. He turned and tried to sleep again, but his mind refused. He tried to confront the fear, forcing his mind to relive the attack, to face his fear and defeat it, but he could not! Even in his sleep, he always woke before the climax, as if his mind could not bear to relive it.

He lay awhile remembering as his mind recalled the first time he had gone hunting, as a young man of 18. He had been accompanied by the best of the Pharaoh's hunters. Those who always accompanied his stepfather, on a hunt. He had been attacked then! Why had that attack not recurred in his dreams? He had been in equal danger. But now he understood. In that first attack he had not looked into the creature's eyes. Not like this time, when he was woken from heavy sleep by the unearthly scream of his horse. The lion had already wounded his gelding. The horse could not escape, hobbled as it was. He must have shouted and attracted the attention of the of the beast which now watched him ready to spring. The horse's blood coated its mouth and mane. The attack must have been savage. Slowly he felt for his knife. He must not break eye contact with the creature. That would be fatal. He had the knife now, in his hand. This was the moment of life or death. Suddenly the lion sprang. Senenmut lived it again, just like the first hunt all those years ago. The stinking fur in his face suffocating him. The tearing of his arm by razor claws. But this time the hunters were not with him. This time he was the one who must plunge the knife into the animal's chest.

He felt the warm rush of blood as the knife went home. The beast shuddered and fell back. Now there was fear in its eyes. It snarled and turned to limp away into the undergrowth. It would not get far. Blood was pouring from the wound drenching the ground. He had remained completely calm, mechanically examining his arm. There was blood everywhere but not his own. The injury to his arm was superficial. Fumbling for his water skin he washed the wound. It would heal. He lay back again and found himself sobbing uncontrollably. His mind ran over the events. He had killed a lion, and no one would know but himself. This time there would be no accolades. This was the real world, the harsh world of life and death which he now inhabited.

The gelding was no longer fighting and lay slumped on the ground. He remembered it all. He searched for the stallion in desperation. The copse of trees was small. The horse could not be far away, hobbled as it was and would be visible if it had ventured out into the fierce sun. He was frantic. The stallion was his lifeline. But he found it hiding among the trees shivering with fear.

He left the place at once, leaving the gelding where it lay. Anyone finding it would recognise where it was from. It bore the brand mark of the Royal stables. So be it. He could not remove the mark and he could not bear to stay a moment longer in this dreadful place. He moved on to Ezion-Geber[32]. There he sold the stallion. The traders recognised it immediately as a valuable animal from the Royal stables of Egypt. And it was not a gelding. It could sire young. New blood from which to breed valuable animals. The men were not good men. Not men you could trust with an animal. It showed in their twisted smiles; innately cruel. But they would not mistreat a valuable animal. He could count on that. And he must sell. Keeping the horse made him a marked man.

With some of the money he bought a mule and joined a large train of mules and camels travelling north, which would pass through the Edomite capital. It brought him here, to this Caravanserai, a hard ride from the port. He did not want to be alone as the news spread that he had been paid a good price for his horse. He chose to go north to fool his pursuers. He would go even further north with this caravan, to Edom's capital at Seir[33] which was the meeting point of many trade routes. In such a bustling centre he hoped to avoid notice. He would stay there and quietly wait for another caravan going south. Anyone searching for him would learn that a man had sold a valuable horse in Ezion-Geber and gone north. North was the obvious direction to take for a man such as he, and he must think as his pursuers would think.

The settlement of Seir was utterly unique. The track leading into its centre would be difficult to find without prior knowledge. The mule train entered this narrow defile with its high walls rising sheer above them. But they were not walls made by men. On both sides, to a height of 50 feet the walls rose, showing clearly how they had been cut by surging water in its ancient past. A channel cut deep into the rock by the sheer force of the water. On and on it led until suddenly the high walls gave way to an open marketplace, swarming with people and animals, with every manner of thing being bought and sold. The Caravan train made its way to an Inn cut into the sheer rock bordering the marketplace. Caves accommodated the travellers while the animals were penned outside.

Even in his distressed state, Senenmut was astonished by the city around him. It was a fortress built by nature herself. And the unique entrance was not its only security. The city had no other entrance. Locals, of course, knew how to find a way up through the surrounding cliffs, but no enemy would find them. And even if they did, the tortuous access would limit entry to very few men at a time. It was impregnable. But Senenmut knew that for that very reason he would not be safe here. He was a fugitive. He would be hunted. This enclosing city which gave security to others, would for him be a trap from which there was no escape. As his tired mule followed the others to the Inn, Senenmut knew that this place with its pleasant welcome would be the first stop at which his pursuers would enquire. A trap within a trap. In this city, where there were other choices, he must go elsewhere. He wandered along the main street as it rose in a gentle incline above the marketplace and found an ill-favoured hostelry where for a few coins he was given a straw filled sack on which to sleep and provender for his mule. His hostess offered him thick gruel and a crust of bread. It looked unsavoury, but was hot and filling, and the acrid wine accompanying it would purify it from any corruption.

The next day Senenmut returned to the sprawling marketplace which had opened to his sight so suddenly the previous day after the long narrow entry into the city. Every conceivable thing was on sale. Fresh fruit, vegetables, caged birds for food and asses for labour. Baked goods extended their fragrance for free while competing with the pungent smell of freshly cured leather. Pottery bowls and jugs of every size were on offer, and set in a prominent place, almost a place of honour, was a cache of lethal looking weapons, knives and spears and curved blades for war. They would command a good price.

Observing his surroundings Senenmut could identify the main buildings where the centre of power must lie. Distinguished men in flowing robes were presenting themselves to the guards at the entrance to a tall building on the south side of the marketplace seeking admission. He had heard of the Kings of Edom. An old lineage, chosen on merit, not birth, who had fostered good relations with Egypt by treaty and trade. No, it would not be safe to settle here. His identity would not remain hidden for long.

He thought again of Reba, the friend he had in Midian and realised, now that he had time to think, that he must make a decision. He could make a much more comfortable life for himself in the north rather than Midian. But could he be hidden in the north? Certainly, he would not be safe here in Edom or Moab, or one of the city states of Canaan where Egypt's control was strong. His pursuers would search, and demand promises from all these dependant states, that they were not harbouring him. That was normal practice with wanted men. But further north, perhaps the king of Naharin would give him sanctuary as Egypt and Naharin were jealous rivals for power. Naharin may be glad to offer employment to a man who had been high in Egypt's army, an Egyptian courtier. Or he could move on to Mesopotamia, to one of the growing centres of the east. Life could be good in the city of Susa or Nineveh. No educated man would go south to Midian. He saw that now. But for that very reason, was it the better choice? To disappear. If he held a position in any court, he would never be safe from the silent assassin's blade. But no assassin would look for him in Midian, a land devoid of scholars. A land of labouring men, shepherds, fishermen and copper smelters.

It was two months now since he had made his decision and joined the caravan going south from Seir travelling through Midian. It was a humble affair calling again at Ezion-Geber then following the trader's route along the eastern margin of the Edomite Sea, the sea by Aqaba along whose eastern shore, the Midianite settlements lay. All the settlements were on the coast, Haql in the north followed by others of dwindling size and importance. They sprang up in the gullies between the mountains where forests of date palms grew[34], whose deep roots could find the fresh water hidden under the sand.

Senenmut had known lands as desolate as Midian. The Nile travelling from its source in the south, flowed through dry desert where no rain fell. But the river itself provided abundant fresh water. And there were expanses of fertile soil on either side, exposed when the river fell. These could be used for crops. But Midian had no river, only the salt sea, and streams which flowed for a brief season in the early summer carrying melt water from the snowy peaks of the huge mountains to the east. He wondered why anyone would live in this harsh land with no permanent river and almost no rain. Even animals would find slim pickings in its vast wilderness. But Senenmut knew how the Midianites made their living. Every Midianite man grew up knowing how to build a furnace and smelt copper, as they had done for a thousand years. And Egypt needed copper to build her military arsenal, because with copper and tin, bronze was made.

Senenmut remembered his impression of the first settlement within Midianite territory, when the mule train arrived at Haql, the principal town, which announced its welcome in advance by the pungent smell of fish hung to dry in the parched air. It was a large settlement, and the manner of dress and style of life clearly showed its frequent contact with Ezion-Geber. The traders stayed one night in the Caravanserai, spreading their wares out for sale in its cavernous entrance. But that night, as Senenmut ate his meal alone, he was conscious of men watching him, and his sleep was disturbed by an instinctive warning of danger. This place would not be safe for a man alone and he was glad to leave it behind and head south when the traders moved on the following day. They journeyed for 3 days, pressed hard to the water's edge by the mountains which allowed them only a narrow path, before finally reaching the last settlement.

Maqna was just a sprawl of black tents by the sea, huddled under another swathe of Date Palms. The land itself was dry and rocky, the colour of a fired pot, with a scattering of shrubs and trees climbing the slopes. But here, the layers of rock created pools and springs of clear water which broke through the red soil giving life to man and beast.[35]

It was a strange end to his journey when the mule train arrived at the settlement of Maqna, an hour before sunset. He would do as the other travellers would and spend the night under the stars, together. There was no Caravanserai building here. The inhabitants were all tent dwellers. But before darkness fell, he wanted to look around. To see what else was here. To see if anything drew him. To see if in his heart, he still wanted to find Reba.

He had climbed the slope east of the settlement and was watching a group of shepherd girls leading their flock down to be watered. He remembered his mule. It too would need water. He approached the watering hole and waited as the girls filled the troughs. He would water his mule when they had finished. The girls did not cover their faces, as the Shasu[36] women did, and Senenmut observed the elegant, chiselled features he could not fail to admire. 'Beauty wasted in such a place, where few would ever see it,' he thought.

Suddenly another group of shepherds approached at speed down the slope. Young men this time, hurrying their sheep to water. They had waited until the girls had filled the troughs intending to drive them away and use the water for their own flocks. Without thinking, Senenmut stepped in.

"Stop this nonsense. Let the women finish."

The men stopped. His Aramaic was clear enough. They understood his meaning. But he was just one man, and they five. It was a risk. Why did he do it? Perhaps because he had seen too much injustice and would not allow more? The men hesitated. He spoke as if he must be obeyed. They stepped back, uncertain, and the first flock took the water. Then the girls left, taking their flock and their excited chatter with them. The men ignored Senenmut as he rested, then watered his mule when they had finished. Now he must join his fellow travellers. He may no longer be safe after offending the local youths. But the girls were returning and with some embarrassment, approached. Their leader, identifying him as Egyptian, spoke in the Egyptian tongue. Her words were halting but clear.

"Our father asks will you eat? Our tent is near," she said, pointing.

Senenmut's instinct was to refuse. His feelings since leaving Egypt made him no longer want the company of other men. But this first touch of human kindness after Egypt had cast him aside overruled his reserve. He would accept their offer.

"Thank you. I will come," he said bowing briefly.

He followed the girls to a nearby tent. An old man emerged and welcomed him.

"You helped my daughters. It was a kindness," said the man speaking clearly in the Egyptian tongue. "Please eat with us and rest the night. May I know your name?"

Senenmut thought quickly how to answer. He must not disclose his identity. He could no longer use the name Senenmut. He would use his childhood name, the name given him by Hatshepsut naming him as her son.[37]

"Moshe. I am Moshe," he said bowing.

"And I am Jethro," said the old man. "I am the leader of my people, so if I welcome you, all will welcome you."

---

[32] Ezion-Geber was an Edomite city on the north coast of the Gulf of Aqaba

[33] Seir was the name of ancient Petra, an Edomite stronghold.

[34] Historically there were vast groves of date palms at Aqaba where springs rise from huge aquifers of water, to this day, in the underground rocks.

[35] Maqna today still has fresh springs, still fed by the huge aquifer under the Saudi and Jordanian deserts

[36] The Shasu were Bedouin who lived in the Mafkat (Sinai).

[37] The name 'Mose' means 'son' in the Ancient Egyptian language, and it was his adopted mother who named him.

CHAPTER 6

REBELLION IN THE NORTH

UP IN SYRIA, IN THE city state of Qadesh[38], Durusha[39], its king had called a clandestine meeting. He did not like the growing power of Egypt spreading north and he was ambitious for his own territory. Why should Egypt have the lion's share of wealth that passed along the trade routes between nations? They passed through Syria and the Levant. The crossroads of the world. Egypt was to the south and should content itself with taxing its own territory. No, it was time to challenge Egypt's ambitions. And the first challenge would be for mastery of the northern city states of Canaan which Egypt had controlled for too long. The leaders of the Syrian cities and many from Canaan had gathered and were ready to listen. He stood to address his countrymen.

"I have called you here today because we have reached a critical moment in our history. Now is the time to act if we hope to stem the tide of Egypt's ambitions." He paused as he surveyed the leaders around him.

"Pharaoh Hatshepsut is dead. Her wisest councillor Senenmut has been forced to flee Egypt. This is the best chance of victory we will have in a lifetime."

The leaders of the other city states watched and listened with bated breath. They knew the power of Egypt was growing. In just fifty years she had gone from defeat to victory. She had expelled the Hyksos invaders and regained control of all her territory. Then in punishment for the invasion, the greatest of her warrior pharaohs, the first Tutmose, had even taken his army into Syria and subdued many cities there also, travelling as far as the great river, the

Euphrates. Besides this, he had overpowered Canaan, punishing her city states for their support of the Hyksos. But he was dead, and through his son's reign, Egypt had kept a light touch on Canaan, allowing thoughts of freedom to grow. Now the third Tutmose was pharaoh, a young man of little experience.

"Our campaign must start in Canaan," said Durusha. "The city of Megiddo has welcomed us. Both the city and her king want to be free of Egypt," he continued. "If we support Megiddo now, while this new young Pharaoh is still finding his feet, we can break the strangle hold Egypt has on Canaan and gain a share in the revenue that should be ours. At present, Egypt controls them alone," he added.

Durusha knew he must rouse these neighbours to join forces and fight alongside Megiddo[40]. This ancient city in northern Canaan was desperate to rebel against Egypt her overlord. The willy old king knew that the promise of gold was his greatest argument. But his real interest was self-interest and if Megiddo could be freed from Egypt's rule, his own city, only a little further north, would gain much from the altered balance of power.

Durusha knew his words were dangerous. There had been a standoff between Egypt and Syria over control Canaan since the time of Pharaoh Tutmose 1, the father of Hatshepsut. But then, during her years in power, Canaan had been content to accept Egypt's control. Her city states had paid their tribute without dispute all through Hatshepsut's reign. It brought security. Egypt may be a hard master, but she defended her own. And Egypt's security depended on controlling Canaan. She would never forget the invasion of the Hyksos armies from Syria. From now on, she must keep Canaan as a buffer zone between herself and this constant danger to the north. But the other leaders had their doubts.

"Majesty, we know nothing of this young Egyptian king, Tutmose lll. He was trained by his brother Senenmut. He may prove a good soldier."

Durusha had thought these thoughts himself. But he didn't believe them. Tutmose had been raised in the Temples. It was difficult to create the mindset of a soldier in a prince whose years had been spent in study. And he had been a sickly child. He was unlikely to be a powerful soldier. But Durusha understood his task. He must use logic to persuade the other chieftains to support him.

"Megiddo is a valuable prize. And for us it is a near neighbour while Egypt will have to march her armies for two weeks to reach it. It is inconceivable that she will wage war here in the north. She is rich, yes, but no state has unlimited resources. She cannot raise armies year after year without impoverishing herself. It is not worth her while. Tutmose and his advisers are not fools. Even if he is victorious once, the distance is in our favour. Tutmose cannot defend land so far in the north if the cities of Syria work together. He cannot hope to overcome the power of a united Syria. He does not have the resources. No one does."

"But my Lord, our spies tell us that Tutmose is training many men," said the generals.

"Listen to me!" said the king. "His soldiers are peasant farmers. They can only join their pharaoh for war after the harvest and must return to their fields again as soon as the inundation has passed, to plant food for the following year. They will never be skilled soldiers," he paused. "And if we act together, and act now, we are sure of victory."

If only Durusha could read the future. Then he may have been more circumspect. But he knew nothing of the potential in Egypt's slaves. A huge force of free labour. Freeing Egypt's peasant farmers in their tens of thousands to train for war. To train well. To become Tutmose's crack troops. To take cities and garrison them. Other farmers could be trained as ship builders to build a large navy to transport Tutmose's troops quickly and easily to the port cities of Syria. But all this was, as yet, hidden from him.

---

[38] The city of Qadesh or Kadesh was located on the Orontes River in western Syria. It is mentioned for the first time in Egyptian sources when Tutmose lll defeated a Syrian insurrection under the leadership of the prince of Kadesh at Megiddo in Palestine. It remained an Egyptian outpost until it came under Hittite rule (c. 1340 BCE, during reign of Akhenaten). King Shutatarra of Kadesh was one of the foreign rulers mentioned in the Amarna letters.

[39] Known from history.

[40] Megiddo was a major city state in northern Canaan, a site of archaeological investigation. It is in the 'plain of Megiddo' which has given its name to the place of the final apocalypse of Amageddon as outlined in the Bible.

CHAPTER 7

TUTMOSE'S 1ST CAMPAIGN YR 23

TUTMOSE LEFT WASET[41] THE FOLLOWING day bound for Avaris[42]. There he would meet his generals and agree the final plan of attack on Megiddo. All along the Nile men were hard at work bringing in the wheat harvest. The barley was already in. Wheat for bread, barley for beer, the staples of Egypt. In some places the cultivated land stretched for miles to the east and west, land that was flooded by the river at its height, then drained as the river fell, leaving the perfect conditions for growth. Moist earth and warm sun. No need for ploughing. The farmers would simply broadcast the seed directly onto the waiting soil, then release their pigs[43] to trample it into the ground. But harvest required manpower, and this dictated the time of year that the Pharaoh could go to war. His soldiers must harvest their grain, then they were free to follow their lord into battle. This was how it had always been, but things were changing.

Entering the delta, Tutmose looked out across the vast flat expanse of fields cut by the divisions of the River[44], stretching as far as the eye could see. Grain ripe for harvest. But this was not the work of Egyptians. This was the work of Habiri slaves. The men his brother Senenmut had tried to free.

But ever since Senenmut had fled the country, during the declining years of Hatshepsut, Tutmose had been making plans. With Hatshepsut living in the south, in Waset, Tutmose was free to take control of the army in the north. He moved the leading generals of the Northern army from Men-nepher[45], to Avaris, his new centre of operations, and here they made their plans.

Tutmose's idea was to use the Habiri slaves as part of his war machine. The idea was so simple, but it was a masterpiece. He realised that enough grain could be grown by these slaves to feed the whole country if properly organised[46], freeing thousands of peasant farmers to form a well-trained, permanent army.

First, he extended the store cities of Ramesses and Pithom[47] to accommodate the grain. Then he conscripted the first cohort of peasant farmers to Avaris to train as full-time soldiers. Then another cohort would be called up, and another. In this way he grew a standing army of 10,000 men. Enough to defeat any rebellion in Canaan. And enough spare men to garrison every defeated city. Now he was ready to face rebellion. And it was sure to come when Hatshepsut died. But would Egypt's enemies discover his plan? Surely no spies would report back to their masters that Egypt's slaves were growing large quantities of grain, no matter how much they grew. They may notice the peasant farmers being taught soldiering skills, but this was not new. Egypt had always used peasant farmers as soldiers during the months of Akhet, when their fields were under water. So the difference was not easy to spot. And all the while, Tutmose was assembling his assault force. Thousands of peasant farmers, well trained as full-time soldiers, while their families were fed with grain grown and stored for them by the slaves. It was a system that could continue indefinitely. Soldiers lost in war would be easy to replace. Egypt had hundreds of thousands of farmers. And the slaves who fed the country would never be in short supply. Hard work seemed only increased their numbers.

As the barge continued north, Tutmose remembered that making sure his people had food was the first duty of a Pharaoh. But with his army of slaves, he would not fall short in this duty. The capacity of the store cities was vast. And he need not fear the Habiri slaves, though their numbers were huge. With Senenmut gone they no longer had a champion.

The journey to Avaris gave Tutmose time to assess the situation, and he realised that his plan was ready just in time. War was upon him and this battle at Megiddo was one he must not lose. The future of Egypt's control of Canaan rested on it.

For the last 30 years, Egypt's lands in Canaan had been subject to the creeping influence of Naharin[48], the most powerful state in the north, in Syria. All through the reigns of his father and stepmother Hatshepsut, it had been growing in secret. And now with Naharin's backing, half of Canaan was in rebellion. Egypt must win this fight, or she would lose control of Canaan forever. These facts defined this campaign. This first strike, this first Campaign would concentrate on Megiddo, but it would affect the whole of Canaan. Success here would free him to move against the cities further north, that were inciting the rebellion. He must consolidate control of Canaan first, then attack Qadesh[49]. Then slowly move east to challenge and defeat Naharin itself.

THE ROYAL BARGE REACHED THE dock outside the Palace of Avaris. This Palace was now familiar, but he remembered his astonishment on his first visit. It was built on a huge platform 15 cubits[50] above the level of the river[51]. And it was built for luxury, in the style of Thera[52] and Crete. The life-like art of these cultured neighbours was exquisite. Very different from the formal art of Egypt. And it was the height of fashion. The palace felt spacious and stylish, and passing through its beautiful chambers, Tutmose asked himself if he should make this his primary residence. Would his courtiers be content to leave their homes in the south? And most importantly, would Nepherure be happy here? If he must go repeatedly to war in Canaan and Syria, this was the place to live. He took a detour from his own apartment to assess the quality of the queen's rooms. The walls were decorated with charm and delicacy with pastoral scenes of animals and birds, beautiful women, and children at play. Yes, they would appeal to a woman.

Having toured the palace, Tutmose stood at the window of his chamber, looking out over the pleasant gardens, musing. He was hungry and was struck again by the strangeness of this recurring theme[53]. To have found the appetite of a growing youth after a childhood of nausea at the thought of food, was strange indeed. He summoned a servant.

"Bring me wine and bread," he said. "I am hungry." He thought again of how his appetite and strength had grown in the last few years. It was a joy to be well. Never in his life had he felt so well. It made him feel fully a man; confident, intrepid, powerful. But that was not the only cause. A smile crossed his face as he remembered. Yes, he could finally hope to make Nepherure his queen. He felt sure of it. That more than anything made him feel like a king. He felt as if he had launched this campaign on the strength of it! She may or may not give him children, but he knew now that the greatest prize she could give him, was herself. He loved her as he would love no other. He would make her life as content as it was possible for him to do. He would ask no more of her than that.

With a day to spare before meeting his generals, Tutmose resolved to visit the harbours built in the Hyksos years, along the coast. They were better situated than the Egyptian harbour at Men-nepher[54] which was built in a lagoon off the river. Being away from the coast, the harbour at Men-nepher kept the ships safe from enemy raids but was of little use during the months of the year when the river was too low to allow the ships to reach the open sea[55]. But from this Hyksos harbour in the north, ships could leave the port at any time of year. Tutmose paused to take in the whole site. He had to admire these men. Egypt hated the memory of the Hyksos, but they were clever men, and Egypt had learned much from them. They had introduced chariots to Egypt which were now foundational to his army. Their knowledge of horses and how to train them was previously unknown in Egypt[56]. And the design of their composite bows had given Egypt a huge advantage when fighting the renowned bowmen of Nubia who still used the simple bows[57].

But now Tutmose must turn his mind to this campaign. His first test. The culmination of all his training. This battle that would prove if Egypt had it in her to beat the best in the world. Could she defeat the combined armies of Qadesh, and the princes sent from Naharin?[58] Soldiers from all the major Canaanite cities had gathered at Megiddo. If Egypt lost this battle, she would lose control of Canaan. She would lose the security of the buffer zone between herself and the north and the revenue from the trade routes they controlled. The region generated great wealth from olive oil, and wine; from the wool they produced and silk they wove,[59] for which they were rightly famous. Canaan produced the elm and birch woods needed for chariot building. But their most valuable trade was in purple dye highly sought after by the merchants of the east. And all these cities were in rebellion led by Qadesh, the leading city of Syria.

Megiddo was strategically placed in the valley dividing Canaan and Retanu. All the satellite towns looked to Megiddo and its rival Hazor for leadership. All had mobilised their armies in defiance of Egypt. To be free of the relentless demand for tribute. To be free to rebuild their cities with strong walls as they had been when the Hyksos ruled, before the crushing vengeance of Egypt's first Tutmose had destroyed their walls and taken their people as slaves and their cattle as booty. Canaan had used the peaceful reigns of the second Tutmose and Hatshepsut to rebuild and recover their populations. And now a new generation was in power. A generation that had not known the brutal punishment Egypt could inflict. A generation who did not believe that an untried young Pharaoh would risk his neck against the massed armies of Canaan, Qadesh and Naharin itself.

While the generals met the King at Avaris, the army mustered at Tharu. To be sure of victory Tutmose had mustered his whole army of 10,000 men. He must overwhelm the enemy. And he needed enough men to effectively garrisons Megiddo after the battle.

Setting out, they moved from Tharu, the first fort along the coast road, each a day's march from the next. It was a ten-day march to Gaza, Egypt's military base in Canaan which she had garrisoned throughout the two previous reigns. Discipline would be tight. One night only in Gaza, then move on to take the costal town of Joppa. Leave it garrisoned then move on. Eleven days march to Yehem, another city under garrison which had remained loyal to Egypt, where the generals and the King made themselves ready for their final Council of war.

"Majesty, we await your decision. Do you intend to approach Megiddo from the north or the south?" they asked.

But there were three routes leading from Yehem to Megiddo. Two were easy to traverse for both chariots and infantry. The King considered. He knew that enemy spies had followed his every step since leaving Tharu. But now there was a chance to outwit them. There was a third road that the rebels would not expect his army to use, and he wanted to add surprise to the attack. To the astonishment of his generals the king chose the central route, for the infantry to take. A direct route leading northeast, but one made difficult by a narrow ravine which must be passed in single file.

"I wish to lead the infantry myself, by the central route through the narrow pass. The rebels will not expect this."

The generals were horrified.

"Majesty, we cannot advise it!"

"Why so?"

"Lord, that route, at its narrowest, hardly allows a chariot to pass! Only one at a time for sure."

"But it is a shorter route and would bring us directly to the city itself. I will use a light chariot and take only the foot soldiers who would slow the progress of the chariots if we travelled together.

"Majesty, but what is your will for the rest of the army?"

"The chariots will divide, half taking the northern road and half the southern, and you will drive the enemy to me at Megiddo. I wish General Djehuty to lead the northern section and General Amenemhab to lead those using the southern approach. Tonight we will send out spies to see where their army is mustering. With that information we will decide. Have your men ready to move out at dawn."

Spies were sent out into the night. They returned at dawn and reported that the rebel army was camped outside the city, ready to defend it.

"I am decided," said the king. Move out as instructed."

As the sun rose the army divided. The chariots set off to follow the main roads on their circuitous routes to approach Megiddo from opposite directions. The king and his infantry entered the narrow defile. All day they marched, and as the sun moved towards the west, Tutmose and his army emerged opposite Megiddo, and camped beside the stream across from the city. The rebel army's spies were alarmed. They alerted Durusha to their miscalculation, but night was falling, and all must wait the return of the sun. As dawn broke Durusha and the rebel forces prepared to confront Tutmose's men, but now found that they were in the path of Tutmose's chariots approaching the city from both north and south. Suddenly they realised that they were under attack on three sides!

"Where have all these soldiers come from?" Durusha shouted to his generals in astonishment. "There must be 10,000 of them! We can never defeat such an army!"

"We are surrounded," my lord!

But even as he spoke a cry went up from his men. All courage failed them as they saw the number of men ranged against them. The rebels hardly struck a blow but turned and ran for the city leaving their horses, chariots and even their weapons as booty. But the rebels were now in terrible danger. The city dared not open her gates, with Tutmose's army so close to her walls and her own men in disarray. But throwing ropes down to the soldiers below, the citizens on the walls started hauling up the desperate men[60]. Durusha looked on in dismay as his plans melted away before his eyes. His army was in confusion. There would be no attempt made to oppose this Pharaoh! But he himself would not enter the city. He had enough experience of war to understand the horrors of a siege. The city would be a death trap. He would take his chance to escape. Shouting orders to his bodyguard to follow, he turned his chariot and fled the field.

Tutmose and his generals watched incredulous as the battle was won with so little fighting. But as they watched, expecting to see the enemy surrender, they witnessed instead a total breakdown of order among the Egyptian troops. Their inexperienced soldiers, dazzled by so much booty[61] turned from their work of pursuing the enemy and fell on the booty left behind, allowing the rebels to escape in large numbers into the city. Tutmose was beside himself with rage. All the careful planning that had placed this rebel army in his hands was wasted. He stormed at his generals.

"How is it that trained men will leave off pursuing the enemy, to fall on the spoils?" he railed. "Is this how you have trained your men?"

"Fools! To capture Megiddo is to capture 1,000 cities! The chiefs of all the cities of the region are shut up in it.[62] We have thrown away our advantage!" he shouted. "Megiddo has sealed its gates and now we must lay siege, possibly for months, to defeat it! Your soldiers will pay for their crimes. They will dig a moat around the city. They will cut down every tree in the district until they have built a wall of timber to place it under siege. All who have entered the city must remain imprisoned there[63]."

The generals were silent with shame. Tutmose had led them to triumph but had been betrayed by his own men at the point of victory.

"It is a disgrace Majesty. We are mortified. We will go through the camp, and every man found with booty shall be punished."

But Tutmose would not vex himself further by remaining at Megiddo. Taking his bodyguard of 400 men he left the city in the hands of his generals and moved north. He was too angry to stay. The cities of the region were undefended. Their armies had gone to Megiddo leaving them easy prey. He travelled through Lebanon, storming, and punishing three of its cities. Yenoam, Nuges and Herenkeru, known together as the Tripolis. Many other defenceless towns also felt his wrath. They were stripped of their able-bodied men, their goods and the harvest lying ripe in their fields. Only those who had fled to the mountains escaped the wrath of the Pharaoh.

But to build on this victory, Tutmose knew he must create a divide between the city states of Syria and those of Canaan. He knew that 330 princes of Naharin had supported this rebellion at Megiddo[64]. He must block their future access to the south in support of Canaanite cities. He would build a fortress[65] in the central valley of Lebanon as Pharaoh's before him had built fortresses in Nubia to subdue the populace. Men taken in the battle and from the surrounding cities were put to forced labour. Many were unused to heavy work but were brought to the task by the Egyptian whip. The thing was built, and by the time Tutmose returned to Megiddo after 6 months, the starving citizens and soldiers holed up in the city would agree to anything for food.

Leaving his generals to deal with the aftermath of the siege, Tutmose entered the city. He would examine the palace of this king who had defied him. He wished to see how he lived and the palace he maintained. The city archives may be in the palace. They would be searched, and maybe he would find evidence of his brother in this city, or correspondence from him. There was a chance. His heart was divided as he thought of Senenmut. But if he was here, he would be found.

With his bodyguard attending him, he entered the city. All around was the chaos of terror and death. Ignoring it all, he followed the main thoroughfare which climbed to the palace at the highest point of the city. The gates had been flung wide and he entered and crossed the outer court. Before him stood the large audience chamber, deserted. All around was disorder and chaos. He followed the central corridor which led him to the private apartments of the King and Queen. Entering the latter, Tutmose halted. The rooms were hung with yellow silks in elegant contrast to the ebony furniture. The stone floor was covered with fine wool carpets, richly woven in yellow and blue. All was silent in contrast to the tumult in the city below. A large bronze mirror, beautifully made, adorned one wall, and beside it, standing ready for use was a tall loom of carved ebony inlaid with gold. He had not seen a loom of this upright design before[66]. In Egypt, women of the royal house enjoyed the occupation of weaving. They were famed for the fine linen and sashes of intricate patterns that they made. After employment in the temples, weaving was the one occupation permitted for a lady of the royal house. He would take this beautiful loom as a gift for Nepherure from the palace of Megiddo. He turned to a captain in his bodyguard.

"Find some palace women who know how to use this loom. See that it is brought, and others like it along with skilled women to Waset as a gift for my queen."

With the fall of Megiddo, Tutmose's own men received him like a god. A large garrison would be left in the city while the rest of the infantry were free to return to Egypt. But Tutmose was also free. Free to indulge his love of hunting before returning home. He was within striking distance of the Orontes River and the territory of Niy, where his grandfather had hunted elephant after his military victories[67]. Taking sufficient charioteers as a bodyguard he set out for the famous swamps. There he found elephants by the score and brought them down with the power of his bow. Their tusks were removed and carried back to Egypt as trophies of the king's power[68]. Lions were found in equal number and fell to Tutmose's arrows. Their beautiful pelts, thicker by far than lions found in Egypt, were added to the booty. Having enjoyed his leisure, Tutmose and his men travelled south punishing every fortified city that had played a part in this rebellion. Hazor the first, was fully involved in the rebellion. The city was stripped of its wealth and the leading citizens who had remained in the city were taken as prisoners to Egypt. Further south, Shechem in the foothills, and the cities of the coastal plain, Aphek, and Gerar must also pay for their disloyalty. When he returned on his next Campaign, these cities would learn to submit to the rule of an Egyptian garrison.

The army returned to Egypt in triumph with their prisoners and much booty. Tutmose chose a chariot embellished with gold for his return[69]. The young god returning in the strength of his gods. Carts rolled through Avaris carrying hostages. Sons and brothers of the those left in power to rule in Canaan[70]. This victory would be spoken of far and wide and cause the rising powers of Ashur[71] and Shinar[72] to the northeast, and the Great Khatti, king of the Hittites to the west to think soberly of this new power in Egypt. All would send tribute to honour this young king whose gods had given him such a victory.

In Waset, the best of the plunder was given to Amun in thanks, but Tutmose, forgiving the folly and inexperience of his troops, ruled that every soldier would be rewarded. Each could then return home with goods to display and stories to tell. With such prizes, men would be eager to follow their lord to war another year. The booty was paraded through the city; 340 slaves, 2,000 mares and 200 foals. General Djehuty, Tutmose's chief of staff received the gold chariot[73] of the king of Megiddo. But over 900 other chariots were given to his officers. Soldiers who had displayed marked skill or bravery received battle bows, and even the least of them received a small bullock. 20,000 such cattle had been taken, but the best of them, 2,000 beautiful well-formed animals were given to Amun while an offering of gold was given to the temple of Ptah, in Karnak. Ptah, the oldest of the gods, would have his wooden temple rebuilt in stone[74]. If in time he had sons, Tutmose would raise one to be a High Priest of Ptah, a fitting tribute to Egypt's oldest god.

Tutmose surveyed the triumphal parade from the 'Window of Audience' as it wound its way through Waset and past the palace. The campaign had been a resounding success. With this victory, Canaan had passed from the control of Naharin to the control of Egypt. Each step had been recorded by his personal scribe Thaneni on a leather role[75] which became one of that man's prize possessions and would be buried with him in his tomb.

Tutmose had done his duty. He had presented his offerings to Amun and Ptah. Now he would put off the hardness of heart that ordered the brutal destruction of rebels. He would put off his soldier's garb and become mannerly and gentle and would woo the girl he wanted as his queen.

---

[41] Waset is the ancient name for Thebes
[42] Avaris was the capital in the north east Delta from which the army started out for Canaan and the north

[43] Information from Heroditus

[44] Egyptians referred to the Nile simply as 'the River'.

[45] Ancient name for Memphis

[46] Field work done by Hebrew slaves. (Exodus 1 v 14)

[47] Pithon, one of the store cities built in the delta whose name means Per Aten; the estate of the god Aten. The god was later worshiped solely by Akhenaten.

[48] Naharin was the rising power in ancient Syria at this time. Called Naharin in Egypt and the Bible, it is often referred to as Mittani in other records.

[49] Quadesh was a famous city of ancient Syria

[50] The Egyptian cubit measured 52.5 cm

[51] Read in the book 'Amenhotep lll' by Kozloff

[52] The island of Thera was a centre of exquisite art and culture before its destruction by a massive volcano in around 1450 BC. It is thought by some to be the legendary Atlanitis

[53] Tutmose was a sickly child.

[54] Men-nepher was the ancient name for Memphis

[55] This is historical fact

[56] Historical fact

[57] Historical fact

[58] Naharin had sent 330 Princes with their men, to fight at Megiddo

[59] Breasted Vol 2

[60] This account follows the historical record

[61] This follows the historical account

[62] Quote from Breasted Annals of Tutmose lll's 1st Campaign

[63] Durusha King of Qadesh did escape, but his son was among the prisoners taken to Egypt.

[64] Factual

[65] Historical fact

[66] Upright looms were introduced to Egypt from Syria

[67] Historical fact

[68] Historical fact

[69] Recorded fact

[70] Historical fact .This was normal practice.

[71] Assyria

[72] An early name for Babylon

[73] Recorded in Breasted Vol 2. Figures taken from Breasted Vol 2; 18th Dynasty

[74] Factual

[75] Factual

CHAPTER 8

MARRIAGE YEAR 23

IT HAD TAKEN ALL JALA'S wit and kindness to shepherd Nepherure out of her hopeless despair. She had known from the beginning, that to allow the girl to move with her household to the Harem would have sealed her fate. She would never have emerged again. Never married. Never borne a child. A child that would give her something to live for. Something to love, and for which to build a future.

Tutmose had taken Jala into his confidence. The strangeness of his childhood had taught him to read people well, and he saw in Jala an ally with whom he could work. Together they surrounded Nepherure with kindness. Tutmose brought the princess a sight hound[76] as a plaything. A vulnerable creature that shared her need for affection, and which elicited from the girl her first smiles since her life had lost its joy. Slowly the question of marriage became acceptable to the girl. When her mother, Hatshepsut, had made herself Pharaoh, Nepherure had been advanced to fulfil the duties of the Great Royal Wife. So she had already experienced the offices of queen. That was not new, and it held no fear for her.

Nepherure and her household moved to Men-nepher months before the marriage would take place. Jala treated it as an adventure, to allay the girl's fears. Nepherure had spent some early years there and the memories were happy ones. Senenmut had visited her there, and she talked of him now as she would talk of one dead. The man she had loved and lost. Slowly, in her mind, a resolution took place. She had loved Senenmut and would never love another. Why he had fled Egypt she did not know. She had never understood her mother's words that there had been a conspiracy. But he was gone. And Tutmose had gone out of his way to be kind. Life with him may in time, bring at least contentment. The old Palace Harem at Men-nepher had not changed. Nothing changed in Men-nepher. The garden, stretching to the river wall was as it had always been. The bathing places were unchanged. All had seen her mother in her young life. The very earth remembered. It was part of her.

The marriage ceremony in the incense filled haze of the Temple of Ptah, was long and exhausting. But the girl was beautiful with her waiflike fragility. Her wide eyes were fixed on the face of the brother she had come to trust, as she walked the length of the Temple, hardly aware of the courtiers and priests present. Jala wept. She had come to love this fragile girl. And watching her fulfil this simple act required of her to become Egypt's queen, which had always been on a knife edge, flooded her mind with relief. She had achieved it. Now she would step out of the girl's life for the moment. Tutmose must be her companion now. Her first friend. Her trusted friend. Until in time a marriage could be made between them.[77]

---

[76] A breed of dog known in Egypt at this time.

[77] There is evidence that Tutmose and Nepherure were married for a short time.

CHAPTER 9

SHOCKWAVES REACH MIDIAN 1484 BC

THE SHOCK OF TUTMOSE'S WARS spread far and wide, even reaching to Midian on the far side of the Edomite Sea. The Midianite tribesmen heard it first at their gathering in the north at the oasis of Aqaba on the seashore. But the news brought a swift end to their annual gathering. Everyone knew that this news would come one day, but still it struck fear. The old Pharaoh Hatshepsut was dead and Pharaoh Tutmose now held power alone. Fear had spread like wild fire across Canaan because revenge was in the air. For the last 2 years Tutmose had been building his army and now the punishment had begun. The city states who had dared to rebel had only felt the first wave of his anger, but for months now, Canaanite families who could, had fled south to Edom, to find safety in the towns of Eloth[78] and Ezion-Geber. Here they should be safe, because Egypt had no quarrel with Edom. But the towns were overflowing with desperate people.

Of the Midianite women, Zipporah was the first to hear the news. Her father Jethro trusted his eldest daughter to listen and be quiet. Once the other women of the tribe were told the news, the wailing would be unstoppable. But Zipporah's response had been silence, as she digested the facts. The news was certainly true. Some of their tribesmen going to the gathering had passed through Eloth and Ezion-Geber only a short distance west of Aqaba. They had seen the panic first-hand.

Jethro left the tent, leaving the girl to continue her work. She could think while she worked, but her heart was racing. Were they in danger? Surely here in their settlement at Maqna, far to the south of Aqaba accessible only by a narrow coastal track, there could be no danger. The northern town of Haql just south of Aqaba could be at risk. But one of the few blessings of this barren land that her people called home, was its position well to the east of the military road connecting Egypt with Canaan. Surely Egypt would not invade Midianite territory. There was nothing to take except people to enslave. And Egypt already used Midianite men, working them as hard as slaves, to smelt copper. The Midianites must find their bread somewhere. Their land could not feed them, and Midianite men were famous for their skill in copper smelting[79]. They worked for Egypt and were paid in grain. The work provided essential food for their families, but no one spoke of the health cost of the work. That the acrid vapours from melting copper would shorten their lives. It was the price they must pay to live in this land. But its isolation gave them safety. Where in the wide world could safety be found but in this wilderness with little water and hemmed in by mountain and sea. Living was tough but at least here they were safe.

Since the rise of this new dynasty of Egyptian Pharaohs, which were in fact the old family of Egyptian kings, who had hidden away in the south of the country while the Hyksos invaders held sway in the north - since their rise to power, nothing was safe. Egypt was as powerful now as in her golden age and was determined to conquer all who questioned her authority. Her armies could crush everything and everyone. Even cities with high walls could not stand against her.

But Zipporah knew enough of the situation to stay calm. As her father's favourite, with his quick mind, and because she wanted to learn, he had taught her about the wider world. She knew the danger of Egypt and the need for diplomacy. She knew about Edom, to the north, whose wise kings did not war with their neighbours but grew rich by offering safe haven to the thousands of traders who passed through their territory every year. Her father had taught her the language of Egypt and the Egyptian counting system, so she could deal confidently with the traders who passed through their settlement. Her tribe traded everything they could, to live. When no rain fell the sheep could not find pasture and food was short. The fear of famine was always present. The dread of hungry children with their pitiful wailing. They would not all survive.

Fish could be plentiful in a good year when storms did not churn the deep ocean to the south. And the women worked long hours to make anything the traders would buy. Most prized of all were their textiles. Beautiful work. Patterned rugs of sheep's wool coloured with natural dyes and woven by hand on large wooden looms. There were always some rugs, the best, that were kept as currency to be exchanged for grain when famine reared its ugly head. Or very rarely if times were good and it was festival time, a few rugs may be exchanged for precious spices. But Zipporah knew that her life would continue in the same pattern as that of her mother and grandmother. Nothing could change here, in this place of isolation. Nothing for good or for ill.

---

[78] Ancient Eilat
[79] Midianites were famous copper smelters, employed by Egypt.

CHAPTER 10

AMENEMHAT

FROM HIS HOME IN IUNY[80], Amenemhat[81] heard the news that had exploded in the corridors of power. He learned of Senenmut's speech at the Great Council, where the great and good of Egypt had hung on his words. Where he had so nearly won the argument that would slowly allow leading Habiri slaves to become citizens; but how in a moment of madness, or fury or conceit he had told the Council that he himself was an Habiri. That he was an example of what these men could be, and be for Egypt, clever, loyal, and hard working. Amenemhat had seen it so many times in their years together. Senenmut's inability to see danger. His belief that he was invincible. That even his enemies could not fail to listen. But he had failed to see that the poison of jealousy could wilfully blind men to the truth.

Amenemhat had wept for his friend – his brother. Had he escaped? Where was he now? The frenzy of interest in him had slowly died, bereft of fuel to fire it. Amenemhat heard all the news. The death of the Pharaoh. The rise of Tutmose lll as Egypt adjusted to her new reality. The rebellion in Canaan which had been expected as night follows day. The mobilising of the army after harvest. News travelled even here to his foundry in this quiet backwater of Iuny where he worked with his half-brother. Rebuilding the business had kept his mind from losing its moorings. But he never talked, and his brother Parry[82] knew better than to ask. Fear silenced the lad. Any connection with the traitor Senenmut would send them to the mines, or worse. There was safety in silence.

Slowly the news at the city gate where men gathered changed to war. The young Pharaoh was a man of action. Canaan was in revolt, spurred on by the kings of Qadesh and Naharin. Egypt must act. The younger generation were eager to go. To see the world. To follow their Pharaoh. To come home with booty and maybe a slave. The optimism of youth always prevailed in the minds of the young. Amenemhat knew better. He had seen war, the carnage, the horror. The strangeness of a body so alive then dead. So little changed, yet in a day, passing from the beauty of a fine physique, a man active and strong, to a stinking corpse. Parry had heard enough of war to know better than to follow the King. Amenemhat did not need to forbid it. Together they worked on, half-brothers, skilled men, making a living at their forge.

As the years passed, their work expanded. They took local lads as apprentices. Well-built boys who could work hard. They came to the foundry and learned their trade, until after a few years, Amenemhat could ease up. Take some respite. The business paid well, but what should he do now that he could raise his head from the daily grind. Should he take a wife? Not from here. Not an Egyptian girl. He lived like an Egyptian but wanted a wife who knew his real world. But it set him thinking. Was it now safe to go north? To seek out the world he had come from. To see if Senenmut had found their family before he became an exile. He knew Senenmut had started to search for their roots. He would not have rested until he found the truth and discovered his story.

The Festival of Opet[83] was approaching. Businesses would close. Everyone would go to Waset for the Festival. His absence would not be noticed. Now was the time to go.

Amenemhat set his house in order, leaving Pairy and the lads with clear instructions. He would be gone for a few weeks. The Northern army base was now in Avaris. He would use this reason for his journey. His story was that he was trying to procure army contracts for the business. Metal workers were essential. Amenemhat could show them weapons he had made. His business could expand beyond domestic and farm implements. He could make arrow heads, spear heads, helmets, war axes, although he preferred to make defensive not offensive items. Forging a battle axe brought back too many memories. But he would make whatever his customers wanted. He lived in the real world.

With the river running beside the town, transporting goods north would be easy. It would take a few weeks to reach Avaris, but the river was always flowing. On reaching Avaris, Amenemhat was determined to put out of his mind, memories of his brother. He had lived the last 6 years with the constant ache of guilt. He himself was the connection between Senenmut's two worlds. He had been the cause of Senenmut discovering his slave heritage. Ever since Amenemhat realised that Senenmut was the brother he had lost in childhood, he had put a guard on himself to prevent Senenmut from learning the truth. But he had failed. Caught for a single moment off guard, he had betrayed himself and thrown Senenmut into the downward spiral of discovery. The knowledge that his was of slave blood.

Reaching Avaris Amenemhat was astonished at the change. There were new buildings everywhere, where the quiet old town had been. The new King had moved the headquarters of the Northern Army there, with extensive new barracks for his men. And he was extending the docks and building ships to transport his army to the ports of Syria. Once built, the ships were moved to the harbour of Perenepher[84] in readiness for war. Only under the Hyksos had Avaris been so exalted. Never by the kings of Waset, or any before them. But to control Canaan it was necessary to use Avaris. Tutmose would continue to honour his family's god above all. His capital would remain at Waset. Amun and his great temple at Ipet[85] would not be neglected. But daily life for the army must now centre on Avaris, while the king spent most of his time at Men-nepher, the nearest royal city.

The noise of stone workers could be heard on every side. It was rumoured that Tutmose would take the port cities of Canaan on his next campaign. Then he could transport the army and supplies by ship to the coast of Syria.

One rumour that Amenemhat heard and believed, was that Senenmut had received sanctuary from someone in the Habiri community in Avaris. Without it he could not have made his escape. He must have contacted the Habiri leaders and found sanctuary with them, and this was where Amenemhat would start searching for his family. He wandered through the town following the river, observing the people around him. The city was a melting pot of races and soldiers of every rank. A new campaign into Syria was expected as soon as the harvest was gathered, and preparations could be seen on every hand. Armaments were arriving by ox waggons. Messages must be carried to and fro, and woe to the farmer with his laden donkey passing along the thoroughfares as chariots tore past, oblivious of man and beast.

On the edge of town Amenemhat noticed a group of workshops by the river. It was a poor district and few of the men wore wigs. Nor were their heads shaven, as were all Egyptians. He began to hope he had found the Habiri settlement. He approached an old man and greeted him in Hebrew, the language of his early home in Men-nepher, before they had moved to Iuny. The man hesitated, looking round to see if they were alone.

"I don't know you. Where are you from?" he asked.

"I live in the south", Amenemhat replied, again in Hebrew, and the sensation was strange.

"What do you want?" asked the old man, still nervous of this stranger who was flouting the rules by speaking in the language of the slaves.

"I speak in Hebrew," said Amenemhat, "because I am looking for the free Habiri community. I know some of them live in Avaris."

"How do you know about the Habiri community. Who do you know? Give me some names."

Glad of the progress, Amenemhat continued.

"My family lived in Men-nepher when I was a child. My father was Amram, of Levi's house, but he died, and my mother married a man named Ramose. My mother's name was Jocabed, and she was also of the family of Levis."

The old man's expression changed. Gone was the air of suspicion, but in its place was one of fear.

"Why should I believe you? Tell me about this family. How many children were born to Amram?" he asked in a strange voice.

"My sister Mirjam was the first, then myself. I was known as Aaron. Then my younger brother was given the name Manasseh,[86] but was not known by that name".

Now an extraordinary thing happened. The old man who had been sitting quietly outside the workshop, got to his feet without a word, and hobbled as quickly as he could inside, leaving Amenemhat alone. No explanation was given. He was simply left where he was, standing under the acacia trees outside the workshop. He waited, not knowing what to do, then after a considerable time, another man emerged.

"I am Simeon," he said. "I am happy to talk, but would you come with me? My home is nearby."

Simeon's manner was reserved but mannerly. Amenemhat followed him a short distance along the path fronting the river, where they entered a modest house. Simeon turned and spoke the words Amenemhat was longing to hear.

"If you wish to know of your brother, the child who was adopted, I can tell you that he must have reached the fortress at Tharu and made his escape."

Amenemhat sat down, staring at Simeon.

"I never thought I would hear those words," he said. "If my brother escaped Egypt, he is probably alive."

"And you must be Aaron," Simeon said gently after some time. "I am your mother's younger brother."

Amenemhat stared at his host. He could hardly believe his ears. A flood of pain filled his mind as the sudden realisation of all he had lost, came to him. For a long while he could not speak.

"I never expected to find any of my family again," he said after a long silence. "Our life in the south gave us food and work and let us live as free men, but we lost all experience of community. Our neighbours were fair but distant. They knew we were not local, and Iuny is a proud town. Proud of its connection to Egypt's royal house[87]".

"So you wish to return? asked Simeon. The old Pharaoh is dead, and her son is gone. There are none who will remember. You could return and live here as a free man."

Amenemhat considered his reply for some time. His half-brother Parry would not wish to move north, but his sister might.

"My sister has returned to my house. She was married but her husband is dead. He was Egyptian and she wanted to be as others, but now she has returned. We live as Egyptians, but she knew the old life most of all of us. She was nine years old when we left the north."

"Have you married?" asked Simeon.

"No. I do not want to marry an Egyptian girl and have no other choice in the south. But if I took a wife from this community, she would find my home alien indeed."

Amenemhat and Simeon talked long into the night. They talked of family past and present, of the community of Avaris and the freed slaves who lived there. Amenemhat talked of Senenmut and of the strange way they had met as boys. Of the uncomfortable feeling Amenemhat had always had about Senenmut. His likeness to his brother, then the discovery of his birth. They talked of the new Pharaoh and his campaign in the north. Of the new army base at Avaris and all the changes taking place. Avaris would grow profoundly as a city now that it housed the army headquarters. He may find permanent work here. Perhaps a move to the north would be possible. He would discuss it with his sister Mirjam on his return home.

---

[80] Iuny was a city south of Thebes
[81] Senenmut's Habiri brother known later by his Habiri name Aaron.
[82] Parry was a half brother of Amenemhat and Senenmut
[83] An important religious festival in Waset
[84] Perenepher was a large harbour on the coast north of Avaris
[85] Karnak
[86] The Septuagint in Judges 18 v 30 gives Mose's original Hebrew name as Manasseh. Josephus also says this.
[87] The Tutmoside royals were originally from the town of Iuny

CHAPTER 11

ZIPPORAH LISTENS

ZIPPORAH WAS WEARY AFTER HER day with the sheep but must now apply herself to her evening duties. She snatched some warm bread for herself hungrily as she attended to the food for her father and his guest. Her labours would probably stretch into the night with little time to attend to herself. But as the eldest daughter of the family this and many other responsibilities fell to her. She had been with the flock all day, managing not only the sheep and goats but her sisters as well. Now she must serve her father and his guest, because Jethro had found in their new guest, a man whose company he valued, and he wished to eat with him alone. He wanted news. This man would know what was happening in the world. He had an Egyptian name. He must be Egyptian. Everyone in the Mafkat, in Midian, and in every city state of Canaan, lived in dread of Egypt. How could they not? Egypt had no equal. Her rule stretched for hundreds of schoeni[88] to the south, all along the great River[89] into Nubia and Kush. These kingdoms had been controlled by Egypt for a thousand years despite the innate strength of the Kushite men and the size of their armies. Tall and strong, Kushites were renowned as deadly bowmen, but still Egypt had overcome and cowed them into servitude, plundering their gold, cattle, ebony, and ivory and enslaving their people. For hundreds of years the whole length of the River, south of the border had been studded with Egyptian fortresses to keep control of Kush. Each fortress the size of a city, and housing thousands of soldiers behind impregnable walls. And not content with controlling Kush, the father of the female Pharaoh Hatshepsut, had invaded Canaan also. Both north and south had remained obedient until her death, but now there were rumours. And as leader of his people, Jethro must discover what was happening in the dangerous world beyond his borders.

"The great Pharaoh Hatshepsut is dead. This is what we hear," said Jethro, hoping his guest would have news to give.

"Yes, she is dead," said his guest quietly.

"She was a strong ruler for 22 years since her husband's death. In fact, she was the real ruler since her father's death," Jethro added. "It is well known that she was the power behind her husband's throne." He paused and continued, hoping to draw Moshe out.

"Will her nephew Tutmose be a strong ruler?"

Moshe knew he must not appear reticent. It would be bad manners, ungrateful. He forced himself to speak of Egypt, and the tired girl serving them heard it all.

"Will Tutmose be content to control Canaan, or will he wage war in the north, as the rumours tell us?" asked Jethro.

Moshe was silent. He must turn the subject somehow and ally his host's fears.

"Pharaoh Tutmose is building up the army to go north," Moshe replied and paused.

"He has been well trained," he added, as the memory of his own part in it came back to him. Remembering the skinny boy that he himself had taught to drive a chariot! Taught to use a bow. And now Tutmose was Pharaoh and leading the army!

"Yes, we hear that the army base has been moved entirely away from Men-nepher to Avaris the old Hyksos capital," mused Jethro.

"It is some years now since that move was begun," said Moshe. Ahmose[90] himself started the move north by building a new palace on the site of the old Hyksos palace[91]. Now the Northern Army has its base in Avaris, while the harbour at Peren-nefer will be restored and extended as a military harbour."

"A palace in the north where the army is stationed is much better of course, said Jethro thoughtfully. "Then the pharaoh is ready with his army within easy striking distance of Canaan," he added.

"You understand the situation well," said Moshe quietly. "The Southern

Army must remain in the south to control Kush, but the focus is now on the north, to control Canaan."

Jethro pondered for a while in silence. The thought of Egypt building up her forces just across the Mafkat from Midian, was disquieting. Perhaps his guest would know about Egypt's intentions.

"Should I be concerned, that Egypt might cast her eye over Midian?" he asked.

The tired girl had paid little attention to what was said so far. She could understand the Egyptian tongue if she concentrated, but in her weariness, she had hardly listened. But now, hearing her father mention Midian and the Pharaoh in the same breath, her attention was riveted on the two men. Night had fallen, and the light of the fire between them, glowed on their faces. Over the past two hours, the girl had been a silent shadow as she served them bread and oil, followed by the rich stew of vegetables and goat meat which the other women had made earlier that day. The girl had been too distracted to observe them. Now, as she served the remaining course of ripe figs with curds of sheep's milk, she watched. She must miss nothing.

"Egypt will not invade Midian," said their guest with no hint of doubt.

"It is a relief to hear you say so with such certainty, but how can you be sure?" asked Jethro.

"Egypt is pleased to use your men to smelt copper, a skill known here far better than elsewhere." He paused. "Some smelting is done in Nubia, but the purity of the copper dug out in the Mafkat is superior to that of Nubia. And there is no sense in taking it to Nubia for smelting."

The girl noticed that she was holding her breath as she listened. For Egypt to turn her attention to Midian and send in troops would be the stuff of nightmares. She had heard what they did to women and children in Canaan while the men would be butchered if they resisted and enslaved if they did not. She moved quietly to her cooking fire to boil water. The men would want drinks before they went to their rest. She stood silent and still, waiting for the water to boil. Jethro too was silent, listening as his guest continued.

"You have no reason to fear an invasion by Egypt," he said. "The stability of your village system means there is a constant supply of boys reaching maturity. And you train them yourselves to be competent workers, then send them to the Mafkat ready to work. We use unskilled slaves to do the mining, but we need skilled men to smelt the copper."

Jethro observed his guest.

"You speak of yourself as Egyptian. Do you think you will return?" he asked, regarding the bronzed muscular man in front of him.

Moshe laughed, a bitter laugh, noticing for the first time the slender girl moving in the firelight as she brought him a bowl of steaming tea. It smelled of herbs with a hint of spice.

"It hardly matters how I speak of myself," said Moshe softly. "Perhaps I will always be Egyptian in my mind, but my heart can no longer belong to Egypt. And I will never return."

One Egyptian 'Schoenus' = 10.5 km

[89] The Nile was simply called 'the River'

[90] Ahmose was the first king of the New Kingdom. He defeated and drove out the Hyksos.

[91] Ahmose's palace has recently been discovered at Ezbet Helmi

CHAPTER 12

ZIPPORAH LISTENS AND LEARNS

JETHRO AND MOSHE CONTINUED TO eat alone, and the news continued to spread of the arrival of an Egyptian stranger, befriended by their leader. The story was told by the girls among the women of how he had helped against the shepherds. The stranger aroused much more interest than the usual excitement at the arrival of the camel train from Ezion-Geber. This was always welcome, as no one else ever passed this way, but its scope for news was limited. It visited the large community at Haql in the north, and this small community at Maqna, where Jethro's tribe lived because of its abundant water. Then it continued far to the south to the shore of the vast sea and to the mysterious lands further east where tribes of other races lived. But it rarely had news of Egypt.

As the days passed and the stranger stayed in the camp, even the men took notice. Who was he? Was he a guard from the Egyptian mines of the Mafkat?[92] None of the men remembered him, but there were only retired men here. And the stranger had shown kindness to Jethro's daughters which was not the action of an Egyptian guard from the mines who were without exception, beasts not men. The old men speculated that Moshe was from the army. It was said that Egypt's young Pharaoh Tutmose was preparing for war. Perhaps their visitor had fallen foul of the Pharaoh. And amid the speculation, Zipporah too became fascinated by the stranger. She alone had heard the discourse between himself and her father. This man was in a class of his own. She knew her father was head and shoulders above the other men in the tribe, educated as he had been in Egypt, and with an understanding of the outside world. But he was not exceptional when compared with the stranger. Of course, her father wanted their guest to stay. There was no one else in the tribe with whom he could share his mind. None of the women with their petty quarrels or even the men who had no ambition. There was none to match her father. Even his eldest son, Hobab had no interest in the outside world, despite his time at school in Egypt[93].

Zipporah was of marriageable age, but no one was chosen for her, and she had no doe eyes for any of the young men. But watching this Egyptian with her father as she served their food, she listened, fascinated. Here was a man with wide horizons who knew much of the world. A man of learning and understanding. But listening, night after night, she realised he carried a burden. And slowly as she continued to listen, it gradually became clear to Zippporah that he was a hunted man.

What was his story? Was he from the army as the men speculated? He was certainly not from the mines. And he was not a trader. He had a natural authority. And, like her father was a man of culture. Egyptian, but without the pride and arrogance that was their hallmark. She listened to the words and nuances that passed between the two men. They ate alone or with Hobab but rarely with the other men, as they spoke in the Egyptian tongue, with occasionally a little Aramaic. She understood it all. The silent presence. Trusted by her father. Unnoticed by their guest.

"I was a General in the army," he said.

"You served under Tutmose?"

"I served under the Pharaoh Hatshepsu[94]".

"But now the young Pharaoh reigns alone and he wants his own way. I see," said Jethro. "And some of his stepmother's generals do not suit him."

"That is not the whole story Sir, but may I reserve that for another time?"

"Of course. With a change of leader there are always changes. I understand," said the old man.

Moshe was silent. But the listening girl was transfixed and could think of nothing else. So he had fled Egypt! Her thoughts were totally consumed by this man she had known for only a matter of days. And if there had ever been thoughts in her mind of another man, they now withered on the vine.

Night after night the two men shared their minds. Jethro had found a man who was his equal. Who surpassed him in knowledge of the world but was his equal in mind. They discussed widely.

"Have these lands always belonged to Midian?" Moshe asked.

"The Midianites have only been a separate people for 400 years. The land we have here is poor, but it is secure, and with our able-bodied men away working in the Mafkat, we need security for our women and children." He paused.

"Here we are away from the military road connecting Egypt to the north. That brings us security. To the east we are protected by a vast empty wilderness. Only traders pass this way. We are separated from Egypt by the Mafkat and the sea," he paused, then continued.

"The land can sustain sheep and goats if it is grazed carefully. But it is poor land, not like Canaan. Not worth fighting for. It is barren, with rocks and mountains and little rain. We have abundant water, but it is deep in the ground[95] and finding it is a skill not known to many."

"So your people found the land empty of men when they came here?" asked Moshe.

"Yes. Our tribe moved south from Canaan and found the isolation here gave them protection. There are a few nomadic tribes beyond these mountains to the east," he said indicting the huge monoliths lit by the last rays of the sun against the darkening sky. "But it is a trackless wilderness."

"But it provides for your needs?"

"The land itself cannot feed us, but our men are skilled in working with copper and earn their bread smelting copper for Egypt." said Jethro.

"And Egypt is glad to employ them and pay them in grain," said Moshe.

Jethro laughed. "You understand the situation," he said. But then became more sober. "Since living here with steady employment supplied by Egypt, we have grown in number." He paused as the new thought troubled him. "This is good, of course. In the last few years there has been no famine and our numbers have increased again. We now have more lads reaching working age, but that has caused a new problem." He paused again. "They are more than can be employed in the Mafkat. While food is sufficient all is well, but if we have famine as we have in the past, our people will suffer." He hesitated. "There are few things so terrible to see, as starving children," he said.

Moshe listened. He knew well that Egypt mined the Mafkat and had done so for millennia, supplying the Pharaohs with both turquoise and copper. But he did not know this land or its extreme barrenness. Reba had not told him. Maybe he could stay here, and if he did, he must find ways to help these people. He liked Jethro and realised how fortunate he was to have found such a welcome. It could be the perfect refuge for him. A place to hide. Near to Egypt, but out of sight, where no one would think to search for him.

MOSHE LAY IN HIS TENT thinking. He had been woken by his recurrent nightmare, but it was past. He was now safely in Midian and told himself to view his position as good fortune. He had learned that Reba was dead, but Jethro had welcomed him, indeed he was glad to welcome this cultured stranger. He rose and quietly left the tent. The Midianite settlement still slept. Dawn would be an hour yet, but the eastern sky was growing lighter. He walked silently away from the surrounding tents. He wanted solitude. He must think. His mind was questioning his decision to stay here. Was it the right choice? He was safely hidden but should he have gone north and found a purpose for his days in the Court at Sumer or Ashur?[96] They would have used his skills and his knowledge. But he would be the continual target of assassins. He would never know peace. Here they could search, but what for? For a man with no name, no position? If they did not find him in Canaan or the east, they would conclude he was dead. Staying here might buy him safety for his body but it would be death for his mind. What would he do with his life? He was still a young man in strength and mind despite his 40 years. And life would be unbearable with no purpose.

Moshe's gaze moved south away from the eastern sky. The light was spreading, and the huge mountains to the south were silhouetted against it. He had never seen such giants. They were bigger even, than the mountains of the Mafkat. Some showed blackening at the top. He had heard of mountains that spewed fire. Were these fire mountains? He had watched them before, and their raw power and blackened peaks drew him. If he must spend time in Midian, he would venture that way one day. The raw grandeur of those peaks would help him accept the "littleness" he had become.

[92] Mafkat is the ancient name for the Sinai peninsula, where Egypt mined copper and turquoise for millennia.

[93] It was a normal practice for the sons of leaders in the nations surrounding Egypt, to be schooled in Egypt.

[94] Written this way Hatshepsut's name removes the female element.

[95] Even today there is a vast aquifer under the Saudi and Jordanian deserts.

[96] Two of the earliest cities of the ancient East.

CHAPTER 13

TUTMOSE'S 2ND CAMPAIGN; REGNAL YEAR 24; 1480 BC

ONLY TWO YEARS HAD PASSED since the beginning of Tutmose's sole reign, but in that time, he had become, in truth, a man and a king. He had led his first Campaign into Canaan and seized a resounding victory, a thing not attempted on such a scale since the time of his grandfather. His extraordinary victory had been acknowledged by all the emerging powers to the north and east. Yes, the campaign was an unquestionable success. Before it, Canaan was falling under the control of Naharin. Since that campaign, Egypt was Canaan's undisputed master and the world acknowledged that Tutmose was his grandfather reborn.

But there was another reason that contributed to his new self-belief. He had married the girl he wanted. The girl his brother had loved. She was also the Royal heiress, and marriage with her confirmed his right to rule. But it was the girl herself that mattered most. In a life that had known little of love, he had found that rare thing. Someone he truly loved. When he remembered the failing child that he had been, and how he had idolised his brother, he could hardly believe the turn of events that had raised him so high and cast his brother from Egypt, a fugitive. Clearly the gods had made their choice.

But now he faced another challenge. His second campaign. To prove that the first was not simply chance. The rulers of Syria had been seriously frightened by that first Campaign. They had not expected to meet such a force. Now, on hearing that Tutmose was again taking his army north they were truly afraid. What had they done to wake this sleeping beast that was Egypt! They had miscalculated. Tutmose had men enough and to spare. He could garrison the defeated towns, so could build on his victories year after year. Now he was returning north only a year after his previous Campaign! Where would it end?

But Tutmose was resolved that at this stage he would not attempt to gain more territory but would consolidate his previous gains. Taking his army north would remind the city states of Canaan that Egypt was their lord. He would extract another year's tribute. The people of Canaan were cattle and must be driven to obedience. Never would they be allowed to forget their crime in supporting the Hyksos in the past, and Naharin so recently. The humiliation that the Hyksos had brought on Egypt would never be forgotten and never forgiven. This tour would be of Canaan only, to remind these cities that their land was subject to Egypt. With Megiddo still broken after the war and the siege, Hazor was the leading city of the region south of Qadesh. He would visit this city in all his pomp and teach them to fear him.

The army crossed the Mafkat to Gaza and on to Yehem. The open road now lay ahead leading to Hazor. It was a good road, built for chariots. The hours crept by, but the drive was pleasant. They would push on to cover the ground and halt to camp on the north side of a large inland sea, the Sea of Chinnereth half a day's drive south of Hazor.

The sun was moving west sending out its slanting rays, and in the distance Tutmose could see a line of blue water filling the horizon, with low hills beyond. A beautiful sight, restful after the long day. The horses were weary and could smell water making them restless. Tutmose brought his chariot to a stop on a slight rise above the lake and stepped down from it wearily. He walked down to the water's edge leaving his driver to attend to the horses. Small waves lapped the shingle beach. A restful sound as they washed over tiny shells deposited on the shoreline. Separated from the proximity of his men, Tutmose was aware of the peace of the place. A timeless tranquillity in marked contrast to his reason for coming here. It felt almost a sacrilege to disturb this peace. But he turned away. Thoughts came to his mind that he did not wish to consider. He refused to think of them. But his eyes were drawn again and again to the tranquil water. A sight totally at odds with the pent-up force in his mind, driving him on to punish these cities that had dared to rebel. It came to his mind, that peace was a thing of beauty, a thing to prize. War may fill Egypt's coffers and make her great. War would bring tribute to the temples and please the gods. But peace held a beauty he would never find in war. He paused. His men were gathering now. The camp would soon settle in for the night. His generals were waiting. He could not stay. But in later years these thoughts often returned. They entered his dreams and asked him again to answer the question. Was peace a thing to prize?

CHAPTER 14

MERYET[97]

JALA WAS WARY. IN A short while, Nepherure's half-sister, Meryet was to pay a visit. Jala had never met this young woman but sensed that there was no real friendship between the girls. They had been together only as children and their friendship had faded. But now with Hatshepsut's death Meryet was determined to make gains from the connection.

Instinct had always warned Nepherure of the latent jealousy in her sister. Although not of the Solar Blood, Meryet would have been a candidate to be queen. She was half royal. She was young. She was considered a beauty. But once again the spoils had gone to Nepherure and now the green eye of jealousy burned even more strongly in the young rival.

When Meryet heard that Tutmose's queen, Satiah had died, she hoped that Nepherure, the obvious candidate, would stay out of the contest. Nepherure was in deep mourning for her mother and Senenmut. Meryet hoped that if she left her sister unsupported, she may simply retire from court to the Harem and leave the field open. So she had hoped. But her plan had failed! She realised now that if she had come to Nepherure at her time of need and wept with her, she could have shepherded the girl to the Harem herself. But now Nepherure was queen, and all her own status and royal blood was of no use. She was an un-needed extra, who would fade into insignificance. And here were sown the seeds of her hatred. For Meryet was no fool. She knew the potential power of her position. After Nepherure, she was the logical choice for queen. And Nepherure was stupid! To remain loyal to that man Senenmut after his fall from grace, when the King, the holder of the throne, wanted her as his queen, was utter folly. What was the value of sentiment when put in the balance against power? Power and position! To be queen was to have your name and likeness carved in stone on monuments up and down the land, to stand for eternity. Carved in palaces and temples. The Great Royal Wife of a powerful Pharaoh. He was not yet powerful, that was true. But Egypt was rising to new heights. She would soon be as great as she had been in her golden age 400 years ago, before the Hyksos invasion, when Egypt's iron fist had taken control of Kush and Nubia. When she had built a garland of fortresses along the Nile to keep these vast lands under her heel. And with the slave population of the Delta, to do the work of feeding the country, Egyptians were free in their tens of thousands to become soldiers. With such an army, Egypt could make Canaan, with her rich city states as much a slave as Nubia. And Nepherure would have given it all away for the love of a man!

Meryet knew that she was not such a fool. But she had been a fool! She had allowed Nepherure to recover after Senenmut's departure. Allowed her to charm and please Tutmose. Had allowed Nepherure to bring herself to the task sufficiently to marry Tutmose and become his Great Royal Wife! Meryet could hardly believe her own stupidity. She should have befriended her sister when she was vulnerable. When she could so easily be persuaded to live out her days in mourning and weep her life away. Then she, Meryet would be queen! She knew Tutmose did not care for her as he did Nepherure, with her soft feminine face. But Tutmose had no need of love in a wife. He could fill his Harem with beauties to his taste. And Meryet knew she would have been a perfectly good wife to Tutmose. Much less trouble than her delicate sister. But she had lost her chance! Her one chance! Unless – unless - could it be remedied even now? And this was her reason for visiting Nepherure today. She would be charming and warm. She would share her sister's joy at her marriage. She would enthuse. She would pretend. But hidden in her pretence she would drop the fatal words that would undo this marriage of convenience.

MERYET ENTERED THE APARTMENTS THAT had belonged to Hatshepsut. The best apartments in the palace. And as she did so, the old bitterness in her heart awoke. She loved beautiful things, and these apartments had always called to her. She had even envied Hatshepsut. Why should she herself not have such things? And now again she would be denied them, for now they belonged to her sister. Here the lamps were of alabaster, while her own were simply of faience[98]. The walls here were hung with sumptuous fabrics encrusted with jewels. Every couch for reclining was decorated with lapis lazuli and gold, and low ebony tables were piled with plates and wine jars imported from Crete and Thera. Huge vases of lotus blooms filled every corner, and as if that could not provide scent enough, expensive frankincense was burning to sweeten the air.

Jala went to meet the queen's sister smiling a welcome, but no matter how much she covered her face with smiles, Meryet's eyes were as hard as stone.

"You come to congratulate your sister on her marriage," said Jala. "How kind. Nepherure has been alone in her sorrow, but now you are come," she added intending to convey the hint of rebuke in her greeting. But Meryet swept past. She knew of this Nubian princess who had performed some heroic deed and been welcomed in Egypt. But she was Nubian, and Meryet would waste no time on a Nubian, not even one of royal rank.

"Where is my sister?" she asked without looking at Jala but gazing round the room at the many things she admired.

"The queen is expecting you," Jala replied. "I will tell her you are come."

She led the way into the smaller of the audience chambers. Meryet took this as a personal insult. Was she not fit to be entertained in the best room? But she said nothing.

Nepherure was reclining on a sumptuous couch, her gaze stretching across the palace gardens to the River, where sunlight was dancing on the moving water. At the sound of voices, she turned to see the curvaceous figure of her sister enter the room. She rose at once to greet her. Meryet scanned the scene before her, as she inwardly mocked this girl who would rise for anyone, when she was queen of Egypt. She produced her smile again, but Nepherure had seen that smile many times and knew it for what it was. She had no great hopes for this meeting. Their years together had taught her the sum of this sister, but she held out her hand and smiled. Meryet seized the hand offered to her and bowed to kiss the delicate fingers. She must play this role of 'caring friend' to the best of her ability.

"Welcome," said the new queen lightly, as she looked into her sister's face hoping, just hoping that there had been a softening since she had seen her last.

"I come to bring homage to our new queen," said Meryet trying to smile. "You have fulfilled your mother's wish, dear sister, she added, watching as her words found their mark. A shadow crossed Nepherure's face. This was no fulfilment of Hatshepsut's dream and they both knew it. But Meryet would take her time.

Nepherure spoke of the Coronation at Men-nepher. Of the great expedition underway to take the army into Canaan and put down the rebellion. Jala did not join them, sensing that she was not wanted by the proud Meryet. But she ordered the servants to bring wine and honey cakes to sweeten the time the girls had together.

"Yes, my husband is determined to repeat the victories of our grandfather and bring honour to his great namesake," said Nepherure. "Our grandfather's victory over Naharin, when he crossed the Euphrates, is printed on the King's mind. To repeat it is his great ambition," she said, trying to show an interest in warfare which was in fact anathema to her.

"May the gods be with him," replied the other. "May all Egypt's enemies flee before him," she said, looking knowingly at the queen.

Nepherure hesitated. The thought of Senenmut fleeing Egypt as a fugitive burst on her mind disturbing her peace. She looked at her sister who sat smiling at her, a cruel smile. Suddenly her tranquillity was broken. A sob escaped her, and she jumped to her feet and would have fled the apartment had not Jala come to her aid.

"My Lady, what has distressed you so suddenly?" she asked, catching Nepherure in her arms.

The queen stopped and turned, staring at Meryet.

"I think you should leave us," she said softly.

But Meryet had not yet delivered the full pay load of her ammunition and would not leave until she had.

"What have I said?" she protested. "Surely we all wish that Egypt's enemies be vanquished," she added.

Jala could see signs of real danger and was determined to prevent catastrophe.

"Lady Meryet, you know the queen is still weak. It would anger the King to know that she had been distressed by your visit," she said, refusing to lower her gaze from Meryet's face. But Meryet was also determined.

"I think the King would not undo his command to the High Priest of Amun to hound that Habiri traitor from the country. Ask him if you do not believe me," she said, as she rose, turned on her heel and swept from the room. A terrible silence hung in the air as she departed. The servants stood transfixed. Jala was frozen to the spot as she held the swaying form of Nepherure in her arms and stared after the retreating figure. Suddenly a great scream tore through the room as the queen slid to the floor and collapsed in a swoon on the cold tiles.

Now panic broke out on all sides. Servants lifted the queen and bore her to her couch. Jala fanned her face and offered her wine as soon as her eyes opened. But the poison of Meryet's words had done their work. Never again would Nepherure acknowledge her title as Great Royal Wife. Never again would she acknowledge the husband she had taken. Now she knew his guilt, that he was implicated in the plot to drive away her love, she would never see him again. She would leave the Court and live out her days in the Harem at Mi-Wer with Jala as her companion, and only once, in the far distant future would she ever return to the royal court, when all her youth and beauty had gone.

---

[97] Her full name is Meryetre-Hatshepsut. When I wrote my 1st book, the general thinking among Egyptologists was that Merytre was Hatshepsut's second daughter, mainly as she shares the name Hatshepsut. It is now known that her mother was Huy, a temple adoritrice. Her father is unknown, but it is clear she is from the royal harem, so I have made her a harem daughter of Tutmose ll, making her a half-sister of Nepherure, and for convenience I have shortened her name to Meryet.
[98] Faience is a material similar to opaque glass made by heating sand with different chemicals to create a variety of colour.

CHAPTER 15

NEPHERURE LEAVES WASET

JALA ATTENDED ON NEPHERURE IN the days that followed, but all the joy and contentment that the girl had found in her new life, had turned to stone. She would do as Jala bid her. She would eat a little and drink when asked. She slept and she woke, but she hardly spoke a word. The king had gone north with the army three months after his marriage, and all had been well until Meryet had told Nepherure of her husband's complicity in the banishment of Senenmut.

One morning, Jala came to the queen's rooms to find her dressed and walking in the palace gardens. Hope rose in her heart, but looking into the girl's face, Jala saw that the change was not for the better. Then with unaccustomed firmness, Nepherure spoke to her friend.

"I have decided that I will stay no longer in Waset. The King could return at any time, and I wish by then to be far from this city, and far from the Court." She reached out a hand to her friend and smiled weakly. "If you wish to stay here, I perfectly understand. I will give you an allowance which will make you free to live as you choose." She paused and became serious.

"You must marry and build a life for yourself as you have tried so hard to build a life for me."

Jala could bear no more. Her long-enforced self-control was utterly broken. All her work to coax Nepherure back into the land of the living, had failed. But she would not leave her now.

"My Lady, you are the only friend I have, or care to have. I promised you once that I would be your companion, and that I will be, wherever you wish to live."

At the kindness of this stranger, Nepherure could not contain her tears, and once again, these two desolate women wept together.

"Where will you go, my Lady? Is the only choice to bury yourself in the Harem."

"Yes, I will go to Mi-wer[99]. I no longer wish to live in the world of men."

"But you are queen, my Lady!"

"I am no longer queen," she said softly. "My sister's purpose in coming here was to break my trust in the King, and she has succeeded. He may now make her his Great Royal Wife, and perhaps then she will be content."

"But my Lady, isn't Mi-wer an uncivilised place? Surely the Harem in Men-nepher would be a better choice," said Jala.

"You are right of course, but I know that the Court will be spending much time in Men-nepher in the future." She paused. Despite her disinterest in politics and war Nepherure had a shrewd knowledge of what was current in Court matters. She had served with her mother many times in the Councils of State and understood the needs of Egypt looking forward.

"The north is what draws the King. He wishes to subjugate Canaan as our grandfather did. So he will be much more often in Men-nepher. I do not wish to be near him, so have decided that Mi-wer will suit me better.

The removal of the queen's household to Mi-wer was a simple matter. The river was high and the weather pleasant. Jala looked out across the parched land that was Egypt and longed for her homeland, but as they entered the Fayum[100], slowly the countryside around them turned green. Jala could hardly believe it. Never having been to the Delta, in all her time in Egypt she had never seen such verdure. She rested her eyes on the swaying crops and found peace, of a sort, from the turmoil of her broken dreams. But as they followed the canal into the basin of the Fayum such sights met her eyes as she had never imagined possible. A huge pyramid stood in the middle of the vast lake and beyond it stretched another building of enormous size. She had heard of the famous Labyrinth of the Fayum built centuries before. But how was it possible to build such things? The scale was beyond belief[101]. But reaching the Harem itself, the contrast with the majesty of these buildings was shocking. There was no the luxury here! The simplest of buildings supplied the wants of these minor royal women. And was it here that the queen of Egypt was to spend her days! Jala was appalled, but Nepherure gave no sign of her thoughts. For her it was sufficient to have escaped the intolerable situation of being married to a man who had betrayed the thing most precious to her in all the world.

They settled quickly into the apartments allotted to them. As queen, Nepherure could command the best, and Jala made sure that she received it. But the best Mi-wer had to give was meagre indeed, and to add to that distress, Nepherure's health was becoming a concern.

It was two months now since the King had left for Canaan. Nepherure had determined that she would never see him again. But what ailed her? She was exhausted. Every morning she was violently sick. She could eat, and her delicate frame was not wasting, but her paleness and lethargy frightened Jala. Her own health had always been robust, and although she tried, she had little understanding of the ailments of others.

The days passed. Slowly they were settling into this new life. But the queen's health was not improving. One morning Jala was sitting with her friend who had not yet risen, and was troubled again by nausea, when one of the Harem attendants asked to speak to her alone. Jala followed the woman out of Nepherure's chamber as asked, but could not contain her anger.

"Why are you disturbing me at this time? You can see that the queen needs me."

"I am sorry my Lady, but I must speak to you. I have attended on many ladies, and I am certain that the Lady Nepherure, rather, the queen, is with child."

Jala stood transfixed! "What did you say?"

"The queen is with child, my lady. I would swear to it."

Jala turned and ran back to Nepherure's chamber. She stood rooted in the doorway watching as the girl threw up again, then lay back exhausted. Calmly she went to the bedside and sat beside her, but now her heart was singing. Nepherure opened her eyes and looked at her friend. She tried to speak but burst into tears. After a moment she calmed herself.

"I have never been ill like this before. When will it stop!" she said with a sob.

Jala ran her mind over the memories she had of her girlhood at the Harem in Semna[102] and made a calculation.

"It will start to improve in just a few more weeks my Lady," she said with a smile. "Be brave until then."

Nepherure heard the words mechanically, then turned her puzzled face up to her friend.

"You know what ails me? Since when have you studied physic?"

"I did not know what ailed you, my Lady, but you are in the very place where is it best known. This is a women's world, my Lady. A place where children are born, and you are with child."

---

[99] Mi-wer was a royal harem in the district of the Fayum which grew in importance during Tutmose lll's reign.Today the area is known as Gurob. The name Mi-wer means 'Great canal', after its siting on the Bahr Yusef canal which ran from the Nile into the Faiyum. A town built up around the Harem. The site was dug by Flinders Petrie 1888-9. Sobek was worshipped in the Faiyum. The sacred crocodile was called Petsuchos, a huge Nile crocodile encrusted with Jewels.

[100] The Faiyum Oasis is a depression or basin immediately to the west of the Nile south of Cairo in Egypt. The extent of the basin area is estimated at between 1,270 km^2 and 1700 km^2.
It has a large freshwater lake and in the past was a rich farming area.

[101] In the second book of his History, the Greek writer Herodotus states that the Labyrinth "surpasses even the Pyramids."

[102] Semna was an important city in Nubia on the Nile where we can assume that Jala had spent her childhood in a royal harem.

CHAPTER 16

REGNAL YEAR[103] 25 TUTMOSE RETURNS FROM HIS 2ND CAMPAIGN

TUTMOSE ENTERED THE PALACE AND went straight to the queen's apartment. He had hoped Nepherure might have come to greet him on his arrival home after his long absence, but perhaps she was unwell he thought. Then casting his eye around the queen's apartments, his disappointment turned to alarm. Hardly a servant stood in attendance. All the furniture was covered with linen sheets. There was no incense burning, no flowers filling the huge vases, and standing in solitary state in the centre of the room as if forgotten, was the tall gold and ebony loom he had sent as a gift to his queen from Megiddo. It had arrived but looked lost and without purpose standing there in the silent room. A gift unseen. Slowly a cold fear entered his mind. 'Where was Nepherure? She was a delicate little thing. Had something happened to her?'

"Where is my wife?" he shouted at the servants he found removing linen sheets from the furniture at his coming. One terrified servant stammered a reply.

"The queen is gone Majesty!"

"Gone! Dead! My bride dead and I am not told!"

"Not dead my Lord the man stammered but gone from the city. She has left Waset and gone to the harem at Mi-wer."

"Why has she left? What has happened that she has left me?" he shouted at the servant, but the man was mute.

Tutmose stormed out of the apartment to search for someone who could answer his question. Finally, the palace steward knelt before him.

"Get up man and tell my what has driven my wife away!"

The steward was terrified. How could he tell the King what had happened when all that he had to say was unsubstantiated gossip?

"Majesty, the queen left with no explanation."

"But something must have happened. Did anyone visit her?"

Now the steward was unable to escape. He dare not lie to the King.

"She did receive a visit from her sister, Majesty, the Lady Meryet, but I was not party to what passed between them."

Tutmose's mind considered these words. He knew his half-sister well enough to know that jealousy of Nepherure raged in her heart. But what had she done?

"Find the Lady Meryet and send her to me here - at once!" he shouted.

It was not long before Meryet arrived. She was wearing her finery and an exotic perfume.

"Greetings brother," she said lightly, kneeling before him.

He left her there for a long time. He was burning with anger but was determined to control himself. He knew that if he was to gain any truth from this woman, he must make her afraid. After a long while he bade her rise.

"Stand up madam." He said without looking at her. "I have some questions for you."

Meryet stood. Fear was now pounding her heart and written on her face. She realised she had miscalculated in her actions, but she would not cower. She, also, was of the royal house.

"You visited my wife shortly after I left with the army." He emphasised the word 'wife'. He wished her to acknowledge it.

"I visited my sister, yes, to congratulate her on her marriage, my King."

"We have been very happy together," he said looking her full in the face, confronting her.

"I love my wife very much indeed and I want her to be happy," he added.

Meryet lowered her eyes. Even she could feel the stab of conscience for what she had done.

"Since your visit to the queen she has been very distressed. So distressed in fact as to leave Waset."

"I have no idea why she was distressed," she lied.

"Did you mention my brother Senenmut?"

The girl winced and could no longer answer. He seized her arm viciously.

"Madam, if your words have broken the health of the girl I love, you will pay dearly for it."

But Meryet's jealousy and bitterness were burning also. She turned on him with fury in her words.

"You must take care my Lord. For if my delicate sister cannot give you sons, you will need to find another woman of the royal house who can!" she said, as she raised her eyes to his face in defiance.

But he knew these facts only too well, and his interest went far beyond the narrow world of her ambition.

"Lady, if I ever make you my queen, I promise you will not be the happier for it! I will use you to give me children, but I will honour as many women as I choose and acknowledge them all as my Royal wives!"[104]

He flung her away and strode from the room with icy self-control. Meryet stood alone for a moment, then breathing a short sob, fled the apartment.

Tutmose put aside the clamour of praise for his successful campaign from his Court and Generals and left Waset immediately for Mi-wer. If it was at all possible, he must see Nepherure. He reached the Harem anonymously and was shocked at the primitive apartments it offered.

'This is a dreadful place for my wife to live, even for a short time,' he said to himself. 'Something must be done. I will order a Palace fit for her to be built he resolved. And the place needs to live, to have industry and purpose'.[105]

Night was falling. He was desperate to speak to Jala and discover the facts, but he must wait until morning. He went to the King's apartments and summoned the Chief Eunuch.

"The queen must not to be told of my coming," he said, "but notify the Lady Jala that I wish to speak to her in the morning."

Next morning early, Jala came immediately at his summons. She was shocked to see the misery in his face and could not hide her fear.

"Madam, I want to know why you have removed my wife from Waset without my permission."

Jala fell to her knees before him, shocked at his words, but she must answer.

"My lord, please do not think that I have done this thing! I hope you know my Lord that it has been my greatest wish that Nepherure become your wife and achieving that end has been a great joy to me."

"Then why has she now left me!" he asked and could not hide the anguish in his voice.

"Majesty, the queen received a visit from her sister Meryet." She hesitated. If she chose the right words, perhaps he would not be angry, but to choose the wrong words would put the blame on him!

"Majesty, Meryet was party to information I did not know, so I cannot know the truth of it."

"But what did she say?"

"She said that you had instructed Menkheperraseneb, the High Priest of Amun to hound your stepbrother Senenmut out of Egypt."

Tutmose was stunned. It was cleverly done. He could hardly deny his dealings with the High Priest. It was not the whole truth, but it contained more than a grain of truth. He had indeed allowed Menkheperraseneb to test Senenmut's loyalty regarding the slaves. He knew now that Menkheperraseneb had used trickery, but the result was the same. Senenmut had fled Egypt, and that alone was enough to poison Nepherure against him. He thought about Jala's words a long time. She had been his ally he knew. He resolved to trust her with the truth of his own weakness.

"I was the dupe of the High Priest just as Nepherure has been the dupe of Meryet", he said simply, the anguish sounding in his voice. "He played on my fears, just as Meryet has played on Nepherure's fears. But I cannot be free of Menkheperraseneb and nor can I dispose of Meryet! Life is strange. The all-powerful pharaoh is in fact controlled by others.

"My Lord I fear the queen will never see you, or ever leave this place again," said Jala. She feared to speak, but the truth must be told.

"She feels she can no longer trust anyone, except perhaps me alone, and for her sake I must remain worthy of that trust."

Tutmose put his head in his hands.

"So I have lost her!" he said, and there was pain in the words. "And perhaps I must now make Meryet my Great Royal Wife!" he paused. "She has won! I must have sons. I have lost the one son I had by Satiah. Children die!"

He paused. "But Meryet will gain little from me. She may give me children, but I will give her no joy!"

Jala stayed silent as Tutmose said these words. Without Nepherure's permission she did not have the right to tell him that Nepherure was with child.

Tutmose left Mi-wer that day never to return. The Court was told that Nepherure's health had failed and that she had retired from her roles as Great Royal Wife and God Wife of Amun. That she would live out her days at Mi-wer and would not return.

---

[103] Ancient Egypt had no fixed point from which to measure years, such as our Year O, the birth of Christ. So they measured the years passing by reference to the number of years the king had reigned. Tutmose lll became king as a child in 1504 BC and reigned for 54 years until 1450. Hatshepsut reigned with him for the first 22 years so Tutmose's sole reign started in his 23rd Regnal year at the age of about 25.

[104] Tutmose took a number of women whom he acknowledged as his wives.

[105] It was Tutmose lll who developed the harem at Mi-wer into a luxurious palace with a thriving weaving industry where the royal women were employed.

CHAPTER 17

MOSHE JETHRO AND HOBAB TALK

THE HEAT OF THE DAY was fading to gentleness and a breeze from the north
stirred the evening air. Night would soon be upon them. Moshe stood outside
his tent watching the western sky with the last rays of the sun still red after the
dust storm which had passed through a few days before. After this brief
twilight, the sky would be a blaze of stars. Then it would be time for the men
to gather and eat.

As the first stars became visible Moshe moved away from the firelight of the
camp to the shadows at its perimeter. The vastness of the dark sky spread above
him and suddenly he was back at the temple of Ra in Iunu[106] remembering the
awe with which he had first gazed with understanding at this self-same sky. He
had been a scholar then, studying these wonders, all their power and mystery.
He had also been Senenmut, the son of the Pharaoh. It seemed an age ago. Far
from him now in time and space. He looked at the vast canopy above him
spangled with stars and planets. He could name them all, from 'the Imperishable
ones'[107] in the northern sky, across to where the decan stars[108] rose in succession
every ten days along the southern horizon, marking off the weeks of the year.
Had there been nothing in these stars to tell of his fall from power? He who had
stood so high in Egypt. Had the gods known nothing of his future? That he
would never be Pharaoh? That he would be an outcast? These powerful gods
who claimed so much but gave so little! And now he was a fugitive, fleeing for
his life, glad to find refuge in this desolate place. In the vagaries of life even the
one man he had set his hope in, Reba, was dead. But he had found a friend in

Jethro, who had been glad to welcome him, awed to have the companionship of a cultured Egyptian. So he had found sanctuary at least, and a welcome. Surely he should accept his lot. He was lucky to have found it.

Jethro himself was fluent in the Egyptian tongue. The other men of the tribe spoke enough to get by when working in the Egyptian mines, but Jethro had spent some time at school in Egypt, and his understanding was excellent. The tribesmen were in awe of Moshe. They speculated that he must be an army general who had fallen foul of his Pharaoh, but Jethro knew he must be more than that. Even a senior general in the army would not have the breadth of education that Moshe clearly had. With his wide understanding of the world, he had the knowledge of the priests as well. Even the highest priests. The real scholars. The ones to whom the whole world flocked to gain learning. And he hoped against hope that Moshe would stay. He longed to speak with him more, of the wider world and its learning. His own sons were outdoor men, not men of learning. They must earn a living, and their eyes were closed to the search for knowledge. They were too young to see its value as he could. He had been taught the value of learning as a boy and educated for some years in Egypt. Of his own sons only Hobab had spent time in Egypt and had learnt the language at least. And Hobab, as his heir did not spend time working in the Mafkat, but even he had limited horizons. He knew many languages and could deal effectively in the world of trade and barter. But Jethro wanted more than that. His active mind needed access to a world beyond the narrow confines of Midian.

The weeks passed and far from diminishing, fascination with this newcomer was growing in the tribe. The men ate together around the fire, but Jethro wanted his guest to himself. The two spent long evenings together and Jethro tried to draw him out. To learn the news of Egypt and so much more. Everyone wanted news of the court and the Pharaoh. But he must be patient. And he must not pry.

But there were times when the two of them were alone, when despite himself Moshe could not hide the pain and longing in his voice. He told Jethro privately that he had fled from danger. That he was guilty of killing a brutal slave master to protect a slave. He had not hidden these facts, and his kindness to Jethro's daughters showed that he was a man who hated injustice.

Jethro knew he must be patient, but he could hope and plan. Clearly Moshe had no plan, so Jethro would plan for him. He had no wife, but Jethro could provide a wife. He had daughters. It would be an honour for any girl to marry such a man. And as time passed it became less and less proper for a man to live in their community unwed.

Tonight, the two of them and Hobab had shared their evening meal and all three stayed drinking spiced tea under the stars. It was a world without walls, silent but for the murmurs from the women's tent and the restless sounds of the tethered mules grazing on the perimeter of the camp, watched by the boys.

Moshe held his cooling cup between his hands watching the glow of the fire between them as Hobab reported to his father on the business of the day. In this quiet backwater there was no threat from marauders. There were no buildings filled with possessions to attract raiders and the dry wilderness was impassable except to those with local knowledge. Even the camel trains never strayed from the coast road.

"Word is, that there is a surge in the crowd of fugitives flocking to Ezion-Geber. The lucky few to escape the wars in Canaan," said Hobab. "But it will soon be over. Egypt cannot hope to hold Canaan as she did in the days of the first Tutmose. The city states have experienced a taste of freedom under his son and the female Pharaoh, and they will fight to keep it."

Jethro glanced at Moshe then shared his own thoughts.

"But this Pharaoh seems determined to stamp his authority on Canaan," he said.

Moshe was conscious of the kindness of his hosts. They asked nothing in return. He would of course leave them gifts if he left, in payment. But did he wish to leave? And if all they wanted of him was to share his knowledge, he must give them something of what he knew. It was time to break his silence.

"Naharin[109] in the north is building her strength," he said glancing up. "And Naharin wants control of Canaan," he said and paused. "But Egypt needs Canaan. Her city states are an essential source of revenue and goods for Egypt," he finished, as his gaze returned to the fire.

"But surely Egypt cannot hope to overcome Naharin and her allies," said Hobab.

"It is true that Egypt has an enormous task to overcome the combined strength of Canaan and the other states loyal to Naharin," said Moshe. He paused then continued.

"Canaan wants to break free of Egypt. She has been held under by force alone, not loyalty. While some Canaanite cities have a blood connection with Naharin, none have a blood connection with Egypt."

"So how can Egypt hope to succeed if there is nothing to make the Canaanite cities stay loyal to her?" asked Jethro. "She may win a few campaigns but will have to face many more to overcome Naharin," he added. "Surely she cannot afford the cost of a long war. And the distance the Egyptians need to travel to reach the north all adds to the challenge."

Moshe hesitated. He knew exactly how Egypt paid for her army, but did he want to open the subject of the slaves? He waited, but he owed them a debt. He must speak.

"Egypt now has a large standing army that is a match for the combined force of Canaan, Naharin and her allies," he said. "Tens of thousands of men who do not return to their villages to plant and harvest every year. Elite soldiers must train. They cannot be farmers for most of the year if they are to be ready for war. These soldiers do not grow the food for their families, they are paid in grain that others have grown. Grain grown in vast quantities in the delta and used as their wages," he hesitated, but he had started now, so must finish. "This is how Egypt can train a powerful fighting force. Her peasant farmers can be full time soldiers because Egypt has a huge workforce of slaves who grow and store vast quantities of grain in the rich lands of the delta," he paused. "And this pays her army," he said then fell silent.

"And this is how she will subjugate Canaan!" said Hobab with anger in his voice.

"An elite army maintained by the work of slaves," added Jethro thoughtfully.

Silence hung between them. Jethro sensed that it had cost Moshe something to speak of the slaves and wondered why. But Moshe had not finished.

"War is costly, but Egypt is determined to maintain what she has gained. She cannot afford to lose Canaan because its foundries cast many thousands of bronze weapons and much bronze armour. And Canaan grows the Elm and

Birch trees needed in the building of chariots. These are woods which Egypt cannot grow herself."

Hobab and Jethro stared at their guest in silence. He had an intricate knowledge of Egypt. They listened spellbound. It was like the clearing of a mist to see the truth as it really was. Hobab was astonished at the revelations and listened with rapt attention. But he was weary after his active day and knew the morrow would equal it. After a time, he bade them goodnight, but Jethro would not retire yet. Slowly a thought crystallised in his mind which made him speak.

"You mentioned the slaves," he said. "The Habiri slaves held in the north of Egypt are related to Midian," Jethro said and paused.

"I know," said Moshe with his eyes on the fire. He hesitated. But perhaps this was as good a time as any to own the truth.

"You know a good deal of what passes in Egypt, I think," said Moshe. "Do you know of the slave child adopted by the female Pharaoh?" It hurt too much to speak her name.

"Of course, although we did not know the secret of his birth until recently," said Jethro. He paused and continued. "Perhaps no one knew it except the Pharaoh herself and the High Priest," he paused again. "But she raised him to be third in the kingdom. Under her he ruled Egypt," said Jethro. And as he spoke, a thought flashed across his mind! Suddenly he realised who this man was who had such an intimate knowledge of Egypt! But Moshe was speaking again.

"He tried to champion the Habiri slaves, have you heard that also?" asked Moshe in a hollow voice.

For a time Jethro was silent watching his guest as his thoughts exploded with the enormity of what he now knew. Was this man, whom he had welcomed here in Midian, this self-same 'Ruler of Egypt'! But how much should he say? The fire burned low. The night breeze was cooling rapidly.

"He had to flee for killing an Egyptian slave master. Have you heard that also?" asked Moshe.

Jethro knew he need not answer that question, but it covered another question that he must answer.

"You have already told me that you killed a man. You need add no more".

Now Moshe looked at his host, at his fine weathered features, flushed with the light of the fire.

"And am I still welcome"? he asked.

"You are now doubly welcome", said Jethro. "You are no longer a stranger. If you are Habiri, we are of the same blood."

---

[106] The ancient name for the city of Heliopolis

[107] The 'imperishable' stars were the ones which never passed out of view from Egypt as the tilt of the earth's axis altered the night sky

[108] The rising of the decan stars every 10 days marked off the Egyptian weeks which were of 10 days.

[109] Naharin, also known as Mittani, was Egypt's great enemy at this time

CHAPTER 18

NEPHERURE YEAR 25

DESPITE HER DELICATE FRAME, NEPHERURE carried her child in good health, and as the child grew and began to move in her womb, a bond formed between them even before he was born. She brought him to birth in the seclusion of the Harem, where many another royal child had been born, and he thrived. Days turned to months, and the child delighted both his mother and her faithful companion. But the Princess would give him no name and would not allow herself to think of his future. The trauma of discovering the treachery of her husband, and the strange isolation of the Harem affected her mind and made her obsessive. Her child was the only light in her life, and she could not allow thoughts of his future to spoil the present. But Jala must. Slowly by gentle words, she convinced Nepherure that Tutmose must be told of his son. The child was royal, of the Solar Blood, the son of the King, and could not be allowed to be lost in oblivion.

Finally, with Nepherure's permission, Jala left Mir-wer for Waset. She had sent a message to Tutmose asking if she might speak with him and received a favourable reply.

The journey south was always slow, moving against the flow of the River. But to be away from the Harem, to visit Waset again, was a relief after more than a year of incarceration.

Jala had found contentment in her life. She loved Nepherure and she loved the child more than she could express, but a change of scene was restorative. She reached Waset and was met by Tutmose's attendant. The audience was for the following day in the King's private chamber. Waset was hot compared with Mi-wer and Jala laughed at herself. She had not prepared for the heat of Waset although she should have remembered. But in truth she had little time to think of herself.

The next day dawned and Jala was summoned to the King's apartment. The rooms were plain and although answering the need of function, in no way answered the need for beauty and rest. One item only was of intrinsic beauty, a tall, exquisitely carved ebony loom, embellished with gold stood in one corner and its unchallenged beauty drew the eye to it immediately. The king saw at once Jala's eyes drawn to it but made no comment. How could he offer a gift to his bride now she had rejected him? His face looked drawn, and even with her downcast gaze, Jala noticed he had aged. But his tone was kind.

"Welcome Madam. Why have you come? I assume my wife needs my help in some way."

Jala was touched by his words. In his heart Nepherure was still his wife. It boded well for her mission.

Jala had agonised much over how she would tell the king of his son and had never fully resolved it, but she must speak.

"I come on a strange errand my lord."

Tutmose glanced at her. Was there a chance that Nepherure had relented? But his pride would not ask such a question. He waited, and Jala knew she must be bold.

"You were married to my Lady for a short time only, My Lord, and when she left Waset she believed that all she was taking from you was herself." She paused, and the King's face strangely changed. His quick mind realised what was to follow.

"Within a few days of our arrival at the Harem my Lady became very unwell and I feared for her," she said. "But in truth there was no need to fear," she added glancing up at his face, hoping he may understand. "One of the midwives at the Harem alerted me to the fact that Nepherure was with child." She stopped. Tutmose strode towards her and seized her shoulders.

"Look at me! Tell me again," he said, his voice shaking.

Jala raised her eyes to the King's face.

"My Lord, your son was born a year ago. He is your child my Lord, of the

Solar blood. He is a healthy beautiful boy and has brought great joy to his mother and to me." She paused. Tutmose put his head in his hands, but she was not finished.

"Majesty, he must be acknowledged as your son."

Tutmose was speechless. He was both shocked and delighted, but there crept into his mind another sensation. A sense of foreboding.

"Who else knows of this?" he asked, "because I fear for his safety!"

Now it was Jala who was shocked. Her only fear had been that the King might not acknowledge the child and confirm his life as a Royal Prince.

"But who would harm him my lord?" she asked in astonishment.

"Meryet may harm him if she knew of him. She still harbours hatred of her sister and ambitions to be queen, and Nepherure's son of the Solar Blood would out rank any child of hers. If she knew of him, the child's life might be in danger!"

Jala stared at him.

"The midwives in the Harem know, my lord. They were witnesses to his birth, as was I, and the Chief Eunuch knows of him, but outside those few it is not known. Nepherure does not mix with the other harem women, and her servants consider all dealings with her as sacrosanct. The secret is safe.

"And so it must remain," he said with strong emphasis on his words as he looked into her face. "I will have his birth registered in the Temple of Ra in Iunu as my son. I will not trust the High Priest of Amun here in Waset, nor his nephew who will replace him. They are from the same mould and cannot be trusted. But I can trust the High Priest of Ra in Iunu, and all royal births are registered in that Temple." He paused again, looking at Jala as he spoke. He was silent for some minutes as his mind ranged across the many issues involved. Then he returned to the subject of the boy.

"Then I must think of the best way to introduce him to the court."

But Jala had more to say.

"My lord I must ask your indulgence further because the Princess wishes to keep her child with her at Mi-wer. He is all she has in the world, and she needs him."

Tutmose could listen to no more. He sprang to his feet and moved away from her. Jala felt her pulse pounding in her ears.

"And what of my love, and my needs? The love I bear my wife! The love I already bear my child! May I not have them with me!"

Jala was dumbstruck. There was no argument she could make. But her silence softened him, and after some minutes he spoke.

"Very well, if this is her wish, I will make no claim on either my wife or child for the present. I understand her position." He paused. "Have no fear madam."

For a time he was silent. This discovery was so new and he must think of what it would mean. But some things were clear.

"Tell his mother that I name him Amenemhat and will register him as her son and mine at the Temple of Ra in Iunu as all royal children are registered. The world may not know of him for the moment, although in time he must have a military title. But he may live with his mother in Mi-wer until his 8th birthday, then he will come to me to train as a soldier."

At the first part of this speech Jala felt a wave of relief, but at the mention of soldiers, her heart sank.

"My lord, my Lady would be terrified if her child were destined for the army. She is not strong in body or mind, my Lord, and to suggest her child becomes a soldier is the queen's greatest fear. She cannot bear the thought of her beautiful son fighting and killing. It is abhorrent to her. It was partly for this reason that she has refused me permission to come to you until now."

Tutmose could hardly contain his fury at being so set about with refusals, but he hesitated. He would be taking a new wife. He may soon have other heirs. Life was uncertain. He knew that many things could change before it was necessary for his son to be trained. He would not insist on it for the present.

"Very well, I will register his birth with the Temple but not openly. The High Priest of Ra must know everything because in time he must be acknowledged as my son and the child of Nepherure. But for the present he can be given a civilian title and can train as a priest from his 8th year. Indeed, such was my training until..." His voice trailed off, but Jala finished the unspoken sentence in her own mind. Yes, Tutmose had known only the training of the temple, until Senenmut made a soldier of him.

"When my son is old enough, I will take him to Men-nepher where he will train as a priest in the Temple of Ptah[110]. I will be in the north often in the future as I must set my mind on developing the army base and the military harbours north of Avaris," he paused. "There, I can get to know the boy." He paused again. "I am greatly in your debt lady," he said, his face serious. "And now I must entrust another that I greatly love, into your care. Serve them well."

---

[110] Tutmose had a son who was a High priest of Ptah and it is not known who his mother was.

CHAPTER 19

AN IDENTITY FOR NEPHERURE'S CHILD YEAR 26

AFTER JALA LEFT HIM, TUTMOSE'S thoughts remained with his son. The news was overwhelming. How marvellous and yet it brought its own sorrows. He wrestled with the problem of how to deal with Nepherure's fears. To honour his promise to her, and yet give his son the future position that was his by right. He summoned the Chief Eunuch from the Harem at Mi-wer, to discuss with him his concerns. When the Eunuch arrived, Tutmose immediately put to him his fears. But the man was silent and seemed preoccupied.

"Do not be afraid, Ipu," said the King. "I do not consider that you have fallen short in any way. But I need your help as you know the workings of the Harem."

But the man's demeanour did not change. There were grave concerns he must convey to the King.

"Majesty I fear I already bring bad news." He paused.

This alarmed the king.

Are my wife and child safe?" he asked aghast.

"Yes Majesty, your queen and her son are safe. My news does not concern the Lady Nepherure or her child. They are well."

He paused as Tutmose waited.

"My news concerns your young concubine Betamun who, as you know, gave birth to a daughter a few months ago. She is in very poor health, and her child is dying, despite all attempts to help them. I fear for both their lives."

Tutmose regarded Ipu intently. He had not seen this child, but the thought of a young life struggling for survival, distressed him. He remembered Betamun fondly. A sweet girl, far too young to die.

"The world of women can be a dangerous place Ipu, every bit as dangerous as the battlefield."

"Indeed Majesty. Despite our best efforts, sorrows come."

Tutmose thought over the Chief Eunuch's words, but his overwhelming thought was for Nepherure. Not only was there the concern for the safety of his child, but what could be done at Mi-wer to create a place fit for his queen to live? Proper living conditions must be provided at the Harem now that Nepherure had chosen it as her home. He compared it with the Harem of Men-nepher where he had spent his childhood. That harem was a huge complex, like a small town, providing interest and occupation for the women. There were thriving industries based there and no expense was spared to encourage the royal women in the weaving of fine linen. The Harem produced linen of the highest quality, fit for temples and palaces. And this was repeated in many other ways with workshops producing jewellery and perfumes, and vineyards to make wine, all to enrich the lives of the harem ladies. These industries must be established at Mi-wer also. He would direct Ipu to set to work on this immediately.[111]

But the question of Nepherure's child continued to concern him and it could not all be dealt with at once. He must meet with his Generals and deal with urgent questions concerning his next campaign in Canaan, and it was days before he could again summon Ipu. Finally they met. Tutmose knew the situation of his son needed immediate attention, but they were again interrupted by a messenger asking for an urgent audience. Tutmose was angry and rounded on the messenger.

"I will not be interrupted without appointment like this!" he shouted at the man. The messenger knelt before the King, not daring to raise his eyes from the floor, but did not leave.

"Well what is it man?" shouted the King

"I come from the Harem, Majesty with news. The Lady Betamun is dead as is her child."

Tutmose felt his stomach turn as a feeling of sickness swept over him. He dismissed the messenger, and was silent, then spoke to Ipu.

"Why is it so many royal children die, Ipu," he asked, his head in his hands.

Ipu was silent. He knew the question was not an accusation for a failure of care. But he had no answer. Both were silent for some time, then Ipu spoke.

"Majesty, this loss of Betamun and her child is a tragedy, but it could provide a solution to the greater problem we are facing."

"Go on," said the King.

Ipu felt his way forward. He did not wish to insult the memory of Betamun with glib suggestions, but this loss could prove helpful.

"Majesty if we tell the world that Betamun died, but her child was a boy, and that he lived, the Lady Nepherure's son could take the identity of Betamun's child. Everyone knows that Betamun's child was yours. But she was kept in seclusion during the birth. And knowing that she and her child were dying, no one asked if it was a boy or a girl," he paused then continued.

"If it was said that the Lady Nepherure had adopted Betamun's child, it would remove the risks to his life, while still acknowledging the child as yours."

Tutmose stared at the man. It was a brilliant deception. Life in the Harem, this world of women, had taught Ipu the way women thought. The way they could be led.

"But could Nepherure accept such a thing?" asked Tutmose.

"I believe she will do anything to protect her child," said Ipu. "And it would be said that she had taken this motherless infant to her heart and wished him to be regarded as her son."

Tutmose was silent as his mind examined the plan. But it was without fault. It would answer the need entirely. Surely in time Nepherure would allow the child to be known to the world, and it may even serve some purpose, as yet unknown.

"Then I authorise you to carry out this deception," he said. "Use the Nubian Princess as your ally. She is entirely trustworthy. I will leave the execution of the plan with you. I have had the child registered secretly by the High Priest of Ra, whom I can trust. The child has been registered as my legitimate son, born to my queen, Nepherure. Born of the Solar Blood." he paused. But we must keep this secret from every other person, or the story will be out. Do not trust the High Priest of Amun here in Waset, or his nephew who will be High Priest after him."

Having settled in his mind and given instructions to Ipu about what was to be done for his child, Tutmose wrote a letter to his wife which would be conveyed to her by Ipu. On his arrival at Mi-wer, Ipu delivered the following letter to the Queen.

"Dearest Lady,

The child you have borne me has been registered in Iunu, in secret, in the Temple of Ra, as our child, but to the world he will be known as the child of Betamun, adopted by the Lady Nepherure. I have named our son Amenemhat. I trust you will be content with this. And my best wishes go with you both."

---

[111] It is known historically that Tutmose lll was the pharaoh who developed the Harem at Mi-wer.

CHAPTER 20

MOSHE AND THE QUESTION OF MARRIAGE

MOSHE KNEW THAT IN MIDIAN he had found safety, but his mind could not be free of the continual nagging question – was it the right decision to stay? Could he really settle for this slow pace of life with no challenge for his mind? Even with Jethro's kindness, it frightened him! It seemed impossible to settle the question. There were many things that haunted him. With no use for his mind, what could he achieve? Nothing! He would be nothing! The arguments went back and forth. Even though he was held in high regard by all, and had as a friend the leader of the tribe who prized him. More than that, these were people connected with his own blood. If he would find a home anywhere, surely this answered most closely to his needs. He would have an identity of sorts. Maybe in time even a sense of belonging. And as the weeks turned to months, he did all in his power to build in his mind a resolution to stay and find a purpose for his days.

But as time passed, an issue arose between himself and Jethro, mild at first, but it must be resolved. He knew what it was. Jethro was determined he must marry, but Moshe could not countenance the idea of marriage. He would remain alone. He had loved once, and although it now felt a lifetime away, that love was sacred. It would be a mockery to enshrine anything else in a rite of marriage. But Jethro was undeterred, stating gently but firmly his feelings on the subject.

"You need a woman to manage your life, my friend; your food, your tent, water for your needs and the care of your clothes," he said presenting his case with clear logic. But Moshe protested.

"Indeed, I have many needs but surely a servant is the answer, an older woman to whom I will not be required to fulfil the claims of a wife," he said.

But Jethro knew his people and his community. At first he did not insist, and provided Moshe with the servant he wanted, but as time passed he knew he must persuade his friend of the seriousness of the situation.

"You need to understand that it is not proper for a grown man to live unwed in such a community as this. Every man must have his wife"

And Jethro had determined on the solution. With his knowledge of the world, he knew that any girl would be honoured to be the wife of a man such as Moshe, and his eldest daughter, Zipporah, was the most eligible girl in the tribe. Jethro offered her to Moshe, hoping to find his acceptance, but Moshe could see that the problem would not lie just with himself.

"Please understand me, my friend that it is a difficult thing for me to view any woman in the role of a wife when I still have so clearly in my mind the memory of the girl who was to be mine," he paused. "I have nothing to give another woman and she would know that full well." He paused again, then continued, hoping that his words would speak to Jethro.

But Jethro was no sentimentalist.

"You know as well as I, that few men marry for love. They marry for convenience, and the girl must accept that."

But Moshe had other concerns.

"At present your daughter stands high in your community. She would have married well, making her choice of the best of the young men and would have been highly valued as a wife. I am not a young man and that will weigh in the mind of a girl." He waited, hoping to convince his host.

But Jethro saw things differently.

"She will be honoured as your wife. Many a girl is married to an older man. It can be a good thing, and an honour where he has gained standing in the community that will give her status and attention. And few women can choose whom they wed."

"But she may not see it in that light. She has held a high position as your eldest daughter and will feel the fall in dignity. I am an outsider. I am not one of your tribe. And living as my wife may be very different from what she would expect. Who knows what my future will be? If you wish me to marry, perhaps one of your younger daughters would be happier as my wife."

"No, I will not allow you to be slighted. You are a man who is to be honoured and I will give you my best."

"Even remembering that I am a fugitive? And the reach of Egypt is wide and long? Who knows if I might be found by them?"

"These thoughts are not new to me," replied the old man, "You may rely on that. And I still consider my daughter will be privileged to marry you.

There was nothing more that Moshe could do or say on the subject. Jethro believed he knew his daughter well enough to know that she would be pleased to marry such a man. It would give her status. Moshe could have married an Egyptian lady of noble birth, but instead he would take her as wife.

"Very well my friend," said Moshe. "I understand what you are saying. Your kindness towards me has been beyond anything I could have hoped. I accept the arguments you have presented, and must agree in principle, but please have patience with me a while longer."

NOW THAT HE HAD DISCUSSED the matter with Moshe, Jethro knew he must prepare his daughter for the prospect of marriage. He saw little problem. Zipporah would marry the man he chose for her. He knew that she prized learning and would value it in a husband. So he was astonished at her reply.

"Father I do not think you are right to encourage this man to stay."

"What I decide will not come from consultation with you," her father replied with annoyance. But the girl was angry and was driven to say more than she intended.

"Father you know how our community lives so near to starvation. Children in our tribe often die of hunger. You know that father. And yet you welcome an able-bodied man and invite him to your table and to stay when he is unable to contribute to the needs of the tribe! He will simply be another mouth to feed!"

"I will not be spoken to like this by you. We have large numbers of children, more each year, and at present they are fed and healthy."

"Forgive me father, but this is my very point. We have had six or seven years of good rains and the seas have had an abundance of fish so yes, we have many children. In fact we have a large number of boys who will soon come of age. But Egypt has a set quota as to how many she will employ. Egypt will not employ all these boys, or if she does, will demand reduced rates of payment for them. Egypt never gives anything for free. And if we now have a year, or a succession of years with no rain, we will have starvation. We cannot feed another man who does not contribute to the tribe."

Jethro was silent for a moment, but he too was angry.

"I will hear no more of this. I have offered you to him, and in essence he has accepted."

"On what altar have I been offered!" asked the girl, careless now of anything she said. "And do we even know if he will stay? I may not have the alure of Egyptian women!" But the last phrase she muttered to herself as she left her father's tent, and he could only guess at her words.

CHAPTER 21
1479 – 1477 BC
TUTMOSE MARRIES THEN LEAVES ON HIS 3RD CAMPAIGN

TUTMOSE WAS PREPARING TO RETURN to war in the north. He knew it was time to launch his next campaign. But before setting out, he must find himself a new queen. He must have another wife and was determined that Meryet would not gain from her treachery.

He alerted the High Priest of Ra at Iunu to search the records for a suitable girl as it was in the great temple of Ra in Iunu that records were held of all royal births. Then the girl must be found. She would be working in one of the great temples as a chantress or adoratrice as this was the only work permitted to a royal woman[112] outside the harems, and as a singer or a priestess, she could earn a modest stipend. Then she must be assessed for her suitability.

The search was commenced swiftly and carefully. As queen she must be young enough to bear children and royal enough to be the' Great Royal Wife'[113] of the Pharaoh. And Tutmose added his own requirement. She must be gentle on the eye.

The priests worked methodically and soon alerted the king that a candidate had been found. Working modestly in the great Temple of Ptah in Men-nepher, a girl was found who was suitable in every way. Nebtu, as she was known, was plucked from obscurity, and brought to Waset. There with little explanation and without ceremony, she was ushered into the presence of the king.

As she entered the king's apartment, Nebtu's appearance satisfied the king's last requirement. She was gentle on the eye. She was past the first flush of youth but would be less troublesome for that. Tutmose smiled at the girl before him who was utterly bewildered to be in his presence. He wanted an informal meeting so pre-empted her deep bow with words of welcome.

"Welcome Madam. I trust this summons has not distressed you."

"No, my Lord, but why have I been brought here?" she asked fearful of causing offence. Tutmose knew he must bury his pain. The world must not know that Nepherure had refused him. The King of Egypt could never be refused by a woman. And the woman before him seemed pleasant enough. He turned and smiled again. The girl showed intelligence. She was pleasant, and he settled in his mind, that as the one woman he wanted was denied him, this one would do as well as any.

"Madam I will explain," he said pausing.

"You see before you a King without a queen, Madam," and again he paused.

"You are of the Royal house, and are as yet unwed," he said smiling again.

"Do you think between us we could make a marriage?" he asked, amused at her astonishment and confusion.

The girl was shocked by his words, but she must answer. She could not refuse such a request from the King, and did she wish to? Finally, she stammered her answer.

"If this is your wish my Lord, it will be my wish also."

'So it is done,' Tutmose reasoned with himself. 'My heart must release Nepherure and I must take Nebtu instead.[114] I must have heirs.

"Thank you, Madam. I will endeavour to make you content as my queen. You will find me often absent as I must continue the wars in the north. Indeed I must go north very soon, but this will give you time to adjust to your new position."

The ceremony took place in the very temple where Nebtu had been employed. The temple of Ptah in Men-nepher, where all royal marriages took place. And the familiarity of the surroundings helped to calm the girl. It was a simple ceremony, and Nebtu, wide eyed and mute, fulfilled the task of presenting both herself and her gift, the sacred Lotus blooms, to her Lord, without faltering. The nuptial feast followed in the palace itself, where she took up residence in the queen's apartments.

Tutmose now had his queen, but would she prove fertile? He had proved himself a warrior, as a Pharaoh must, but now he was required to provide Egypt with heirs. Only then would he have fulfilled the two most vital requirements of kingship.

HAVING PROVIDED HIMSELF WITH A new queen Tutmose turned his mind to war. But in the year since his second Campaign his generals had not been idle. Thousands more peasant farmers had been trained as soldiers. Soldiers who would garrison the towns already under Egyptian control. Gaza, Joppa, and Megiddo were already garrisoned. But Ashkelon, Gezer, Shechem, Taanach and Hazor must be secured to form a base from which to strike north. His first campaigns were only the beginning, only setting the stage. Step by step he would gain control of the Hyksos heartland and finally defeat Naharin. These northern powers must never again be allowed to threaten Egypt. Fear of them had shaped the reign of his grandfather, the first Tutmose, but their treachery had been uncovered. Kept secret during the reign of Hatshepsut, they had waited until an untried youth reigned alone. But they had misjudged this youth. Tutmose knew he had the manpower to destroy Naharin and her allies. He would achieve victory even if it took the whole of his reign.

Tutmose had studied the history of the region to understand the present. The great powers in the north had, in years past, been Ebla[115] and Mari[116]. With their demise Naharin and her allies had risen and were growing in strength, and until they were defeated, Egypt's control of Canaan and her wealth would never be secure. Tutmose must lay his plans with care.

His first Campaign was a decisive response to an emergency. All of Canaan was in rebellion and needed a crushing blow to turn the tide. The following year he repeated his tour of Canaan to remind those city states that he was not to be trifled with. Now it was time to take more territory. To make another strike against the cities of the north. First, he would take control of the remaining ports along the Great Sea. The most powerful was Byblos, but all of them, from Dor in the south to the coastal Island of Arvad[117] in the north must be brought into submission. Any city that did not bow to his rule could be a knife in his back when his attention was turned east to deliver the death blow to Naharin.

With control of the ports, Tutmose could use ships to transport his men. But it had not yet been tried and must be tested. Every move must be known and understood. Thus, on his third Campaign he transported his army by sea to Joppa, the port he had taken in his first Campaign. It worked well, and now he, his generals, and every rank of soldier were familiar with this system and ready for the next step. He was ready to extend his reach into Retjanu[118].

After the harvest of his 25th year, the King and his army boarded the Byblos boats lying at anchor at Perenepher[119], the port on the coast north of Avaris. All went smoothly. The soldiers, chariots and horses disembarked at Joppa, and the army followed the coastal plain north, on their tour of inspection. They would visit every major settlement, and if they met resistance, punishment would follow. But they found the cities still submissive and obedient. There was no resistance of any kind. The princes he had placed in power were desperate to please, remembering that their children were held hostage in Egypt. He questioned the leaders again if there was a man of Senenmut's description known in Canaan, but no one knew anything of him. The cities were garrisoned and must feed these extra mouths on their limited supplies. They would pose no threat to the kings plans to move north in the next Campaign.

Tutmose marched the army as far as the three cities of the Tripolis near the coast. All around the countryside was in bloom with flowers of great variety. Beauty he had never seen in Egypt. The king was fascinated. Records must be made of these beautiful plants. He ordered his scribes to make drawings of these exotics and take them back to Egypt[120]. The success of the campaign put the King's mind to rest. He had achieved his first objective. Canaan was no longer in rebellion, and to be sure of its continuing obedience, he would repeat the same tour the following year. Then he would move on to the greater task of defeating the cities of Retanu. But for now, he would put the subject of war out of his mind and return home to his new wife.

---

[112] Royal women were restricted in the sort of work they were allowed to do.
[113] Great Royal Wife was the term Egypt used for their Queen.
[114] One of Tumose's wives was called Nebtu
[115] Ebla was an historic state in north east Syria

[116] Mari was an early state in central Syria

[117] Known now as the Island Jaziat Arwad

[118] Syria

[119] The military harbour on the coast north of Avaris

[120] A record was made on the temple walls at Karnak of these new plants seen in Canaan

CHAPTER 22

THE SEARCH FOR COPPER

THE SETTLEMENT OF MAQUA IN the southern part of Midian had one benefit as a site for a village. It was blessed with an abundant supply of water. The huge mountains to the east were blanketed every winter with deep snow, which, melting under the blazing summer sun, percolated down through the superficial layers of rock, until they struck the impervious granite beneath. From here the water flowed in underground streams to the valley floor and was collected in huge cisterns, dug into the bedrock by previous generations. Rough vegetation grew in the valleys, but few crops could be grown in the intense heat, so the land could only support nomadic livestock. Shepherding of the animals was done by girls and young lads, until the lads reached manhood when they were sent to work in the Mafkat. There they would spend their working lives, smelting the copper ore dug out of Egypt's mines by foreign slaves. Moshe could not work in the Mafkat. He would be known. But he observed and listened to the old men as they talked. He knew that Egypt did not pay the Midianite men the true value of their labour, but they had no power to change their situation. The copper they smelted was from mines in Egyptian territory. Egypt owned it and could employ whoever she wished. But Moshe knew the value of copper. He knew the insatiable need for bronze. Every army needed bronze, and the main component of bronze was copper. Copper and Tin. Even during his short stay in Seir, Moshe remembered the high prices paid for weapons in the marketplace. Slowly a thought crystalised in his mind. The Midianites owned vast tracts of land. Land very similar to that of the

Mafkat. If the Midianites could find copper on their own land, they could make a better living from it. They had the skills. They could mine, smelt and find a market for the copper themselves, then their labour would be properly recompensed. He questioned the old men. They all knew the land. Taking flocks to pasture in their youth, hunting game and travelling across it to tribal gatherings, they knew it well.

He started with general questions.

"How do you recognise rocks that contain copper?" he asked the elders one evening sitting by the fire.

The old men were pleased to talk and share their knowledge.

"Do you know any rocks in your own lands that could bear copper?" he asked.

"When copper is near the surface of the ground the rocks are green in places. This is the copper ore," said one. "I have never seen evidence of it in these mountains here in the south", the old man continued, "Sometimes I have found pieces of ore in the gullies, but not near here," he finished.

"Rocks lie in layers, and in most places the ore bearing rock is covered by other layers," said another, then hesitated, and another took up the story.

"If pieces of ore are found in gullies it shows that the rocks contain ore. Then it is worth the work of digging away the surface to search for ore," said a third.

"Do you know of any such places?" asked Moshe.

"Yes, to the north, just before reaching the territory of Edom," they agreed.

"And is it in Midianite land?" asked Moshe. "Or does Edom claim it or Egypt?"

"No, it belongs to Midian," the old men agreed. "It is 8 days ride north of this settlement," But they were warming to their subject.

"There is marshland north of Ebion-Gezer. You need to know the way past it to reach Timna[121]. There is a specific place you must leave the camel trail," they agreed

"Is 'Timna' where the copper lies? Moshe asked.

"Yes, there is copper at Timna," said the main speaker. He paused then continued.

"We have never considered mining the rocks at Timna because the site is a long way north of our settlement" he said.

"And what would we do with it?" asked another. "We cannot obtain tin, and tin is needed to make it into bronze."

Moshe listened with interest. This sounded hopeful. The men knew where copper could be found.

"Your men travel north every year to meet the other Midianite tribes at Aqaba," said Moshe, hoping to spark their interest in his plan.

"Yes, but that is a special time, and Egypt makes sure our men do not have any other time to spare from the work in the Mafkat. They do not want us to find our own copper."

Listening, Moshe realised this was probably the real reason why no mining was done. He knew well the strategies used by Egypt to control subject peoples. But he was determined to find a way. He at least could go, and a few of the old men could travel and be his guides. And some of the older shepherd lads could come to do the heavy work. It was possible, and if it succeeded, it would be a contribution he could make for his welcome by the tribe.

---

[121] Timna is an ancient site for mining copper, north of Aqaba.

CHAPTER 23

TIMNA

MOSHE KNEW HE MUST SATISFY himself as to the suitability and legality of his idea to extract copper at Timna. So he chose his moment with care, when he spoke to Jethro and Hobab.

"Midian has grazed the eastern portion of the Arabah[122], which includes Timna for the whole of living memory," said Hobab. "Edom would not dispute our claim."

"And would other Midianite tribes resent your mining the copper and making money from it?" he asked and was relieved at the answer.

"The area near the mines is poor pastureland. Shepherds avoid it as little grows there", Hobab assured him.

Moshe was pleased. He now had the approval of the tribal leaders, so he readied himself to visit the area and see for himself, accompanied by some shepherd boys and several of the old, retired miners to guide and advise. They travelled north, passing Haql and Aqaba and skirted Ezion-Geber, then headed for the rocky outcrop at Timna eight days out of Maqna. As they approached, the men pointed to an area of rocks ahead, which from a distance seemed unremarkable. Then the lads got to work, moving away sand which covered the underlying rocks, and with the sand removed, a clear seam of green ore could be seen in the rocks below. The seams of ore had separated in places forming fractures in the rock, which with a little work could be removed.

Camping in the open for a few days and nights gave the lads enough time to free a section of ore, while some of the old men travelled back to the springs at Aqaba to refill their water skins. They had brought a supply of flour to make flatbread over the campfire, and Moshe used his bow to supply them with game. In a few days, enough of the green veined copper ore had been dug out to fill all the available space in the mules' saddle bags. It was time to return to Aqaba. There, using the ready supply of palm trees, fuel was plentiful and the process of crushing and smelting the ore could begin. Before leaving Timna, they covered the mine workings with sand to hide their prize and hoped it would not be discovered before they could bring more men there to work it.

Back at Aqaba, the old miners were in their element. They took pride and pleasure in building a furnace. It brought back memories of how they had earned their living. Now it was the turn of the young men to watch the skill of their elders, and to learn. They had brought with them from Maqna, a pottery crucible to hold the ore, and a pair of leather bellows. One man worked, standing with his weight first on one then the other of the bellows to keep a constant flow of air to the fire[123]. The fire was hungry for fuel, but slowly the heat grew until these experienced men knew it was hot enough to have melted the ore. A plug in the side of the crucible was withdrawn and the hot copper flowed, glowing like fire, to cool in a pottery basin. Moshe had never seen, at first-hand, how smelting was done. It was hot work. But every phase was of interest. They left the copper to cool overnight, and the next day, pleased with their first consignment of copper, they returned home to the settlement to consult Jethro.

"The purity of the metal is excellent," said Jethro as his experienced eye examining the heavy ingot. Moshe was silent. He must gage the reaction of Hobab also. As future leader, it was his response that would drive or oppose the project. Moshe could sense that Hobab was reticent.

"I can see that the copper is good," he said. "But what is our purpose in working copper for ourselves? We have all the work we can do in the employ of Egypt. And we need this work. We must under no circumstances offend the Egyptians."

"I do not wish to change the agreement with Egypt in any way, or remove men from working for them," said Moshe. "The work at Timna would be secondary."

"We have more boys reaching manhood in the next few years than we have ever had," said Jethro. "Egypt will not need them all."

Hobab looked at his father in silence.

"So would we use some of the lads for this task?" asked Hobab.

"They could be supervised by the retired men," suggested Moshe.

"This first consignment is of top quality," said Jethro, musing as he handled the ingot again. "If Moshe wishes to take it to Edom to sell, I think we should accept his offer," said the old man.

"As long as we do not jeopardise our relationship with Egypt," added Hobab.

"There should be no risk of that if you continue as you are doing," said Moshe. "Midian should be free to use the resources of her own land, as long as it does not affect Egypt," he finished.

So it was agreed. A small delegation would go to Seir to find a market for the copper. Moshe was delighted that Hobab agreed to be one of the party.

"Take men who can understand a little of the Egyptian tongue," said Jethro to Moshe.

"Thank you, yes, and with your permission I will take the lads who did the mining and the elders who smelted the copper ore," he added. "I can translate for them, and we may need their report."

Now all that stood in their way was the cycle of the seasons with the flocks. They must wait until the breeding season was past. Then Hobab and the young shepherds would be free to journey to Seir. So for the present, Moshe must be patient.

---

[122] The area of land just north of Aqaba

[123] This was the method used. There is evidence that Timna had been worked for the production of copper from the 4th millennium BC.
 See page 127 of the article below;
 file:///C:/Users/User/Downloads/Egyptian_Timna_Reconsidered_2014.pdf
There is mention of desert tribes, Midianites and Edom extracting the copper, and as shown in the article, it was later taken over by Egypt.

CHAPTER 24

JETHRO AND MOSHE TALK

JETHRO AND MOSHE HAD FINISHED eating, and the short twilight had passed. It was late and the community was going to its rest. But Moshe could not rest. His tent was hot, while the air outside was soft and cool. Only Jethro, remained outside, resting, and taking the night air. He also was wakeful. But Moshe knew he must get away, to the water's edge, to think. The thoughts in his head could not be spoken here where he would be heard. Tents had thin walls. He must leave the camp for a while. He loved the beach with its isolation. There was always peace there at night, listening to the sound of the waves on the shingle. Here in Midian, where the sea had no outlet[124], the waves rose gently on the shallow beach with only a ripple. A gentle sound. Even the wind could hardly stir the swell. Like breathing. Regular, almost imperceptible. Yes, he would go to the sea. It was no distance, but he must not forget his manners. He must bid 'good-night' to Jethro before he left. He approached the old man.

"Good night, Sir," he said smiling, and the smile sounded in his voice.

"I will walk a while, I think. Good night," he said again.

Jethro turned. "May I join you? It is a beautiful night."

Moshe hesitated. He wanted to be alone. To think. But he must not refuse.

"Of course."

The moon was showering a steady light on the track which sloped gently down to the beach. Around them were the muffled sounds of weary animals. The occasional bleat of a goat. A donkey stamping. They walked in silence.

Moshe glanced up at the moon. It was a dying moon, wasting away, to be reborn in another week. But it lighted their path.

"Do you still follow the gods of Egypt?" came Jethro's voice with its sudden question.

Moshe laughed, a bitter laugh, which sounded harsh.

"Egypt has no use for me, nor do her gods," he said with more sadness than anger.

"But you served them once?"

"Of course. They were my world. I studied for five years at the temple of Ra in Iunu[125]," he said then was silent. To study at Ra's temple was the pinnacle of learning for an Egyptian, and Jethro would know that.

"So you worship no god?" asked Jethro.

Moshe did not answer. What could he say? He had made his challenge once to the Hebrew God when he learned he was a Hebrew. But as all his attempts to serve the Hebrew people had failed, what would their god want with him now? How could he serve him? He had nothing to give to any god.

"And you?" Moshe asked. "Reba told me of his God. The God of the Hebrews also. Do you and your tribe serve him?"

Jethro paused.

"The Midianites, like the Egyptians, serve many gods," he said thoughtfully. "We worship the god of this mountain", he said, glancing round to his left at the huge monolith beside them. "Its name is Horeb," he said thoughtfully. "Some of our tribes, those in the north, worship the gods of Moab, the Baals and the Ashtaroths," he paused. "I and my people worship the God of the Hebrews in our own way, but he has not helped my people as he has helped the Hebrews."

"Helped them!" replied Moshe in astonishment.

"Yes, he has helped them," Jethro replied. "They are now a large and powerful nation, and in such a short time. Hardly four generations."

"But they are not powerful!" said Moshe fiercely. "They are cowed by the whip to serve Egypt!"

"But there are prophesies," said Jethro. "They are slaves now, yes, but this was all foretold[126], and also that they would be freed and leave Egypt and return to the land of their forefathers."

Moshe laughed, but there was no joy in his laughter.

"If I, with the high position I held, was unable to release a few of them to become traders, it will be a great marvel indeed if they are ever freed." He paused then continued. "Egypt needs them. They are part of her war machine. She will never free them," he said and was silent.

They had reached the water now where all the fishing craft lay hauled up on the beach, leaving an unbroken sweep of shining water stretching far to the south on their left. Moshe turned to glance across the stretch of sea ahead of them, where a dark line was all that marked the coast of the Mafkat at its junction with the sea. Beyond it lay Egypt, its deserts and farmland, where the Hebrew people would wake again tomorrow and the following days to slavery. But Jethro was speaking.

"We shall see," he said quietly, watching the pale moonlight on the water rippling at their feet. "I would love to see Yahweh act again in my time as he has in the past," he added wistfully. "And you must listen when our young men sit round the fire and recite the story of the beginning," he said. "Every lad in the tribe must learn it and recite it. It is an important mark of manhood," he added.

"It is very different from the stories of Egypt regarding the beginning," said Moshe respectfully. He did not wish to offend his friend.

"Yes, but both speak of the deluge I think?" said Jethro, hesitating then continued.

"Our stories have passed from generation to generation. Most men cannot read, so our history is kept alive by every youth, who must learn to recite the stories, word for word, corrected by his elders, round the fire at night. In this way our story is passed on, unchanged and never forgotten."

Moshe hesitated. He thought about this God, the God that Reba had called 'The Great God'. He remembered Reba's words which had seized hold of his mind when he learned that he was Habiri. Hearing about this God, who was the God of the Habiri as well, had given him hope! Learning that the Habiri were not a worthless people, but the leading family of these tribes, had freed him from the self-loathing that assailed him when he discovered he was of slave blood, Habiri blood. He had tried to serve his people, but it had come to nothing. He had achieved nothing for the slaves and his efforts had cost him everything he had, and almost his life! He could not go over it again. It was too painful to remember. None of it was true. He did not believe it. This God, if he really was a God, if he had any power at all, had mocked and betrayed him just as Egypt's gods had done.

But Jethro was speaking again. And listening, Moshe realised he was asking him to do something that only he could do.

"Would you consider using your skills to make a record of the story of our people? I fear that it will be lost. I am sure that the story has been lost among the Hebrews themselves because of their servitude. I can write a little, but my eyes are old and none of my people have the command of the Hieratic[127] script as you do. I fear that the common language, the Aramaic language that the traders use, which my people speak and can write a little, will be lost in time. I want it recorded in the Hieratic script which will always be known. Would you consider the challenge of this task?

But Moshe was horrified at the request. How could he write the history of this God when he did not believe it? How could he honour him, when this God had mocked him and destroyed his life! Taken everything he had! When he himself had tried to serve the Habiri! It would be worse than mockery to write it, both for himself and for them. And it could not be true. No, he would do no more to serve this God who hated him.

But he must find a way to answer Jethro without telling him the truth. He was stalling and he knew it, but he must delay. And there was a way out.

"Your story is known only in your own language Sir, and forgive me, but as yet I do not speak your Aramaic dialect well enough. I cannot record it in Hieratic when I do not fully understand it. It would be a poor result"

But the thing was important to the old man. He wanted a record made.

"I could translate it for you. It would be possible, I am sure."

But Moshe was playing for time. If he could avoid the request now, he may escape it altogether. Jethro was old. He may die, or forget his request.

"Can I ask you to delay it Sir? He asked, hoping that delay would save him. "I am making progress with your language, slowly building on what I already knew. And now I live here, I will be fluent in time, I think," he paused. "I can read the classic Aramaic script because it is written as it is spoken, unlike Hieratic and Hieroglyphics which are picture languages. So learning your dialect should not be difficult." He paused to think. "When I know it well enough to do it justice, I will write it for you," he finished.

"Very well, "Jethro conceded. "When you are ready will be time enough."

---

[124] Gulf of Aqaba
[125] Heliopolis
[126] The promise given to Abraham in Genesis 15
[127] The script used in daily life by the Egyptian scribes. Hieroglyphs were kept for religious purposes.

CHAPTER 25

MOSHE RAILS AGAINST EGYPT'S GODS

MOSHE HAD NEVER LIVED A solitary life. He had lived his life in temples and palaces surrounded by his fellow men, but now he needed solitude. His mind could not cease from continual questioning, demanding answers he could not find. His heart also pleaded for answers. Why had the gods acted against him? What had he done? Surely he had done right in his treatment of Tutmose! Why was he punished for doing right? On and on it went. Was it simply that Egypt's gods had no concern for any who were not true sons of Egypt?

It became his habit, at sunset, to find a place of solitude. Often he would find himself inwardly railing at the great sun god as he watched him move away to the west to sink below the horizon into the body of Nut[128]. But the great Ra never answered. Watching him again tonight the thought came to him in all its shocking truth. Ra was no god at all! Neither was Amun! None of Egypt's gods worshipped with such devotion had any power at all! And was Yahweh the same? This god of the Habiri and the Midianites. Was he also powerless? He was certainly indifferent, even after Moshe had tried to help the slaves. And this god had not helped him when his own life was in danger, and he had to flee Egypt!

These thoughts, which were in mockery of the gods, acted as a salve to his broken spirit. The gods of Egypt deserved none of his devotion. He would turn from them in every thought and deed. He would live in defiance of them all. He would live his life determined to believe that power lay in the hands of men alone for good or ill. It was men who decided what was right and what wrong. From now forward he would decide his own fate.

As these thoughts settled in his mind, Moshe found a kind of peace. Like the peace that comes after the turmoil of bereavement. When the thing one loves has gone and will never return.

He could find peace of a sort in the wide-open spaces of this harsh land. The very harshness of it agreed with his state of mind. Physically he had escaped, but his experiences had torn the heart out of him. Everything he had been, was gone. His heart and mind were raw and at times he needed to escape from his fellows. Taking the sheep out to the solitary wastes gave him rest from his pain. Relief of a sort. He would wander to the east in search of forage for the flock. The sheep were safe with him. He was good with his bow and could keep the lions and jackals at bay and feed himself with game. The challenge was to find vegetation, which only grew after the short rains had passed through. And the flock must keep moving as the scrubland could not be grazed more than twice in the year. Overgrazing would destroy it forever, reducing the land to desert.

There were other shepherds who grazed their sheep nearer to the settlement. Lads not old enough to be sent to the Mafkat, and young girls followed the sheep until they married. They must all stay close to the safety of the settlement. But Moshe could take his sheep further afield. And this was his preference. But now the year had turned, and it was time for the sheep to bear their young. At this time they were vulnerable and could not remain out on the mountain slopes. They would be a magnet to the wild beasts. So for the time being, he must return to the camp.

MOSHE KNEW HE MUST NOT leave Jethro's request unanswered. It would appear as more than laziness. It would be an affront. It was an honour to be asked to record the history of these people. He could not simply excuse himself and turn away. So before he left for Seir, Moshe must face his reticence and speak his mind to Jethro. The opportunities were easy to find. Neither man liked to waste the most beautiful part of the night after the men had eaten together and gone to their rest.

"Can I ask you to indulge me, Sir?" said Moshe approaching the old man.

"Would you walk with me?" he said, hesitating. "I must speak with you, regarding your request. You asked me to record the history of our peoples," he paused. "I have things I must resolve," he said, and paused. "But please understand that in no way do I wish to give offence."

"I understand completely", Jethro replied. "In its own way your hesitation shows that you respect our history. And the fact that you wish to ask questions shows that you want to believe it if it proves true."

Moshe was silenced for a moment looking at the old man before him. What would his friend say if he knew of the anger fighting for mastery of his mind?

"Your kindness will make my task easier," he said. "Thank you, Sir."

But still he hesitated. Could he find the words to adequately answer the thoughts and feelings of his mind? His problem might amount to stark disbelief of the whole story. The whole history of his people! A tale to cover the failure of this God, Yahweh to rescue his people. Was it simply that other gods were more powerful and could enslave the Hebrews against his will? But he no longer believed that the gods of Egypt had power. Some power he had seen. Dark magic bought at a terrible price by dangerous and evil men. But beyond that, all was simply priest craft. Deception to hold the people and even the Pharaohs in thrall to themselves. But what if Yahweh had no power? How could he live in this community, living a pretence? It would be unbearable. And now, without giving offence, he must explain his position to Jethro.

He turned to his friend. He would start with the most pressing question.

"How do you answer the problem we have right now with the enslaved Habiri? With respect Sir, I cannot accept that it is enough to say it was foretold and will be resolved in time. The question is, how can it ever be justified to allow people to be enslaved at all? Surely it shows simple impotence on the behalf of your God?"

But Jethro was not offended.

"The question of suffering is one we must all face," he said. "I think there is a reason why it was necessary to allow the Hebrews to become enslaved," he paused. "But that cannot be shown yet. Your question is one of allowing suffering at all."

"Yes, if Yahweh is truly powerful, and has good intentions towards his people, why does he allow this suffering? To me it speaks of weakness or moral failure. There is no other excuse."

"I will not try to explain it as I see it at present," said Jethro. "To do so would only be my theory." He paused then continued.

"But there is another story about suffering I would ask you to consider first. It is a well-known among my people and all the people here in the east. The story of Jobab. He was a good man who knew great suffering. His story is known and preserved among his people in Edom but is known by us also. You could listen as the boys recite it, but you are going to Seir. This history is from Seir. Perhaps the time to hear it is when you are there. Then we could discuss it."

Moshe hesitated.

"Why would any man continue to serve a God who had tried to destroy him?" he asked, shocked at the directness of his own question.

But Jethro was not shocked. He believed that his God was both good and powerful and yet, allowed suffering. Moshe decided that if there were answers to be had, he would give them a hearing.

"I will certainly look into this history, Sir. I am grateful to you. But can you tell me something of his story?"

"I will tell you the circumstances, and then you can follow it in Seir.

"The man Jobab lived some hundred years ago. He was a king in Edom soon after the nation of Edom was established. He was a follower of Yahweh, the God of his fathers, although, due to intermarriage with Canaanite women, many Edomites worshipped the gods of Canaan." Jethro paused. He wanted Moshe to have time to think about the story. He did not want to tell it all now. But he had promised to explain a little.

"Jobab was extremely wealthy. His wealth was in large herds of livestock, and he had many servants. He was well known in all the lands of the east as a good and just ruler. He had a wife and a large family and lived an honourable life, teaching his children to follow his God."

"A man to be admired," said Moshe. "His God must have been pleased with him."

"As you say, Yahweh was pleased with him. A man without fault. But the accusation was brought, that Jobab only loved and served his God because of the blessing and protection he gained. Without that protection, would Jobab turn against his God? Was his love purely mercenary? Did his devotion, in any way, grow from love?" He paused.

Moshe was silent. He could see the implications of the story. Even in human terms, true love must be given for itself, not for gain. Despite his anger, Moshe felt drawn to this story. He had tried to follow this God and had lost everything! Even becoming an outcast! He had expected protection, and success in his ventures not to become a fugitive. But even if Yahweh was a good God, fulfilling all that a God should be, would he have followed him for himself alone? Or would he only follow a God who gave nothing but blessing? No challenge. No hardship. No striving. Even if Yahweh was a 'Good God' as Reba had said of him, was that enough? Could Moshe love his God for what he was, not just what he gave?

They returned to the camp and the night's rest. But already Moshe found that he was impatient to hear this story.

---

[128] Egyptian mythology taught that the sun entered the body of the goddess Nut at sunset and passed through her body during the course of the night to be reborn at dawn.

CHAPTER 26

AMENEMHAT IN AVARIS

AMENEMHAT SAT WATCHING HIS WIFE, with the child at her breast. A scene that had become a regular part of his life. A picture of domestic contentment that had eluded him for so long but was now restored in such abundant measure since his move to Avaris fifteen years ago. He was weary after his day's work, but the child would soon be sleeping, and then they would eat.

With Simeon's help he had found a place to set up a foundry among the free Habiri of Avaris. And his sister, Mirjam had joined him. No longer wanting to live in the south with no community to which she belonged, she too had moved north and as an unwed woman, lived with her brother.

It was in this community that Amenemhat had found his wife, Elisheba. And she had given him children, four sons and two daughters! The astonishing miracle of life. His sons were his pride. What a gift for a man who had been so alone. But his daughters had given him something else. Something he could not name but which had entered his heart, making him more vulnerable but more human.

He had stayed in Avaris, and besides finding a wife, he had found a whole new demand for his skills. He could build chariot parts as well as any of the expensive imports from Canaan. The officers who came to his workshop showed him respect even though he was now known to be Habiri. His skills commanded respect. They wanted the best chariots, and he built the best.

So with lucrative work he had money, money to spend. And there was one thing above all that he had never had and was determined to give to his sons as soon as they were old enough: education. He had seen it in his brother Senenmut, and the lack in himself created an almost physical pain. With money he could have his sons educated by the best. They would learn to read Hieroglyphs and the Hieratic script. They would learn to write. They would learn mathematics from the best masters. It meant sending them to the Temple schools where they learned far more than writing and numbers. There they learned of the Egyptian gods. But at home he taught them what he could of their Habiri God, YWH. He knew the stories of this God, even if first-hand experience of his God eluded him.

Looking back, he realised how close he had come to never knowing this new life. It had only been the wish to find out what had happened to Senenmut that made him venture to Avaris. There, fate had brought him to the one man who knew. Simeon had harboured his brother before his final escape. If Senenmut had been caught, he would have been paraded as an enemy of the state. No, he had clearly made his escape.

Finding Simeon made it possible for Amenemhat to reconnect with his Habiri roots. He even reverted to his childhood name, his Habiri name, Aaron. And of all the cities of Egypt, Avaris was the place to build a foundry. Here the Pharaoh was building the army on a scale not known before and needed chariots and weapons without number. Amenemhat had told his half-brother Parry, of the chances available in the north but Parry[129] wanted no connection with the Habiri. He wanted to be an Egyptian and was still afraid of the connection with the traitor Senenmut. He wanted to stay in the south and blend in. To marry an Egyptian. So they had parted, dividing the business and going their separate ways.

---

[129] Egyptian records tell of other brothers and sisters of Senenmut, not mentioned in the Bible. These I have assumed to be half siblings. The children of Jocabed by a second marriage. Parry is one of them.

CHAPTER 27

TUTMOSE MARRIES AGAIN

RETURNING FROM HIS 3RD CAMPAIGN, Tutmose had married Nebtu and found contentment of a sort. He could not fault her. If fault was to be found it was in himself, but he was not long at home before duty called him once more to the north. Slowly but surely he was tightening Egypt's stranglehold on the lands of Retanu. With persistence he would finally defeat Naharin. He returned home with a measure of contentment, but a new sorrow awaited him.

Tutmose could not believe the news. He was surely unlucky in his queens. Satiah was dead, Nepherure had left him and now Nebtu also had died. They had been married for only a few years. She had borne him no sons, and now she was dead. He had lost his son Siamun, by Satiah, and only Ameny remained, and unless he was prepared to break the heart and fragile sanity of the girl he loved, he could not take her child from her and raise him as his heir. He must marry again.

Nebtu had been a good woman, a good wife, and a good queen. His heart had never quickened in her presence as it did in those heady days when he held Nepherure in his arms. No, Nebtu ruled no part of his soul, although he had grown fond of her. But now she was dead, and once again he must consider the question of marriage to Meryet. He would summon her and see how she behaved herself. Six years had passed in which she had been forbidden to marry. He would see if she had learned a little humility.

He had just returned from his 4th Campaign. He had never lost a battle. He had grown as a man, a confident man, and was a supremely successful soldier.

More successful even than his grandfather. He would listen to no waspish nonsense from this woman. She answered the summons promptly, but he would not treat her with any care.

"So madam, you are learning some obedience," he said.

Meryet stood with downcast eyes, but her pulse was racing. If she offended the king again and she were forbidden to marry elsewhere, she would die childless.

"I gladly obey my Pharaoh," she said.

"Gladly? Have you learned some manners in these last six years?" he asked.

"I am sorry to have offended you my Lord," she said humbly.

"You are mistaken madam. I am never offended by a woman. Angered? Yes, I was angered by your insolence."

Meryet reddened. She had been a fool! After believing Nepherure a fool, she herself had been a greater fool to offend the King.

"Can you forgive, my Lord," she asked, now raising her eyes to his own. Hers was a sober face. Were there tears?

"My wife has died," he said shortly. "My third wife. Not the one you caused to leave me."

"I am sorry my Lord."

"Sorry that my wife has died, or sorry that you caused Nepherure to leave me?"

"Both, my Lord," she lied.

"So you have found a heart, now that you have learned to suffer a little."

"I have suffered my Lord".

He was silent. He still disliked what she was, but she had the sort of charm that would please a man. More pleasing in that way than Nebtu had been. And if she were fertile, he may have sons.

"Remember what has passed between us today, madam, or I will call you to account for it."

She looked at him in confusion. What was he saying?

"I have decided to make you my wife. You have a chance to prove yourself useful. But take care not to anger me. I will not forgive again."

Meryet was stunned into silence, looking at him with astonishment written on her face. He laughed out loud at her surprise. But she would not take offence. She would seize this chance to please him. He was offering her a dream come true. She would grasp it with both hands.

"So madam, you will be the highest woman in the land - but for one." He paused and Meryet held her breath as her pulse raced. Who would stand ahead of her? She who had been a deceiver might expect to be deceived in return.

"I am raising the rank of my mother to be acknowledged as the Great Royal Wife of my father[130], may he live."

Meryet breathed a sigh of relief. What had she feared? That perhaps Nepherure would be named again as his Great Royal Wife? Not that at least. And for the King's mother Isis, Meryet would be gracious. She would not mind standing behind Isis in rank, even though everyone in the land knew Isis had never been the Great Wife of Tutmose ll. Hatshepsut alone held that position. But Meryet felt herself relax. She need not bear this for long. Isis was old. She would not stand in her way for long.

Tutmose married Meryet and made her his Great Royal Wife[131]. And as Nepherure had retired from her role at the Temple, Meryet was also given the role as God Wife of Amun, a title previously only held by ladies of the Solar Blood. Tutmose knew that his High Priest would object on that ground, but as his half-sister, Tutmose decided Meryet was royal enough, and the role would keep her out of his way. She would have duties to perform at the Temple. Suddenly Meryet was almost the highest woman in the whole of Egypt. Maybe in time she would also be content. But for her husband, a return to war would free him of her company.

TUTMOSE WAS A MAN WHOSE head could be made to rule his heart. Where action was called for, even action against his own desires, he could act. Had he not done so already? The one man he had loved, he was prepared to destroy. Senenmut had been more than a brother to him. The throne was his for the taking, but to do so would have sealed Tutmose's fate. But more than that, Senenmut had trained his rival to be a soldier! Creating a King and a warrior out of a failing child whom no one had expected to live. Tutmose was fully aware of these facts. But when the power to act was in his hands, and in the cold light of day he understood the threat Senenmut posed to Egypt, Tutmose could turn against his friend. Because Senenmut was a traitor by birth. Adopted from the Habiri people, Tutmose knew he would not rest until he had freed them from slavery. But to free them would open the flood gates. There were thousands upon thousands of them. Men controlled by the taskmaster's whip. And with nothing to lose but their lives, these fierce hardened men would have fought for their freedom and might have seized power. No, Tutmose's first duty was to protect Egypt, even if to do so he must destroy a man better than himself.

IN LIKE MANNER, HE TOOK Meryet as his wife although his heart railed against it. She became his wife with all the required ceremony but without celebration. Within a week he had left for Canaan on his 5th Campaign with no regrets for his new queen.

Meryet felt like a thing discarded. The King had married her, but with no feast of celebration it seemed almost an insult. Now he was gone, and she must hold her head high in the Court, knowing there would be much whispered mirth expressed in secret. But she hardened herself, daring any to express their ridicule openly. The king was gone, but the trappings of royal life remained. So why have regrets? With the king in Canaan, the Palace was hers at last. And now she would have the apartments of the queen, which she had always coveted.

Meryet left the public part of the palace and walked deep into its heart to the quiet strictly private rooms which had always belonged to the queen. She knew them in every detail. They had belonged to Hatshepsut, then so briefly to Nepherure and now would be her own. She had come alone to claim her prize. She had waited so long. The best rooms in the palace. She hesitated before entering. Even now it felt like hallowed ground which to enter was like a trespass. But boldness took her forward, despite her racing pulse. She gazed round at the ebony furniture, the alabaster vases, the wall hangings of pastural scenes worked in fine tapestry. She had spent most of her childhood here as the companion of Nepherure. Part of the family, but not a part. A companion but not a daughter. She had loved everything she had known here, the voices, the laughter, the contentment. But today something was missing. Not the objects, but the atmosphere of the place. Its spirit had gone, and as she looked again around the sumptuous rooms before her, the very thing she wanted seemed to elude her.

Perhaps she had mistaken the source of her envy. She had coveted these trappings of luxury, but now that they belonged to her, they did not fulfil her dream. A cold thought crept into her mind. Was it in fact the luxury that she had wanted? Her heart had ached for what she had been denied here, but perhaps it was not the luxury! With a stifled cry she realised. It was the welcome she had craved. The welcome of a family into their home. To belong. Where Senenmut and Nepherure had been welcomed by their mother, while she was forgotten. Silently her gaze took in the audience chamber before her. She could hear their voices again, as memories from childhood returned. The voice of the queen debating with Senenmut, each challenging the other. Equals, friends, not merely mother and son. And she, the silent child, unnoticed unwanted. She waited, remembering. Painful memories.

But the feelings passed as Meryet faced the memories and forced herself to take control of her mind. She would not dwell on the past. She would not indulge in self-pity. She would not allow herself to be pitied even in her own heart. Pity was for failures, and she would not fail. She cast a defiant glance around the apartment and turned away. She was now Queen of Egypt. The Great Royal Wife of the Pharaoh. The highest woman in the land. She laughed at herself and her momentary weakness as she retraced her steps. She had not failed. She would produce an heir, and then, what was the most important work she must do? She must build a tomb fit for a queen. Unlike her sister, she would be a queen for eternity.

That very day Meryet summoned the architect who had built the King's tomb. Tutmose had already been king for 26 years and his tomb was long since complete. Its position was a guarded secret, but she knew where it was. He had chosen a very remote point, at the far end of the first branch of the King's Valley[132]. Even beyond the tombs of their parents and grandparents. She understood why. Wasn't the whole purpose of these burials in this remote place, to hide them? To conceal them from grave robbers. The burial itself, with its valuable grave goods must be hidden, but the Mortuary temple, where the dead king would be worshipped would be built for all to see[133].

Tutmose had chosen his grave site well and she would do the same. The

Valley had other branches. Perhaps there was a place at the end of the next branch of the King's Valley. She would visit the site with the architect. He would identify a good site. One that could be easily concealed. Where the rock was stable enough for tunnelling and would not collapse. This was a project she would enjoy. Choosing her home for eternity. Then she could plan the design and decoration. Her sarcophagus would be cut from quartzite, the preserve of the royal house. She would have her burial chamber carved in the shape of a cartouche to emphasise her royal title[134]. And her grave goods would contain the full quota of 401 shabti[135] to serve her in the afterlife.[136] Yes, now she could have a tomb built for herself that was fit for a queen.

---

[130] Historical fact

[131] Meryet-Hatshepsut, (her full name) became Tutmose's Great Royal Wife

[132] Tutmose lll's tomb has been found

[133] Tutmose's Mortuary Temple was built beside that of Hatshepsut at Deir el Bahri. It was named Djeser Arket. It is no longer standing.

[134] KV 42 is a tomb sited at the end of the second branch of the King's Valley. Howard Carter uncovered foundation deposits of this tomb identifying it as built for Meryet. It is the shape of a cartouche and had a celestial ceiling decorated with yellow stars on a blue ground, but Meryt was never buried there. There is a mystery as to why Meryet was never buried there, which can be explained as the story of the next generation unfolds.

[135] Shabtis are small figures about 20cm in size, buried with a person to act as their servants in the afterlife. Egyptians believed that by magic they would grow in size and perform tasks to help their owner.

CHAPTER 28

YEAR 29, TUTMOSE'S 5TH CAMPAIGN

FOUR TIMES, TUTMOSE HAD TAKEN his army north, and slowly but surely his objectives were being realised. The whole political landscape of Canaan had changed from loyalty to Naharin to loyalty to Egypt. Canaan was now firmly under Egyptian control and would remain so, leaving the king free to focus on the second phase of his plan, which was to take the renowned, and strategic city of Qadesh.

To be thoroughly ready, Tutmose allowed two years preparation, delaying this 5th Campaign until the 7th year of his sole reign. The docks at Men-nepher continued to build Byblos ships, as the harbour at Perenepher was extended to moor them. A magnificent fleet, to transport his troops with both speed and efficiency. The troops would reach Retjanu fresh and ready for battle, avoiding the long march through Canaan. And travelling by ship was second nature for Egyptians, whose lives had always centred on the River[137].

With his fleet ready, Tutmose set sail. They would make landfall on the Phoenician coast. Passing Joppa, the next major port was Dor. These two cities had been brought to heel and garrisoned along with the wealthy island city of Tyre after the first campaign. Sidon, the next port submitted without a fight, and leaving a garrison there, Tutmose moved north seizing Berytus[138], and finally the great trading centre of Byblos. Egypt was renowned for her skill in naval warfare. With the River as her thoroughfare, and all her major cities situated along its banks, the Egyptian army was more familiar with storming a city from water than from land. Indeed, it was from the river that the Egyptian army had overcome the last Hyksos resistance at Men-nepher and Avaris. The King of Byblos, along with the rulers of all the port cities had heard tell of Egypt's victories and submitted without a fight.

Now the only remaining port was Arvad, a well defended island city off the coast, lying near Qadesh. The island was surrounded by high walls which could withstand most attacks, but would she submit? Egypt could not afford to have a hostile city behind her back as she laid siege to Qadesh. But wisdom prevailed, and rather than be punished by the Egyptian army fresh from their other conquests, the King of Arvad opened his gates to the Pharaoh.

Having gained control of the entire coast, and garrisoned its cities, Tutmose took the army inland. Qatna fell and was garrisoned, as was Tunip further south. The Egyptians now surrounded Qadesh on three sides. Further inland, Ardata, an ally of Naharain closed its gates against Egypt so Tutmose burned the city's entire wheat crop standing ripe in the fields. This broke their resistance[139]. They opened their gates, but the city was pillaged as punishment, with the strongest of its citizens taken as slaves. A large garrison was left here also, leaving Qadesh surrounded and ripe to fall in the next Campaign. In every city Tutmose enquired of the nobles and scribes if a man of Senenmut's description was employed anywhere in the city. But none knew of him, and Tutmose's fear grew that his brother would be at the centre of the rebellion, residing in the capital city of Naharin itself.

But Tutmose had achieved all the aims of this campaign. At Byblos he ordered the building of a large fortress,[140] where goods raised as taxes, and tribute arriving at the city could be stored and guarded by an Egyptian garrison. Indeed, having garrisoned all the ports and inland cities he had taken[141], Tutmose sent his victorious army home overland. The first leg of the journey took them to Yenoam, Nuges and Herenkeru, towns near the coast where an abundant harvest was just ripening. Grain and wine; fruit in abundance from the magnificent harvest was liberally enjoyed by Tutmose's soldiers. Having had their fill and taking all they could carry the troops set off, destroying the fruit trees of every city they passed on the long march home[142]. The troop ships, now being free of soldiers, were able to carry vast quantities of booty back to Egypt. Much was given to the temple of Amun where large numbers of cattle and sheep were sacrificed in thanks for the victory.[143]

[137] Egyptians did not use the name 'Nile' simply referring to it as 'the River.'

[138] Ancient Beirut

[139] Recorded by Breasted

[140] Historical fact

[141] Egypt kept control of defeated cities by garrisoning them. How did Tutmose have the manpower to do this? Answer; the large number of Hebrew slaves in the Delta grew enough grain to feed the country, freeing Egypt's peasant farmers to be trained as Tutmose's crack troops in vast numbers.

[142] Recorded by Breasted

[143] Facts taken from Breasted.

CHAPTER 29

JOURNEY TO SEIR[144]

THE ANIMAL BREEDING SEASON WAS over. It had been a good year, with almost the full quota of breeding ewes and goats producing one healthy kid, and occasional twins. The first weeks had passed, and the new mothers had bonded with their young, while the experienced ewes settled to the familiar task of mothering afresh. Hobab was now free. He could leave the flocks to the care of the youngsters and accompany Moshe to Edom.

It was a group of six men that set out along the coast road to Aqaba, dressed in their best, and riding sturdy mules. This road was safe enough. No one would rob them here, and for the road beyond Aqaba, they would join a mule train going north into Edom and Seir. The two older men had been to Seir briefly in their youth, as had Hobab, but the lads were desperate to see this famous city, cut out of living rock.

Moshe had become accustomed to the dress of the tribe. They lived almost entirely in the open, and a head covering and a loose robe were essential clothing living under the fierce sun. Eight days were spent in reaching Aqaba, but each night found them a welcome in one of the Midianite settlements along the route.

Aqaba itself was teeming with beasts and men, and Moshe noticed on every hand, desperate men looking for opportunity to steal goods or mules or even men, as slaves. He wondered how he had escaped them when he came alone to the city having fled Egypt. Perhaps there was, after all, a benign presence taking pity on his plight. But as they had no business in the city, and the day was drawing towards evening, they passed through as swiftly as they might, and found accommodation at the large Caravanserai beside the northern gate of the city.

The next day, they and their fellow travellers gathered at dawn, ready to start crossing the open plain of the Arabah, but the increased number of travellers multiplied every delay, and this shorter distance took almost the same in time as the first part of their journey. Finally Seir came into view ahead of them. An outcrop of rose red rock, rapidly turning to a deep orange by the light of the setting sun. They entered the city through the narrow defile, a source of astonishment to the young men, but the abrupt arrival at the Souq after the winding passageway was a moment to savour for them all. Night was falling fast after the short twilight, as Moshe led his fellows to the humble inn he had found previously. Here they were presented with a hearty meal which was all they needed to send them to sleep after the long day.

As the noisy clamour of the Souq woke him, Moshe recognised his surroundings. He remembered his first visit to the city, when danger stalked at every turn. But this time he was not alone, and the sense of belonging came to him now for the first time since leaving Egypt. Now he had a new identity to hide that of the fugitive he had been. Now he could approach the centre of government in safety as part of this trade mission.

Dressed and breakfasted, the party set out for the buildings on the west side of the Souq, marked as important by the large group of soldiers guarding the entrance. Hobab and Moshe approached and spoke to the soldiers, producing the letter sent with them from Jethro, written under Moshe's guidance. It was the introduction they needed from the leader of their Midianite tribe, endorsing his son, Hobab to speak for him. Moshe had agreed with Hobab that when the question of his own name arose, he would use the name 'Reba'. The name 'Senenmut' was infamous, and 'Moshe' was clearly an Egyptian name which would call for explanation.

The guard carried their letter inside, returning in a while with an official.

"Show me the copper you have brought? I wish to see it," he said.

Taking the ingot from Hobab, the man inspected the metal. He was clearly impressed.

"Will you leave the ingot with me? I will show it to my master," he said.

Hobab was happy to comply, and it was agreed that they would return later in the day for the verdict.

Now they were free, for a few hours, to visit the city and the markets, although they had no goods to barter. The lads wanted to see everything and had to be constrained from setting off alone. It would not be safe. So as a group, the men walked the length and breadth of the city, so different from any settlement they had ever seen. They were awed by its rock cut dwellings, some high in the rockface, accessed by precipitous paths. But it was the market that drew them the most, with its seeming endless variety of goods, many unknown to these men from the backwater of Midian. There were singing birds in wicker cages, jewellery with polished stones, fine glazed pottery, and most interesting of all, the assortment of bronze weapons and knives, beautifully made. The stalls were filled with the trappings of luxury fit for residents or visitors to this sophisticated city, but nothing was within their reach. Their limited means must be kept to buy food. But this at least was plentiful and cheap, and its smell became more enticing as the day progressed. As time for the mid-day meal approached, they found a stall selling hot pancakes cooked in a flat pan over an open fire, and generously filled with a mix of goat's cheese, vegetables and garlic. They had refilled their water skins from jars at the inn so could forgo the services of the many water carriers hawking and calling around the streets.

But the time had passed, and they must present themselves again to the guards. Hobab and Moshe were invited inside for a formal interview, and entering, were taken to a spacious room cut out of the rock, with windows facing the front of the building, towards the Souq. The room was welcoming, with whitewashed walls and the floor spread with rugs and cushions. They were offered spiced tea, steaming in fine pottery cups, and settled themselves on the cushions to await their host.

Moshe had expected to meet a low-ranking government official, but the man who entered was clearly otherwise, well-mannered and of noble bearing. Clearly a man of high standing and probably high birth. Neither young nor old, he had the air of someone familiar with taking command and making decisions. He bowed briefly with a smile and settling himself opposite them, opened the interview.

"I am Zerah," he said speaking, to Moshe's relief, the classical Aramaic with which he was familiar, not the Midianite dialect which Moses still had difficulty following.

"I am interested in what you have brought. I have examined the ore and find it to be of high quality." He paused. "And have you mined and smelted this yourselves at Timna?"

Hobab deferred to Moshe to answer.

"Thank you for receiving us, Sir," he said, and receiving a smile from their host, continued.

"Yes, our men have both mined and smelted this ore, and yes, it is from Timna," he said. But now he must tread carefully. He must show that Midian claimed ownership of the site at Timna, but without offending their host.

"As you will know Sir, Midian is a nation of shepherds, who cross all their lands regularly to find pasture for their animals," he paused. "But they also understand rock formations. They recognise copper bearing rock and have known for some time that the rocks at Timna contain copper ore." He paused again and continued.

"Timna is part of our land, as you will know Sir, but it is near our northerly border, and so is at a considerable distance from most of our settlements." He must leave no doubt about who owned the land.

"But until now, Sir, there has been no capacity in our manpower to develop the mine, as all our grown men have been employed by Egypt in the Mafkat."

"I understand," said Zerah, and Moshe bowed with some relief. There would be no dispute as to title. He paused and continued.

"But in the last few years the number of our boys reaching maturity has increased and they are more than can be employed by Egypt. So with this spare capacity we hope to develop the Timna mine." He paused to allow Zerah time to grasp the situation.

"We will start production in a small way and increase as more lads become available for the work," he finished.

"Will you look for other markets for your copper?" asked Zerah.

"We don't wish to Sir," said Moshe. "We will not look for another market if Edom will give a fair price," Moshe replied with a smile.

After a short pause, Zerah spoke again. He liked dealing with these men.

"Perhaps I now have a proposal for you," he said and paused. "If you need time for men to become available, may I suggest a joint project between us? He waited while Hobab and Moshe digested his words, then continued.

"Your men have the skill of smelting, and we have men readily available to do the mining of the ore." Again he paused, but then made an even more extraordinary offer.

"And I have a second suggestion," he said. "Both of our nations need bronze with which to make weapons, and making bronze requires both copper and tin. Edom needs copper but has access to tin. You have access to copper but not tin, I think. If we work together, both of us can have access to both copper and tin and so be able to make all the bronze we need."

Hobab and Moshe were astonished. Here was a high-ranking Edomite offering to partner Midian in a joint project to the advantage of both. Their trade mission appeared to be a great success.

---

[144] Seir has been identified with Petra

CHAPTER 30

EDOM

NOW THAT AN AGREEMENT HAD been reached, Hobab was keen to return home. He was not made for diplomacy. Being on his own soil, attending to his sheep and sleeping in his own tent made him a happy man. But it was clear that Moshe must stay and approve the writing of the official documents. Zerah was impressed with his business-like approach. They shared a mutual respect, and Zerah invited Moshe to be his guest while he remained in Seir, and young Kerrit was to stay as his assistant.

But Moshe knew he must be more vigilant than ever here as Zerah's guest. Surrounded by luxuries he had sorely missed, he could so easily slip back into the familiar ways of his former life, betraying himself. And the greatest danger would be in his friendship Zerah. He warmed to this fine Edomite who had certainly been educated in Egypt. His heart and mind ached to reach out to him. A man of his own age. A man of learning and culture. A man of noble birth. But he dared not. It would endanger them both. Egypt's spies were everywhere. He planned carefully how he must act to maintain his disguise. He must keep up the appearance of a Midianite nomad, never removing his Keffiyeh[145], even while living inside, in the comfortable room assigned to him. He must choose the simple food he had become accustomed to in Midian. Any of the serving men could be in the pay of Egypt, on the lookout for the noble fugitive Senenmut. Here in Seir he was known as 'Reba', a name used by high-ranking Midianites. This would add to his concealment. And as he could both speak and write classical

Aramaic, the language of the legal documents, he was fitted to do the work in hand.

While the agreement was being drawn up, there were many occasions for the two men to talk. Moshe cast around in his mind for subjects they could discuss that would not expose him. So many subjects would be dangerous, and he could not be continually evasive. But the story of Jobab was something he wanted to investigate, and it would be a safe subject to discuss. After they had dined together on the first night, he broached the subject.

"It has long been a wish of mine to read the famous story of Jobab in the Hieratic script," he said to his host.[146] He paused then continued.

"I know he was a king of Edom, but as I have only ever heard his story told in the Midianite dialect, I want to be sure that what I have heard is correct."

Zerah was surprised at the request.

"I am sorry to disappoint you," he said, "But it has never been translated into Hieratic."

"What a pity," 'Reba' replied and paused. "If I come to understand it, maybe I can translate it myself'," he said.

"It isn't an easy story to understand," said Zerah, "but I can certainly find a copy in classical Aramaic for you to translate," he offered. "We can read it together and may understand it better."

"Can you explain what you know of his story?" asked 'Reba' watching his friend.

"Certainly. It will take some time, but no matter. Where shall I start? He said thinking aloud. "But can I ask what interests you about his story?

Moshe thought quickly before he replied.

"We Midianites worship many gods. Some worship our ancestor's God, Yahweh. It is claimed that he is a good god, a just god. I know that your Jobab worshipped Yahweh and continued to follow him despite many terrible things he suffered. I would like to know his story."

After some thought Zerah recounted what he knew.

"He lived shortly after the patriarch from whom both Edom and Midian descend[147]. He was one of the early kings of Edom."

"So the things recorded about him are historical? They are true, asked Moshe.

"They are certainly true. He is remembered to this day. Places in the city bear his name. His palace still stands. And his descendants live among us. He lived only 5 or 6 generations ago." Zerah paused, wondering how he should present this strange story.

"He lived a long life, and became a very wealthy man, then suddenly, in the space of a few weeks he lost everything."

"And did he turn against his God?"

"He did not turn against him, but he asked many questions, and this is the substance of the writings we have."

A sense of his own overwhelming loss struck Moshe like a physical blow, but Zerah was still speaking.

"Yes, Jobab asked many questions and at the end of the story Yahweh replied, but he did not answer his questions. The extraordinary thing about this story is that in the end, Jobab's encounter with his God was sufficient. He got beyond the need to ask 'Why'. Although Yahweh did not answer Jobab's questions, he answered all he needed to know. He removed Jobab's need to question.

Moshe was silenced by what he heard. Was it possible? Could he ever be free of the grinding question – 'Why'? Suddenly he was aware of a thought, a sensation, a knowledge – that Yahweh had not rejected him! He had not cast him off. That Yahweh would yet have a purpose for his life. In leaving Egypt he had lost everything, but not his life. What if God required even more? What if he wanted him to be part of the answer for the Habiri? That could cost his life! Could an encounter with God be of such a magnitude that even if he lost his life in the process, it would be worth it? [148]

Moshe went to his rest that night with his mind on fire. He had gained so much from his time with Zerah. Not just head knowledge, but answers to some of his deep questions. He could not bear to leave without further time for discussion. Nothing they had discussed was exposing him to danger. Surely a little more time here would not be unwise. So the following day, trying to be objective in his questions, Moshe again challenged his host.

"So with the history of Jobab so well known, why does Edom not follow Yahweh now?" he asked.

Zerah did not need long to answer this question.

"I think you can see why", he said. "Men want their freedom, to make their own decisions."

"So why do men worship a god at all?" asked Moshe.

"Men follow a god who they think will let them achieve their own ends. They worship Molech[149] and Chemosh because they believe they will help them. They imagine that power and wealth are in the gift of these gods."

"But surely, a true God is of more value than what he gives," said Moshe quietly.

"Yes, that is the challenge," said Zerah laughing.

"What I look for is a God at least as good as a man," said Moshe.

"You mean one that is not cruel and self-seeking!" replied his friend.

"I mean one like a good father, who loves his children. He may discipline them – for their good, but he provides for them and plans for them."

"I think most men are driven by fear, not love," said Zerah honestly. They worship a god like Chemosh because they have been taught to fear him."

"I have seen too much of that," said Moshe then stopped himself. The gods of Egypt ruled by fear. They demanded gifts and gave fear in exchange!

"So is there no god worthy of our worship for what he is?" Moshe asked quickly. "Because he is good, trustworthy? Because your soul loves him? I am sure you have known human love. The love of a girl? You love her for herself, not for what she brings".

"You are a fortunate man if you have loved so," replied Zerah.

Minutes passed in silence until Moshe added.

"I have loved so. And something of me died when I lost her."

But Zerah did not reply. He was starting to fear that he already knew too much about this man for the good of them both. Pure philosophy was safer.

"Well, I wish you well in your search for a God worthy of your heart," he said at length. But he was serious now. "I can see that in theory a God should surpass men in goodness and power, but I do not know if Yahweh is such a god".

---

[145] The Keffiyeh was the traditional headdress worn by Middle Eastern men
[146] Writings which accompany the Septuagint identify Job as Jobab an Edomite king.
[147] Abraham

[148] Job 1 describes him as being from the land of Uz. Lamentations 4 v 21 equates Edom with Uz.

[149] These were the gods of Moab and Ammon, and probably of Edom.

CHAPTER 31

MOSHE RETURNS TO MIDIAN

WHEN THE FIRST PARTY OF men returned from Seir, the tribe heard the news. Hobab told them of the agreement with Edom, to work the mine and make bronze together, but the tribe could hardly believe it. Now Moshe had returned with written documents to prove the agreement. And simply having him present, stating the facts of the contract, with no sense of drama, finally convinced them. But it was hard to take in. The fact that Midian would have her own bronze to sell! Bronze, the most highly prized commodity, that no nation could get enough of. She could provide a little for herself also. She could move away from being totally controlled by Egypt. Perhaps in time the fear of famine would disappear. She would be able to feed her children even in the lean years, when fish were in short supply and drought caused the flocks to miscarry. The tribe were awed at what had been achieved, and the lads who previously had no prosect of employment, would now have work. They could contribute to the tribe. Now they would have the chance to marry, in time, and raise families of their own, a thing not approved for men without work.

Zipporah was astonished. Shocked that she had been so wrong about this man, this stranger whom she had resented - against every rule of hospitality. He had brought hope! Practical help. Food on the table. A future. A chance for the tribe to grow and thrive! It would no longer matter that they lived in a dying land. The land was giving them its special bounty. Metal from the ground. No longer would they eke out a meagre living with the ever-present fear of famine.

But the contract with Midian was not the only document Moshe had brought back when he returned. He had the copy of Jobab's story that he and Zerah had translated, and Zerah had given him sufficient papyrus sheets to make a second copy. When completed, Moshe would send it to his friend. A small thanks for his kindness.

As the year unfolded, Moshe found satisfaction working on the plans for Timna. The older lads were marshalled into action by the retired men to learn their trade. These men who had worn out their lives scratching a living in the service of Egypt found a new joy in life as teachers, passing on their skills for which they found renewed enthusiasm. The boys were desperate to learn. To be the best. To be in the first group chosen to work at the new mine. It was only right that Kerrit and Ephah who had mined the first of the copper and seen it smelted, should be in at the start. Hobab was now committed to the project and the two lads accompanied Moshe and Hobab back to Timna ahead of the others to make plans. True to his word Zerah sent a cohort of miners to Timna to meet them. They were instructed to take their orders from Moshe to prevent disputes, and report directly to himself any problems that might arise. Within the year, Moshe could step back and leave the management of the mine to Hobab. He must now set his mind on the next phase of his plan, finding ways for Midian to trade her newfound wealth more effectively.

"I hear good reports from Timna," said Jethro the next time he and Moshe met to eat. "The work is progressing well they say".

"It is indeed," Moshe replied, "And on that point I had something to discuss with you".

Jethro laughed. He had learned to expect the unexpected with Moshe.

"Tell me," he said.

Moshe hesitated but knew what the next move must be for the tribe.

"I would like to visit Aqaba again and see what can be done about a harbour there," he said. "With valuable commodities to trade it is a pity if we do not have a proper harbour of our own that can be used by bigger vessels. No proper ships can use Aqaba at present, only fishing boats." He paused. "We need a deep harbour." He paused.

"If we are forced to sell our wares through Ezion-Geber we must pay trading taxes. If we want to avoid taxes, we need our own harbour."

The logic was clear. Jethro was taken by surprise but could see the force of the argument.

"You may be right", he said. "You have my permission to speak to the other settlements and with Hobab. He may agree, but I am not sure."

"I think there is a chance that we would pick up other trade that at present uses Ezion-Geber," Moshe added. "The overland route from the northeast, the route the traders use, would more naturally run to and from Aqaba than Ezion-Geber," he added. "Aqaba has the more direct route."

But Jethro hesitated.

"Can we be sure it is worth the cost in man hours?" he asked. "Is it justified? We may only have modest quantities of bronze to sell."

"No question," said Moshe. "A port of our own will open up a market for many things. Midian should not be known only for working with copper. We can trade many things once the port is open to us – salt, dates, dried fish. The women have many skills. They are famous for their textiles. Their rugs are highly prized. They make leather goods. Leather water bottles are needed by everyone. The women grind wheat and spin wool. With a proper harbour, we can trade our goods to a wider market, not just passing traders. That way we will realise their true value".

"You are right of course," said Jethro. "I see the problems rather than the opportunities," he said laughing to himself. "And I can see the advantage of developing Aqaba. Few places have fresh drinking water coming out of the ground in quantity as it does at Aqaba, so freely available for man and beast.[150]" He stopped. Moshe had turned towards him and was listening with attention.

"Of course," said Moshe. "I had not thought of that. With such good water supplies, it is a natural place for animal markets. With such an abundant water supply, animals can be safely corralled there, waiting to be sold".

"But before you build this harbour at Aqaba," said Jethro, cutting across his last remark, "Please will you settle the question of your marriage?" he added.

Moshe looked at his friend. He had been taken off guard by this last request. It was a subject he had been avoiding. But thinking again of his position in the tribe, he knew now that he wanted to belong. These people were the nearest he would ever know to his own blood. He had made this land his home. Now something told him that he must make an unbreakable commitment. He needed his own home. And the centre of every home was a woman.

---

[150] Even today, there is a huge aquifer under the deserts of Jordan and Saudi Arabia. The city of Aqaba has used this as its main water supply up to the present time.

CHAPTER 32

REGNAL YEAR 31 AMENY IS NOW 6 YEARS OLD

THE DAY TO WHICH JALA woke in the Harem of Mi-wer, that first day of Peret[151], awakened in her a longing for her homeland. The air was hot and dry, but as she looked out across the grain fields to the west, a distant haze, almost a mist, distorted the scene. A pang of longing filled her as she watched. It was so like the mist she remembered every morning in her homeland of Kush[152]! Water vapour hanging in the air, until it was burnt off by the strength of the sun. But watching for a moment longer, Jala knew this could not be moisture. This was dust. The dregs of the sandstorm that had passed through 3 days ago, blown in from the western desert.

A feeling of longing rushed in upon her. Longing for her homeland. The beautiful highlands of Kush which was all she had ever known until she was 19. There, all was lush and green. There no dry desert wind ever blew. She had not valued her home in those days. Had not given it a second thought. She had been privileged, yes, the beloved only daughter of the king. That was why she was still unmarried at 19. The king wanted her with him to run his court since the death of her mother. Yes, she had been lucky in so many ways, but she had never given it a thought in those happy days, hardly aware of the beauty of the world around her.

But Jala did not have long to indulge her longing for her lost home. Rarely did she wake like this, free of the noise and presence of the small boy who had taken charge of her heart. And he did not delay long, even today. She heard him coming with his mother to waken her. This child she had hoped for and prayed for. Not for herself but for Nepherure. But he had become the fulfilment of both their lives.

Amenemhat was 6 years old today and this was the cause of the delay. It was his birthday, and the entire Harem had come to wish him joy. Now he had come to demand his right of Jala also, because after his mother, for whom no words could express his love, Jala was the most vital person in his life. And she was different. She seemed to understand boys. All the boys in the harem looked to her as their leader. She was the one who could make even the dreary lessons of their Tutor in the Kap[153] bearable. She arranged rewards and incentives which made learning palatable, removing the need for the whip, the preferred choice of their tutor. And as the special companion of the Princess, Jala had influence, and could always have her way.

The child burst into the peaceful chamber of his adopted aunt, but she had heard him coming and was ready. The noise seemed to take bodily form as both it and his small frame arrived together. Hardly had she heard him than she knew he would be upon her, resting for a brief moment in her arms to stake his claim, then away to investigate the next thing to catch his eye.

"You are dressed already this morning Jala. Is it in honour of my birthday?" asked Ameny not really needing an answer.

"Of course, Ameny," she said. "It is a most important day. Our royal prince is 6 years old."

"If I am a Prince, will I be a King?" he asked suddenly, his question forgotten almost as soon as asked, as his butterfly mind moved on to his next thought. Jala glanced at Nepherure. How should she answer? But the slight hesitation caught the child's attention. He stopped and turned from his onward pursuit and observed his mother closely. Nepherure said nothing and Jala was silent. But instinct told the child that he had stumbled upon a mystery.

"Is someone else going to be King?" he asked hardly stopping for a reply.

"Who is king anyway? And aren't most of the boys in the harem the king's children? Why aren't they all Princes?"

As Nepherure stood stock still, Jala was forced to speak. To try to curb this talk before it ran completely out of control.

"You know that the Pharaoh Tutmose has been king for many years."

"Is he my father? Why don't I see him? I'm 6 now. I should be allowed to see him."

"Of course you will see him," said Jala trying to remove the mystery from the child's mind.

"Why doesn't he come here? The maids say the King used to come. Isn't he allowed to now? I thought kings could do anything."

Jala tried to steer the child's train of thought.

"When you are 8 you will go and live in one of the great temples to train as a priest. Every Prince does that. You will see the king then. You may go to one of the temples in the north and he spends nearly all his time in the north with the army."

"But I don't want to wait two more years! I should be allowed to go now. I should be allowed to see my father!"

Jala looked at Nepherure, but the Princess was frozen to the spot and she was forced to continue.

"Of course you want to see the king. Everyone does. That is why he is so busy!"

"But he is my father and I am called a Prince, so I want to go there!"

The child seemed determined but was clearly not distressed by the subject. Jala thought it best to distract him.

"Your mother and I completely agree. We will talk about it and see what can be arranged. You go with your maids now and play with the other boys. I will come in a moment."

The child left them, immediately forgetting the questions he had asked. Forgetting altogether the words he had spoken which had caused an explosion of panic in his mother's world.

Jala turned to Nepherure who was staring wildly.

"Forgive me my Lady! What could I say? I have no wish to distress you."

"What have you done! You have reminded my son that he has another parent! A parent who will make a soldier of him! Every boy dreams of being a soldier. My son will not rest until he finds his father!" she said staring, wide eyed. "For a boy, his father is his hero. For Amenemhat his father will be his god!"

[151] Peret was the 4 month long season, following the inundation of the river. The time of planting and growth
[152] Kush was the old name for Ethiopia
[153] The Kap was the harem school

CHAPTER 33

YEAR 1473 TUTMOSE'S 6TH CAMPAIGN

TUTMOSE KNEW NOTHING OF HIS son's words. For him, this child was still unknown. The child he loved with a passion, and yet was still unknown. But there was no time to think of his child, or the girl he had loved, for once again he was facing war and must focus his mind on the next military campaign. Trouble had been reported in Retanu and he must give these reports serious attention. The powerful alliances of Retanu supported by Naharin gave the city states there the courage to rise against their garrisons and break the treaties they had signed with Egypt.

But Tutmose knew that he had the means to wage war. The Habiri slaves in the delta were freeing the peasants from their farming. Peasants whose families had worked the land from time immemorial could be released from that task and trained as soldiers. The slaves could grow more than enough food to feed the families of these drafted men, and the soldiers themselves. And any surplus grain would be preserved in the store cities of Ramesses and Pithom, built for that purpose, the storing of grain. Tutmose also knew that despite their servitude, the Habiri population was growing year on year. As their numbers increased, more Egyptian farmers would be freed to join his army. The system worked well. There was never a shortage of grain, or of new blood to swell the ranks of his army.

Shemu,[154] the season of harvest, was wearing away and the river was sinking to its lowest ebb. Priests and people alike silently watched for the return of Sopdet[155], to restore the flow of the river and usher in the New Year.

As the river rose, so would the heat of Ra, and the warmth he gave with this abundant supply of water, boded well for the next harvest. This cycle of planting and harvest would continue. This he could leave in the hands of the gods, but it was time for Tutmose himself, and his army to go north. The rebellion in the north was centred in the Island city of Arvad. Qadesh, knowing that she was the next target, and desperate to break the stranglehold of Egypt on the cities around her, had emptied her coffers to buy the help of this island state. With Arvad in rebellion Tutmose would have to redirect his campaign.

After discussion with his generals, Tutmose decided to land his army on the coast, south of Qadesh. Then they would approach Arvad from the landward side. Egypt was known to prefer to attack by ship and all the island's defences would be arranged to counter this, so their attack would have the advantage of surprise. He knew also that Arvad's ruling family were from Naharin[156] but ruling a population of local people. When he had defeated the city Tutmose would take the women of the ruling family as booty, and their sons as hostages back to Egypt, so the punishment would be felt in Naharin also. The city would lose all the possessions that had previously been spared when they had submitted to Egypt, its valuable livestock and luxury goods. Defiance must be punished to teach every city the folly of rebellion.

Within a matter of months, Tutmose had achieved his aims. Arvad was brought into submission. Its goods plundered and as always, enquiries were made for any man fitting his brother's description, but none was found. The king and his army could return home having completed another successful campaign, and once again offer to Amun in his shrine at Waset, thanks for the victory.

Tutmose entered the Temple of Amun through the last great gateway[157], erected by his grandfather. As the procession moved slowly forward, he was free to think. He had now reached the 30th year of his reign. A milestone for every Pharaoh. The year when he would celebrate his Heb Sed[158]. The ceremony at which he must show that he was still fit to be king. Tutmose laughed to himself as he thought of his physical strength. With his constant campaigning in the north, he was fitter now, in his 30th year on the throne than he had ever been. The procession moved slowly forward towards the shrine of Amun, as Tutmose followed the priests. He passed between two huge obelisks[159] also erected by his grandfather and glancing up he could see the sun reflected from the gold of their capstones pointing to the sky. But how should he celebrate this important year? His grandfather had been a great role model. Why not commission two similar obelisks here in Karnak. That would be fitting[160].

The procession continued slowly forward, and the very slowness wearied the king. He hated these routines that constricted him. They were like a cage around him. He had arrived back from the north and must before all else conform to the routines of Karnak. He must offer his thanks to Amun for victory, of course. For the booty taken and the prisoners captured. This he knew. While he hated the ceremonies of the priests, he knew he must not be slack in bringing his thanks and his offerings to this god who had given his family control of Egypt and raised himself to the throne. But the world of priestcraft wearied him.

The booty he had set aside for Amun had been arriving at the Temple for the last hour to a fanfare of trumpets. Hundreds of slaves, among them strange people, pale skinned and blue-eyed, people of Mari descent[161]. Tusks of ivory freshly cut from the beasts he had hunted in celebration of his victory on the journey home through the plains of Retanu; hundreds of them. Lion skins, sacks of wheat, the entire harvest of Retanu. Its cities would go hungry. Just punishment for their rebellion.

Leaving the outer Court, the procession entered the Hall of Pillars[162]. Massive trunks soaring above him, each carved with the story of Egypt and her gods. Huge cedars brought by sea from Lebanon and carried here by river. More building done by his grandfather to stand in honour of Amun and grace his house. The slow pace continued, but he was glad to enter this section of the Temple away from the fierce heat of the sun. Here it was not open to the sky but covered by a stone roof high above him. He relaxed in the shade it provided.

The priests continued their processional pace, further and deeper into the Temple. Here were the obelisks raised by Hatshepsut, and ahead of him, another of her works, unfinished at her death. The red and black granite shrine[163] built to house 'User-Hat Amun', the sacred ceremonial barque of the god, used when his idol was taken out of the temple at festivals. The priests to the right and left did not alter their pace as they conveyed the king through the Temple. But while he must follow, the king's mind was free to muse. Should he remove this unfinished barque shrine erected by his stepmother? It would please the High Priest if he did, as it bore carvings of Hatshepsut on many of its stones. And Menkheperraseneb wanted every memory of Hatshepsut removed. But he must curb the ambitions of this priest. He had been guided by him long enough. No, he would not remove the shrine. In fact he would finish it in honour of his stepmother.[164]Let the record of her coronation remain. It could do him no harm now. She was dead and her son Senenmut gone from Egypt. Besides, looking at it again his eye caught sight of the elegant carvings of the girl he loved, Nepherure, serving with her mother. No, he would keep it and cherish it, along with the few memories he had of her. Seeing these reliefs each time he passed this way would bring back memories - bittersweet, but his life held little that was sweet. Glancing again at the carvings of Nepherure reminded him of the son he had never seen, her son. The evidence of their brief union. His thoughts moved on. The child must be half grown. When would his mother release him to attend school at the Temple of Ptah in Men-nepher? He could only hope she would.

Finally the procession reached the shrine of Amun and there was Menkheperraseneb's smiling face, pleased with the booty garnered from the king's latest campaign. He bowed obsequiously, and there was a rare glimpse of light in the face of this priest whose mind and heart were consumed with bitterness. Why could he not be glad of his life? What more did a man need to be content? He was Hight Priest of the most powerful Temple in the land. Why allow his mind to relive the few plans that had failed? Tutmose mused. His mind was free while his body must be present to perform the ceremonies. Then he remembered. Menkheperraseneb had no sons. Perhaps that had embittered him. And without sons he must pass his prized position of High Priest to his brother's child, only a nephew. Maybe theirs was a rivalry that had raged all their lives, and one which the High Priest would lose at his death when his brother's son would replace him. Tutmose neither knew nor cared, but he knew this nephew, and knew he would continue to be a thorn in the side of his Pharaoh, trained as he was in the fierce family pride of his uncle.

[154] The 4 month season of low river

[155] Sopdet was the Egyptian name for the star Sirius. Egyptians believed that the star Sirius controlled the rise and fall of the Nile. It disappeared below the horizon for 70 days as the river started to fall and reappeared when it returned

[156] Details from Breasted's accounts of Tutmose's wars

[157] The pylon gateways of today at Karnak are different from how they were in Tutmose lll's day. The first pylon encountered in Tutmose's day, we now call the 4th Pylon and was built by the first Tutmose

[158] The Heb Sed Festival was celebrated by the Pharaoh after he had reigned for 30 year and again every subsequent three years. It was an occasion on which the Pharaoh would show he was physically fit to rule.

[159] These obelisks erected by Tutmose l, have been lost

[160] Tutmose raised at least 4 obelisks at Karnak. One, known as Cleopatra's needle stands on the Thames Embankment, London. One in Central Park NY. One taken to present day Istanbul by the Emperor Theodosius, and the last, known as the Lateren obelisk stands in Rome.

[161] A statue from ancient Mari in the Louvre Museum shows a blue-eyed king of Mari.

[162] The Hypostyle Hall, but in Tutmose's time the pillars were of wood not stone

[163] The Red Chapel

[164] Tutmose finished the Red Chapel, the upper part of which bears his name, but later replaced it with a wider barque shrine of his own.

CHAPTER 34

PRINCE AMENY; YEAR 31

NEARLY A YEAR HAD PASSED since the celebration of Amenemhat's sixth birthday. Now he approached his seventh, but still, Tutmose had not seen his son. He had counted the years, as they passed, hoping that Nepherure would agree to release the child to train at the Temple of Ptah in Men-nepher when he reached his 8th year. It was the tradition for all royal princes, to train in one of the great Temples from their 8th birthday, and if he came to Men-nepher, to the Temple of Ptah, Tutmose could finally get to know this child whom he loved already, but had never seen.

The king spent most of his time in Men-nepher, when not on campaign. There he could focus on the next campaign. His army generals and government employees resided there, and every courtier with ambition to ingratiate himself into the Pharaoh's favour, moved there also. But the Pharaoh lived a solitary life when not on campaign. He lived alone in the old palace with just his attendants for company. The isolation of his childhood had made him thus, and as no ties of the heart kept him in the south, he was glad to be free of the court and his queen, in Waset.

Tutmose felt that the weight of responsibility for his wars, was always with him. He must continually be planning for the next campaign. His generals had developed a powerful standing army which must regularly train new men to replace those lost in battle. But Tutmose had found a new interest in building his navy and wanted to be in daily contact with the great dockyard at Men-nepher. The plan was to build 50 ships, which, as they were finished were moved to the new harbour at Perenepher on the coast. Egypt had a long history of boat building but had needed to learn new skills to build her war ships. These were sea going ships, built in the style of the famous imported Byblos boats[165]. Tutmose would visit the yard in the early morning and watch the carpenters and chandlers at work. He loved being involved and having used the navy in his latest Campaign he understood that there was a balance to be struck in building a ship, between the need for strength and the need for speed. A lighter ship which sat high in the water could move with greater speed, but this must be balanced against the advantages of a heavier ship with greater stability which could withstand the battering of storms on the Great Sea. The cedar wood from which they were built was a vital resource from the forests of Lebanon in southwest Retanu. Egypt had learned the value of ships for a sudden strike at the enemy so she must retain control of these forests. They were now an essential part of her war machine, not just for domestic use. Cedar had no equal. It contained oils that made it proof against the destructive effects of water. Perfect for ship building. Another reason why Egypt must keep control of Retanu.

Despite his busy schedule, Tutmose had it in mind to visit the High Priest of Ptah[166]. He must discuss the training of his son if he was to come to Men-nepher after his 8th birthday. Scenes of his own childhood came to mind as his thoughts turned to his son. Vague memories of his mother and the harem where he was born. The tearing of that comfortable world when he was taken to Karnak to be under the tutelage of Hapuseneb[167], the High Priest of Amun. He had never been able to unmask the real Hapuseneb, cold, clever, neither his friend nor his foe. And his day-to-day tutor, Menkheperraseneb, who always wore a guarded face, and in all his childhood gave nothing but endless lessons to the small boy who longed for human kindness. The memories cast a pall over his mind. He remembered it all. The meticulous ordering of his food, the pain in his belly that became a constant companion. The weariness. The loneliness. Remembering, he was determined to make a better life for his son. The boy must not be shut away with one tutor as he had been. He must continue to learn with others as he did now in the Harem at Mi-wer.

Having visited Waset briefly after his last campaign to pay his respects and deliver booty to the temple of Amun, Tutmose was returning to Men-nepher.

The year had turned. Sopdet[168] had been seen in the dawn sky, heralding the New Year, and causing the river to rise[169]. He waited until the water was deep enough for the Royal barge to pass safely upstream from Waset to Men-nepher. Concerns about his son played on his mind constantly, and the enforced rest added to his anxiety. As the barge passed the wide Canal leading to the Fayum and the harem at Mi-wer, Tutmose was filled with remorse. How he longed to see his wife and child. He knew he would never see Nepherure again, but may he hope that in a year's time, Jala would bring his son to him in Men-nepher? He must write to her. He longed for contact with his child. He had known so few close relationships in his life and all of them had ended sadly. Nepherure had belonged to him for such a short time, and Senenmut his half-brother whom he had loved and betrayed. He turned his mind away from the pain of remembering. Perhaps he could find healing in the love of his child.

Reaching Men-nepher the king's barge found its mooring in the royal dock. The palace was deserted, but always in its silent apartments, the tangible presence of past Pharaohs and their wives lingered. Tutmose thought of his mother, Isis. She had never lived in this Palace. Her home had been the Harem, and all through the reign of Hatshepsut, Isis had been excluded from Court. Only with Hatshepsut's death had he been able to give her the official title of Great King's Mother and a welcome at Court in Waset. Now she was content to remain in that city and enjoy the company and gossip of her ladies. She had only ever taken a formal role at Court. As a Harem wife, she felt her lack of standing among the nobles, despite being the mother of the King. But she was glad to be free of Men-nepher and would never return. But how could this dismal palace be brought to life and made ready to welcome his son. Both palace and Temple must show a ready welcome. Amenemhat would be studying at the temple of Ptah, and if he proved himself a scholar, Tutmose would send him to finish his education at the great Temple of Ra in Iunu. There he could learn the greatest secrets in the world.

Jala received the letter from the King, with a heavy heart. How could she hope to persuade Nepherure to give up her child to the Temple of Ptah? Her life revolved around the boy, from dawn when the child burst upon the sleeping world, to the hour when he would fall asleep from sheer exhaustion, leaving all around him with a sense of quiet relief. But Jala's duty was not only to Nepherure. Hadn't she, Jala, played a part in bringing this child into existence by persuading Nepherure to marry the King? And the child was fast outgrowing the Harem. At only seven years old he was pushing every boundary. He loved working with his tutor and formed his hieroglyphs with great care. But with his schoolwork done for the day he seized his freedom, becoming once again the active child he was. The harem and the village beyond its walls had many industries now. In the course of the last 8 years, the Pharaoh had endowed it with ample funds for gardens and pools, farms and vineyards, and all the trades that went with them. Both inside and out, the buildings of the harem were beautified, and industries had been established to make it a hive of activity. The extensive vegetable gardens, benefitting from the rich soil of the Fayum, produced food as fine as any in Egypt, and Ameny insisted he try his hand at everything. Grapes were brought in abundance to be processed into wine, and on a visit to the winery with his maids Ameny discovered the process in operation. He was transfixed and after each subsequent harvest, considered it his duty to assist in the trampling of the grapes. Flax arrived in its raw state and the child watched with rapt attention the various processes of soaking, drying and spinning the thread into different grades. The finest would become linen garments fit for a king or priest, while the coarser grades would become towels or bandages or a variety of other useful cloths. But the looms on which it slowly, as if by magic became cloth before his eyes, held him spell bound. Weaving was an occupation allowed to royal ladies and his mother spent many contented hours weaving sashes of brilliant colours for her own use. Indeed, he remembered the day when the most beautiful loom he had ever seen arrived at Mi-wer. Carved of ebony, and embellished with gold, it was of a different design from the one his mother used. But the loom arrived with others of the same design, and women skilled to teach the ladies how to use them. Having learned the new style of weaving, this beautiful loom became his mother's most treasured possession.

So the years of the young Prince in the harem passed slowly away. The potter was one of his particular friends, and with great delight the old man allowed Ameny the use of his wheel. After months of effort for both himself and his maids, who must restore him clean to his mother, he presented her with the evidence of his genius, along with a clear explanation as to why a jug without a handle could be as useful as one blessed with such an addition.

JALA READ THE KING'S LETTER again and decided that subterfuge was required if Nepherure was ever to release her child to live the normal life of a Prince. Nepherure herself knew well that every royal Prince was destined for the temples or the Army and would instinctively choose the former for her child. So this was where Jala must start her own campaign. She pretended it was natural that Ameny would leave Mi-wer on his 8th birthday and it was just a case of choosing where he would go.

The two women had dined and were enjoying the beauty of the short twilight when Jala made her move.

"My Lady, I heard today from Minmose's mother that her son is faring well in the Temple at Waset."

Nepherure looked at her friend but did not reply. Minmose was a boy born to the king in the harem of Mi-wer before Nepherure's arrival there, and was only a year older than Ameny. But Jala continued.

"It is a pity that the child must make his way alone as his father is now spending so much time in Men-nepher."

Still Nepherure was silent. Jala glanced at her, and looking directly into her eyes, with a smile on her face, covering the fears in her heart, continued.

"If Ameny were to go to the Temple of Ptah in Men-nepher, we could be sure that the Pharaoh would not leave him alone or afraid."

A smothered cry escaped from Nepherure as she thought of her child lonely or afraid. But Jala must elicit an agreement, not just a response from his mother.

"Is it always the lot of a royal prince to leave his childhood home, my Lady?" asked Jala with feigned uncertainty. "It has certainly been the case with all the boys here, I think," she added with a question in her voice. "I could go with him of course, to put your mind at rest, and stay as long as he needed me. But I think Ameny will find his way in the world," she added with a smile.

Nepherure was silent again, but she had denied nothing that Jala had said. She knew in her heart that the world of women would never suffice for her son, and after some time she spoke. She was unable to lift her eyes from the floor but spoke with only a waver in her voice.

"Perhaps you are right. Perhaps Men-nepher would be best, where Amenemhat will have his father to see that he is loved." She paused. "And if you take him and wait until he is settled, I will be content," she finished as her voice faded to a whisper.

Having delivered herself of the most difficult speech she had made in all her years of motherhood, Nepherure melted into tears. Jala said nothing. She must not undo Nepherure's resolve with careless words but placed a comforting hand on her shoulder then added in a cheerful vein.

"Our little Prince will be excited at your decision, I think. He will go out to meet his life eagerly, and I think he will find it."

IT SEEMED AS IF THE months became only days that separated Ameny from his 8th birthday. Nepherure hardly spoke of his leaving. She knew that Jala was right to approach the inevitable with cheerfulness. And it was in this way that Nepherure spoke to her son.

"The Temple of Ptah in Men-nepher is probably the oldest Temple in Egypt."

"Don't old things fall down?" asked the child.

"Not when they are built of stone," she replied.

"Is this palace built of stone or will it fall down?" he continued.

"Only Temples are built of stone Ameny, because they must last for millions of years."

"Do the gods live for millions of years?"

"The gods never die, my love. Only people die."

"But the Pharaoh doesn't die. He just goes into the sky with Ra."

"That is why a palace is not made of stone because it is not needed forever," replied Nepherure wondering how close she was to failing in her theology. But the child was not interested in eternity right now. Right now, he wanted to play with his mother's sight hound, a creature who was always hoping and waiting at his heels for the boy to play with him.

The turn of the year was soon upon them. Ameny would travel to Men-nepher with Jala as soon as the river was safely navigable. Tutmose had been on campaign again, his 7th, and had just returned. Words could not contain his joy when Nepherure wrote in reply to the letter Jala had received, informing him of his son's imminent arrival. Tutmose had made arrangements in great detail with the High Priest of Ptah. The old priest was mystified at the care taken by the Pharaoh for his son. The child was not even of a royal mother. But Tutmose had lost the son born to him of his first queen and queen Meryet had borne him no sons as yet. So the boy may prove to be important.

Ameny was beside himself with excitement at the prospect of a journey in the Royal Barge. His young mind could not think beyond the excitement of the barge itself. He knew he was going to live at a very old Temple in an important city, but the beautiful barge was physically present in all its splendour, waiting at the Palace docks, while the Temple and its city were far away and could not even be imagined. Jala had schooled him repeatedly that he must hug his mother properly. He must look into her face and say he would miss her - but that she 'must not worry because he would be back soon'. Without her instruction Jala feared that the excited child would leave his home and his mother with hardly a thought, consumed as he was with the thrill of the journey.

But Ameny played his part well. Nepherure wept a little but smiling bravely hugged her son and told him to be good. He turned on her his winning smile and kissed her roundly while glancing repeatedly at the marvellous barge being loaded at that very moment. He was not heartless. It was simply that for him, this was not the real wrench he must face. He had the security of Jala, still. She had been to him a second mother all his life, and she was to go with him on his great adventure.

Tutmose found himself pacing the corridors of the palace checking and rechecking the rooms he had chosen for Amenemhat. He could hardly recognise himself. He had been sole Pharaoh of Egypt for the past 10 years. He had just returned from his 7th Campaign in the north where he had again secured all the seaports of Retanu. Every battle he had engaged in, he had won. He was almost ready to strike at the heart of Naharin and her King, the climax of all his campaigns. So why did he wait with trepidation for the arrival of a child? He knew that no other child would ever matter to him like this child. How strange were the secrets of the heart? But his heart was not long in disclosing its secret. This was Nepherure's child. The child she loved. And if he were forbidden to love her, he could at least love her child.

The first part of the journey from Mi-wer was along the canal and happened in stages from lock-gate to lock-gate[170]. The water rose with the land around it, up and out of the basin of the Fayum. The water did not flow towards the river, and oarsmen were needed to take the barge forward. Even when it left the canal and entered the river itself, the oarsmen remained, to drive the boat forward in the sluggish river. Ameny was fascinated by every detail of the lock-gates, never missing a moment of the process, as the gates were closed and the basin filled, raising the barge to the higher level for the next stretch of the canal. He watched the oarsmen, and when he tired of that, he watched the farmers working the land as the barge passed. He knew the names of all the river birds, the Heron, the Kingfisher, the Ibis and the delicate white Egrets, and also knew the many strange stories about them. There was always something that could hold his attention and Jala was relieved. The child occupied himself well throughout the journey. She thought of his tutors and a measure of anxiety entered her mind. But if his tutors could contain his exuberance, she thought, they would be delighted with him. She prayed he would delight his father also.

They reached the royal dock at Men-nepher on their 5th day out of Mi-wer. The child was tired and disorientated by yet another Palace rising before him. They had slept at four different Mooring Places[171] on the preceding nights of their journey and here was yet another. The boy was half asleep when they arrived but was far too heavy for Jala to carry. She too was tired, and gratefully accepted the help of a man who boarded the barge and lifted the sleeping child into his arms. She followed mechanically, hoping through her tiredness that the Pharaoh would wait until morning to greet them.

The Palace was a strange building, clearly very ancient. She could feel the presence of innumerable royals and their guests whom it had welcomed within its broad walls over the centuries. But it seemed happy to welcome this little party also, arriving as it did with no pomp or ceremony as dusk was falling. The corridors were cheerfully lit, and Jala followed her guide through a maze of corridors, to a comfortable suite of adjoining chambers with windows overlooking the gardens as they stretched away to the river. This she took in at a glance, for her gaze hardly left the sleeping child in the arms of her guide, who laid his charge gently on a couch and covered him with a linen sheet. Jala turned to thank the man and request the few items she needed, only then realising it was the Pharaoh himself who had carried his child into the Palace. He smiled briefly at her shocked expression and bade her good night, promising that her requests would be attended to. She stared at the retreating figure of the Pharaoh then turned to check on the sleeping child. A feeling of relief overcame her as she considered the extraordinary thing the King had done. She was too tired to resist the rising emotion that engulfed her, but they were tears of relief and joy. She need no longer fear that the Pharaoh would be indifferent to his child.

The King came to their chambers the morning after their arrival with no ceremony and a small gift for his son. The boy had slept well and was back to his effusive self. With a momentary hesitation only, he glanced into his father's face and thanked him for the gift. It was a model chariot, complete with its horses, which the child received with unaffected delight. He knelt down immediately, with his head on the floor, watching the chariot wheels turn as he moved his toy along. Jala observed silently as father and son discovered they could talk together. Ameny was fascinated by the chariot as it moved, and after a moment, shared his thoughts with his father.

"The chariot should have a driver, really," he said, "But it doesn't matter because I can push it," he added, as an afterthought.

He was so much at ease that Tutmose also relaxed, and the evident pleasure on the face of the King, spoke of new joy after years of loneliness. With Nepherure's son with him in Men-nepher, Tutmose had at last found something more than family ambition to fill his life. He had found a salve for his wounds. He had lost Nepherure but could see her smile every day in the face of her child, and it rapidly became clear to all, that this child was his special treasure. Ameny was not the son of his Great Royal Wife but was the child his father loved.

So from his 8th year the boy was discovering a new world, a world of men. In the temple, with his father, and with the army generals who were regular visitors to the palace, he grew to understand this world. He was popular, even among the old priests at the temple of Ptah, who were captivated by his open face and ready smile. Growing up in a world where he was loved, with the devotion of his mother and Jala, it was normal for the boy to be open and friendly. He made friends easily at the temple, cajoling his fellow pupils into cheerfulness. Not taking offence. And the priests, accustomed as they were to boys with closed faces, closed by fear and awe, could not fail to respond, especially as they also found him to be a ready scholar.

"How is it that you already know so many signs?" asked Jenner, the boy who had attached himself most closely to the prince as to become his shadow.

"You can already read the hieroglyphs on the temple stelae!" he added.

"I learnt them at the Kap, in the Harem," replied Ameny, unimpressed at his own brilliance.

"They are not difficult to learn. Even my mother and Jala know them, and they are not clever at all," he added cheerfully.

His numbers he knew also. But there was much knowledge of the gods, known to the priests of Ptah which was an unknown world to the boy.

"Father, have you studied the teachings of Ptah?" Ameny asked his father a few weeks into his time as a temple novice.

"Not very much," his father replied. "I know he is the oldest of the gods. He is the great builder who fashioned the earth and the heavens at the beginning, but that is all I know."

"Why don't you study him more, father? Why do you worship Amun and Ra more? Ptah is older. So if he is before them, surely he is greater?"

Tutmose considered for a moment. He was pleased that Ameny was committed to his studies at the temple, that was only right. But he knew in his heart that he and his family owed their position and power to Amun. It was a delicate subject. And if he harboured any hope of Ameny following him on the throne, the boy must switch his allegiance. It was Amun who was giving him victory in Retanu. It was Amun who received all Egypt's thanks for these victories in gold and slaves. It was Amun whose temple he would extend and adorn when he had finally defeated Naharin.

But now he must prepare for his 7th Campaign, and before the year had reached its zenith Tutmose was travelling north once again. He watched with pride as his well-appointed ships made their exit from the harbour into the open sea. He was pleased with the efficiency of his men and the harbour was proving itself fit for purpose. His spirits rose high despite his wish to spend more time with Ameny. That time would come. Naharin was not yet defeated but he was on course to bring it about. He could feel victory in the air.

Tutmose watched the coast of Canaan pass as he sailed north to Byblos. As his ship turned to enter that harbour, he could see the outline of the fortress he had built to house the garrison and provide secure storage for the tribute from these subject lands. Grain that would feed his army while on campaign, and feed the garrison left behind. As his ship entered the harbour, the temple of Hathor came into view beside the fort. Here she was known in another guise as 'the Lady of Byblos[172]', worshipped and honoured by many living in the city. Native born, but also wanting the protection of Egypt's powerful goddess.

The king stayed only a few weeks at Byblos. He must show the strength of his fleet in all these coastal cities of the Phoenicians and receive their tribute and homage. Now more than ever the supplies of grain must be securely stored, ready to supply his troops when he turned east to take the heartland of Naharin.

---

[165] Byblos boats were traditional sea going boats developed by the Phoenicians and built at the port city of Byblos, for which the city was famous from ancient times.
[166] Ptah was considered the oldest god of Egypt, the god of creation and building
[167] Hapusneb was High Priest of Amun under Hatshepsut.
[168] The star Sirius
[169] Egyptians believed that Sodet / Sirius caused the rise of the river.
[170] Lock-gates were used in ancient Egypt
[171] Mooring places were Palaces spaced along the river a day's journey apart for the use of the royal family
[172] Hathor, the Egyptian goddess was known and worshipped in Byblos

CHAPTER 35

MOSHE MARRIES ZIPPORAH[173]

MOSHE HAD NOW BEEN LIVING in Midian for five years. When not occupied with other things, or on the dark days when he was assailed with feelings of all he had lost, he would take the flock of his father-in-law away to the mountains in the south. There the sheep would find fresh grass, and from these heights on a clear day, he could see right across the sea that bordered Midian, to Egypt on the far side. It was less than two schoenui[174] distant, and he could see the outline of the huge beach called Nuweiba, jutting out into the water, guarded by an Egyptian fort[175] on the north side. He knew that beach. It was easy to recognise. Its delta shape showed how it had formed from silt, washed down from the wadis and mountains beyond, over many centuries.

The sea was a beautiful sight. It was known, locally as the Sea of Edom,[176] the Red Sea, and from his vantage point he could watch the fishing boats hauling in their nets on the Midianite shore below. Of more interest were the ships which passed up and down to the ports in the north, and occasionally other small boats, that crossed from Midian to the Egyptian shore; fishermen selling their catch to the soldiers in the fort. It hurt to see life continuing in the wide world from which he was excluded. But taking the sheep away to the south, to make use of the fresh grass growing there, was a service few others could do. Only a grown man, competent with a bow, could go alone so far from the camp in relative safety.

But his settled life was about to change. At the turn of the year Moshe had married Zipporah and she was now heavy with his child. As her burden grew, the light in her eyes visibly softened. Her whole demeanour changed from that of a determined girl, to that of a woman, who despite her heavy burden, had discovered a contentment that lodged deeper still.

For Moshe, seeing the growth of his child increasing with the passing months awoke strange memories. The faint memory of his own mother. Of sleeping beside her on the reed mat in those hazy days before he was taken to the palace. He remembered her smell even now. The smell of milk. The comfort that filled his young mind with the certainty of belonging without question. Blissful years, torn apart when he was taken to the palace to become the plaything of a spoilt child. A girl whose command was law. He remembered the terror of loss. But his instinct had told him that only in this girl, who now ruled his world, would he again find safety and security, and the comfort of a sleeping form beside him at night. By his sheer need of her, he won her heart. A girl who had no heart, who cared for no one, became as devoted to her adopted child as any mother born.

But the promise of a child was to be denied Zipporah. All was well until the start of the birth. The experienced midwives detected nothing amiss but as the hours passed and the child became inactive, a strained silence settled over the tent. Darkness had fallen when the child finally entered the world, but there was no cry to announce him. Even in the pale lamplight the face which would have been beautiful, was stained blue and was silent. The cord tight around his neck told it all. Instead of joy the birth tent was a place of heartbreak.

Moshe could not bear the constant sound of sobbing. Memories of his own pain from far-off days, of losing his mother, returned, and woke in him a kindliness that had been missing in his feeling for the girl he had married. If his presence would comfort her, he would give it, regardless of the protocol that excluded men from the tent of sorrow, but was in reality, hallowed cowardice. As the days passed and Zipporah could accept his presence, a new bond formed between them. On his side pity, on hers, numbness still, which became in time the beginning of gratitude, the real beginning of their marriage. It had been no more than a contract, little more than convenience, but their shared pain became the beginning of their shared lives.

In the terrible days that followed the loss of her child, not even the request of her husband would persuade Zipporah to eat. She hardly drank, and for the first weeks simply slept, to find oblivion. One night she rose and while the community slept, left the tent. As the tent flap closed, Moshe woke, aware only of footsteps outside. He rose and followed, as the girl led him through the darkness towards the wild lands to the south. No dog barked as he followed unnoticed. For hours she walked on and on until the darkness of the eastern sky slowly lightened towards dawn. As the piercing light of Ra broke on the horizon, the girl turned towards it, only then noticing the man who followed. She intended to die out here in the wild land. He could see that. To lose herself in the wilderness and never return. To be free of her pain. But seeing her husband, she turned towards him. This man who would not let her die! It was his child that had died, but he had known loss before. How else could he survive such a thing? He claimed to believe in God. Let him ask his God now what had happened! She turned towards him screaming with all the fury that raged inside her.

"Your God has taken my child! Yahweh has killed my child! He is no better than the gods of Moab whom we despise for demanding the sacrifice of children!"

When he did not reply, she looked wildly round, and seeing the cliff to her right, left the path and rushed towards the precipice. Moshe responded, catching her in his arms before she reached her goal. Unable to escape, she sank to the ground like a broken thing.

For a long time, they sat, she huddled on the ground as he watched Ra rising in his fierce brilliance. He was hardly aware that he had started to speak but found himself thinking his thoughts aloud.

"The world is broken, Zipporah. It is not as Yahweh made it to be. I understand that now", he paused, looking down at the girl in his arms. "In this broken world we die, and those we love will die," he said. "Things have been set in motion - forces unleashed - that control the world. Perhaps man caused it by his rebellion. Perhaps we have opened the door to evil, and now it is beyond our power to defeat it," he said. But the girl made no reply.

"I now know that Yahweh is powerful, and despite what I see in the world, I believe he is good." He was talking to himself and was surprised when the girl responded.

"I do not believe he is good! I will never believe any god is good!" she said with a sob.

"I understand. I know I cannot take away your pain. But I have bound myself to you," he said, then paused and added quietly, "Will you let me help you face today?"[177]

---

[173] This is recorded in the Bible; Exodus 2 v21

[174] The schoenus was the Egyptian measurement of distance; plural schoeni; one schoenus measured 10.5 km

[175] A fort was called a Migdol

[176] Edom means Red

[177] The bible says nothing of any daughters Moses might have had, or any children he may have lost. It only tells us that he had two living sons.

CHAPTER 36

MOSHE AND JETHRO

THERE WAS NO LONGER AN option for Moshe to leave Midian and find his life elsewhere. He was married and his wife needed him. In the months that followed the death of their child, he remained in the camp, not allowing himself to escape to the south for solitude as he had before. Zipporah needed him. She needed many things that he could not give her, but he must give her what he could, his physical presence, even if it fell far short of her needs.

The two of them ate alone, food brought by other women, but they hardly spoke. As Zipporah's body recovered and the unwanted milk was not taken, it ceased to form in her breasts. Her figure returned to that of a girl, slim, but now too slim. She had lost her bloom but neither noticed nor cared. Moshe observed it all. She had been a beautiful girl, but he had not married her for her beauty, nor rejected her now, for its lack. The village watched and waited. Life and death were no strangers here. But this newcomer, who dispensed with village customs, who took care of his wife, not just leaving her to the women, while he kept away in the company of the men, was observed by them all. The village took note. This was leadership. A new sort of leadership. Leadership with heart. This man could be trusted with human lives.

Moshe was unaware of the verdict being passed. Nothing was said, even by Jethro. But being the eldest daughter of the tribal leader, with her mother dead, Zipporah had no woman above her. No one in a position to give natural support or guidance. She was alone, and without the support of her husband, could not have survived.

Often, they walked together. He would take her down to the water at twilight, when all was still, after the village children had returned to their tents and before the fishermen went there to prepare for their night's work. Observing them, Jethro would stay away, but when Moshe walked alone he would seize his chance.

"When the men next go to Seir with the consignment of copper ore, we must purchase parchment and ink. Perhaps you have time now to record the story of our people?"

Moshe hesitated. The last time Jethro raised this subject his mind recoiled from it. But to his surprise his feelings had changed. He was no longer desperate to avoid this history. Having learned the story of Jobab, he too was able to set aside the need to know all the answers. He no longer needed to ask why. He would listen to Jethro. He would listen to these records of the beginning. Of the origin and place of the Habiri and the Midianites. He was part of it now. He would live and die here in Midian, and if he had gifts to use, he must use them to do this service and leave a legacy for his people.

It was many months before Zipporah told, even her husband of the new life moving in her womb. Her restoration to the world of the women was now complete. She had never contributed to the gossip they shared. She had never been at the centre of their world but had regained the place of belonging that she had lost. Now as a quieter version of what she had been, with her status diminished, as was that of every married woman who remained childless, her contribution to the work of the village and her silence were accepted in equal measure.

One morning Moshe and Zipporah were woken early by a storm. There was no purpose in rising so early so lay listening to the rain. Suddenly Zipporah spoke.

"I am with child," she said abruptly. He sat up at her words. "It has been moving for one moon cycle, so there will be 5 more moons before the birth," she said avoiding his gaze. "I have told no one yet," she said and was silent.

"And the women have not guessed?" he asked.

"No one has guessed."

"Then I will remain silent if that is your wish," he said quietly.

But with Zipporah restored to the world of the women, Moshe and Jethro had the freedom to spend evenings together to eat and talk under the stars while the women ate together as a group in the privacy of their communal tent.

Jethro opened the subject. He was keen to move on with his request.

"Will you be able to make a record now, of the beginning and the deluge? You have no problems regarding them, I think but I know that the story of Abraham has concerned you," he said, regarding this man whose company he so much prized. The man who had become his closest confident, yes, and now a son, but one who felt closer to him than his own sons. Moshe had been unable to hold his gaze, and Jethro had guessed his reasons for the delay. But he need delay no longer.

"Yes, the records you have of the beginning of the world are different from those of Egypt, but Egypt has lost the true story, I think," said Moshe. "But the memory of the deluge is everywhere. Changed of course, but it is there. Gilgamesh[178] has other names for God but the story is the same." He paused. There were so many parts of the sacred record of his people that he hardly knew and certainly did not understand.

"I will need you to explain to me the story of Abraham," he said.

They were watching the fading light as the sun set in the west. Jethro turned his eyes away from the light and looked behind him, towards the north.

"There lies Canaan," he said thoughtfully. "There Abraham wandered as a nomad. He owned no part of the land except the burial ground he bought from the Hittites to bury his wife."

"And yet he believed God had given him the whole land – to his descendants?" asked Moshe.

"Yes, he did, but he had no descendants at the time, nor for years, as you know. Ishmael was born when he was over 80 years old, but Isaac, the child of Sarah, the child God had promised, was not born until he was 100."

"Why did God make Abraham wait so long?" asked Moshe. "He was finally given the son God had promised, but he never saw his descendants owning the land. That promise is still not fulfilled even now, 400 years later!"

Jethro was silent for a moment, thinking before he replied.

"I think Yahweh has bigger purposes than simply giving land and descendants to a man who pleased him. I do not know what he plans, but by giving Abraham a son by Sarah when she was no longer able to bear children,

God showed he has the power to fulfil the next part of the promise. To give Canaan to the Habiri. But he will do it in his own time".

"Can he destroy the Canaanites? I have seen the powerful armies of Egypt and even they and the Pharaohs of Egypt have found the Canaanites hard to defeat!"

But now the night was upon them, and a cold breeze was blowing. Moshe knew that Zipporah was alone in the tent and he must go to her.

"I will leave you now Sir," he said. "We must talk again. I need to understand this history if I am to do as you ask. Goodnight."

---

[178] The Epic of Gilgamesh is a well know record of the flood, written on stone tablets from Babylonia

CHAPTER 37

MERYET AND HER DAUGHTERS

MERYET SAT IN THE SHADE of the Palace courtyard watching her daughters at play. It was hot, unbearably hot, as it always was in Waset. Her girth, which had been controlled in girlhood, had spread with the birth of her daughters, increasing her intolerance of the heat. She groaned inwardly, longing for the cool of evening. But she knew there was a simple solution to her discomfort. If she were permitted to reside in the north as her husband did, in Men-nepher, the cooler temperatures there would make life far more agreeable. Tutmose had left her in Waset, while he remained almost continually in the north. She was queen, and wished to be seen and heard at Court, and although he knew her wish, Tutmose did not invite her to live in Men-nepher. He said that the court there was merely a military headquarters, not suitable for his principal Queen, but in truth it had become his capital in everything but name.

Since her marriage, Meryet was sufficiently in fear of her husband to curb the sharp words for which she was famous, but still he found her presence oppressive. They had been married for eight years, and although she had borne him Nephertari and Iaret, two girls in their mother's mould, she had given him no sons. Meryet's ambition was to bear the future Pharaoh but with their continual separation, she feared she would fail. And Tutmose seemed content to give up his quest for another son, to be free of her. He had taken three Canaanite wives in the last few years, Menhet, Menwi and Merti[179] and they were honoured as minor queens at the court in Men-nepher. And although

Meryet held the title of Great Royal Wife, while she remained with just the pretence of a Court in Waset, she felt lonely and ridiculous.

The children had tired of their game and were quarrelling loudly. They were still young, just seven and five, and provided little companionship for their mother. But they were all she had, and she must take solace where she might. She tried to calm them.

"If your game is spent, let us leave the garden and take some refreshment," she said, but received no reply.

"Nephertari, come with me now and Iaret will follow. We can refresh ourselves with a cool drink then perhaps play Senet[180] inside, until I must dress for the feast".

But her elder daughter had, in her short life, heard sufficient cruel words from her mother, to learn how to use them, and this chance was too good to miss.

"Why do you bother dressing up for the feast? The King is not here, and all the clever people have gone with him to Men-nepher. Your court is filled with the boring people who are left behind."

Meryet was stunned and mortified. Nephertari understood the situation exactly and cared nothing for her mother's feelings. She knew her father despised his queen, and it amused the girl. But the shock of her daughter's words stunned Meryet. With terrible clarity she saw her own likeness writ large in this heartless child. But the girl had more to say.

"If you had a boy," she added, "you might please our father a bit". With that she finished, knowing she had made the deepest cut of all.

Meryet's ears stung from the merciless barbs of her daughter. But what she said was the simple truth! And if the child knew how things were, how was it possible that the Court did not repeat words in a similar vein for their amusement also. She was mortified at the thought. How could she continue to face these courtiers, day after day all the time sensing their mockery? No, she must act. She must find a way to go to Men-nepher and get herself a son!

Suddenly, Meryet made her decision. The King was on campaign again. It was his 7th raid on the north. He was reaching ever closer to the moment when he could close on Naharin itself. This was her opportunity. She would no longer live with the pretence of the court at Waset. Her daughter was right.

Only the dregs remained there. Those who had not the means or ambition to move north with the king and ingratiate themselves into his favour. She was indeed left with the old, who could not stir from their familiar homes, or those too poor to set up another household in the north, or those too indolent to stir themselves to do so. She was an intelligent woman, although she had used her mind for little that was worthy of it, with her scheming and bitter reflections. But among those remaining at court, there were almost none to raise her thoughts any higher or encourage her in useful reflections. One, however, had become a friend.

Eset was a sensible woman who, when needs must, had become a nurse to the royal children in the harem at Mi-wer on the early death of her husband. Now she had retired, and attended the court at Waset, living on a small pension granted for her services. Her company became a refuge for the queen away from the mindless flattery of the rest. Besides, she knew the harem at Mi-wer and could give Meryet information about her sister's life. But she was a genuine soul, free of bitterness, and this, Meryet admired. Whatever the basis for this unlikely friendship, Eset and the queen became firm friends, and spent many hours together. Their hours became fruitful as they shared their love of weaving and embroidery. Even Meryet's daughters could be persuaded to sit and learn, or at least to sit and watch. And the pleasure of creating something useful gave purpose and fulfilment to the long weary days.

But it was not only Eset's company and skill that came to bear on the queen's mind. Eset was a faithful friend to many ladies who remained at Mi-wer. And in her time there raising children, she had learned the rudiments of reading and writing as a means of passing the time. Now she corresponded with her friends, and thus became the innocent conduit between Meryet and her sister, with information passed, but only one way. Nepherure never knew that the private life of herself and her child was known in detail by her sister, living so far away in Waset. That Ameny was a fine intelligent boy, loved by all. That he was destined to continue his schooling at the temple of Ptah in Men-nepher where his father could pay him frequent visits. All these facts were stored in Meryet's heart, where they became a corrosive poison for her mind.

Still Meryet had produced no son for the king, nor would she, if she remained here in Waset, leading a life of celibacy. Nepherure's child was adopted, she knew, so he was not of the Solar blood. But none the less, he had become precious to the king, and many a Pharaoh was the child of the King's concubine, not his Great Royal Wife. The thought racked Meryet's mind night and day. Tutmose could choose Ameny as Pharaoh! She must not be a fool again and allow her sister to seize the ultimate advantage. No! With or without the king's permission, she would remove herself to Men-nepher. She would take her place in the king's bed and get herself a son. If she, his Great Royal Wife gave him a son, he would not be such a fool as to choose Ameny over the son of his principal queen!

And so it was done. With the king away on campaign, Meryet moved her household to the old palace of Men-nepher. She found that the King's apartments were a tired remnant of the past, uncared for, and unwelcoming. In a few weeks Meryet transformed them. She knew what he liked and provided it with skill and good taste. Bright rooms, sumptuous couches, urns of scented flowers. And for the night? Lamps burning incense and scented oils. Gentle light and a welcoming fragrance. She created a home for the king, filled with beauty and tranquillity. In fact, everything that she was not. But she would hold her tongue. She would not challenge. She would make requests not commands. Tutmose would never be deceived by her, she knew that. He had known her too long. But if she curbed her tongue in his presence and did as he required, perhaps he would tolerate her.

IN THE SPACE OF THE last ten years, Tutmose had become a seasoned general. His careful planning had removed the threat of invasion from the north. And success had helped to steel his mind against the inevitable fear of each new battle. The war was not yet won, but the city states of Retanu were regretting what they had done. They could never have guessed that this young Pharaoh would win every battle he joined. How was it possible to continually pour new, well-trained men into his wars? And then to leave large garrison in the defeated cities![181] Those who had listened to Durusha at the beginning heartily wished they had not. And now Durusha was about to face his own worst nightmare. His city of Qadesh was surrounded by other cities defeated and garrisoned by Egypt. He had lost his eldest son at the beginning of these wars when Megiddo had fallen, when he himself had only escaped by chance. But now in a desperate attempt to defeat Egypt he had sealed up his city. He had emptied his coffers to buy the help of a large army from the east. And with it, a secret weapon. Huge elephants impervious to Egyptian arrows, or so he hoped. Now the battle was upon him. He would address his generals for the last time.

"It is the king himself that we must target," Durusha said to his generals. "Find this king and destroy him. Without their leader the army will flee."

The day of the battle was dawning. Tutmose's army was moving in formation, facing east, to meet the enemy. He had despatched Djehuty and the other generals to lead from the front, while he remained on the southern flank with his second in command Amenemhab, a younger man but one whom he knew he could trust. As the sun rose, Tutmose's men were at first dazzled by its power and, focusing on the enemy immediately in front of them, did not see the strange creatures along the flanks of the opposing army. But Durusha had identified the one man he wished to target. Sending a message to his men he ordered the elephants to charge the southern flank of the Egyptians. The huge beasts came on trumpeting their fury. One was heading straight for the king, its rider singling him out. Amenemhab did not stop to think. Wielding his sword, and hardly noticed by the man riding high behind the elephant's head, he stormed towards the beast just as it lifted its trunk to repeat the deafening noise. But instead of the expected blast of sound, a terrible scream broke forth, as the poor creature stopped in its tracks, waving what remained of its severed trunk. It turned and fled in a state of terror through its own troops scattering them on all sides. Amenemhab's action had saved the life of his king[182].

The path of the fleeing elephant cut a swathe through the troops of Durusha's army, and seeing what had passed, all valour left them. Before their eyes, they had seen the gods of Egypt protecting the Egyptian Pharaoh and fighting against Retanu. Those who could, turned and fled the field. Those who could not were cut down by Tutmose's men. Before Ra had reached his zenith, the battle was over, and Qadesh had fallen. The city opened its gates to the victorious king. But he was weary of battle and would leave it in the hands of his generals. He hardly cared to search the city for his brother Senenmut.

Only those whose life was tied up with Quadesh would have stayed to face what they must have known was inevitable defeat.

BUT WITH QADESH SECURED, TUTMOSE was free to return home. On reaching Men-nepher, his first thought was to find Ameny, but then discovered that Meryet had made herself at home in his Palace.

"I do not recall giving permission for you to travel to Men-nepher", he said by way of welcome when she appeared at his summons.

"Forgive me my Lord. I am continually conscious that I have failed you, my Lord."

"You have failed in many ways madam. In which way especially?"

"To give you an heir, my Lord."

"I have a number of heirs," Tutmose replied knowing full well her meaning.

"Forgive me my Lord but as your queen, I should give you heirs."

"And what makes you so sure you can deliver on your promise?" asked the king rounding on her.

Meryet felt the blood rushing to her face. Even the house servants were present! But she hid her anger and swallowed her mortification.

"With the kindness of the gods my Lord, a son may be given us."

"And the kindness of myself, madam," he said grinding her further into the ground.

Meryet said no more but remained with her eyes averted as her husband strode from the chamber. But she had not been banished. And she resolved to make no demands on the king. When he departed on campaign year on year, she would not murmur. If he wished to promote soldiers from the army into his domestic household, she accommodated them without question. In every outward detail she conformed to his wishes without comment. But she could not control her heart and watched with a jealous eye the ever-growing bond between Tutmose and Nepherure's child. He was nine years old when Meryet came to Men-nepher. A likable child whose pleasant nature made all who knew him, love him. And she saw daily, the fixed place he commanded in his father's heart. When Ameny came to the palace, Meryet could see a physical response in her husband. Ameny made no demands and few requests, but it felt to her as if his father would give him the throne if he but asked!

Meryet held her tongue, but she could not tear herself away. She must know everything that passed between them. Remaining mute when she saw them together while her heart screamed to know Why! Why did Tutmose love this harem child with such devotion? And would he respond in this way to the sons she longed to bear? Would he? Could he ever love another child as he loved Ameny?

---

[179] This is historical fact

[180] Senet was an Egyptian board game.

[181] My understanding is that Tutmose had this ready supply of men because the Hebrew slave population freed thousands of peasant farmers to train as full-time soldiers. This was possible because the work of these farmers, to feed the country, was being done by the slaves.

[182] This incident and the bravery of Amenemhab is recorded in the annals of the king and is listed by Breasted.

CHAPTER 38

VICTORY WITHIN HIS GRASP; 1471 BC

TUTMOSE SAT LISTENING TO THE beat of the oars as the barge carried him north to Perenepher, his new naval port on the coast. There his troops were gathering once again, and there he would join them.

But after 12 years when his only objective had been war, his heart now told him of another claim. Something he had not known before. That this second claim should come now, just when the first was reaching its climax and needed his total commitment, caused turmoil in his heart and mind.

Ever since he came to power, Tutmose had been driven by the ambition to wipe away the insult done to Egypt by the Hyksos invasion. By taking the war to them and their allies and defeating them in their own homeland, as they had done to Egypt. Every campaign of his reign had been directed towards this end. He had planned it in detail over the past 12 years, starting with the crushing of Canaan. Then his objective had been to defeat the power of Naharin, the silent supporter of the Hyksos and the key to controlling the whole of Retanu.

Meticulously he and his generals had planned every Campaign. Each one brought him a step closer to defeating[183] his great enemy. This vile people who had spawned the Hyksos, giving them the audacity to invade Egypt. They must be repaid in full for their crime. He had waged 7 campaigns, and now the great goal was within reach. Every supporting satellite city of Retanu had been defeated and garrisoned. He had now reached the borders of Naharin. Beyond were the cities of Carchemish and Aleppo[184] which he had placed under siege.

By now they would be starving and ready to open their gates. He had subdued all the ports along the coast of the Great Sea and taken the harvest of every defeated city to feed his garrisons, depriving Naharin's capital, Wassukanni of the means to withstand a siege. His hand was raised to make the kill! His heart should be singing at the prospect of his greatest victory. A victory to end these wars. But his heart was divided! Not by fear of danger or failure. He would not fail. But that for half a year he would not see his son. This child who was the embodiment of everything he wanted in a son. Open hearted, running to meet life, and turning his smile freely on all he met, his beautiful smile, his mother's smile. These two great longings dividing his heart. The longing to be with his son after long empty years of waiting, and the need to focus all his attention on this climactic battle ahead!

Reaching the port of Perenepher, Tutmose found everything prepared. The soldiers were eager for war. They could smell victory. Everything was ready to sail at his command. The wind was set fair to carry them to Byblos where they would arrive fresh and ready for war. His soldiers would know no shortages of food while, all of Naharin, including its great capital Wassukanni, would be starving. But none would guess the new weapon he was about to employ.

The fleet reached Byblos as planned. There, part of the army moved out immediately to take Carchemesh while Tutmose stayed at the dock, watching as the ships that had brought them north were loaded on to wheeled bases. Under cover of darkness, they set off in the wake of the army, with teams of oxen[185] pulling the loaded boats. Carchemish fell, followed by Aleppo. Tutmose left scribes in each city to assess and collect the booty from the broken people whose only longing was for food. With their cities under siege there had been no planting and no harvest. But now rations of grain were given to those who submitted to Egypt's rule and lists of hostages and useful slaves were drawn up. With the cities garrisoned, the army, and the accompanying boats were sent northeast to meet the river upstream of the capital. From there they would navigate downstream for a surprise attack on Naharin's king in his citadel.

Washukanni was well positioned for defence, with a strong wall built hard against the swift waters of the Khabur river. The city lay downstream from where the Khabur separated from the Euphrates, and with the water forming a protective barrier to the east, all eyes in the city were turned west from whence the attack was expected. But Egypt had a history of storming cities from the water. Ahmose had sealed the fate of the Hyksos at Men-nepher and Avaris by these very means. It was common practice for them. And Egyptains who had grown up harnessing the power of the Nile would not be daunted by the power of the Euphrates or its tributary. But they must wait for nightfall to make their move.

The flotilla travelled quickly in the fast-flowing water, and after only an hour the lights of the great city could be seen on the west bank, stretching away many furlongs to the south. Night was wearing away with only a short time remaining before dawn. Silently the generals motioned the craft to shore where a narrow shelf of rock was all that lay between the water and the city wall. The bulk of the men silently gained the shore ready to march on the main gates which lay on the west, while skilled climbers stayed at the river's edge, preparing to mount the walls. The marching soldiers carried with them a huge tree trunk which they had floated downstream to use as a battering ram. All was ready. The men reached the main gates and raised a great cry, which was the signal to the climbers to throw grappling irons over the wall and start their climb. Taking out the guards, they moved quickly down to a side gate, and while the eyes of all were drawn to the pounding of the battering ram on the main gates, they opened the side entry to Tutmose's army. It was still dark when a forward battalion entered the city followed by Tutmose and Djehuty. A search was made of the royal apartments and king Parsatatar[186] and his family were seized. In the confusion, some of the younger nobles escaped, and reaching the Euphrates, crossed to other strongholds in the east of the country. But the city was vanquished bringing an end to Tutmose's campaign which had raged for 12 long years.

Tutmose seated himself on his rival's throne and King Parsatatar and his family were brought before him. Tutmose had never seen this king in the flesh but had heard him described by envoys as a man of 50 years of heavy build with blue eyes and light brown hair fading to grey. He had rarely seen a man with blue eyes and this fact had held the description in his memory. But the man before him now, although dressed in kingly robes, was none of these things. Clearly a change had been made to allow the king to escape. But looking at his supposed rival Tutmose grew angry. This man may be a loyal servant, but he would die for his pains.

"Where is your master?" he asked quietly watching the man's response. But the substitute was not fool enough to continue with the ruse.

"I believe he has fled the city, my Lord[187]," he replied, now turning his eyes to the ground. He would not anger the Pharaoh further by meeting his gaze. He started to remove the great chain of office around his neck but stopped at the king's command.

"As you chose to don your master's clothes," said Tutmose, "You may die in them." He nodded at Djehuty who quickly despatched him.

At this bloody action the princes fell on their knees.

"Extend mercy great king," they pleaded. "We have much booty for ransom."

"You have nothing at all my lords," said the king. "Your booty is mine. But I will spare your lives for the moment.[188] Take them away and guard them well".

Tutmose's fury took time to abate. He had looked forward for so long to this moment of victory when his enemy would stand before him. And to lose Parsatatar would leave the door open for his friends to regroup around him. But Tutmose thrust the thought aside. He held Parsatatar's three sons and their wives. And he would send spies to follow the trail of this King. He would make a search. He knew his rival would go east and maybe find refuge in the rising power of Asshur[189] to the east.

But there was one thing remaining for Tutmose to do which would drive out of his mind the loss of his quarry. He would do as his grandfather had done. He would cross the Euphrates River and leave a victory stella as the first Tutmose did when he too had routed Naharin. The victory stella he had planted there on the east bank of the river held a powerful superstition over the minds of the local tribes, and still remained. Now he would plant his own monument beside it in memory of this victory[190].

But with victory achieved Tutmose felt suddenly empty. There was nothing more for him to do. Even knowing that his victory would send shockwaves through Shinar[191] to the east and Hattie[192] to the west, who would speak of this victory with apprehension and send costly gifts to buy peace[193], Tutmose wanted more. He could return home leaving Djehuty in control, and his scribe Amenemhab[194] to collect booty. He had fulfilled the demands of his family and surpassed the achievements of his grandfather, the greatest Pharaoh of them all. But he would not make an immediate return. No, he would find a gift for his son in recompense for his absence. A gift worthy of a prince. He would follow the example of his grandfather once more and return via the swamps of Retanu. Here were elephants as large as any in Nubia with enormous ivory tusks. Yes, he would find a trophy for his son from among the beasts of Niy[195]

TUTMOSE RETURNED TO EGYPT TO a hero's welcome. It had taken 12 years and 8 campaigns to finally overcome Naharin and seize its capital. As news of the victory preceded him, citizens in every town massed together to welcome their returning hero. Tutmose could feel the reverence of his people. Adoration that he had seen exhibited by the whole army, from every General to the common soldiers. On reaching Avaris which had found greatness as his army headquarters, the love of his people was most apparent They were beside themselves with joy, and all along the river as he travelled south to pay a tribute of thanks at Ra's Temple at Iunu[196], the cheering people welcomed their king. Even the priests at this famous Temple, inherently proud, bowed in true reverence. But for such a victory he must pay an equal due. To please both priests and Ra himself, Tutmose commissioned 2 lofty obelisks to be raised in this city already replete with obelisks[197].

And what of Meryet his queen, watching the homecoming of the army? Never before had she seen the people honour Tutmose as a god. She had learned long ago to fear her husband, but admire him? No. She had known and despised him all through their childhood. But now, watching from the "Window of Audience," the King's return to Men-nepher and knowing what he had achieved. That he had routed Naharin and her King, causing him to flee the battle. How he had set up the stela proclaiming his victory beside that of their grandfather. Suddenly Meryet was overcome with admiration for this man she had spent her life despising. And her second thought was close upon it. She wanted his admiration in return. How had she been so blind! More than ever, she longed to be the woman who would give him an heir.

9th Campaign; Year 34 1470

TUTMOSE HAD LIVED WITH THE hope that the defeat of Naharin would bring an end to his wars. With well-equipped garrisons billeted on the defeated cities to maintain order and oversee the collection of tribute, there should be no need to continue his campaigns. But Egypt and her temples had become greedy. Her peasant farmers were proud to be soldiers. Farming was toilsome labour just to live. Far better to leave the slaves in the Delta to grow all the grain the country needed. And every soldier loved to bring home booty from the wars. The priests of Amun lived like nobles off the spoils of Retanu, and the High Priest grew so wealthy and powerful, he considered himself equal to his Pharaoh.

And with a sinking heart Tutmose realised that Naharin would never rest under her servitude. Their king had escaped and would continue to be active. A thorn in Egypt's side. So despite achieving his goal of overpowering his enemies, Tutmose must continue his wars in the north, albeit at a lesser level. Taking his large army would mean there was never defeat, and he must continue to show himself strong. The people of Retanu must feel the iron grip of Egypt on their cattle, their gold and copper. They must see the best of their people taken into slavery, year after year, bleeding their strength to keep them obedient.

The very next year after taking Naharin, Tutmose returned, and from one district alone seized large quantities of livestock, oxen and calves; 500 bulls; asses; huge logs of cedar; 2,000 jars of olive oil, 600 of wine, male and female slaves[198]. And so it would continue year after year until Tumose had raided Retanu 15 times. He missed the birth of his heir, Meryet's first son during his 9th campaign and would miss her second during his 14th. Time that he could have spent with Ameny was lost. In fact he realised that he himself was a slave. A slave to Egypt's avarice. A slave to the greed of Egypt's gods, most of all Amun, with his huge temple at Karnak feeding and housing a thousand priests and their families. The temple employed hosts of young women to sing and dance in entertainment of Egypt's preeminent god. For centuries Egypt had lived well on the best of Nubia and Kush, but her appetite was insatiable. Now she would consume the life of Canaan and Retanu as well.

[184] Its ancient name was Halab

[185] This is historical fact

[186] This name is recorded

[187] King Parsatatar managed to escape

[188] 3 royal princes and 30 of their wives were taken as booty to Egypt.

[189] Asshur was the name of the early kingdom of Assyria.

[190] Tutmosse lll left a victory stella beside that of his grandfather.

[191] Ancient Babylon

[192] The Hittites

[193] This they did.

[194] We know the name of his scribe

[195] Both Tutmose l and Tumose lll hunted elephants in Niy after their wars in Syria

[196] Heliopolis

[197] (Heliopolis was known as the city of spires because of the large number of obelisks there. These 2 obelisks left Egypt in the 1800s. One, now known as Cleopatra's needle stands on the Thames Embankment, London, the other in Central Park NY.

[198] Items listed in Breasted, 'The Ancient records of Egypt' vol 2

CHAPTER 39

A DAUGHTER BORN

THE MONTHS PASSED AND DESPITE her silence, the women realised that Zipporah was with child. This second child coming so close after the first, arrived with minimal warning. A beautiful healthy girl, and her mother loved her[199].

Zipporah knew by instinct what her child needed. She was a natural mother from the first, and in her care, the chid thrived. But still she felt a failure and it was a feeling she could not voice. She had borne a daughter having lost a son. But Moshe was bewitched by his child. The world he lived in told him that a daughter was of little consequence, but his heart said otherwise. She even felt part of him. How was that possible?

The years passed and Moshe's pleasure in his daughter grew. It was not long before another female child was born, and another. The tent had to be extended, and Zipporah learned how to laugh again.

With his wife's hands full of life and joy, Moshe was free to develop his understanding of the records held sacred by his people. Jethro was aging. Moshe had been part of the community for nearly 20 years and the two men provided each other with a continual source of friendship and challenge. But understanding this history and its significance was slow for Moshe who still carried the training that had ruled his mind and his life all his years in Egypt. He knew of gods who were fallible and selfish. Was Yahweh any different? The gods of Egypt could do evil. They were greedy. They demanded much and gave little. Gods who must be appeased. Gods he could not honour but must fear, and now had come to despise. Heartless, made of stone in nature and substance. And against this lifetime of learning he was faced with a stark alternative. He had seen among the priests of Egypt the corrosive result of power and knew that the power of the gods, if it were real, was yet more dangerous. He had seen that power corrupt nearly all who held it, so was it possible that a God, with total power over men could be good? Where was the evidence? In his heart he wanted to believe it, but could it be true? Was it possible that Yahweh was a God he could honour?

The village was a hive of activity. Moshe sensed that the whole nature of the village was changing. The income from the copper mine brought innovation and new industry. A foundry had been built to make blades with some of the copper. The deep-water harbour at Aqaba was bringing trade directly to Midian saving taxes on her goods passing out and claiming taxes on goods coming in from other sources. The fear of famine was receding. Both the men and the women sensed a change. Life could be lived more by hope than by fear.

But twilight had fallen. The day was at an end. Moshe washed his hands and directed his steps to Jethro's tent as he always did, to share the evening meal. Questions had been rising all day in his mind and soon after they had eaten, he put them to his old friend.

"I remember asking you once before sir, what Yahweh's purpose could be in allowing his people to be enslaved? You did not answer me then. But I have seen them. They suffer. They have no hope. And while I have been with you here in safety, a whole generation of men will have been reduced to cruel labour as part of Egypt's hunger for power", he said, knowing he posed a hard question for his friend.

Jethro was silent, but Moshe sensed he had an answer and was trying to put it into words.

"I know the first thing Yahweh said to Abraham, was that he would create a new nation from his line. After Isaac it was Jacob's line, but his sons were riven by jealousy. A family like that will never stay together. Judah, one of the leading sons had already left the family homestead and married a Canaanite woman. They were breaking apart. They would never have become the nation God planned." He paused and continued.

"But in Egypt, where they were outsiders, and later when they had a common enemy in their task masters, they were forced to unite." He paused again. "Perhaps the slavery could have been avoided if the brothers had behaved differently. But they could not or would not. And now, despite them, Yahweh has created a large nation of Abraham's family. In time he will give them their land." He glanced at Moshe, but he had more to say.

"The Canaanites live in a beautiful land, but live wicked lives and their wickedness will be their doom."

Moshe pondered this reply. Did it give sufficient reason for slavery? The more he considered it the more he could accept it. How differently facts could be understood! Perhaps even slavery could be used for good! Even for the people who must bear it.

They had finished eating and the night was beautiful.

"Can we walk to the shore? Moshe asked. He loved the feeling of space looking out over the sea as the light of Ra faded and the moon rose. This was the place that always drew him after dark. His eyes followed the waves lapping gently on the shingle beach and knew that his mind could accept this explanation. It was an answer. But it was only part of the answer.

"But what is the purpose of Yahweh setting up a new nation? How would this nation be different from any other, seizing territory from their neighbours, killing or enslaving? Stealing from anyone they could defeat in battle. Is there anything better to be hoped for from this new nation and their God?"

A breeze was blowing cool now from the south, from the sea. It carried the smell of the sea, a richness, a 'greenness,' salty and cool. Moshe lifted his face towards it. The air was beautiful. The world could be so beautiful. Scents and sounds. The vision of his wife with her child. The passion of young love. But so many times, the world he knew that should have shown beauty and innocence, showed corruption instead. He could not keep the thought to himself.

"Is there any hope that your God can inspire goodness, not corruption in his people?"

Then Jethro was speaking again.

"I have asked myself these same questions," he said, "and it is because of the conclusions I have reached that I am trying to follow Yahweh." He paused. "With your knowledge of the gods of Egypt, you may have found things that trouble you. You can answer that better than I. But when I look at the gods of Canaan and Moab, I find things that I hate. Things that offend me deeply. I do not wish to serve a god who demands the sacrifice of children, as Chemosh, the god of Moab, and the Baals of Canaan demand. And to require young girls to serve the pleasure of worshippers at the shrine of Ashtaroth. I abhor such things."

The anger in his voice said even more than his words could say.

Moshe felt only admiration for this old man who strove to live by high principles. He found an echo of Jethro's words in his own mind. There were practices in Egypt that were repellent to him. Brought up as he had been as part of the royal house, he had not allowed himself to dwell on the things that related to the royal house. But there were things that disturbed him. He saw it clearly now and faced the truth of it. The practice of a young girl being made the wife of Amun, as his mother and sister had been. To be required to undress and appear naked for the delectation of the idol, had never sat happily in his mind[200]. And was this practice taken further in other temples? He had not cared to know. But there was no denying that sacrifice was made of defeated kings, and princes of subject nations who rebelled. Yes, the gods of Egypt had dirty hands and dirty hearts.

"But how do you know that Yahweh is not the same in what he requires?" asked Moshe.

"I think, that on this point I can be sure," Jethro replied without hesitation.

Moshe was silenced. Was the worship of Yahweh really different?

But Jethro was speaking again.

"It seems that our forefather Abraham left his home, and the goddess worshipped in his city to escape such practices. The worship of Nina, the Moon Goddess of Ur required every woman and girl to serve time in her temple for the pleasure of her worshippers[201]. Yahweh told Abraham to leave the city. Maybe he was spurred on by the wish to spare his beautiful half-sister Sarah, whom he loved and who later became his wife, from this practice." He stopped and looked at his friend. In the half-light he could see Moshe's face.

But now Moshe must ask the hardest question.

"And what of human sacrifice, is that forbidden also?"

But Jethro's gaze was unflinching.

"Yahweh made that very clear by a graphic action that will never be forgotten." Moshe was silent, listening.

"After leaving Abraham childless for so long, he finally gave him a child in his old age. When the boy was about 15, God told Abraham to sacrifice this precious son Isaac as a burnt offering."

"What! I thought you said Yahweh did not allow human sacrifice!

Jethro did not reply but continued his narrative.

"Abraham obeyed without question. He knew that Yahweh had promised that through Isaac, his family would grow. And he reasoned that if Yahweh could create a child for a woman of 90 years, he could raise the dead."

"But did he do it?"

"Abraham carried out every detail. He went to the place Yahweh told him. He built an altar. He bound and placed his son on the altar. He was about to kill him when Yahweh stopped him."

"What can be the purpose of that?" said Moshe horrified.

"By stopping him at the very moment of sacrifice, the story will never be forgotten.

Yahweh has written in stone that human sacrifice is forbidden.

Moshe listened in silence. If this were true, he could follow this God. But he had found something else. Something he had longed for without knowing it. He had found a role model. Abraham's faith astonished him. And he wanted to learn to live and to trust, as Abraham had. His heart rose at the thought. He had longed to find men in his own lineage whom he could admire. He needed men worthy to be his heroes and mentors. And he had found one. Not just any man, but a man from whom he had received his own life! His heritage! The heritage of all the Habiri!

Moshe was silent for some time. But there was a further question that formed in his mind.

"If this God does not require us to give him the lives of our children and their innocence as sacrifices, what does he require?"

Now Jethro hesitated.

"Beyond these things I do not yet know, but this is because he has not yet established the Habiri people and given them his laws. But in time he will. And then we will see what he requires."

"But does he have the power to decide when these things will happen?" asked Moshe. "Do you really believe he can defeat the gods and Pharaohs of Egypt and force them to free the Habiri?"

"That is a big question," said Jethro. "But I want to believe it. To believe he has the power, and that when the time is right, he will act," said the old man.

Thinking of all that had been said, Moshe knew, that if this were true, these things could not remain for him simply an argument in his mind. If these things were true, he knew his own heart also would be drawn to serve this God. But this evoked another question.

"If what you have said is true, and Yahweh even has power, beside goodness, why do not all men follow him?" he asked.

Jethro hesitated.

"There you have asked a question more about men than about God," he said.

Moshe was mystified and his face showed it.

"Look into your own heart," said Jethro. "To follow a God who requires you to be just in all your dealings; to be just to your servant who is in your power; to honour and love your wife even if she has failed you. To require a way of life that is right, rather than the freedom to follow gods who feed your lower instincts; this is not for all men." He hesitated and turned a wistful face to his companion.

"There seems to be a pull in the heart of men to do wrong rather than do right. We see it in ourselves," he said and smiled. "I can understand why few men wish to follow Yahweh.

---

[199] We are not told if Moshe and Zipporah had daughters but they were married for over 40 years, and it was usual to only note the birth of sons.
[200] This was the case in the practice of making a girl the god wife of Amun
[201] Read in Halley's Bible handbook.

CHAPTER 40

A SON BORN

AFTER HER EARLY YEARS OF infertility, Zipporah's body had become as good at bearing children as any woman in the village. She had borne three daughters after the loss of her son, and now was once again with child. She had ceased to allow herself to hope for a son. Bearing her son had only brought heart ache, while her beautiful daughters filled her life with joy. Perhaps it was her very contentment that gave her such fecundity. She was strong, and although no longer young, carried this new child with ease.

She had learned how to handle the pain of childbirth. From mild beginnings, the force of each contraction built in intensity, and with it the pain. But there was a way through. She must set her mind to wait. Allow the wave to build. And when the peak had grown to an intensity that was no longer bearable, it would start to decline. Wait for that moment. Do not give in to fear. Allow it to come for then it would pass.

Only in the throes of childbirth could a woman remember that pain. Afterwards the memory faded. Until the next time. But once again it was upon her. That remembered pain allowing no space to think of other things, even of the child and the joy it would bring. Just the pain. But while she held her mind and body together to enter this battle once again, deep inside her a new thought made its presence known. This was a boy she was bringing to birth and this boy would live! It gave her new strength. She heard nothing around her as she entered the red zone of pain, gasping for breath as the contractions blurred into a continuous wave. And then the cry. A lusty cry. A cry of complaint, of shock. A cry of fear which woke in his mother the fierce primaeval protective bond of a mother for her child, the pain forgotten.

The birth of his son was for Moshe a moment of sober reflection. A daughter would grow up to marry and bear children to her husband and his line. But a son was a step in the long march of history, to be like his father and his father's father before him. But what was this boy's heritage to be? He was not of Midian. He was not of Egypt. He was Habiri. What was his future? What was his people's future? At best it was unknown. Here in Midian, he would be as his name, 'Gershon'[202], a stranger in a foreign land as was his father.

It was strange that the birth of a daughter brought harmony between Zipporah and her husband while the birth of a son would bring division.

"He must be circumcised," said Moshe to his wife as he watched the sleeping child. "It is required. He is Habiri, and even they, who have lost all understanding of their God, know that this must be done. It is the agreement between Yahweh and his people."

But Zipporah turned on her husband in fury.

"Never! I will not allow my son to be bloodied by the knife of any man or priest! Isn't it enough that your God took our first child? He will have no part of this one."

"But if he is to be my son it is required," said Moshe gently.

"Who requires it? Not our gods. I will not follow a god who requires such a thing."

Moshe tried again. Circumcision was normal in many cultures.

"Even in Egypt boys are circumcised when they come of age[203]," he said.

"This is not Egypt," came the reply.

"To perform the rite while he is an infant is much less painful than when he is grown," Moshe reasoned.

"It will not be done now or in the future," replied his wife.

Moshe could not or would not overrule his wife. Even Jethro admitted that the custom had been lost in Midian, so Moshe had no ally. His son had been born in Midian and would be raised a Midianite.

[202] This was the name of Moses' first son

[203] Certainly among some social groups, circumcision was performed at the coming of age ceremony in Egypt.

CHAPTER 41

AMENY

EIGHT YEARS HAD PASSED SINCE Meryet had removed herself to Men-nepher. She lay on her couch as the wave of nausea surged to its peak and slowly faded. She counted the days. This was her third month. Surely the sickness must soon pass. But as she lay not daring to move, she thanked the gods again and again, as she had knelt and thanked them before. This was her second pregnancy since coming to Men-nepher. She had given Tutmose one healthy son, and even if this child were a girl, she could still look her sister in the face and laugh. She had won. She, not Nepherure had borne the next Pharaoh.

She remembered the first. All the pain of the birth forgotten as she held her child, her son, Tutmose's heir in her arms. His hair was still wet from the birth. His skin red and wrinkled. His cry, that pleading sound of a newborn, helpless, yet so powerful. Begging to be held close and safe, and awakening the instinct to protect in every woman who heard it. His father had named him 'Amenhotep'. 'Amun is Satisfied', and that was the word that summed up Tutmose's response to his son. Meryet was beyond joy, while her husband? Yes, he was 'satisfied'. He was pleased to have a son, but there seemed an added poignance to his 'satisfaction', which she could not understand.

It was a boy, this second child. He would be named 'Ahmose'. Two sons she had given her husband since coming to Men-nepher! Amenhotep the eldest was now 7 years old and would soon leave the Kap[204] in the harem where he had already received a substantial education – and become a novice at the temple of Ptah here, beside the palace itself.

FOR EIGHT YEARS MERYET HAD performed her part and reaped the rewards. Tutmose had given her two sons, and the eldest, Amenhotep was the most magnificent child she had ever seen. But now her boy was to become a novice at the great temple, the temple where Ameny shone as a scholar and friend of all. She could not bear that these half- brothers would be compared. Her son, Amenhotep, being so much younger than Ameny, would be at a disadvantage. It seemed that Amenhotep was always at a disadvantage when compared to his brother, and no more so than in the affections of his father. So many times, she had watched Tutmose with his sons, somehow controlling her pain and remaining mute when she saw Tutmose and Ameny together. Her heart and mind forced to silence the inward scream – why! Why did Tutmose not respond in this way to her own magnificent son! Why! Why! Why not? And she was not alone as she noticed the bond between the king and Ameny. Her boy, Amenhotep, the king's heir saw it too. He was just a child, but instinct told him that his father did not love him as he loved Ameny. And as he grew in years this knowledge would never leave him. It would enter his consciousness and make him a failure in his own eyes. A knowledge of falling short that would haunt him to the end of his days.

But Meryet knew she must act. Ameny had completed his studies at the temple in Men-nepher. He was now qualified to serve as a priest. He had received the rite of circumcision and come of age. It was time for him to move on. There were temples to Ptah throughout Egypt, where he could be employed. Indeed, the temple of Ptah in Waset would be a good choice and would keep him away from Men-nepher. Meryet could only hope that her suggestion would be acceptable to the King. She would speak to him that very day.

Meryet timed her audience with the king as well as she could, judging that he would deal with her more happily after he had eaten his evening meal and indulged in the wine he loved. She entered his apartment.

"I hope I find you well my lord?" she said bowing low.

"To what do I owe this pleasure," asked the king wearily, looking at her while the sarcasm cut through his words.

"I wish to speak to you regarding your heir my lord."

"Indeed Madam? I was not aware that I had chosen my heir."

Meryet allowed this slight to pass and continued.

"I wish to speak to you about our son who will soon be moving to the temple to start his training, my lord," she paused then broached the subject of her son's rival.

"I understand Prince Ameny has completed his studies, my lord. A great achievement. He has completed his studies and received the rite of circumcision. May I ask what plans you have for him?"

"You may ask," said the king and paused. But he understood immediately what she feared.

"You want him out of the way of your son, I suppose," he added.

"I was thinking that if he were placed as a sem-priest at the Temple of Ptah in Waset, he would be nearer to his mother whom he could visit more easily."

"Perhaps Waset would suit," said the king. But he had his own thoughts. He was anxious to leave war behind as soon as possible and spend time with Ameny. Waset was where he himself must go when his wars were over. It was there in the temple of Amun and the King's valley that his building work must be done. They could be together in Waset and Ameny could share with him the building of his monuments.

"How kind of you, Madam, to think of such things," said the king sarcastically. "I will give it some thought," he said. But he had said all he wished to say to Meryet. The sooner he could be away from this woman and living in Waset the happier he would be! There were things to be completed in the north, in Canaan and Retanu but then he would be free. And he had plans for Ameny. He could start his training as a sem-priest in Waset, yes, but after that he was to be elevated to be High Priest of Ptah here in Men-nepher. Ptah was the oldest of Egypt's gods, and it was a position of particular honour, often reserved for the pharaoh's eldest son, his heir, to be the High Priest of Ptah. But for the moment he could serve as a sem-priest in Waset. The High Priest there had a safe pair of hands to guide his boy. Yes, he could place Ameny there and enjoy some years with him in his old age. And when he was ready he would make him High Priest of the highest temple of Ptah in the land. The temple here in Men- nepher.

And so it was arranged. Ameny took up his new role as a priest of Ptah at

Karnak, giving him more opportunity to visit his mother in the harem at Mi-wer. But life in his mother's quarters for long hours bored him. He was 16 and had just escaped the confines of school and found the quiet of his mother's rooms a place of tighter confinement even than school. But there were other attractions at Mi-Wer, beside the company of his mother. At 16 years old the 'beauties of the harem' were suddenly very visible to him. His mother spent her time alone with Jala and just a few servants. But the young prince was welcomed in the other parts of the harem. In fact, besides raising royal children, harems existed for the pleasure of royal men, and as a son of the King, Ameny was welcomed to eat and drink; to listen to the playing of the blind harpist and watch the dancing girls. One girl in particular caught his eye. Tiaa was her name. Her dress was not grand. She was only a commoner, but her smiles and her company pleased the young prince. He was delighted with his discovery, but it was not long before Nepherure heard of her son's liaison.

"What are you doing taking such a girl? She is a nobody!"

Ameny was shocked. He had never been reprimanded by his mother in his life. But Nepherure was adamant.

"There is nothing royal about her. She has no royal blood even from her grandparents!"

"But mother, what need have I of royal blood?"

"You are my son! I will not hear of you taking a commoner."

"But mother I am not of your blood! My mother was not royal."

Nepherure hesitated. She could not bring herself to disclose the truth."

"But you are the son of the king," she said, continuing the challenge. "You carry his blood."

"But so are many children of the Harem. If I carried your blood, the true Solar blood I could understand your anger. But I do not."

Jala listened to all that passed between mother and son but kept her gaze on her work. Nepherure hesitated again, gazing at her son, this child whom all the world believed she had adopted. She could say no more. But Ameny must speak again even if it would incur her wrath.

"Mother, Tiaa has been with me for some months now. I cannot abandon her. She is carrying my child."

Now even Jala stopped her work and gazed in shock at this fine young man they had raised with such love. Nepherure sat as a statue, looking at her son, as a solitary tear escaped her eye unheeded, and fell on the embroidery in her lap.

"Then it must be," she said, knowing that she herself had denied her son his heritage, living in fear as she had. Fear that he would be Pharaoh. Fear that he would go to war.

Once again Tutmose must hear the news of his family while on Campaign. He learned of Ameny taking a wife while on his 16th Campaign, and of his first grandson's birth during his 17th. But this would be the last.

During his last battle, Tutmose had had the closest brush with death in all his years. It was a sign. Once again, the leaders of Retanu had targeted the king himself, and once again it was general Amenemhab who had saved his life. The enemy, desperate to break the ranks of Tutmose's chariots drove a mare on to the field of battle to distract the stallions. The chariot stallions immediately caught her scent and all thoughts of the battle left them. Turmoil raged. One chariot spun completely round as its stallions, ignoring the whip of their driver, pursued the terrified mare as she bore down on the king. Rushing in front of her, at risk of his own life, Amenemhab slashed wildly at the belly of the creature killing her outright. She fell to the ground in a pool of blood. The mesmerising smell of the mare changed to a stench of blood and carnage,[205] freeing the stallions from their trance. But Tutmose took note of this second sign. He would go to war no more. If the Temples demanded funds, he would tell them to reduce their quota of priests. They were overrun with them. Able bodied men fit for real work but living lives of ease, feeding off the tribute his wars exacted from Kush and Canaan.

---

[204] The Kap was the Harem school
[205] This incident is recorded by Breasted

CHAPTER 42

TUTMOSE MOVES TO WASET; REGNAL YEAR 43 1462 BC

FINALLY HE WAS FREE. TUTMOSE closed his eyes with relief as the thought came to him again. Free of war! Free to live. Free to leave campaigning behind him! Free to be with his son. Free to build. Finally, he could leave the north in the hands of his generals and their garrisons. He could go to Waset and be with Ameny. He still had the gift he had never given him. The magnificent ivory tusks from the hunt in Niy. He would present these to Ameny now in celebration of the end of war and the beginning of their time together.

The river was flowing swiftly for so late in the season. The high-water mark had been very high, and the decline of the water was slow, making southbound travel heavy work against the current. The pattern of the winds was in general from the north, but even with a north wind and under full sail, the oarsmen of the royal barge must work against the flow of the river Tutmose was impatient. He would be attending an important festival in Waset, but he wanted to arrive in good time. And then with Waset once again as his home, he could see his son daily. He could finally build the monuments by which posterity would remember him, and make a record of all his wars.

The key Festival of the year in Waset, the 'Beautiful Feast of the Valley', was held in honour of the deceased Pharaohs who were buried in the Valley of the Kings. But it included everyone, even the common people. Because just as the deceased Pharaohs were celebrated, the ordinary folk could celebrate their own family members who had passed on into the afterlife.

Along the river, harvests had been gathered in, melons, garlic, onions, beans, lentils, cucumber and cabbage were grown by many. With grain produced so abundantly in the delta, less was grown here, leaving room for livestock as well. But it would soon be the hottest time of the year, and the land was dry. It was a long time since Tutmose had seen the fields wearing this tired garb after the harvest. It was a long time since he had travelled south at this time year instead of going north to war. The harvests of Canaan would only now be ripening, and the population, who had worked all year to raise their crops, must harvest and send the best of them to Egypt to grace the tables of the King and his court and the offering tables of the gods, in temples up and down the land. Canaan was fertile. It was a land where rain fell, unlike Egypt, which never saw rain, and food was part of the tribute Canaan paid to her overlord. These payments, arriving year after year, to feed Egypt's elite, underlined her dependence on these city states that she could not afford to lose.

But to ensure that Egypt would always control these lands had cost Tutmose the best years of his life. Since Hatshepsut's death he had taken the army, almost every year, to war in the north. Almost every spring the army had moved north, living off the harvests of Canaan as they progressed overland, or going directly by ship to the port of Byblos, and eating the produce of Syria as they waged war. But he would not go to war again in the north. He had taught Naharin and her allies to leave Egypt's territories alone and was finally free of war.

Tutmose watched the banks of the river as they crept by. He told himself to relax, to take his ease. It mattered little how slowly they sailed. They could go no further than the Mooring Place[206] at Abydos[207] today and would reach it long before dusk. He had a special affection for this Mooring Place. Nepherure had stayed with him there on the return from their marriage in Men-nepher. Losing her had made it sacred to him, and he had taken none of his other wives there, only her son. Yes, he had enjoyed time there with Ameny, getting to know his son. Denied the chance to see him for too many years, the time they now shared was precious. And Ameny was now living in Waset and had a family of his own. A wife and a son! Tutmose felt a pang of regret for the lost years of Ameny's childhood. But he would see Ameny now, and in due course his grandson[208] who remained with his mother at the harem at Mi-Wer. Ameny at only 17 was distinguishing himself as a sem-priest and learning all he would need to take charge, in time, as High Priest of the great temple of Ptah in Men-nepher.

"But why accept that Ameny would only be a priest when as his eldest living son, and of the Solar Blood Ameny should be Pharaoh. The thought tormented Tutmose. His mind could not let it rest. He had long ago agreed with Nepherure that Ameny would not be Pharaoh and had accepted it. It was assumed by all that his heir was Meryet's son, Amenhotep. Indeed, comparing it with his own life, was the life of a High Priest not a better choice than to carry the responsibility he had had to carry as Pharaoh? For Amenhotep, it would be his greatest joy to one day be Pharaoh. But he had no understanding of the weight of kingship. 'Let him discover the dross of his dream', thought Tutmose. Indeed, with his mind moulded by his mother Meryet, Amenhotep was driven solely by ambition. 'Maybe in time he will learn', thought his father. 'He certainly has much to learn. But life and hardship might yet teach him'.

Tutmose reached Waset two weeks after leaving Men-nepher. The day was fading fast but the Palace was alert for his coming. A welcome homecoming. There was a month yet until the festival, but he would meet the High Priest of Amun in the morning to discuss it.

Since the overthrow of the Hyksos and the restoration of Waset as capital of Egypt, 'the Beautiful Feast of the Valley', had become the highest point of the year in the south. Citizens poured into the city from all the countryside around, to see the idol of Amun carried in its sacred Barque[209] to the river, then across it to the temple of Mentuhotep on the west bank. Then everyone from the highest to the lowest gathered at their family tombs to feast together.

Hatshepsut had changed the focus of the festival from the temple of Mentuhotep when she built her magnificent new Mortuary temple of Djeser Djesere[210]. The idol of Amun was now carried to her Mortuary Temple instead, to pass the night in the sanctuary there, before returning the next day to Karnak.

Tutmose had now been sole ruler of Egypt for longer than Hatshepsut's entire reign but had not yet turned his mind to building his own Mortuary Temple. It must be completed before his death or others would decide what was built. And he must make sure that this important Festival would acknowledge him as well as these other Pharaohs. Now he had retired from war, he must plan. A Mortuary Temple was known as 'a House of Millions of Years' as it was the place where the Pharaoh would be worshipped as a god for eternity. And it must include a shine for Amun as he held first place in Tutmose's devotion. But building his Mortuary Temple was only the start of his plans. He must build a new Hall at Karnak large enough to record all his campaigns. A 'Hall of Festivals', he thought. And changes must be made to the shrine that housed the Barque of Amun. Its wall must tell his story, not only that of his predecessor. But his Mortuary temple must take precedence. And now he was in Waset, he had summoned the High Priest of Amun and his architect to make plans.

It was a great relief to Tutmose that there was now a new High Priest of Amun at Karnak. His old tutor, Menkheperraseneb, who had held the post for so long, had died, and was replaced by his nephew, another Menkheperraseneb. Tutmose disliked the new man as much as the old, but the order of seniority was now in his own favour. The first Menkheperraseneb had at first been his tutor and he had never broken free of the control of the old man. But with this nephew, Tutmose would insist on his own way. Rekhmire[211], the architect was also new and Tutmose summoned him also to hear his ideas.

Looking out across the river at the splendid temple of Hatshepsut, where the procession would finish this year, Tutmose voiced his frustration.

"I have been pharaoh for nearly 50 years, far longer than either Mentuhotep or Hatshepsut. Their grand Temples stand here in pride of place opposite Karnak", he said pointing across the river. "And yet where will my temple stand?" he asked turning his frown on the two men. "How will future generations recognise my reign?" he asked, aggrieved.

"Indeed majesty," said Menkheperraseneb having no better answer.

"The procession will take the same route this year, I suppose?" said the king looking again at the High Priest hoping for more. "We cross from Karnak and process to Djeser Djesere as usual I presume?"

"Indeed," said Menkheperraseneb. "And then, will my Lord visit the temples of his father and grandfather for the feast?"

"I will visit my father's temple for a short time, but we shall hold the feast at the temple of my grandfather", said Tutmose, looking again towards the west bank.

"And my son Ameny will accompany me", he added on a more cheerful note, then hesitated. All knew that he loved Ameny, but if his heir was Amenhotep, it would be expected that he would be part of the ceremony. But Tutmose put it out of his mind. Amenhotep was still young. He could leave that decision for another year at least. He turned to look across the river again at the route he would follow to Djeser Djesere for the festival. Hatshepsut's temple was always a beautiful sight, with its elegant lines in keeping with the temple of Mentuhotep. But where, he wondered, could he build his own mortuary temple! The situation angered him profoundly but looking again he could see that there was no space to build unless he moved further south. But then the connection with Karnak would be entirely lost. He turned to his architect.

"Where should my Mortuary temple be built so I can be part of this Festival?" he asked. He did not expect a very pleasing answer, but he would sound the man out.

"The space is limited, Majesty," said Rekhmire and paused. This was something Rekhmire had thought about very carefully. Now was his chance to show his skill to the king.

"To attempt to build between those two temples opposite Karnak, would seem to result in a less important temple, Majesty."

"Seem to?" said the king with anger rising in his voice. "You are not employed to state the obvious man," he added with impatience, as Menkheperraseneb smiled to himself. But Rekhmire had more to say and knew he must say it quickly.

"If we were to raise a third temple on a platform between the two existing structures Majesty, it would add a pleasing symmetry to the whole, and being higher would show the pre-eminence of your majesty," he added.

Tutmose looked at his architect with interest. The man did have some intelligence after all.

"Of course," said Tutmose, thinking aloud. "A higher building, that stands above the others is showing its superiority by its position, even if not by its size[212]." He was silent, looking towards the west bank of the river again. His old eyes were better able to see distance.

"And if it is for the worship of Amun and your Majesty alone, there is sufficient space to make an excellent shrine."

The king was clearly pleased, but Rekhmire had more to add.

"And it is time, my Lord, that the focus of the Festival of the Valley be changed from Djeser Djesere, to a temple for my Lord."

Tutmose turned to the architect again. "But how can we change the route of the procession away from Djeser Djesere? We would be removing the primary function of that temple and would offend the Ka of my stepmother Hatshepsut."

"No offence would be perceived if it is done for the greater honour of Amun, my Lord."

"Go on," said the king. This man's ideas were worth hearing.

" I understand that my Lord has plans to build a more splendid Barque to carry the idol of Amun? If the Barque is made wider, my lord, then a wider gateway would be needed for the Barque to pass through, and the gateway to Djeser Djesere would be too narrow. So the procession could no longer pass to Djeser Djesere, but would pass instead to your new Temple, my Lord." He paused, knowing his idea was brilliant[213]

"As the change would increase the honour of Amun, it would cause no offence to the dead Pharaoh" repeated the king, musing.

Tutmose looked at his architect. This was a stroke of genius. He had made a good choice in this new man, Rekhmire[214]. He would use him again. Indeed, he had hardly started on the building he would do at Karnak. Building would be an excellent occupation to fill his last years when he was no longer going to war.

Rekhmire knew that his future in the king's service, indeed any future he might hope for, would stand or fall by the quality of his work on the king's new Mortuary temple. It was to be named 'Djeser Arket', "Holy of Horizon", and would be of great importance to his Pharaoh. He could picture in his mind's eye the symmetry he could create, with the two existing temples and his masterpiece between and above them. It would be a fitting monument to his master and add a final glory to the whole site. But the king was impatient.

"I want all work on other projects to stop so that both you and the entire labour force can focus on this Mortuary Temple," he said.

'The king has realised his own mortality', Rekhmire thought to himself. 'Yes, even kings must die, and he has already reigned 44 years. But he said no more and determined to start work immediately.

The priests performed the ceremony of the 'stretching of the cord'[215], and the foundation deposits were buried deep in the earth[216]. Then with the foundations laid, the great platform was raised above them. Vast quantities of stone and rubble were carted to the site to fill the cavernous space under it. Solid flanking walls were built with revetments all the way round to support the massive weight of the temple above. Indeed, so high was the temple to stand above its surroundings, that the platform on which it stood would be level with the uppermost floor of Hatshepsut's temple. It would be a splendid sight! The finest limestone blocks were being cut at this very moment, shaped, transported, and placed in position. Only then would their surfaces be smoothed and carved. The King who greatly admired the delicate carving on the temple of Hatshepsut, wanted his own to be as fine[217].

While the work on the temple was going apace, men were set to work to lay a ramp, a processional way, leading from the river to the entrance of the temple. The route from Karnak itself to the point of the river crossing was chosen and laid, and a larger pylon gateway was built through which the procession must pass. When the temple was near completion the Barque shrine built by Hatshepsut[218] in the centre of Amun's temple complex, was carefully taken down and a wider one built in its place to house the splendid new, Barque, larger and grander, with its coat of Nubian gold, another gift from Tutmose to his god.

The king visited the site daily. The structure grew quickly but would require years to complete. He was residing almost entirely in Waset, leaving his son Amenhotep to the supervision of his mother, in the north, and the army in the hands of his generals.

But at 16 years of age, Amenhotep, having finished his schooling, was consumed with a passion for the army. His father had not yet named him as his heir, but to impress his father, Amenhotep trained hard. He was longing to be named as his father's heir and was determined to be seen as superior to all the officers. He boasted loudly of his prowess as a bowman and a charioteer and continually found ways to engage the soldiers in new exercises. He wanted to keep the army always on war alert, causing tension between himself and his generals. Tutmose knew of this but knew also that at his death, Amenhotep and the generals would no longer have an arbitrator between them, so decided to allow them to adjust to each other while he still lived. Without active war, no men were being lost in battle, so their numbers were not diminishing. But Amenhotep still wanted to train more recruits to increase the size of the army. He was like one obsessed, and with only General Djehuty daring to question his actions, Djehuty soon found he no longer had the favour of the young Pharaoh. Amenhotep spent his time between the army base at Avaris and the naval base at Perenepher. He longed for his father to give him permission to go on Campaign. This would be a signal to all that he was the chosen heir. Tutmose was glad to leave the maintaining of the army to his son, with the supervision of the generals. But still, he would not name his heir.

While his queen and her son remained in the north, Tutmose was enjoying the company and advice his favourite son. Time was passing and Ameny was now the father of another son whom he named Tutmose, in honour of the father he loved. Tutmose saw in Ameny and his family everything he wanted in his heir and could not resist speaking to Ameny openly of his wish to make him Pharaoh, but Ameny was astonished.

"Father how can you think such things? My mother is not of the royal house as is Amenhotep's mother. And my brother loves war while I am a man of peace. He will be delighted to pull down the strongholds of those who rebel against Egypt, while I follow the teaching of Ptah, the great builder. No, we are each suited to the roles we have."

---

206 Palaces a day's journey apart for the use of the Royal house.

207 Abydos was no ancient capital of the country and believed to be the burial place of Osiris the god of the dead.

208 Webensenu was born around **1463**

209 A ceremonial barge used to carry the idol. It was itself considered sacred. Known as 'User-hat Amun', it had a shrine built to house it.

210 Known today as Deir el Bahri

211 Rekhmire is recorded as being Tumose's architect.

[212] I heard this said by a Polish archaeologist.

[213] Rekhmire did build a larger barque requiring a larger shire to house it, and a wider gateway leading to Djeser Arket, the Mortuary temple of Tutmose lll which was then used for the festivals.

[214] Rekmire was Tutmose's architect for all his building work

[215] A required ceremony before any building was done.

[216] Another required ceremony.

[217] Only the ruins of Djeser Arket remain today.

[218] Known as the Red Chapel.

CHAPTER 43

TUTMOSE BUILDS HIS FESTIVAL HALL

TUTMOSE WAS FINDING THAT AFTER his years of war his mind was at last finding rest. He revelled in being in Waset with Ameny but realised that he would never persuade him to take the throne. The disappointment was like an ache inside him. He would so much prefer to leave Egypt in Ameny's hands. But he must be glad of what he had. And he was happy, sharing so much time with his son. It made him feel young again, adding years to his life, and together they planned his building projects.

With his mortuary Temple underway, Tutmose's next ambition was to make a record in stone of his 20 years of war. A monument to last forever. His wars had built Egypt into a powerful Empire. She ruled most of the known world and had more power than any previous Pharaoh had ever possessed[219]. Tutmose was determined that such achievements would be remembered forever. His scribe had recorded the details of every battle on a leather scroll[220], and these records would now be transferred to the walls of a great stone hall with space allotted for each one. Karnak was already a huge complex. But there was space to build on the eastern side of the shrine, towards the sunrise, away from the great pylons. Indeed, if he added his hall behind the shrine itself, he would be adding to its protection by ringing it round with more walls of stone.

But how would he build? He admired Hatshepsut's Temple. His work would only be one storey high, but he could use her design. He consulted Ameny whom he knew had an eye for elegance, surpassing his own.

"A Hall across the whole width of the Karnak temple but in the style of Djeser Djesere," said Tutmose. "I will need that much space to display the reliefs of my campaigns", he added, as the thoughts crystallised in his mind.

But Ameny had reservations. "Father do you not agree that much of the beauty of Djeser Djesere is created by the central ramp? It adds dignity to the whole", said Ameny.

"But my Hall will be on one level only so will not need a ramp," said his father.

Ameny sensed that the loss of the ramp would change the whole effect, but he remained silent. He did not wish to upset the plans which his father held dear.

"It will be built in sandstone as it is so plentiful in the new quarry, "added the King.

Ameny tried to hold his peace, but he had seen recent building done in this new sandstone and thought it too dark to please the eye.

"Would you not prefer to build in limestone father? It is such beautiful stone. Light in colour and can be worked to a smooth finish. That would be my choice," he added.

"Rekhmire is a good man, and he has chosen sandstone," said the King.

"Yes, he is a good man," said Ameny. He agreed that Rekhmire had excellent ideas. He was a good architect, even if his choice of stone was not always aesthetically pleasing. But he would not push the point. He did not want to spoil his father's pleasure. And what would it matter? Of the generations to come, how many would see with an artist's eye and be disappointed in the grand Festival Hall of the great Tutmose?

The king submerged himself in his building projects now, just as he had submerged himself in war. They gave him ample subject matter to discuss with Ameny, and they grew in scale as his grandchildren grew in age. Amenhotep had also married. A girl of semi royal blood living in the harem at Men-nepher. The girl's royal blood brought her the approval of Meryet, but Meryet had no intention of relinquishing her position to a younger queen.

"I am glad you have had the sense to find a woman of royal blood," she said. "My sister will have grandchildren as common as any commoner it seems, for Ameny has made a poor choice in his wife. She has no royal blood at all."

"I am glad you approve mother," said Amenhotep with a yawn. "But as Ameny will not have the throne surely it hardly matters."

"It is never wise to lower yourself in the eyes of anyone," she said. "Even a man such as Ameny should have married well," she added.

"I approve of your choice, but I will not have her take my place at court." She paused to see how her son would respond, as she continued.

"You may bring her to Court after my death, not before. Besides, she needs to attend to her children. Leave her in the harem at present."

AMENHOTEP WAS PERFECTLY HAPPY NOT to honour his wife at Court. He had an aversion to giving women status. He knew what it had done to Hatshepsut, whose folly had led her to raise a Habiri slave child as her own! No, his wives would not be given status in his Court. In his youth he had studied the writings of Middle Kingdom texts that denigrated the role of women in power. He had even taken as a motto for himself the writings of King Amenemhat who denigrated the role of women in public life[221].

Yes, Amenhotep was wary of giving power to women. But he was pleased when his young wife presented him with a son, who in true form, he named after himself. He raised a stela recording the child's birth, placing it in the temple of Ra at Iunu. He would add another at the boy's coming of age[222]. But he left his young wife and her child in the harem at Men-nepher under the watchful eye of his mother.

Tutmose was amused at the fecundity of his sons, and glad that Amenhotep also had a son if he were to be his heir. But it was Webensenu, Ameny's firstborn, who held the highest place in his heart. The boy had just finished his schooling in Men-nepher where his younger brother Tutmose would soon start. Webensenu had received the rite of circumcision and come of age and his grandfather wasted no time in honouring him by making him 'Master of the King's Horse'.

But Ameny was appalled!

"Father how could you do this? This title should be reserved for an heir to the throne!"

"Your son is an heir to the throne whether you see it or not," said the old man without apology. "Besides, I am old. I am near my death, and I wish to honour my favourite grandson. No one will give him titles when I am gone. Meryet will see to that." He paused as his thoughts continued.

"And there is something else I shall put in place before my death".

Ameny was wary. He could see no purpose in Tutmose angering his heir without good reason. It would only cause problems for his family when the old king died.

"What is it you plan father?"

"I have decided that Meryet's daughters, Nephertari and Iaret[223] will marry your sons when your boys are a little older."

"Is it wise father to anger the queen? She has no love for me or my sons."

"Are my grandson not good enough for her daughters?" asked the king.

"Meryet will not think so," said Ameny. "But if it is your wish father, let it be so," said Ameny in some confusion.

"Yes, it is my wish," said Tutmose softly. "When the children are a little older, but before my death. I do not intend to leave Meryet free to thwart my wishes," he finished.

Ameny could not understand his father's words, but one thing was clear to him.

"Very well father. I respect your wishes even if I do not understand them. But it is time for you to name your heir, father. My brother needs to be sure of the throne before your death."

"Your brother does not deserve your loyalty Ameny," said the King. "I fear that Meryet will show her true colours when her son is on the throne. But you are right. I cannot continue to delay."

BUT MERYET ALSO, HAD HEARD of the title given to Ameny's son, Webensenu and had received from the king a command that her daughters were to be given to Ameny's sons. She dared not go against her husband, but she could and would punish this upstart family. They may be favoured by the king. But the king was old. His word would not always rule her. And she would find ways to punish them. Webensenu had finished his schooling in Men-nepher, so had escaped her clutches, but his younger brother, Tutmose, now 7 years old, had recently arrived in Men-nepher and she was required to house the child with his servants, in the Palace while he attended school. But she would not allow this child to live in her domain with the convenience she had allowed his brother. If only the King would name her son his heir! Then she could draw a distinction between her own sons and Ameny's family. But she could and would make life uncomfortable for this second of Ameny's sons, that she was required to house!

---

[219] Under Tutmose lll Egypt's Empire stretched from the Euphrates in the north to Sudan and Ethiopia in the south, a thing achieved by no other Pharaoh.

[220] This scroll was found in the scribe's tomb.

[221] Amenhotep quotes the following against the position of women. "Has any woman ever marshalled an army? Are there rebels nurtured in the palace?" (quote from book Mistress of the House, Mistress of Heaven. Women in Ancient Egypt p34 Markoe / Capel)

[222] A stela celebrating the birth of a Prince Amenhotep has been found naming him as heir to his father Amenotep ll and another marking his coming of age. Both were found smashed and are held as evidence against Tutmose lV by Egyptologists, who accuse him of doing away with his older brothers to gain the throne. But in this study, it will be seen that these facts are explained in a different light.

[223] It is possible that Nephertari married Webensenu, but we know for sure that Iaret married Tumose lV although she was not made his great Royal Wife.

CHAPTER 44

THE JOINT REIGN BEGINS AND AMENHOTEP MAKES HIS 1ST CAMPAIGN; 1451

IT WAS NOW TWO YEARS since Tutmose had named Amenhotep as his heir and raised him to share his throne in a co regency of joint Pharaohs. The joy this brought to Meryet, knew no bounds. It was the fulfilment of her greatest ambition and should finally have made her a contented woman. She would live through her son, enjoying all the satisfaction that had eluded her own life. She could add the title of 'King's mother' to that of 'Great Royal Wife'. Already the highest woman in the land for many years, surely this would bring her the satisfaction she craved. But though she had gained prestige, love still eluded her, even love from the children she had borne. Because shaped in her own mould, they too were unable to love freely as a gift. Love in their eyes was always a down payment for future service that would be demanded.

Amenhotep was a finely built young man of 16 years. He was taller than his father, having gained this from Meryet. Indeed, when regarding this son, Tutmose felt the lad had acquired far too much of her. Her wilfulness and constant complaining were the first things to be observed. As a child, Meryet had been very much as Amenhotep now was. Not as Tutmose would choose his son to be. Not like Ameny. These two sons, so remarkably alike in appearance yet growing into such different men. But he would not complain. Amenhotep would serve Egypt well enough. He would be a good soldier if he learnt some self-control.

But to be Pharaoh fulfilled only the first of Amenhotep's ambitions. His greatest ambition was to be a warrior, to emulate or even surpass his father's campaigns. From the outset of the joint reign, Amenhotep had stelae made of his prowess as an archer[224], as a rower and as a charioteer. He claimed he could surpass any man many times over. He idolised war and dreamed of evoking terror and dread in the hearts of any who opposed him.

It was many years since Tutmose had defeated Naharin and ceased his wars, but he knew that he would have no rest until his son had experienced war. The north was subdued, but a chance soon presented itself in the south. A rebellion had broken out in Nubia, at Gebel Barkal. The king must attend in person, and he took his son with him into Nubia to experience war. Tutmose was ruthless in his crushing of the rebels. This area of Nubia did not conform to the worship of Egypt's gods. They had their own deity for whom they had built a splendid temple. Routing the rebels was only the beginning of Tutmose's plan. Having crushed them, he forced the defeated men to tear down the temple to their god. But even that was not enough. They must in its place raise another, yet more magnificent, for the worship Amun[225]. Amenhotep watched and learned. Defeat followed by humiliation. But for him it was not enough. He would then have executed the leading rebels, not simply enslaved them as his father had done.

But war in Nubia[226] and Kush was very different from war against Naharin. The Nubians were powerful people, but the rulers of Naharin were in a class of their own. Inventive people, constantly developing the art of war. It was they who had first introduced the use of horses and chariots in battle. They also who had developed the deadly 'Composite bows' that had changed the face of war in the last century[227]. But by creating his large armies of well-trained soldiers Tutmose had defeated and garrisoned even Naharin and her allies. Now he had no need or intention of going north again. But to answer Amenhotep's overwhelming desire, he would allow his son to visit the north under the control of generals. But which generals would have the courage to control this young firebrand? Tutmose delayed until he had chosen generals who could. Men without families who could not be threatened. Men old enough to be past ambition. Men who no longer wished to gain the ear of the king. Among them was Djehuty, and these men he hoped, could control his son and bring back a report. Yes, under these restraints, it was wise to allow Amenhotep to go north and experience war.

So in the spring of the 2nd year of the joint reign, the army was ready to march. Indeed, it must march. News had reached Egypt that in Joppa and many of the northern ports, the garrisons had been overpowered, and the towns had broken free, closing their ports to Egypt. The army crossed the Mafkat and reached Gaza in 10 days There they rested, but not for long. Spies returned with news that a rebel army was gathering five days journey to the north. Acting quickly, they marched north cutting off the rebels before their full quota of reinforcements could arrive. It was a decisive victory spurring them on to cross into Syria.

To reach the rebellious ports in the north, Amenhotep and his generals must cross the Orontes River, but here again they faced resistance. Rebels loyal to Naharin mustered their men, but seeing the strength of Amenhotep's army fled away, leaving the Egyptians free to march on the nearest prize, the fortified town of Tikhsi. The town was hardly guilty of rebellion. It had no garrison to overthrow and was completely unprepared for war. Their harvest still stood in the surrounding fields. They could not withstand a siege and offered little resistance. But Amenhotep's blood was up. He would use them as an example. Seizing seven princes from the town on which to exact his fury, he returned to Waset and there, innocent or guilty, he executed them with his own hands in the temple of Amun. A sacrifice to his god[228].

---

[224] Amenhotep ll made more claims to be a great warrior than any other recorded.
[225] This war and these facts are recorded; details available in Breasted's work
[226] Nubia relates to present day Sudan, while Kush relates to present day Ethiopia
[227] This is historical.
[228] Recorded in Breasted

CHAPTER 45

AMBASSADOR FROM GAZA

THERE WERE MANY THINGS THAT Tutmose did not like in Meryet's son, foremost among them being an obsession that he had learned directly from her. Meryet's memories of childhood made her bitter against Hatshepsut and she hated Senenmut who, though not of the royal family, had been adopted and loved while she herself felt herself unloved. Tutmose also, had been outside the centre of privilege in Hatshepsut's domain, but he was grateful to Senenmut for his kindness and would not hate the woman, who though having the power to destroy him, had not done so. When Egypt fell to him, Tutmose had not taken revenge on his stepfamily. He had left all records of them on display throughout the land, but this was a point of contention with Amenhotep.

"Father why do you allow the images of that usurping queen and her slave son to remain in places of honour?" the lad asked on one occasion.

They were words that could have come directly from the mouth of Meryet herself, and Tutmose was angry.

"You will not speak of my family in that way if you wish to be considered part of it!" he said suppressing his anger. The boy was shocked. He did not retract his words, but never spoke of it again, although his thoughts remained unchanged.

For over 50 years Tutmose had ruled Egypt. He could not remember a time when the title of Pharaoh had not been his, spoken in hushed or fearful tones, but with respect always, save only on the lips of his old tutor,

Menkheperraseneb. The irony did not escape Tutmose that his aunt Hatshepsut and her son Senenmut, whom Menkheperraseneb hated, were the people responsible for raising him to his high office of High Priest. But life was full of such ironies. Looking back on his long reign and long life of 53 years, how many of the great events he had witnessed, would he have predicted at the outset? And how many more would there be after his death?

With this last thought, Tutmose's mind returned to the present and his thoughts changed from the reminiscences of an old man to the anxieties of a reigning king. He remembered that he must ready himself today for the 'Time of Audience', to hear, among other reports, that of his envoy from Gaza.

SINCE BEING NAMED AS HIS father's heir, Amenhotep must travel to Waset regularly to be present for the audiences held by the king. Ambassadors also, who previously had only to travel to Avaris to the King's court now had the distance to Waset to add to their journey.

But the hour of audience had arrived, and the king had made himself ready. His old eyes were losing the focus of vision he had once known, but the ambassadors from Gaza who would attend on him today, were well known to the king. He took his seat in the audience chamber, casting only a momentary glance at his son, seated with him, whose face showed in turns, boredom, anger and frustration, in keeping with his sense of status but lack of years.

The ambassadors entered and prostrated themselves before the king. Amenhotep scowled. His pride, which always searched for any suspected slight, was convinced that they disregarded himself, only paying homage to his father. He shifted on his seat, wishing to show his annoyance, but Tutmose held up a hand to admonish him, then spoke.

"What news do you bring us," he asked, the weariness sounding in his voice. The entourage remained where they were while the ambassador rose, and with a bowed head, replied.

"My king, the news from Gaza and the garrison there is without concern, my Lord. Your subjects are loyal and obedient my Lord."

"What of the harvest of the land this year," asked Amenhotep, interrupting the ambassador, who turned to him, maintaining his bowed head.

"The harvest should be plentiful my Lord. The rains have been good and without storms." But he hesitated and Tutmose, with his long years of experience, did not fail to notice.

"You have something more to tell?" he asked, but still the man hesitated. Amenhotep grew impatient.

"Do you come before us unprepared man? Speak out!"

But Tutmose knew better than to rush a report that may be sensitive information. He wanted the whole truth, not a hurried answer. He turned to his son and lowered his voice.

"If you wish to hold audience in my court sir, you will do so in silence until you have learned how to behave!" He glared at his son. "Or you may leave us!"

Amenhotep was beside himself with fury. To be admonished by his father in front of these nobodies was utterly humiliating. He half rose from his chair, determined to leave, but now the ambassador addressed him directly.

"May I ask the young Pharaoh to allow me to speak in his presence also? What I have to say may concern him."

Amenhotep sank back into his chair. The shame and anger on his face subsided and he felt mollified by the Ambassador's remarks, but was there cause for alarm?

"Speak," said Tutmose quietly, all the while observing the speaker.

"My Lords, may I remind your majesties of something perhaps forgotten?" He paused.

"May you recall there was a traitor, a scholar of the royal house, one called Senenmut, who fled Egypt many years ago?" He paused again, feeling his way.

"There have recently been rumours reaching Gaza of a man, a scholar, an old man, possibly Egyptian living among the Edomite or Midianite tribes and accepted by their leaders."

Tutmose shifted in his seat, but Amenhotep became as rigid as a statue.

"My Lords this information came to light because men from Edom came to Gaza and among the things they purchased was a large quantity of papyrus. The garrison, being responsible for goods arriving from Egypt is the best source of supply of such commodities. When I heard of it, it concerned me as it was so unusual. I became suspicious as to who would want such supplies and questioned the men. We found a man in Seir who for money would talk and he disclosed that he had heard of such a man, a scholar, living in Midian. I believe this could be the man Senenmut, who is still living."

There was a long pause while Tutmose stared at the ambassador, unable to speak. Moments passed, then he roused himself.

"If my stepbrother still lives, he is a man of 70 years old," he said quietly.

The ambassador could feel the tension rising in the court. He had been the bringer of trouble, but as a loyal servant of Egypt, he had simply done his duty.

"We searched Edom, my lords without success and intend to search Midian. If he is there, he must be living a simple tribal life. He may be married and have sons. But the Midianites have always been loyal to Egypt, my Lords and would not knowingly hide an enemy of Egypt. The mines of the Mafkat being a vital source of employment for them."

Quite suddenly Tutmose decided that the interview was over. His old mind needed time to think about what he had heard, and he did not wish to show confusion or alarm in front of the ambassador.

"We will speak again," he said. "Wait in the city until I summon you."

He dismissed the ambassador and left the chamber. The shock had brought on a profound weariness, and he needed to rest but Amenhotep followed him.

"Father are you not alarmed? What do you plan to do about this news?" he asked, a mixture of fear and incredulity sounding in his words. But Tutmose would not be drawn. He needed time to think.

"I am not alarmed to find that my brother still lives, living in a tent in the desert," he said trying to put Amenhotep off the scent.

"But he could still be dangerous! He may have sons!" said Amenhotep, determined not to allow the subject to drop. "Surely it is more necessary than ever that we remove his statues and those of that usurper queen from the temples!"

"If he has sons, they know nothing of Egypt, nor does Egypt know them," said Tutmose, turning angrily on his son. "I will not be pushed into any actions I do not desire by you!" he replied.

Amenhotep stared at his father in disbelief as Tutmose continued.

"Senenmut was a man apart. He was reared to rule Egypt. His sons, if he has any, will have been reared as goat herders. No, I do not fear his sons."

But Amenhotep was now really afraid.

"Father, if Senenmut still lives, as Hatshepsut's adopted son he had a claim to the throne! A claim greater than ours! She was of the Solar blood while you and I are not!"

But Tutmose would not be drawn. He was too weary. Suddenly he felt his age heavy upon him. He could not discuss it now. He must silence his son.

"If you are such a fool as to jump at every shadow, you will never rule Egypt!" he said, and passed into his own apartment, leaving his son in a turmoil of fear.

But Amenhotep could not let it rest. He counted the days until he was to see his father again, and while he waited, he searched the army records and talked to all who could inform him. He must find out as much as he could. But what he found was more than even he suspected.

And Tutmose also sensed the urgency of the matter. He saw that he must lay to rest Amenhotep's fears, so summoned him early. The old king had not slept well. The fear of Senenmut's return had been a continual nightmare in his younger days and it now returned to cloud his dreams. He looked tired and drawn, and for once, Amenhotep noticed his father's weariness. He tried to handle his father with care.

"I hope you are well, father," he said with a smile. But such pleasantries were not normal from Amenhotep and put his father on his guard.

"I am well enough to have an appetite," said the king as he dismissed the servants to share an informal meal with his son. A cone of incense was burning on the table between them, and the coil of smoke drew Tutmose's eye as he spoke.

"Let us examine again these questions regarding my stepbrother," he said. Amenhotep was silent, watching his father's face.

"The fact that he may be still alive need not concern us. You have often asked that the statues of my stepmother and brother be removed, but I see no advantage in it. We must not start jumping at shadows."

Amenhotep shifted in his seat uneasily as the King continued.

"Egypt's army is at the height of its powers, and even if the Midianites wished to support Senenmut's claim to Egypt, they know it could not be done." He paused but Amenhotep could no longer remain silent, and his fears tumbled out in a jumble of words

"But father, apart from the fact of Senenmut's claim to the throne, I have learned other facts about these Habiri slaves we have here in such numbers, and of which Senenmut was one." Tutmose listened. He would hear him out.

We know that the Hyksos were from Syria. There have been many people groups living in that area at different times, but I have discovered that the Habiri were also from Syria before they went south into Canaan.

Tutmose listened. This was new to him.

"In Syria the Habiri were part of a people called the 'Arameans'. Their homeland was called Aram."[229]

"There are many little states in Syria. I have never heard of Aram so what does it matter?"

"I know father. These states are known by different names. We call our great enemy Naharain, while others call it Mitanni or something else.

"I am weary of all this talk! Tutmose shouted suddenly. If you have something to say, tell me clearly!"

But by now Amenhotep himself was shaking. The enormity of his discovery overwhelmed him as he tried to share it.

"Father I have discovered that Aram and our great enemy Naharin have been in alliance for generations[230]. The true name by which they call themselves is 'Aram – Naharin'! The two people groups are joined in strong alliance!" He paused but watching his father, suddenly stopped short. All colour had drained from Tutmose's face

"It is the truth father," he said quietly.

"These slaves and your stepbrother are Arameans. People who have long been in alliance with Naharin! And Naharin has an army that is a match for Egypt."

Tutmose closed his eyes but said nothing. His heart started to race as his mind tried to grapple with these terrifying facts. Had he been fighting all his life to destroy Naharin yet all the while allowing a people connected with them, the Habiri, to live and breed right here in Egypt! A sense of horror swept over him. The slaves numbered hundreds of thousands of men! He had spent his life fighting for mastery of Canaan, but now even Egypt may be under threat! If Naharin and her allies rose to put Senenmut on the throne of Egypt, he could not withstand them. Suddenly his years hung heavy upon him. He could not bear to talk of it further. He must dismiss his son until another time.

THAT NIGHT TUTMOSE'S DREAMS WERE filled with foreboding. He had always feared the Ka[231] of Hatshepsut. She had been a crowned Pharaoh. She was a god. She sat with the pantheon of gods who would judge every Pharaoh who attempted to enter the afterlife at death. And was not he, Tutmose near his death? He felt it so, certainly. Weariness and fear filled his days and disturbed his sleep. All his life he had avoided conflict with the Ka of Hatshepsut. He had left the record of her reign and the record of her son Senenmut still, in Egypt out of fear. Must this now change?

Slowly the answer to that question crystalised in his mind. Yes, he must remove evidence of the Female Pharaoh and her son. He must remove all evidence of her reign. Removing that evidence was the only way to remove Senenmut's claim[232]. He must listen to Amenhotep. At this point in his life Tutmose felt unable to resist. He could not face war. He could not return to his life as a soldier. He could no longer confront Naharin. He knew in his heart that what Amenhotep said was true! He had always known that the Habiri were in some way related to the Hyksos. It was the Hyksos who had welcomed the Habiri into Egypt in the first place[233]. And the Hyksos were from Syria and had the support of Naharin. It was all true. This last piece of evidence completed the picture. A dark and terrifying picture. A picture with Egypt surrounded. Naharin in the north with people who hated the name of Egypt. Cities garrisoned by Egyptian soldiers. But these soldiers, like many in Egypt still held Senenmut in high esteem. His fame had only grown with time. And the slaves! The enemy within his borders, the Habiri, who despite hard labour continued to increase in number! Egypt was surrounded! Senenmut lived, and was welcomed by Edom and Midian, so near at hand! Only across the Mafkat[234] from Egypt's borders. If all her enemies rose together against her, how could Egypt hope to stand? In his dream Tutmose could see the face of his brother, Senenmut, with eyes that spoke without words. Dark intelligent eyes. He remembered them now with mounting fear. Looking into his own conscience, he feared this brother he had so grievously wronged.

Amenhotep was right. For Egypt to survive he must risk the wrath of Hatshepsut even now, when he was so near death. He must remove the Royal serpent from the head of her statues and bury all record of Senenmut. If Hatshepsut was shown to be a usurper, no true Pharaoh, then Senenmut's claim had no substance. And would his supporters rise against Egypt, the most powerful Kingdom in the world in support of a false claim? He could only hope they would not. He must grasp this chance. It was not necessary to remove all record of Hatshepsut. She was no threat in her role as Great Royal Wife or as Regent. She had served Egypt well. But her claim to be Pharaoh must be removed[235]. Amenhotep would have to be content with that.

To his father's surprise, Amenhotep was satisfied to have only the uraei, the sign of kingship, removed from the statues of the Female Pharaoh. Stone masons were sent immediately to Djeser Djesere, to Karnak, and to all the temples up and down the land. Every statue of Hatshepsut as Pharaoh had the uraeus removed with care and precision, and every relief showing her as pharaoh was chiselled away. But Senenmut's statues were removed completely from every temple. Tutmose experienced a strange grief in allowing the record of his brother to be wiped away, but Amenhotep saw to it that nothing remained. The court and the common people watched in fear and astonishment at the wholesale desecration. The favourite Senenmut had been gone from the country for a generation but was still remembered and revered. Why this sudden destruction? They watched silently as Senenmut's statues were defaced, smashed, and buried in deep pits never again to see the light of day[236]. But even as he insisted that the change to Hatshepsut's status be kept to a minimum, Tutmose knew that Amenhotep was just waiting. Waiting until his father's death when he would do far more than the respectful removal of the uraeus from the statues of the female Pharaoh[237].

[229] See the book of Deuteronomy 26 v 5. A wandering Aramean'.
[230] Genesis 24 v4
[231] Spirit

[232] Some Egyptologists think that the reason for the destruction of Hatshepsut's statues was because there was a fear that someone from her line would make a claim to the throne. If Senenmut was her adopted son, they may have feared that he would take the throne.

[233] Joseph and his family entered Egypt in the time of the Hyksos kings.

[234] The Sinai peninsular

[235] The first wave of the removal and destruction of Hatshepsut's statues started with the removal of the Cobra Uraeus only.

[236] Senenmut's statues were buried around 1450 BC, and remained hidden until discovered by Winlock in 1927

[237] The wholesale destruction and burial of Hatshepsut's statues happened as a second stage, a later purge against her.

CHAPTER 46

SEARCH MADE FOR MOSHE

MOSHE KNEW HE HAD FULFILLED his part of his marriage contract. He had given Zipporah children. He had given her status. His work for the tribe entitled them to a share in the food and a place in the village. And it was clear to him now that Zipporah wanted no more of him than that. Theirs's had never been a love match. It was a marriage of convenience, and it continued as such. The marriage was not a failure but had never become what it could have been. The arrangement gave Moshe little control of his family. Zipporah did not want his involvement with her children[238]. It was a sorrow he must bear, but it freed him to spend time with Jethro and to record the history of their people which Jethro so longed for.

In discovering the story of Abraham, Moshe found far more than he expected. In Abraham he found more than a hero, more than a mentor. Jethro had become a friend, but Abraham was the father figure he had longed for but never known. He wrote down every aspect of Abraham's story. Of the people who came before him and the descendants who followed. He wrote the history of Joseph. Of his father Jacob and all his family moving to Egypt to escape famine, where they prospered under the Hyksos kings. He wrote it all, but most of all he studied Abraham himself. Every word he spoke. Everything he did. And it drew Moshe to his God. Abraham had been told what to do. God had spoken to him in angelic, even physical form. What an honour! And Abraham had obeyed, had believed, had acted, had trusted through long years. Years of promises, yes, prosperity, yes. Protection also.

But never until he was old, did he see the fulfilment of the greatest promise, the promise of a son.

There was no doubt in Moshe's mind that the story was true. He was surrounded by nations living even now who bore witness to its truth. They owed their origin to this man and his story. Edom, Midian, the Habiri, and even Moab and Ammon were from the same family. The story was undoubtedly true. And it sounded like history, not like the stories Egypt told, which contained only an echo of truth. But what was the heart of the story? It was never claimed that Abraham was a perfect man. He was not. He was subject to fears, and at times made poor decisions. So what was it Yahweh saw in him that pleased him? That was the question that gripped Moshe's mind.

He had now reached his 75th year, about the age when Yahweh had first spoken to Abraham. He knew it was not possible that Yahweh could use him now to rescue the Habiri at his age. Zipporah had borne him a second son, and this time he made no plea for circumcision. It would not happen. Zipporah would not trust herself to his God or obey his commands. His children would not be Habiri.

The light was fading as he stood outside his tent musing. Evening was drawing on and he was restive. His scribal work was completed, and he had given the finished scrolls to Jethro. He had used a great many expensive sheets of papyrus which had been bought in Edom with the proceeds of copper ingots, and Jethro was delighted. The scrolls were his most treasured possession. Moshe himself was satisfied with the work. No one could have done it better, and it gave him pleasure to use the skills he had worked so hard to acquire in his school days in Waset. To write a document to his own exacting standards, gave him a good feeling. It was an achievement. And the story itself had opened a new world to him. The world of his forebears. Of Abraham in particular. A man who stood head and shoulders above all others. A man in whose footsteps he was determined to tread, however falteringly. A man who had believed the words of Yahweh and lived by them. Yes, he, Moshe, had at last found faith in this God. He had found a God he could honour and follow. The God of his fathers. His heart rose as he acknowledged this fact to himself in clear thought. Yes, he would dedicate his life once again to this God as he had tried to do at Serabit 40 years ago before Egypt had cast him out.

Moshe joined his father-in-law as usual, to eat, as darkness was falling. Looking back at the work he had done and at his initial reluctance, he was grateful to the old man for his persistence. Peace had settled over the village. All was quiet. The children had settled to sleep and only the murmur of voices from the men eating together, or an occasional laugh from the women's' tent disturbed the silence. But Moshe and Jethro had just started their meal when the sound of footsteps reached them coming at a steady pace. The sound grew, and soon a group of three men approached from the coast road. It was a strange hour for men to be travelling, and on foot. As they came into view, a cold dread entered Moshe's mind like a warning. This was no routine visit, and to add to the strangeness they were not Midianites. Their garb showed them to be men from Edom.

Jethro rose to meet his guests while Moshe hesitated in the background, watching. The spokesman for the group approached the old man and as he started to speak, Moshe realised his voice was familiar. In the half-light he scrutinised the man. Yes, he recognised him. He was Zerah's servant! And seeing Zerah's manservant, Moshe stepped forward to hear his news.

"My lord Zerah sends me with an important message," said the man.

"Egyptian soldiers have been searching throughout Edom for a fugitive, but without success. Not finding him in Edom they are coming here to search. They are suspicious of the purchase of large quantity of papyrus sheets from the Egyptian base at Gaza, and my lord Zerah sends word to beware", he said and paused.

"The man they are seeking left Egypt many years ago," he continued.

"I do not know if he is dangerous. Egypt thought he was dead, but word reached Egypt that he may be in hiding in Edom or Midian. They intend to search the settlements of Midian and my master sends warning to beware."

Jethro paused before answering.

"Thank your master for his kindness" he said. "With your warning we can take the necessary steps. But it is late. You must rest here for the night?"

But the servant declined.

"Thank you for your kindness", he said. "But my master told us to come with all secrecy and not to delay. We have a boat waiting for us in the bay and my lord Zerah is anxious to hear our report."

"Can we not offer you some refreshment at least, asked Jethro", but the men would not stay. "We have all the supplies we need, and my master bid us return immediately."

"Then give our greetings to your master for his kindness, from myself and my son-in law Reba," said Jethro, including Moshe in the salutation.

"My son- in- law knows your master and will wish to send him greetings."

Moshe bowed to the men, but they would wait no longer, and as they left, a warning came clearly into his mind. 'Leave at once. Take the sheep to the mountains. Go tonight.'

So it had come at last. His pursuers had found him. The unusual purchase of parchment from the Egyptian base in Gaza had raised questions. Who would need it but a scholar? And a reward would bring betrayal. Zerah must have realised that the friend he had made was not in fact a Midianite, but the Egyptian prince being hunted. But who had betrayed him? Not Zerah. He had risked his own position to send a warning.

DAWN WAS STILL SOME HOURS away when Moshe left the camp. The sheep were sufficiently rested and were content to move off to fresh grazing. He watered them well. It would be a long day's walk to reach the corral for the night where there was water. He had not slept. He must organise his supplies. Plenty of arrows and a second bow. A skin of water and a long rope that would serve as a bucket to draw water from the deep wells of the desert. A cover for his head against the power of the sun and a warm cloak. Night was cold in the cloudless desert. But he was sufficient to the task of survival in this harsh land. He had done it many times. And the outdoor life had made him strong. It would not tax his strength, even when he left the path and moved up into the mountains to escape those who may follow. There he could disappear, how long for, he knew not. The important thing was to leave. Leave now.

The moon was sufficient to light the path as it passed near the cliffs bordering the Edomite Sea, the Red Sea, which lay calm and beautiful in its light. Beyond the Sea lay the Mafkat, Egypt's wilderness, so near and yet he had never crossed over from this side to that. The Mafkat with its lucrative mines where in a few hours' time, Egyptian task masters would be shouting orders to weary slaves mining copper and turquoise from its rocks. As the sun rose, he rested briefly and drank some water. There would be none for the sheep until they reached the corral, but the grass was good, and they fell to grazing for a brief moment. Game was plentiful at this time of the year, so the risk of lion or jackal attack was small, and Moshe, though watching for them, saw no evidence of predators. They moved on as Ra journeyed across the sky, flinging his heat over the rocks which reflected it back with almost equal force, until he started to sink towards the west, admitting his own decline. They had almost reached their shelter for the night, when glancing back Moshe saw what he knew to be men following in the distance. The faint outline of mules and men in a cloud of dust. He knew at once that he must change his plan. He could not continue on the path or rest in the corral. He must leave the path at once. He must move up into the pass between the mountains which would hide them from the sight of men passing on this costal path. His body was weary, and his heart sank at the prospect, but fear brought with it a surge of energy which seemed to communicate itself to the sheep. They crossed the rough scrub land to their left and before Ra had sunk behind the mountains of the Mafkat they were out of sight of the coastal path. The wadi they had entered was replete with new grown grass. This would stay the thirst of the sheep until morning when he must find water. From the safety of the wadi Moshe watched the lighted torches of the men as they reached the corral. Here they stopped. He watched as they built a fire. They would spend the night in the safety of the corral. He could see shapes of men moving in the shadow of the firelight. How long would they stay? Would they continue to hunt him, or would they return the way they had come? It was clear that someone from the village had guided them there, so as soon as the sheep were rested, he moved them deeper into the mountains. There was a well in the next wadi he knew. There seemed to be an endless supply of water beneath these mountains if wells were dug deep[239]. And he knew the terrain better that all but Hobab. He had wandered these wadis many times in the last 40 years and had a natural instinct to find his way.

Long before dawn Moshe and the sheep were moving east, deeper into the mountains. As the sun rose, he found the wadi with the well. Now they could rest. A trough had been cut deep in the rock to hold the water which he drew to the surface with his leathern bottle. It was beautiful water, cool and sweet, filtered through these mountain rocks from rain and snow over centuries past and stored deep in the ground. The grass was good and the water plentiful. They were safe and he might land an Ibex with his bow. They would rest here until the grass was gone then move off to find more.

---

[238] This is the impression one gets from reading the biblical record of their relationship.
[239] Even today there remains a huge aquifer under the Jordanian and Saudi deserts.

CHAPTER 47

TUTMOSE; YEAR 52 1452

TUTMOSE HAD GIVEN PERMISSION FOR the uraeus of kingship be removed from Hatshepsut's statues, but he had not realised how terrible it would be to witness. Now that the alterations had begun, he carried a dread fear of this Pharaoh, a god, whom he must meet again at his own judgement. What could he do to appease her? And far more than the alteration of Hatshepsut's statues, Tutmose knew that when his son reigned alone, he would inflict the final and most terrible penalty of all against this woman he hated. When all power was in his hands, Amenhotep would not hesitate to break open Hatshepsut's tomb to remove and destroy her body.

Tutmose himself, as Hatshepsut's heir, had equipped her Ka for the afterlife. Most important of all, was the mummification and burial of her body. Without a body her Ka would wander forever with no place of rest or nourishment. With no body she would be unable to enter the afterlife but instead would enter the second death and be lost forever[240]. The horror of what his son would do overwhelmed him, but how could he prevent it? For days he agonised. His mind was consumed with thoughts of tombs. His own tomb. His father's tomb. Hatshepsut's tomb. Like the woman she was, she had planned it well. She wanted those she loved near her. It would be her home for eternity. She had insisted that Senenmut's secret tomb be placed as close to her own as possible, even inside the sacred space of her mortuary temple. And in addition, she had taken the body of her own father, the first Tutmose and reburied his mummy with her in her tomb.

As this thought passed through his mind, Tutmose knew he had found the answer! He sent an urgent message to his son.

"Eat with me today, I have something to ask of you."

Amenhotep was delighted that his father wanted his company and came at the hour requested.

"I am visiting my tomb tomorrow and would be glad of your company," Tutmose said pleasantly as they ate together and received a prompt agreement.

"If we go early, I will find it less tiring," he said.

Amenhotep obliged. His father had listened to him over the subject of Hatshepsut's statues. He was enjoying the rare sensation of respect from him. The following morning, the royal barge carried them across the river soon after dawn when Ra was still in gentle mode. Sedan chairs were ready and waiting to carry the two Pharaohs the length of the Kings Valley to the hidden entrance of Tutmose's tomb. They approached the tomb and entered. Amenhotep had never been inside his father's tomb before. It had been finished and closed so long ago. He was surprised to see how simply it was decorated. The walls were lined with symbols of the Pharaoh entering the afterlife, but there was no luxury here. The designs were simple line drawings[241] Mathematical, almost. No grand paintings filling the walls of the burial chamber. The site for the sarcophagus was also simple, but beside it, a space had been made for another burial. Amenhotep turned to his father.

"Do you intend that my mother shares your tomb father?" he asked in surprise.

Tutmose tried to hide his displeasure at the suggestion. Never would he want Meryet with him for eternity!

"No," he said hiding his feelings. "Meryet will not lie here.

"Then who will have this place of honour?" asked Amenhotep with sarcasm in his voice. He felt slighted that his mother was rejected. He knew of his father's love for Nepherure and it made him angry.

"I will be moving the sarcophagus of my grandfather to lie here," said Tutmose quietly.

Amenhotep was mortified that he had spoken so hastily, accusing his father.

"I am sorry father," he said humbly. Apologies did not come easily to this young Pharaoh, but it was balm to his angry mind to know that Hatshepsut would lose the honour of having her father, the great Tutmose in her tomb. She did not deserve such honour.

"I am pleased," said Amenhotep humbly.

The day for the moving of the first Tutmose's body arrived. But more would be achieved this day than Amenhotep ever imagined, for this day's work was intended to deceive him. Tutmose knew his son's anger. He knew that once kindled, it burned on and on until, of all that aroused his fury, nothing remained. Tutmose knew that besides the destruction of her statues, Amenhotep intended to destroy the body of Hatshepsut. But he had found a way to prevent it. He knew that the tomb of the royal nurse Sitre was close by Hatshepsut's own, and he intended to move the body of his stepmother to the safety of Sitre's tomb.

"I will open Hatshepsut's tomb and bring the body of my grandfather here," he said, and could read the pleasure on his son's face. But there was more that he did not tell him. He would make a great show of opening Hatshepsut's tomb, and carrying his grandfather's wooden sarcophagus[242], with many rituals, to its new resting place at the far end of the King's valley. But quietly, unobserved, at the same time, he would have the body Hatshepsut moved, in secret, by men he could trust, and hide it in the tomb of her old nurse[243]. There it would never be discovered.

And so it was done. Amenhotep watched delighted as the sarcophagus of the first Tutmose was carried to its new resting place. It pleased him as much as seeing the removal of the Royal cobra from the brow of Hatshepsut's statues. And while he watched, he waited. He waited for the moment after his father's death, when he could destroy all memory of Hatshepsut forever from the temples of Egypt. Cast out, smash, and bury her statues and remove her name from the King lists. He could see it all in his mind's eye. He would watch as the priests removed and destroyed her body. Nothing would be left of her name or her memory. Without a body she would die the second death, the final death, leaving her Ka to wander the world with no place to rest. He smiled to himself as he thought of it. Revenge would be sweet. A just penalty for a woman who had acted as she had.

[240] This was the Egyptian belief as to the importance of the body for the afterlife which is reflected in the lengths they went to with mummification to preserve their physical bodies at death.

[241] When visiting Tutmose lll's tomb I remember the very simple stick like drawings on the walls of the burial chamber.

[242] The sarcophagus of the great Tutmose l was a simple wooden coffin.

[243] The unknown second mummy found in Sitre's tomb KV60 has been shown to be that of Hatshepsut.

CHAPTER 48

AMENY MADE HIGH PRIEST OF PTAH IN MEN-NEPHER; 1451

TUTMOSE HAD GIVEN PERMISSION FOR the removal of all evidence of Hatshepsut's reign as Pharaoh, and all records of her son, but seeing the resultant destruction carried out day after day in this city which had been shaped by them, shocked him deeply. And he was not alone as he watched in horror the destruction carried out by Amenhotep's men. Ameny too, saw it all. He knew the story of Senenmut, who under the Pharaoh Hatshepsut had ruled Egypt wisely. Seeing the images of the great Pharaoh herself being publicly humiliated was bad enough. History was being falsified. But the shameless destruction and burial of the statues of her son, destroyed as if he had never existed, shocked Ameny deeply. He tried to remonstrate with his father.

"The gods will not leave my brother unpunished for this, father," he said. "And who knows! You also may feel their anger," he paused. "Have no part in it!" he pleaded. "Your stepmother Hatshepsut now sits among the gods!

But Tutmose knew things that Ameny did not know. He could not tell him of the news brought by the ambassador from Gaza. Instead, he must remove Ameny from Waset.

"You must leave Waset," he said. "You have done enough years as a Sem priest here at Ipet[244]. You must return to Men-nepher and take charge of the temple of Ptah. The High Priest of Ptah is now an old man. He is ready to retire from office."

Ameny knew he could do nothing to alter his brother's actions and did not wish to distress his father further. His new role as High Priest had long been planned, and in a matter of weeks he was on a barge going north. He would not be sorry to return north but he would miss his father. And the king was old. He did not like to be separated from him.

As he neared Men-nepher, the familiar outline of the ancient temple rose before him. He was expected and welcomed as always in this place with so many good memories. His younger son Tutmose was a novice here and would soon be finishing his studies for the day. Ameny knew everything about this temple school where he himself had been a scholar, and waited where he would see the boys leaving to go to their homes. Young Tutmose was not expecting him. It would be a happy surprise. He waited.

Only their footfall signalled the approach of the novices, as silence must be maintained until they were outside the temple. Then the noise broke. Cheerful greetings as they found the servants who would take them home. But where was Tutmose? Last of all. And where was the happy greeting to his servant of a boy who had reached the end of his day? Instead of a cheerful greeting, the boy hung back. Why was he reluctant to end his day and return home? But Ameny could not hold back. Calling his name, he stepped forward ready to seize his son into his arms. A look of bewilderment crossed Tutmose's face as he looked at his father, but instead of shouts of joy, tears streamed down his face as he flung himself into his father's arms.

It took very few moments and fewer words for Ameny to understand this distress. Tutmose was to return to the palace, the domain of Meryet. But that would not happen again. With no word to Meryet, Ameny sent for his son's servants and belongings. Tutmose would not return to the palace. He would stay in the temple with his father. But a scar was left in the mind of this boy, from Meryet's treatment, that she would live to regret.

---

[244] Ipet was the ancient name for the Karnak temple complex

CHAPTER 49

TUTMOSE ESCAPES TO MEN-NEPHER; 1450 BC

THE ROYAL PALACE IN THE heart of Waset still slumbered, but dawn would soon break over the eastern hills and the hymn of the Lector priest ring out to welcome Ra back to the world of men. Tutmose rose every morning before dawn. The habits of a lifetime would not change now. On campaign, the early morning was the time when action was most needed.

Tutmose had come to Waset after 20 years of war, to live at peace and enjoy some years of rest with Ameny. He had enjoyed 12 years with his son, building together the monuments to his reign. Now he had been forced to send his son away and he missed him terribly, while all around, in this city which had been the seat of Hatshepsut's government, destruction raged on every side. The defacing of Hatshepsut's monuments. The smashing and burial of Senenmut's statues in a pit near the temple he had built for his mother, shocked and distressed the king. Day after day it continued, on every side, in every temple in Waset, the city where they had built so much for the gods. It was a torment for Tutmose to witness it. There was a no escape. By day the continual noise and carnage. Then at night, in his dreams he must look into the eyes of this brother he had wronged. Eyes that spoke so eloquently. Dark intelligent eyes. He remembered them with mounting fear. Eyes expressing the pain of betrayal.

Tutmose knew how much he had wronged his brother so long in the past, and now wronged him again. Allowing his memory to be utterly destroyed. Denying him an afterlife[245]. In desperation he sought the support of Amun. He would raise another obelisk in honour of his god. A tall spire to stand at the entrance of Ipet[246] itself, seen by all who entered and all who passed by.[247] Summoning the High Priest he set the plan in motion. He had raised so many monuments to the gods. Surely, they would support him in the judgement.

But even this brought him no peace. He knew he could stay no longer in Waset. His mind could not bear it. He must follow Ameny to Men-nepher, a city he had never loved, but which would now be a haven, an escape from the horrors of Waset. Rekhmire, his architect, would have to complete the work of his monuments alone. The river was still high enough for travel. He ordered his servants to prepare. He must leave at once.

Tutmose sank back on his couch on the royal barge and closed his eyes. He was alone. A warm breeze blowing from the south assisted the weak current in its effort to carry the barge north. A wide canopy gave him protection from the sun and the servants left him to rest. All was still. Only the sound of moving water broke the silence. The current proved sufficient, and with a little assistance from the oars, would bring them to their first mooring place before dark.

But leaving Waset behind felt to the king as if he were leaving his very life. His power, his throne, his command of Egypt. All through his life, as Pharaoh, his presence had inhabited the palaces and temples of Waset. But no longer. Now Amenhotep reigned there, ordering the temples and palaces as he chose. Ridding Egypt of Hatshepsut's reign. Ridding it of all record of her son. The wide world of Egypt and her subject nations, which Tutmose himself had won and controlled, now belonged to Amenhotep. This child he had never loved, never wanted, yet this son would fill Egypt's throne. How long would he reign? Would pride and recklessness bring him down? Tutmose was glad he could not read the future. He feared how his son would rule, while the son loved and admired, Ameny, who had the wisdom to rule, would live out his days in the service of the gods.

But Tutmose could not bear to think of the future and his heir. A great wave of weariness washed over him. Weariness even of life itself, and as the barge moved slowly north, he made a conscious decision to leave his power and kingship, behind. There was nothing more to do. Nothing more to fight. But here, surrounded by the peace he so longed to feel in his soul, it seemed as if he was leaving a vital part of himself in Waset. Only his body and conscious mind were moving north, while his life force, his Ka, remained in the south. As if his Ka had already taken up residence in the tomb he had made for himself in the Valley of the Kings. The place it belonged. The place where it would reside for eternity. And the further he moved away, the faster the end would come. But he could not remain away from Ameny. Leaving Waset he may be leaving his Ka, but away from Ameny was a living death. In that moment, he made the decision. He would die away from Waset, but he would die in the company of Ameny.

Evening was falling as they reached the mooring place at Dendera. The familiar surroundings and the familiar routine relaxed him, but he knew he must face the next stage of his journey. He must visit Abydos. At this point in his life, he dared not pass by the ancient temple at Abydos without making a solemn pilgrimage. Even a powerful Pharaoh needed the support of Osiris, the ruler of the underworld when facing death. His heart was not in it. His heart was set on reaching Men-nepher to be with his son. But he must make an offering to Osiris for this last time.

Tutmose reached Men-nepher and Ameny was waiting at the royal dock to meet his father. Lining the dock were rows of kneeling officials and priests, the blare of trumpets and the endless chanting. But as the royal barge approached the dock, Tutmose's gaze searched for just one face. It was Ameny's features he needed to see. And there was his son. But beside him were other figures, standing among the kneeling crowd. Tutmose glanced at them. Who else would dare to stand in his presence? But looking again Tutmose saw that he had not escaped from Meryet's children. Here stood her second son, Ahmose, a youth he hardly knew, and her daughters, Iaret and Nephertari. They were no beauties, but at least they did not resemble their mother. Watching them he remembered. He had in the last month betrothed these girls to Ameny's sons. His last act of defiance of his now all powerful queen. And as the barge came to dock, Tutmose watched his children. They, also, had come to greet their father. A show of respect, now in his final days when they could gain nothing from him. When all power now rested with his heir.

But while Tutmose observed his children, Ameny watched his father's face and was shocked by what he saw. In the short time since they had parted Tutmose had changed profoundly, and Ameny had to disguise his horror at seeing his father so altered.

"I hope you have rested on your journey father. You look tired", he said.

The old man did not reply but searched his son's face as if trying to commit to memory every detail of his features. Finally, he smiled.

"There is little rest for me now," he said sadly, "neither in body or mind. But to see your face is good medicine indeed." He smiled again and raised his feeble hand to rest it on Ameny's shoulder.

"I do not wish to sleep at the palace," said the king. "May I attend you at the temple and sleep among the priests?"

"Of course father," Ameny replied in surprise. "But let us eat and talk then find you a chamber for the night."

The king greeted Ahmose and his daughters, but he would not enter the palace again. It had become Meryet's domain. Her son was Pharaoh. She now held power of her own. She would no longer bow to her husband's wishes.

But the temple of Ptah lacked nothing. They dined in Ameny's private apartment and talked long into the night. Other comfortable chambers were nearby, but Ameny's own chamber was wide and airy, with two large couches, and Tutmose requested that they share the room.

"To have your company is precious to me," he said.

In truth Ameny was glad to have his father near him. He sensed that he was fading and could even die in the night. It was late when they finally retired. A cool breeze entered the unshuttered windows, and soon both slept. But their rest was short lived. Ameny woke to find his father awake, with his mind wandering. It was clear he was dying. Tutmose himself knew that he was about to leave this world and enter eternity. But he knew it was Ameny with him and he forced his eyes to focus on his son's face.

"I loved your mother," he said.

"Yes father."

"The only woman I have ever loved," he paused. "You have her smile."

Ameny did not reply. He had never known his mother. She had died at his birth. The only mother's smile he knew was that of Nepherure, a rare and beautiful smile, but he was not of her blood.

"She did not want you to be Pharaoh," said the king. But his voice was feeble now. Ameny's mind too, was distressed. He could not think clearly. This man he loved so much, was dying.

"Tell her for me. Tell her I love her still," came his last words.

AS TUTMOSE LOST HIS POWER of speech, he knew that he was about to leave this world and enter eternity. A world where gold and silver, position and titles had no meaning. Where his heart would be weighed[248] in the balance against a feather, and he knew it would be found wanting. He was a betrayer. And with terrible clarity he knew, he would be judged by the gods. Which of the gods could rescue him? Would Amun acknowledge him after all the gold he had given to enrich his temples? Would Ra send him help? Hadn't Senenmut been a priest of Ra? This man he had betrayed and robbed of his life!

Tutmose closed his eyes. He felt his body fading but his mind was growing clear. He felt as if he were floating, looking down on an Egypt of the future. Not the Egypt he had known. Not the Egypt that had ruled the world since the dawn of time, the Egypt that had built the great pyramids. That Egypt would not endure. Strangers would bleed her of her wealth and the best of her people. The desert sand would bury her temples. His own name would be lost for more than a thousand years, then be rediscovered as a curiosity. A study for scholars. But Senenmut would remain, inhabiting a greater stage. Growing in stature throughout the long march of the centuries. His name would never be lost from the world of the living or of the dead.

---

[245] Egyptians believed that if all record of a person was removed, their spirit would enter the second and final death and cease to exist.

[246] Ipet was the ancient name for the Karnak temple. The latter is an Arabic word meaning fortress

[247] This last obelisk is known to us as the Lateran Obelisk now in Rome. It was not finished in this Tutmose's lifetime, but erected by his grandson Tutmose 1V.

[248] Egyptians believed that the gods would weigh the heart of a man at death against a feather, to see if it was pure.

EXODUS

CHAPTER 50

1450 BC

THE KING IS DEAD

AMENY SAT IN STUNNED SILENCE beside the body of his dead father. He had just witnessed the passing of the great Tutmose lll into the afterlife. The king's Ka[249] had left the body that had held it captive for 54 years - gone to become one with his father, the great god 'Ra', to sail the heavens for eternity[250]. But Ameny could not bear to let him go. He wanted to go back! To reverse this moment. To prevent its passing. Tutmose had loved him with more than a father's love, and Ameny had loved him deeply in return. But thinking beyond his own loss, Ameny knew of a certainty that without him, Egypt would flounder. She had been left in the hands of his half-brother Amenhotep, the new Pharaoh, so proud, so wilful, so foolish. Longing for war. Longing for glory. Ruling without Ma'at![251] Without wisdom!

It was still night. Dawn was yet some hours away. He knew the servants would not enter the chamber until he called. He was fighting within himself as tears coursed down his cheeks. As a son, Ameny wanted to stay by his father's side. To keep him a little longer! But as a priest he knew that the work to preserve the Pharaoh's body must commence at once. The organs must be removed, the cavities cleaned with palm wine and the body submerged in a bath of natron. Already decay would have started, and to preserve the Pharaoh's body for his Ka to inhabit for eternity, work must begin at once.

Ameny flung himself across his father's body as a great cry escaped him. He knew what he must do. His father's body would not remain as it had lived. It must now be preserved to house his Ka for eternity and the work must begin at once. The sound of his cry brought the Sem priests running into the chamber, and immediately they understood.

"My father is dead", said Ameny, forcing himself to utter the words. Such final words. "Summon the priests of Anubis at once to prepare his body for burial."

He turned away as the Sem priests came and went, breaking the last sacred moment he had shared alone with his father. He would wait by the body until the priests of Anubis arrived. Then he must prepare himself for the new day that would dawn on a very different Egypt. The Egypt of his brother. But here in this temple of Ptah, he was Hight Priest, and he would give orders that his father's body not be moved. That the work be done here. That way he could remain in attendance until the 70 days of mummification had passed. Then he would accompany his father on the solemn journey in the Royal barge, to Waset[252], taking him for burial in his waiting tomb in the Valley of the King's Gate[253].

The morning wore on. The priests commenced their work of preparing the Pharaoh's body with their usual efficiency. Ameny was exhausted. He had hardly slept, and sorrow added to his weariness. He forced himself to go to his own chamber and eat a little. When his younger son, his father's namesake, Tutmose, woke, he told him what had passed, and stayed with him while he prepared himself for his day at the temple school.

Tutmose had just left with his servants when Ameny's stepmother, the dowager queen, Meryetre-Hatshepsut[254] arrived unannounced. Ameny assumed she wished to bid farewell to her husband and as a courtesy to the High Priest of the temple, was visiting him first. He welcomed her into his private chambers. He knew her by reputation only. She was known to be sharp in her dealings with those beneath her, but as Tutmose's favourite, Ameny had never received a lashing from her tongue. But now her husband was dead. Ameny was no longer the protected favourite of the king, and her tongue was no longer bridled. Meryet was free. And she had long hated this favourite son whom she suspected of trying to take the position of heir which belonged to her own son Amenhotep. With no introduction she addressed herself to Ameny.

"May I ask the reason for your audacity?" she said looking Ameny full in the face.

Ameny was at a loss to understand her. He had acknowledged her arrival with a deep bow. What wrong had he done?

"Are you stupid as well as audacious?" she said, then paused. "Have you no reply?"

Ameny was angry. But he was determined not make an enemy of this woman, so replied as pleasantly as he could.

"I am unaware of how I have offended you, your majesty," he said with another bow.

"Unaware? How dare you speak to me so! You have presumed to order the preservation of the king's body with no reference to me or his heir!" she said, the volume of her tone rising as she poured out her venom.

Ameny was stunned into silence, but the queen had not finished. She knew of the deep love that had existed between Ameny and his father, a love that ignited fierce jealousy in her own heart. Tutmose had not loved her son as he had loved Ameny.

"You will have nothing further to do with the king," she said and watched with pleasure the shock and pain that crossed Ameny's face.

"His body will be removed to the temple of Ra today, where it will be supervised by priests worthy of the name! And when he is removed to Waset for burial you will not accompany him."

With these words she turned from him and waited until he had left the chamber. Ameny was at first too shocked to understand her words. To move the body of the king, interrupting the work of preservation, would cause deterioration in the corpse. Everyone knew such things. It was not a concern for his preservation but a wish to injure both the king and those he had loved that motivated his queen! But this woman and her son were now the rulers of Egypt and Ameny had no redress against them.

---

[249] Egyptians believed that each person was made up of 5 parts, the Body, the Ba, the Ka, the Name and the Shadow.

The Body
For you to continue to live into the afterlife your body must be preserved. Without it your Ka and Ba would have no place to rest and live.
At death, the soul, made up of the Ba and the Ka split into two.
The 'Ka' was unique to the individual. It was the 'life force' of the individual. It was usually represented in hieroglyphs as two arms stretched upwards. When a person

died, their Ka lived on and required the same nourishment as a living person. This is why the ancient Egyptians painted pictures of food on the walls of their tombs. It was believed that the Ka absorbed the life-giving force of the food represented, so the Ka could go on living.

The Ba was your personality, pictured in Hieroglyphs as a bird with a human head, thought to fly between the living world and the world of the dead.

The Name.

If your preserved body was destroyed after death, or if your name was removed, then your Ba and your Ka could get lost and not find their way back to your tomb. They would wander forever, dying the second death into oblivion.

The Shadow was believed to have the power to protect you like a bodyguard

[250] It was believed that the Sun was the god Ra who sailed across the sky every day in his 'solar boat' and that dead pharaohs joined him forever on his journey.

[251] Ma'at was an Egyptian goddess of harmony, truth and justice.

[252] Ancient Thebes

[253] Now known as 'the Valley of the Kings'.

[254] This is her full name, but in the story I have shortened it to Meryet.

CHAPTER 51

BURIAL AND DESTRUCTION

BEFORE LEAVING THE CHAMBER OF her dead husband, Meryet banished Ameny from the room. The audacity of the woman, to dismiss him from a chamber of the Temple of which he was High Priest was hard to believe, but Ameny complied. Nothing could be gained by staying, and there was no sense in angering the woman further. He left in silence, with a simple bow, and fled with an aching heart to the central shrine of the Temple. Here he would not be disturbed. Here he could think and maybe weep a little.

To transport the king's body to the Temple of Ra at Iunu, a city three shoeni[255] distance, would take time. And at this point, when deterioration of the corpse would continue unchecked, was madness. But he understood. Meryet wished to inflict harm on the Ka of her dead husband in payment for the contempt he had shown her in life. But as Ameny's mind roved over the situation, he realised that all was not lost. His priests had already removed the king's organs, the most potent source of decay. They had already cleansed the cavity with palm wine and packed it with bags of natron. Decay could not occur in the presence of natron. Meryet was too late to do serious damage. And the High Priest of the Temple of Ra at Iunu had been a close friend of the dead king. He would rescue the situation. And Ameny would send a trusted Sem priest to accompany the body and keep him informed.

Slowly the 70 days of mummification wore away. The body of the great Tutmose was ready for burial in his tomb in the Valley of the King's Gate[256] on the other side of the river from the city of Waset where he had lived. Ameny had been forbidden a place in the entourage of his father's funeral, but now a new fear entered his mind. If he did not leave Men-nepher now, and remove himself from her sphere of control, Meryet might command that he stay in Men-nepher and miss the whole event of his father's burial. So taking his young son Tutmose with him, he left the city secretly. He would meet his older son in Waset, where he was at school in the Temple of Mut.

To cover the 75 schoeni to Waset would take time. Ameny realised he must use this time to settle his mind and make plans for his future in this new Egypt ruled by his brother. There were other crafts on the river going south. Sea going craft. Beautiful vessels from Thera and Crete, the island nations north of Egypt. Great trading nations with wide knowledge of the sea. Clearly, they had sent ambassadors and nobles to attend the funeral of this great king.

Ameny had visited his father's tomb many times during Tutmose's lifetime. He could envisage it all his mind's eye. The place for the huge sarcophagus. The walls covered with hieroglyphs and images. Incantations from the Book of the Dead. He knew it well. So to be present for the moment of burial was not essential, he told himself. And he need have no fear that the ceremonies of burial would fall short. The pride of the priests of Amun would make sure that all that was required for their king to enter the afterlife would be provided. But one fear remained. After the burial, the entourage would visit the Mortuary temple of the King to make offerings, and here again Meryet may act to prevent Tutmose's favourite son from serving him. She may forbid him access to the temple. So now was the time to go. Before the dowager queen arrived in Waset. Now was the time to visit Tutmose's mortuary temple and leave a love gift for his father.

Ameny and his young son reached Waset as daylight was fading. Ra had fallen behind the hills across the river to the west, that surrounded the wide plain where the Mortuary temples of the three pharaohs now stood in shadow[257]. But the lightness of their stone against the yellow hills behind, made them visible still. He watched from the moving barge as a feeling of acceptance rose in his heart. It was a beautiful sight. Worthy of his father's memory.

The barge moved towards the royal dock. Without ceremony they disembarked and walked the short distance to the small temple of Ptah within the compound of Ipet.[258] They would find his older son, Webensenu, tomorrow and together would take a barge across the river to visit the Mortuary Temple and honour this man they had all loved.

Dawn was breaking as Ameny approached his father's temple, accompanied by his sons. He and his father had planned this building. A beautiful building, completing the symmetry of the temples of Hatshepsut to the north and Mentuhotep ll to the south. A trio of mortuary temples, fit for the three great pharaohs who had commissioned them. They arrived unannounced but Ameny was recognised immediately by the High Priest, who was surprised to see him coming even before the burial had taken place. Offerings to the dead king were brought after the burial. But he welcomed Ameny warmly. Clearly no edict of Meryet's, banning Ameny's entry had yet reached the ears of this priest.

The boys accompanied their father and together they entered the temple. Statues of Tutmose stood on every side. As they entered the shrine a beautifully carved, smiling statue of the dead king welcomed them.[259] Ameny had seen it many times, but now for the first time noticed its remarkable likeness to his father. There it stood, preserving the very presence of the king as a young man in his prime. Ameny was overwhelmed with grief and knelt before it. His father may have passed on to the afterlife, but while his likeness stood here, in his temple, his Ka would always inhabit it[260].

They moved on, entering the shrine to bring their offerings to a huge statue of Tutmose which stood before them dressed as a god. Ameny could not hold back the tears as he knelt to offer the jars of burning incense he had brought to his deified father. He had offered incense time without number as High Priest in the temple of Ptah, but this offering was so very different. It came from the heart, not as a required ceremony, to this man he had loved. He waited, longing, hoping to hear a word, an oracle, spoken in response. But the shrine was silent.

Time was passing and the deep silence of the sanctuary was a strange experience for the boys. Fear of this unknown thing, called death, made them tense. It was time to leave. Ameny gathered his thoughts together and left the temple, bidding farewell to the High Priest. They may not be permitted to enter this place again. He was glad they had come.

The three figures moved together towards the river where their craft waited. They would leave this shore of the dead and return to the land of the living on the east bank of the river, returning to their accommodation at the temple of Ptah. Ameny knew he could not lay claim to the rooms in the royal palace that had belonged to him for so many years while his father lived. No, they would content themselves with the small temple of Ptah within the great precinct of Ipet. He did not wish to enter the palace again and see the dowager queen and her son, living in this palace that held such precious memories for him. Joyous times spent there with his father.

The burial of the great warrior king was a triumphant affair. The royal barge wearing a new coat of gold brought his body to Waset accompanied by a flotilla of other gorgeous barges, replete with hundreds of priests and many royals. The spectacle was magnificent. A pageant of splendour and noise, led by the High Priest of Amun and the young man who had taken his father's place as pharaoh. Leading the rest of the mourners were Meryet and her daughters accompanied by her second son, Ahmose in a style more of triumph than mourning. There was little of sorrow evident in the faces of the royal family. Nothing suggesting a memory of one loved and lost. Meryet was full of smiles, a thing unknown in her previous life.

The flotilla came to rest on the west bank of the river. There the king's sarcophagus was transferred to an ox cart and carried the length of the Valley of the King's Gate to the tomb at the far end, cut deep into the rock. Watching as he was from the east bank of the river, Ameny was glad he was not part of this celebration of triumph. Glad that he had already paid his respects to his father at his mortuary temple.

For the next few days Ameny stayed in the temple of Ptah spending time with his sons. The burial was over. Never again would this great warrior king ride his chariot to war in the north. Even now he would be entering the Duat[261] where he must face the Judgement of forty-two gods. Every Egyptian dreaded the judgement. Here Anubis, the god of the dead would bring the dead before his judges and give his heart to Osiris, the god of the underworld. Osiris would place the heart, which contained the soul, on a pair of scales where it was weighed against the feather of Ma'at, the goddess of truth. Ameny held his breath as he thought of it. If his father's heart was found to be heavier than the feather, there was no escape. it would be devoured by the crocodile headed demon, Ammit, the 'Gobbler,' and his soul would enter the second death, annihilation.

Ameny thrust these terrible thoughts from him. There was another way! A way to find favour with the gods. And surely Tutmose had bought the favour of the gods. His campaigns in the north had furnished their temples up and down the land with booty and slaves from the cities of Canaan and Syria. Amun, the foremost god had received booty beyond counting from Tutmose's campaigns. Surely Amun would help his father. And if the king's soul was found to be lighter than the feather, then it would be 'justified'[262]. To be justified was what every pharaoh and every Egyptian citizen hoped and prayed for. The gods would welcome a justified soul, allowing him to move on to paradise – 'the Field of Reeds', the place of purification and eternal bliss. And every pharaoh hoped to receive special honour from Ra himself. Every pharaoh was a son of Ra and every justified pharaoh would be invited to enter the boat of the great sun god and sail the heavens for eternity, far removed from the world of men.

Ameny's mind had run through the whole saga and was determined that his father would have the support of the gods. He would be justified and become one with his father Ra for eternity. But those he loved and who had loved him in return must pick up the broken threads of their lives and continue their course in the land of the living.

The burial was over but Ameny could not yet tear himself away from this city. He could not return to Men-nepher so quickly, bereft of his father. And to his surprise, his sons were pleased to remain in Waset. Tutmose, because he had suffered badly in Men-nepher at the hands of Meryet and her children. A little boy, persecuted by his own family. But for Webensenu, there was a happier reason. He had made a special friend. The son of the Master at his school here at Mut's temple[263]. Ameny was delighted with the school. Webensenu was making good progress in his studies and was happy. The Master, Hekareshu, a Nubian, of high birth[264], ran a cheerful and successful institution. This pleased Ameny of course, but what could he do for Tutmose. Was the child old enough to join this school? If he stayed here he would be a long way from his home and parents but would have his brother with him.

Surely that would be better than the torment of his royal cousins at the school in Men-nepher. Ameny decided to approach Hekareshu as soon as he could to discuss Tutmose joining the school.

The evening was warm and sultry. Ameny loved many things about Waset; its magnificent temples; the memories he cherished, but the weather at its hottest was torment. Too hot to work. Too hot to think. Too hot to sleep. With no garden or trees, the temple of Ptah had little relief from the heat. Ipet itself, built of stone, absorbed and reflected back the rays of Ra, mercilessly. Even at night there was little respite as the stone which had received the heat of Ra during the day gave it back during the hours of darkness.

Ameny knew he would not sleep. The night would be passed in wakefulness. But there was one place he could go to find relief. The Mortuary Temple of Hatshepsut, beside his father's temple on the west bank of the river, neglected now during all the great festivals since the building of his father's temple. But still maintaining its beautiful gardens. Built by Hatshepsut for the pleasure of her father Amun[265]. Ameny could go there to get relief from the heat. He would cross the river and be carried by chair up the long avenue to those cool terraces. There he would find the coolness he craved and space for reflection.

The sound of the oars moving through the dark water brought refreshment. To his right, the Valley of the Kings showed black where it cut deep into the surrounding hills. To his left, bathed in moonlight lay the beautiful symmetry of the three Mortuary Temples. They docked on the far side and he approached the temple of Hatshepsut along the avenue leading from the river. The huge sphinxes which lined the route seemed to move eerily as the shadow of the surrounding trees moved in the moonlight. Ahead he could make out the first terraced court, dark with trees and the promise of refreshment. But as his chair moved steadily along the approach road, he saw on both sides of the road, deep pits had been dug just outside the boundary line of the temple. He could see right down into the pit on his right. A pit of great depth. And to his left, the causeway leading to his father's Mortuary Temple had been lifted and a pit dug under it. What was this? A deep anguish awoke in his mind. What did his brother intend with these? Once before such a pit had been dug on the west side of this causeway, at the instigation of his brother. Into that pit had been thrown all the dismembered and smashed statues of the great Senenmut! Could this be another such purge? But of what?

Ameny returned late from his visit to the east bank, but the time he spent there in the cool gardens, had refreshed him. As he crossed the river, the silhouette of Ipet stood out proudly against the night sky. This huge complex was devoted to Amun. Amun, whose renown had grown to unassailable heights in the reigns of Hatshepsut and his father. It was Amun who had given victory against Egypt's enemies all through Tutmose's reign. In his mind Ameny acknowledged the pre-eminence of Amun, but in his heart he remained loyal to Ptah, whom he served as High Priest. An ancient god who over time had built Egypt's strength without the need for war and violence.

He returned to his chambers late and slept heavily. By morning a breeze was blowing through the chamber, moving the curtains. As the sun rose, shafts of sunlight fell across his face, waking him. His head ached. Never did he sleep beyond dawn. But why had he not heard the shouts of the Lector Priest welcoming the return of Ra to the world of men? The whole temple was silent. Why? Where were the servants? Where the boats on the river with the shouts of men plying their trade. Since the burial of his father life had returned to normal in Waset. But now the world had changed again. Something was wrong. Seriously wrong. Something so dramatic that the servants had forgotten their duties. Had some new edict of the king dictated that Ra must rise unacknowledged? That servants must desert their duties? He rang the bell by his bed to no avail. He dressed with no servant to oil and scrape his skin. He felt dirty. Unfit to venture out. But outside his window lay a balcony overlooking the Great Court of the temple. Out there it would be cool for perhaps an hour. He drew back the curtain and stepped out and saw to his astonishment the area below him crowded with a host of silent men. Servants, priests, labourers, standing together in silence, watching.

Following the gaze of the men below, he turned to look east, towards the shrine of Amun. The sunlight was shining full in his face, but there, far to his left he could make out a group of soldiers and oxen dragging a heavy object with ropes and rollers. Slowly they advanced, moving towards the great gate of the temple. From his vantage point, Ameny could see the huge object being hauled along with so little care. He saw that it was a large stone. A statue.

Made of quartzite. Valuable stone, only ever used by the Royal family. What were these men doing dragging a statue of a royal person through the dust? No wonder all had forgotten their duties. This was sacrilege! But whose statue was it? And why was it being dragged with so little respect, and by soldiers? The minutes passed and slowly the object moved closer along its path. He knew this temple well. Surely he would know this statue. He cast his mind around what he remembered of the many smaller shrines enclosed within these great walls, but nothing fitted the scene before him. Then a picture entered his mind. He had accompanied his father once, into the inner sanctuary, the shrine of Amun himself. The holiest of the holy places, where only the statues of the Pharaoh's were allowed to stand for to stand in the presence of the idol of Amun was to imbibe the continual life-giving blessing of the great god.

Suddenly he knew. This was the statue of a pharaoh! A statue of Pharaoh Hatshepsut herself. This great pharaoh, who with his own father had expanded this temple at Ipet[266] to be the huge complex it now was, with all its prestige and renown. What was happening? How could a statue of Hatshepsut be so abused? Ameny stood in silence. Shocked, as the others below him stood. Watching. But the soldiers and oxen with their cargo were approaching, and as they did, Ameny saw that the delicately carved features of the Pharaoh's face had been smashed!

The horrifying scene moved resolutely on towards the outer gate of the temple and as they did so, away towards the sunrise, whence the first group had come, another group appeared. These were pulling a larger object, and as they approached, Ameny recognised a huge granite sphinx of the Female Pharaoh. And with the sight of this second horror, Ameny understood. So this was the meaning of the pits he had seen the night before at Djeser Djesere, the Mortuary Temple of Hatshepsut. It was happening again. The shocking destruction of Senenmut's statues would be nothing to this! Here was clear evidence that his brother was determined to remove all trace of Hatshepsut and her son from the annals of Egypt.

Without pausing for thought Ameny knew what he must do. Was his brother unaware of the danger he was bringing on himself and Egypt? Pharaoh Hatshepsut was now a god. She sat in judgment with all the gods to judge those who entered the afterlife. How could Amenhotep hope to escape her anger?

With his head and his heart bursting with shock and fury, Ameny turned towards the palace. It was a short walk. The king, in all probability had begun his hour of audience. Now was his chance to speak to his brother. He reached the palace entrance and the guards bowed him in. Walking quickly towards the audience chamber, Ameny found his brother surrounded by senior members of the army. The king's voice was raised as if in reply to one of his councillors.

"You will send men immediately to Djeser Djesere[267] and start removing the statues of that woman!"

"My Lord there are so many of them. And the statues of the Pharaoh in the form of Osiris, lining the front of the temple are huge[268]. Many times larger than life. Where can we find space enough to bury them?"

"Are you incapable of doing as I tell you?" shouted the king. "Dig more pits! Dig deeper pits! The statues of that woman must be buried. Space must be found. What cannot be destroyed must be buried out of sight! Remove them all!"

Ameny approached, aghast at what he had seen and heard. As he neared the king he stopped and bowed. As a royal prince himself, he had never prostrated himself before this throne, which previously his father had occupied. Amenhotep saw him and for a moment was silent. He had always admired Ameny. Their father had loved Ameny, and while this had created hatred and jealousy in Meryet, it had created a respect for his brother in the young king. He watched him approach without a word but knew that many words would be spoken before this meeting was past.

Following protocol, Ameny waited for the king to speak first. But he did not speak. Instead he watched in silence as Ameny stood there surrounded by the councillors and men of arms who had gathered earlier. Minutes passed and slowly the king's arrogance and anger overcame his awe of his brother.

"I do not need the advice of any more priests", he said contemptuously, looking hard at his brother.

"My Lord, I do not wish to advise but to warn," came Ameny's reply with pleading in his voice. "The Pharaoh Hatshepsut is a god. She sits with those who will be our judges in the afterlife." He stopped.

The king had leapt to his feet and was shouting at his brother, pointing an accusing finger.

"I will not allow the legacy of that usurper to remain! I will trample her underfoot! Indeed, even now, her statues are being buried under the causeway leading to our father's tomb. Under the very road itself so that every foot that treads that path will crush her." He paused, out of breath, but he had not finished.

"And never again will a woman be allowed to gain such power[269]. I will see to it that her name and the name of her son are never again spoken in Egypt!"

Ameny stood in stunned silence. Power had driven his brother mad. But it was a dangerous insanity! Where would it end? Surely he would be punished by the gods. How could a mortal defy the gods and live?

---

[255] A Shonus was measurement of distance used in Egypt. According to Heroditus, one Shonus was about 10.5km, so this distance was about 30km.

[256] The Valley of the Kings.

[257] Now known as Deir el Bahri, the Mortuary Temples of Menuhotep ll, Tutmose lll and Hatshepsut stood here but only that of Hatshepsut is still standing.

[258] Karnak.

[259] There was such a statue of Tutmose lll, beautifully carved, standing just inside the entrance of the Luxor Museum.

[260] It was believed that the Ka of a dead person inhabited their statues.

[261] The Duat was the underworld

[262] 'Justified' was a term used often in reliefs and inscriptions to express the state all men longed to reach in the afterlife. It meant life, not death for eternity.

[263] The goddess Mut, as the wife of Amun, had a temple beside the Karnak temple complex.

[264] Hekareshu was the master of the school at Mut's temple. He was a high born Nubian. Names with the pre-fix 'Heka' denoted a person of the Royal house in Nubia.

[265] Although physically Hatshepsut was the child of the first Tutmose, she also claimed to be the child of Amun, having the scene of her birth recorded on the walls of her Mortuary temple at Deir el Bahri.

[266] Known now as Karnak

[267] Hatshepsut's mortuary temple

[268] The multiple life-sized statues of Hatshepsut in the form of the god Osiris have been restored to the front of her temple.

[269] Amenhotep ll reflected the anti-women rhetoric of Amenemhat 1 from the Middle Kingdom quoted in the text of 'Mistress of the House Mistress of Heaven Women in Ancient Egypt' pg 34.

CHAPTER 52

AMENY AND AMENHOTEP GO THEIR SEPARATE WAYS

ALL WASET WAS ABLAZE WITH talk of the destruction. The very memory of the great female pharaoh would be lost! But then a fresh wave of panic spread through the city as even more shocking news was heard. Amenhotep had not only instructed his men to destroy the reliefs and statues of Pharaoh Hatshepsut, but now another order was issued. Her mummified body was to be taken from its tomb and destroyed. The fact that she was now deified, that she sat with the gods passing judgement on all who must enter the afterlife was too much for the common people to contemplate. This was sacrilege gone mad!

But Amenhotep did not hide away from the deed. He was determined to be present at the opening of the tomb to witness the destruction. The day was appointed. The priests assembled. He would savour his victory over this woman who had become for him the personification of everything he hated. He would relish the destruction of her mummy, forcing her Ka to wander without rest or sustenance for eternity. The second death so dreaded by every Egyptian.

The day arrived. The tomb was opened with great solemnity as if some evil thing was to be removed from Egypt. The priests entered the tomb in procession, accompanied by the young king. This had been the tomb of Hatshepsut's father, the first Tutmose, where she had chosen to be buried also. Amenhotep knew that the wooden sarcophagus of Hatshepsut's father was gone, moved to his own father's tomb. Amenhotep had seen the ceremony of reburial in the days shortly before his father's death. It was a great honour for his father to have the body of his famous grandfather with him in death.

But as they entered with blazing torches to light up the tomb and carry out the destruction of Hatshepsut's body, they found the grand quartzite sarcophagus containing the body of the hated queen gone! How could this be? Who would dare to do such a thing? And where was it?[270] Amenhotep ordered a raid on every tomb that had been sealed in the vicinity since his father's death. But Hatshepsut's mummy could not be found. Amenhotep's fury knew no bounds. He instructed the masons to destroy everything that could not be removed, then seal the tomb so the place of her burial would never again be discovered.[271]

Days passed. The king and the High Priest of Amun shut themselves away to digest their failure and fury. They must accept that they would never find and destroy Hatshepsut's mummy. But there were other things left from her reign that they could destroy, if they were prepared to risk offending the gods. Every day, at the very centre of Amun's temple, Menkheperraseneb[272] must pass and repass images of this woman he hated. Images of her with her daughter offering incense to Amun, carved on every wall of the sacred Barque shrine[273] in the very centre of the Temple complex.[274] Carvings of her coronation where she was honoured by Egypt's greatest gods, Ra and Amun! Every time he saw it, anger seized his mind. When could he have this shrine destroyed!

Menkheperraseneb chose his words carefully. He knew the times when it was wiser not to make requests of this king. Never when he showed uncertainty. When he questioned himself or was faced with failure or frustration. Amenhotep was a man driven by pride and ambition. He wanted to make a name for himself, greater even than that of his father Tutmose who had made Egypt the most powerful empire on earth. He was determined to prove himself an even better soldier. Indeed, Tutmose had not been a natural soldier. He was a small man and naturally weak. Only self-discipline and constant effort had made him able to ride with his army and endure the hardships of army life. Amenhotep knew that he himself had physical advantages beyond those of his father. He was taller and stronger, and having put equal effort into training, would surpass him. He recorded proclamations claiming his superior prowess as an archer, a rower, and a charioteer, more than any pharaoh before him[275] So the High Priest chose his moment carefully and approached his king at an opportune time.

"Majesty, may I speak to you regarding monuments you may wish to build at Ipet? When my lord returns from campaign and his victories are fresh in his mind, might it be good to have a new pylon ready to have a record carved of your exploits?"

"You may command the cutting of stone in Aswan[276] if you wish to extend your temple complex, my lord," replied the king believing he understood the motives of the old man.

"Thank you, my king," said the priest. "I will do as you say. But some stone is already available, if we remove the remaining monuments of that heretic woman."

Amenhotep looked at the High Priest. Was there more to this request than he realised?

"Tell me what it is you wish to remove," he said watching this ally whom he would never grow to trust. But the priest must tread carefully. To remove a barque shrine made for the honour of Amun was a brave move. It may be seen as an act of sacrilege, an act of folly that may anger the gods.

"The usurper built a Barque shrine at the very centre of Ipet, my Lord. A shrine which your own father replaced with one of greater size and honour. It is therefore unused and could be removed without causing offence."

Amenhotep sat watching the priest. He would agree to the request, he decided, but would let the responsibility rest on the old man.

"I see you are set on removing this shrine," he said as he rose to leave, to escape the company of one so eaten up with hatred. Even his own anger was no match for this.

"Your hand may perform the deed and your heart be weighed for it in the judgement,"[277] he said as he left the apartment.

So it was done. The Barque shrine, built by Hatshepsut at her coronation was dismantled and its stones used to strengthen the new gateway built by Amenhotep[278]. Now both the pharaoh and his High Priest could rest knowing that the legacy of Hatshepsut was gone forever. The List of Kings carved on the walls of the 'Chamber of Ancestors' at Karnak by Tutmose lll had omitted her name. Nothing remained of her legacy as pharaoh. No one in the future who may see her name written as the King's daughter or the Great Royal Wife of Tutmose ll would have any reason to think that she had reigned as a Pharaoh of Egypt. Her line was gone. There was no longer any way that Senenmut could claim her legacy and her crown.[279] In the markets of Waset, little else was talked of. But in the houses of the courtiers the subject was avoided. No one dared provoke the anger of the king, and his spies were everywhere.

But the shock of this wholesale destruction was not limited to Waset. News spread to every temple that honoured the female Pharaoh and threw them into panic. She had poured much of her personal income, inherited from her mother, into restoring temples up and down the land that had been neglected since the Hyksos rule[280]. But all must obey the edict. They must remove and bury her statues. Those at a distance from Waset, while doing what they must, did not deface every image. They feared the living Pharaoh, but also feared to offend this deified Pharaoh.

With all the destruction that was happening, Ameny knew he must go to Mi-wer to comfort his mother. Hatshepsut was Nepherure's own mother! If she heard this news, what would it do to her? Nepherure had been close to her mother all her young life. She was the Royal princess, the Royal heiress at the heart of the Royal family. The only child of the second Tutmose and his Great Royal Wife, Hatshepsut. Then Hatshepsut herself became Pharaoh and Nepherure was required to fill the position of Great Royal Wife, supporting her mother as pharaoh. This was huge. It was from these heights that she had fallen. Now she was old and delicate in mind. If she heard of the shocking treatment of her mother's legacy, it might unhinge her.

School had restarted for Webensenu, and Hekareshu, the Master had kindly agreed to allow Tutmose also, to attend the school. He made a special allowance for the boy as he was so young, inviting him to live with his own family, where over the last weeks Tutmose had made a friend of Hekareshu's young daughter Mutemwia, who was of a similar age.

With the kindness of the Master, Ameny was free to travel to the Fayum alone. The barge moved swiftly with the rising water and Ameny could feel its power as it surged north, carrying the barge like so much flotsam. Despite the horrors so fresh in his mind, the journey calmed him, allowing him to relax and think of other things. Watching the surging water, he understood again, how his forbears had used the power of the rising river to carry huge stones, even obelisks, from the south to Waset and even Iunu[281] in vast numbers, creating there, at Iunu, a city filled with obelisks. A 'city of spires,'* as it was known.

The barge approached the Fayum, left the river, and entered the system of canals and lock gates that controlled the changing water levels between the river and the huge lake at the centre of the Fayum. The canals would carry him there and to the harem at Mi-Wer. The serenity of the rural surroundings was sweet and soothed his exhausted mind after the turmoil that had overtaken his life since the death of his father. Jala was told of his coming and was there to meet him on his arrival. She could not risk him finding his mother, without warning him of her distressed state.

"My dear Ameny!" she said with a sob at his embrace. "We have so longed for your coming. But you must prepare yourself for the sad state of your mother", she added.

"I expected as much," he said. "To hear of the destruction of her mother's legacy must be terrible to bear. Of course she is distressed."

Jala hesitated before answering, looking at him now with fear in her eyes.

"Your mother blames herself," she said. "This is her chief problem."

"But how can she be blamed?" asked Ameny.

Again she hesitated, trying to read his face. She had rehearsed this moment. She chose her words carefully.

"She believes that if she had stayed at court with your father, as his wife, she could have prevented all this carnage," she said.

Her words masked more than she could disclose. But she was sworn to secrecy. There were things that Ameny must never guess.

"But my father Tutmose is dead. It is his heir Amenhotep that has destroyed Hatshepsut's legacy," said Ameny bewildered. "What has that to do with my mother?"

But Jala knew she must halt this enquiry, and her only hope was to ask Ameny not to enquire.

"For your mother's peace of mind, I must ask you not to question more," she said. "Her mind is very unstable."

Ameny knew he must and would comply. He loved his mother dearly, and what did it matter that she was confused. He must do all he could to comfort her, and without further words, the two of them turned their steps towards the queen's apartments. The Harem was a haven of peace, but as they approached the queen's apartments, Ameny detected the sounds of sobbing. He entered and found Nepherure kneeling before a statue of her mother, weeping. She had not heard him enter, so he stopped, waiting for Jala to speak.

"My Lady, you have a visitor," she said softly.

Nepherure raised her eyes and saw her son standing just inside the room. But instead of joy, a look of shock and fear spread across her face.

"I can see no one!" she shouted, turning away.

Ameny crossed the room and took his mother in his arms.

"There is nothing to fear mother! It is I, Ameny," he said with anguish in his voice.

But she pushed him away groaning, avoiding his eyes as a wail broke from her.

"All wrong! All wrong!" she wailed then turned to stare at him.

"Mother there is nothing to fear," he said, but the fear remained in her eyes. Suddenly she became frantic.

"I have done this!" she shouted. "Tutmose would have done what I asked. He would not have destroyed the statues. He loved Senenmut. He honoured my mother!" She paused. Again the anguished sobs burst from her as she continued.

"This terrible man, Meryet's son should not be king! she shouted. "And I will be condemned in the Judgment of the gods for what I have done!" she wailed.

But Jala knew that she must control these ravings before Nepherure revealed the truth.

"My Lady it is all a long time ago. Do not distress yourself for what is past."

Ameny too, tried to comfort his mother.

"Mother, you can never know that by staying with the king, you would have borne him a son. And if you did, he may have been as wicked and wilful as Amenhotep. Please do not distress yourself. You are not responsible for the actions of another."

But listening to his words, Nepherure became strangely calm. Her manner changed and she seemed to see Ameny as a stranger.

"You do not know my son," she said quietly. "He is noble. He is a good man. I deprived Egypt of a man worthy to be pharaoh, and the gods will judge it so," she said in a more normal measured voice. Then her voice rose again in the same dreadful wail.

"But it is too late! Too late!" She was becoming hysterical again. Jala knew she must act. Pleading with Ameny she asked him to leave them. She would come to him.

With an agony of heart Ameny turned and left the scene of fear and confusion. What was the meaning of his mother's words? But as he left he heard Jala speaking.

"My lady please calm yourself. What is done is done and cannot be undone.

As the time came for him to leave Mi-wer, Ameny had to face the new emptiness of his life. His father was gone. His sons must remain in Waset. His common law wife, Tiaa, would be waiting for him in Men-nepher but her sphere was limited to the harem. She was a simple girl who, as a harem beauty had caught his eye and his heart. But she could not share, or even understand his life as one of Egypt's elite. His mother was now beyond his reach, leaving only the kindness of Jala to fill the empty void. What joy or purpose was there left in his life? Would he live out his days at the temple of Ptah, fulfilling familiar routines. Serving a god who showed no need of him?

As Ameny bid his mother farewell, she was distressed but calm. Jala's words had found their mark. Ameny reasoned that it was her sensitive nature that had opened her mind to this misplaced guilt. She was a Royal Princess, but with no power. She had lived her life in seclusion away from the court. She had never known the young man who was now Pharaoh. What could she have done to counter the actions of this wilful young king?

But he must return to his work in the north. His presence at Mi-wer offered no solace to his mother, so delay for this reason must also be set aside. As he bade good-bye to all he loved at Mi-wer his mind turned to the next challenge he must face. The new king and his mother would also be returning to Men-nepher. Their residence would be the palace where the court would gather. But Ameny knew he would no longer be welcome among the elite of Men-nepher. He would be shunned by all who wanted the favour of the palace.

The barge reached its first Mooring place[282] as Ra was descending towards the west and Ameny received a warm welcome in this familiar palace. His spirits had lifted a little by the time he set out the next day. The morning was noticeably cooler after the heat of the south and to be out in the pleasant air, resting under the canopy of the barge as the countryside moved past, brought him a measure of peace. But better was to follow. On reaching the mooring place at Abydos on his third night he received news that the king and his court would not be returning to Men-nepher! Instead, Amenhotep had chosen to make Avaris[283] his residence so he could concentrate on his wars in the north. There was little doubt that Meryet would remain with her son to enjoy the reflected glory of his position, leaving Ameny, in Men-nepher, free of their presence.

And so it proved. Men-nepher became a haven of peace as the court moved north, attracting all who wished to rise in the favour of the pharaoh. Rumours continued to circulate regarding the search for Hatshepsut's body. Soldiers continued to search but in vain. Her body was lost to her enemies. Amenhotep was incandescent with rage that she had escaped his clutches. He had the guards on her tomb tortured for information. But the lost mummy remained lost.

Meanwhile, life in Men-nepher changed for the better. The wholesale departure of courtiers to the north altered the feel of the town. The purpose of Amenhotep moving north was to prepare for war. Not just war, but victory. And for this he must increase the size of his army. Men had been lost in his last assault on the north at the end of his father's reign. These had been replaced, but he wanted an even larger army to gain complete control of Naharin and garrison all her cities. So now instead of the royal retinue flooding Men-nepher, fresh army recruits arrived day after day from the south. Strong young peasants eager for glory, seizing the chance offered them to train as soldiers in the king's army. Here they were assessed for suitability and underwent a preliminary training at the old barracks. Those who were successful, continued on to Avaris for further training.

But another aspect of army governance was to change. The system of generous rations for the troops and the families they left behind, had worked well. But as Amenhotep wanted to increase the size of the army, he must increase the amount of grain grown and stored. The slave masters were instructed to take slaves from field work and use them to enlarge the store cities. They must make bricks and extend the size of the store cities of Ramesses and Per Aten[284] to accommodate the increased quantity of grain. The plight of the slaves was pitiful. They had worked the fields without respite, and now with reduced numbers, must grow even more grain. They were a tough race, but would the policy of removing men to brick making, increase the load of those farming, to breaking point? All Avaris knew of the king's increased demands, and the whole city lived in fear of these downtrodden people, whose only hope for a bearable life was to turn on their persecutors. It was surely just a matter of time.

---

[270] The mummy of an unknown female royal, found in the tomb of Sitre, Hatshepsut's nurse, has recently been identified beyond doubt, as that of Hatshepsut herself.

[271] It is known that Hatshepsut was originally buried in her father's tomb. We also know that her father's body was removed from there and placed in the tomb of Tutmose lll. It has been assumed that it was Tutmose lll that hid Hatshepsut's body from his son to prevent its destruction. But the location of the original tomb of Hatshepsut and her father, to my knowledge, has not been found.

[272] High Priest of Amun at Karnak.

[273] Shrine that housed the sacred boat in which the idol of the god was carried when taken out of the temple.

[274] This barque shrine, made of red stone and was recently restored by French archaeologists who renamed it the 'Chapelle Rouge'. It is at Karnak and can be seen there.

[275] Recorded facts.

[276] Ancient name was Swen

[277] Amenhotep used the stones of the Chapelle Rouge to build the third gateway, or Pylon of the temple.

[278] Stones from this shrine were found in rubble of the pylon built by Amenhotep ll.

[279] The name of Hatshepsut was not included in the first King List written by Tutmose lll on the walls at Karnak, so there was no chance of her name being included in any subsequent lists.

[280] The Hyksos were invaders from Syria who took control of Egypt and held it for 100 years before the rise of the New Kingdom.

[281] Heliopolis

[282] These were palaces along the length of the river a day's journey apart for the use of the royal family.

[283] Avaris was further north, near the coast. It had been the capital in the Hyksos time which would have been the time of the biblical Joseph.

[284] The sore city named in the bible as Pithom is a corruption of Per Aten, meaning ' the house of the Aten', a sun god.

CHAPTER 53

YEAR 7 CAMPAIGN

IT WAS THREE YEARS NOW since his father's death, and in that short time, Amenhotep had changed the face of the country he now ruled. Waset had been the capital of Egypt for the last three reigns but a visitor from his father's time would be shocked at the changes to this ruling city whose very name meant 'Sceptre'. All trace of Hatshepsut's reign and name were gone and the city itself had lost most of its wealthy elite, as the king and his court moved permanently north.

The whole country was being trained for war. As soon as he had dealt with the destruction of Hatshepsut's legacy and moved north, Amenhotep turned his attention to breeding horses to supply his chariots. Horses were bred in large numbers. Mares, to bear the next generation, and colts raised and trained to draw chariots. The fierce chariot stallions of his father's army were legendary. But Amenhotep wanted more. Good land was requisitioned, especially around the town of Akhmim in upper Egypt, north of Waset. It was good land, and had been growing crops, but was changed to pastureland for raising horses. Amenhotep was determined to increase his stallion numbers to over three thousand. Enough to draw 1,500 chariots. And the bloodlines must be honed. He wanted stronger horses, with greater stamina for his wars.

The new pharaoh wanted his son and heir to follow his example as a general and took him north with the army to experience the rigors of army life. The boy, also Amenhotep, was only 10 years old. He had not yet come of age, but to present him to the world, the king had a stella carved in his honour.[285]

The boy's grandmother Meryet, was beside herself with panic for the safety of this favourite grandchild whom she adored. She feared his going with the army, but his father was determined. The boy would accompany him into Canaan, as far as Gaza.

At the beginning of his sole rule, Amenhotep continued with the services of his father's generals. He wanted to learn all he could from their long experience, before dismissing them. But dismiss them he would. He hated these old men from his father's time, most of all, his father's favourite, general Djehuty.

But what could Djehuty do? He had observed this young man who was now king and had long expected dismissal from his post. He was concerned for Egypt's future, but also for his own family and wanted to retain a connection with the army. So he had trained his sons to follow in his footsteps. His eldest, an exceptional charioteer, had charge of training new charioteers, and his second son was Djehuty's chariot driver. He had made these preparations and hoped to weather the coming storm.

But having listened to the advice of his father's generals for as long as he could bear, the king was determined to be rid of them. He hated to be surrounded by these veterans. 'Old men' as he called them. He did not admit to himself that it was because they knew more of war than himself. He saw war as a grand adventure and wanted his own friends, the young men he had grown up with to be his generals and go with him on campaign. He cared not how he dismissed the old guard who had served Egypt so well. So gathering his army leaders together he addressed them all.

"There are going to be changes. Army life is hard and not suitable for old men, he said."

"General Djehuty, you served my father, but you are old. You have trained your son Ramose as a competent soldier, so I will appoint him in your place."

Djehuty was shocked at the callous way he was dismissed but he knew things could have been far worse. He could console himself that his son, because he was one of the king's friends, had been elevated to high rank. General Amenemhab also felt the sweep of the new broom, but his son was not so fortunate.

Now with the young generals in place, recruiting started in earnest. Peasan farmers from all over Egypt must be trained as soldiers. And boys in every village who were not yet old enough to be soldiers, were required to practice archery from an early age. In fact, as far as the king's edict could be enforced, other games apart from archery were forbidden so that even as children they would become skilled archers.[286]

Avaris where the king now resided had but one purpose. To train men in large numbers to be the best troops Egypt had ever produced. An archer, using his composite bow, was expected to shoot 10 arrows every minute and send them a distance of over 50 cubits[287] Officers must train for hours wearing the hot and heavy bronze scaled armour, and every captain and charioteer was equipped with the lighter but still hot, rawhide Keblar vest as protection, in which he must train. Most combat was still hand to hand and the men trained hard to develop the muscle strength required to wield the Halbert and Duckbill battle axes during long battles. Chariots were altered to have six spoked wheels instead of four for added strength and given lighter frames for greater manoeuvrability. Amenhotep loved the sight of his chariots as they drove out in formation and his greatest pride was to ride out with them, surrounded by his 600 strong bodyguard of charioteers, the Braves of the King, the flower of his army.

The king cared well for his army. Every soldier was given the same privilege as the priests, of tax exemption. And those who served for 5 years received, for himself, 12 acres of land as his own, the produce of which would not be taxed. Above this, special honour went to the chariot squadrons, each 25 chariots strong, with 2 men in each, a driver and a warrior, because it was the chariots which always led the attack, using javelins and bows. But closest to his heart was his bodyguard who received additional benefits; a daily ration of 5 mina weight of roasted grain[288], two mina[289] of beef and four cups of wine[290]The 'First Charioteer' drove Amenhotep's own chariot drawn by the strongest and most beautiful stallions.

THE EGYPTIAN YEAR UNFOLDED, FIRST with the flax and barley harvest, followed by the wheat and spelt[291], as the king readied the army for war. They would travel north as the wheat harvest started in Canaan, ready to feed his troops. The battalions gathered at Tharu and set out on the 10 days journey to

Gaza, camping each night then moving on. The first days passed as planned but on the fourth day scouts returned with news that Gaza itself, and the coast north of it was facing invasion from 'Sea People'[292] in their thousands, fleeing violent earth tremors on the Island of Thera which also affected Caphtor.[293] Gaza, with its strong Egyptian garrison had prevented the Sea People from taking the city. But the invaders were asking to be allowed to settle their families along the coast in exchange for the men serving as mercenaries in Pharaoh's army.

On reaching Gaza Amenhotep assessed the situation quickly. Even in Egypt earth tremors had been felt. He knew that the Sea people were renowned fighters. They were tall and strong and well trained in hand-to-hand combat. The Overseer of the Gaza garrison had allowed them to rest and settle temporarily on the beach to the north of the town until the Pharaoh arrived.

But the pharaoh, his generals and the whole garrison at Gaza were astonished to see the terror in the faces of these tough Sea People. The volcano at the centre of their island home had always been alive. Earth tremors, hot vapours bursting out from the ground. Deep fissures forming across fields and dividing villages. All these things were known. And if a village was badly affected, that community might take to their long boats and leave, exploring the coast of the Great Sea until they found a place to settle.

But things had changed. The volcano had entered a new phase of wild activity, and all across the island people were leaving. It was no longer safe to remain. Everyone knew the stories of how volcanos chose to die. Like things possessed they would burst, spewing their molten entrails high into the air until nothing was left of them but a smoking chasm extending deep into the earth. But Thera was an island. If she spewed out her substance, there would be nothing left of her. She would sink beneath the waves forever.

Amenhotep took a few days watching these foreigners and listening to their interpreters. He realised that here was a bargain to be made. These people were desperate. So he could expand his army at no extra cost to Egypt. A deal was struck allowing them to make Canaan their refuge. The families would be allowed to settle in the nearby Canaanite villages and along the coast to the north, while the men would join the ranks of his infantry, swelling Egypt's fighting power to subdue the north. The army he had brought already consisted of three infantry divisions, each of 5,000 men. The divisions were named after one of Egypt's greatest gods, Amun, Ra and Ptah. Now it would be even bigger. Strong enough to quickly force the cities of the north to submit, putting him on course to master Naharin in a subsequent campaign.

Despite the propaganda of his father's reign, Amenhotep knew that Egypt had never gained complete control of Naharin. His father had seized the ports along the coast. Egypt was unbeatable at sea. Tutmose had pushed inland and crossed the Orontes River, then taken control of the trade route that ran through the cities Aleppo and Carchemish, even forcing Naharin's king Parsatater[294] to flee his capital Washukanni[295] and take refuge on the east side of the Euphrates. But Egypt's control of Washukanni was short lived. When Tutmose retired from war, Naharin quietly regained control of her capital and the trade routes it controlled.

Now, with his large army of well-trained men Amenhotep was determined to finish what his father had spent twenty years trying to achieve. He would bring Naharin under Egypt's control as far as the Euphrates River. He would garrison all her cities, keeping control of her trade routes to fill Egypt's coffers. He would take control of Syria, expanding Egypt's empire to the north, just as the great pharaohs before him had taken control of Nubia and Kush creating Egypt's southern empire.

---

[285] This was the 2nd stela made for this Prince. One had already been made to record his birth

[286] I have taken this idea from another place in history. It is not known to be true of Egypt, but this was true in the time of Edward 1 of England; a successful ploy that made the archers of England feared throughout Europe.

[287] 1,000 feet, over 300m.

[288] Mina is a Babylonian measure of weight used by Heroditus in this context. 5 mina = 1.7kg

[289] 2 mina = 0.68kg

[290] Information from the historian Heroditus' in his book on the history of Egypt Book 2 Euterp.

[291] Exodus 9 v 31 barley and flax was followed by wheat and spelt

[292] Philistines

[293] Crete

[294] King of Naharin

[295] Capital of Naharin

CHAPTER 54

AARON / AMENEMHAT

IT WAS YEARS NOW SINCE Amenemhat had left his foundry in the small town south of Waset, in the care of his half-brother Pairy, and moved north to Avaris. As an experienced metal worker, he had found ample use for his skills, here, where the Northern Army was based. Here the need for well-made weapons was without measure or end.

Amenemhat had long wanted to return to the north, to where he was born. As a Habiri forced to live as an Egyptian in the south, he had longed to find the free Habiri community that had grown up in Avaris in the last 30 years. A thing unknown in the south. He found the community - they remembered his family - and welcomed him as one of their own. Here he could throw off the Egyptian identity that had controlled his life. He could even return to his childhood name, Aaron, the name taken from him when his family was forced to move south during his childhood and live as Egyptians.

What a stranger turn of events it was that had led to this exile in the south. The whim of a child, the royal princess Hatshepsut, who at only 10 years old had chanced upon his infant brother and determined to keep him. Her secluded life in the harem at Men-nepher kept the child hidden. The adoption remained unknown in the corridors of power, but as she grew and the child, who was her constant companion, grew with her, he became a vital part of her life, part of her heart. Then with the death of her parents, Hatshepsut gained power of her own. Her brother was made Pharaoh and she, the strong-willed Hatshepsut, became his Great Royal Wife*, the highest woman in the land. Now nothing could part her from her adopted son who was believed by all, except Hatshepsut's nurse, Sitre, to be the child of a royal liaison in the harem. But no questions were asked, and no objections raised to his high position in the royal house. All connection with the child's heritage was long since broken. His Habiri family, Aaron with them, had been forced to disappear and live far to the south so that no knowledge of his slave heritage would ever be discovered.

Aaron's family were given the life and identity of Egyptians, far away from the child that was to be raised as the son of the Pharaoh's daughter. But the turns of fate can never be foreseen, and Aaron had rediscovered his brother in adult life, linking this prince of Egypt with the infant brother he had lost. When Senenmut discovered the truth, he refused to be known any longer as Hatshepsut's son, shattering all her ambitions to make him Pharaoh. But all that was past. Hatshepsut was long dead, and his brother, known now to be Habiri, had been forced to flee the country long years ago.

Aaron had found more than a community and acceptance among the Habiri in Avaris. Among them he had found a wife, who over the last 20 years had given him four sons, his most precious possession. Life was good for him, in the free Habiri community in Avaris. But always at the back of his mind was the horror endured by his enslaved people. Aaron and his family could eat well. He could educate his sons. For himself, he lacked nothing, but could do nothing to help the slaves.

The evening was cooling after a hot day. Aaron and his wife had eaten and were heading for their rest. The window shutters of their small house had been opened as soon as the heat of the day had passed, allowing the rooms to cool a little. And they could enjoy the night breeze in safety as Aaron had added bars at the windows of his modest house. Avaris was a thriving town, but lawless elements remained, who vented their spleen on those on the edge of society. Those without recourse to law. The Habiri community. So this community suffered night raids more than other quarters of the town.

Aaron stretched himself on his sleeping mat and closed his eyes. He had worked a full day and was soon asleep oblivious of all around him. He rarely dreamed. Only when fear encroached on his mind, did he dream. Dark dreams that did not resolve themselves when he woke. Tonight he dreamed again, but his dream was different. Tonight his dream was such as he had never had.

More a vision than a dream. He knew where he was. He knew he was in his house lying on his sleeping mat. But before him stood a man. A being, the like of which he had never seen. It could not be a man. Aaron was transfixed, terrified by this presence. But his mind was alert seizing every word as it was spoken. Words which he knew were pure truth.

"Your brother Moshe lives. He is living in the land of Midian. You are commanded to go to him and help him in the great work he must do."

CHAPTER 55

MIDIAN

MOSHE FOUND THAT HE ADJUSTED easily, living away from the settlement of Maqna, out in the wild lands to the south, shepherding his father-in-law's sheep. He had come to these mountains for refuge, because after 40 years of searching, Egypt had finally tracked him down to his hiding place in Midian. Soldiers had come to the village and even followed him south until the terrain defeated them. So he must hide in this trackless wilderness with its confusion of mountains and valleys. And the mountains here were true giants, with dry valleys between them. Only safe for a shepherd who knew the terrain and who had been shown where to find the wells. Wells dug by previous generations of shepherds who knew of the extraordinary gift of water lying in great abundance in the rocks beneath their feet[296]. Hobab, his brother-in-law had been his teacher. Hobab, who had been born and raised here and knew the mountains as other men knew their familiar streets and dwelling places.

Moshe's days were full, working always to keep the sheep fed and safe. Moving from valley to valley as they devoured the green things that sprouted from the earth. Then move on. Finding another well from which to draw the sweet water from deep in the rocks below. He found enough food for himself also, taking game with his bow almost every day. Ibex mainly, and wild goats. He had killed a young lion once and jackals often, when they came to take a sheep, as an easy meal. Their skins now served to keep him warm, as the nights grew colder.

But how long should he stay out here in the wilds among these awe-inspiring monoliths? Some showed black at their peaks where fire sometimes burned. Times when the mountains themselves stirred and woke from their sleep, shaking the ground around them. Then the village people to the north could see the red glow at night at the mountain's top. A mountain on fire, alive and glowing, like a huge campfire. But so far during his sojourn, the mountains had been at peace.

But the question kept returning. When would it be safe to return? As a shepherd he knew he should return before the season's lambs were born. The ewes were growing in girth and would bear again in a few months time. He should be back in the settlement by then. At lambing time, the work was too much for one man, and the young were vulnerable out in these wilds.

Evening was drawing in as once more he pondered this question. The sheep were moving instinctively towards the base of the cliff where a shallow cave had been hollowed out by the wind. He had lit a fire and started roasting the young Ibex he had shot that morning. He had gutted and skinned it earlier, and drained and buried the blood. The smell of blood would attract predators. The Ibex would take time to cook, and he was hungry, but he must wait. He cast an eye over the scrub land around him. There were no stragglers to bring in. But as his gaze moved back towards the fire, his eye was caught by another glow a short distance from the cave. There, a stout bush grew. The sheep had been cropping its lower branches earlier in the day but now it seemed to be ablaze. It disturbed him. He knew that sometimes the fierce heat of the sun would cause dry sticks to spontaneously catch fire, but it had not been a hot day, and this tree was not dead but green. Could the fire spread after consuming the bush? He wanted to attend to his meal and rest, but he must watch this fire. He may need to move the sheep if it spread.

Leaving his meal, Moshe walked towards the bush to see it more clearly. The fire was not spreading but nor was it dying down. Why did it continue to burn? Surely its branches and leaves should be consumed by now. He moved forward again to get a closer look when suddenly a voice rang out in the silence around him!

"Moshe, take off your shoes. You are standing on holy ground." [297]

Moshe stopped, rooted to the spot, then as if in a dream removed his sandals, transfixed by the voice and the flames. But the voice continued.

"I am the God of your fathers, the God of Abraham, the God of Isaac, the God of Jacob."

At this Moshe hid his face in his hands. He was terrified to look at God! But the voice continued!

"I have seen the misery of my people in Egypt, their slave drivers, and their suffering. I have come down to rescue them. To bring them out into a good and spacious land. A land flowing with milk and honey. The land where the Canaanites live."

There was a pause as Moshe tried to grapple with what was happening. But the voice continued with terrifying words.

"So now – go! I am sending you to Pharaoh, to bring my Habiri people out of Egypt."

Panic was rising in Moshe's mind! This was impossible. And without thinking he replied to the disembodied voice.

"Who am I to go to Pharaoh! How can I bring your people out of Egypt!"

But with great calm the voice continued.

"I will be with you. And this will be a sign for you that it is I who has sent you. When you bring the people out of Egypt, you will bring them to worship on this mountain." [298]

Moshe tried again to counter the commanding voice.

"But who do I say sent me? What is your name?

With calm certainty, the voice continued.

"I Am who I Am. This is what you must say to the people. 'I AM' has sent me. The God of Abraham, the God of Isaac, the God of Jacob. This is my name for ever."

And still the voice continued!

"Go, assemble the elders of the Habiri and say to them – 'The Lord, the God of your fathers appeared to me and said, 'I have seen what has been done to you in Egypt and I have promised to bring you up, out of your misery, into the land of the Canaanites. A land flowing with milk and honey.' The elders will listen to you. Then you and they must go to Pharaoh. You will say to Pharaoh,

"Our God, the God of the Habiri has met with us. Allow us to take a three-day journey into the desert to sacrifice to Him."

There was a pause, then the voice continued.

"I know that Pharaoh will not let you go unless I compel him. So I will stretch out my hand and strike the Egyptians with wonders that I will perform among them. After that he will let you go. And I will make the Egyptians favourable towards you so you will not go empty handed. Every woman will ask for gold and silver and jewels from those for whom she has worked. The things they are given must be hung around their children's necks so they will be carried out of Egypt. In this way you will plunder the Egyptians and receive payment for your labour."

Moshe heard all the words spoken to him, but what could he do with these commands! How could he speak to the people?

"They will not believe me," he pleaded.

But the voice would not accept his reply.

"What is that thing you have in your hand?"

Moshe looked at his hand. He was holding a shepherd's staff.

"Throw it on the ground," came the command.

Moshe threw it down, and before his eyes it became a snake. At that he ran! But the voice called him back.

"Reach out and pick it up by the tail."

Warily Moshe did so, and immediately it was his familiar staff again.

"Do this and they will believe you," said the voice. "But if they do not believe you, take some water from the River[299] and pour it out on the ground. It will become blood."

But Moshe knew he could not go to Egypt. He could not be God's mouthpiece to Pharaoh. He must be excused this impossible task.

"O Lord I have never been eloquent. I am not a good speaker," he pleaded.

But the voice would not accept his words.

"Who gave man his mouth? Who makes him able to speak? Is it not I?"

"Now go! I will help you speak, and teach you what to say."

But Moshe knew he could not carry out this task.

"Oh Lord. Please send someone else!"

Now the tone of the voice changed to anger.

"What about your brother Aaron the Levite. He can speak well. And he is already on his way to meet you. He will be overjoyed to see you. You wil speak to Aaron, the words I give you and Aaron will speak for you to the people and to Pharaoh. But take your staff with you to show my signs."

Suddenly the voice was gone! The bush was no longer ablaze. But in Moshe's heart a new fire had been kindled. For 40 years he had carried the burden of his people in his heart, weighed down with the knowledge of his own impotence to help them. Now hope rose within him. If YHWH[300] himself had commissioned him to this work, he would do it or die trying. On every level it was impossible, but if there was a chance. If all it would cost was his life, he would gladly give it. His time in Midian had not been wasted. He had learned the ways of the wilderness. He had discovered the faith of his fathers. A faith and a God who promised the impossible and had the power to perform it.

Now he would return to the village, soldiers or not. If YHWH wanted him to stand before Pharaoh, he need not fear soldiers. He must speak to Jethro and ask his permission to leave and for his blessing. His own daughters were married. They were part of the Midianite world, but he would take his wife and sons with him.

---

[296] There are, to this day, huge aquifers of fresh water stored in the rocks under the deserts of Saudi Arabia and Jordan. The city of Aqaba is dependent on this water to supply the city's water.

[297] Book of Exodus chapter 3 covers this story.

[298] NOTE; Moshe is in Midian, which is on the east bank of the Gulf of Aqaba, in present day Saudi Arabia

[299] The Nile was just referred to as 'the River'

[300] YWH was the short form of name 'Yahweh' or 'Jehovah', the name of the Habiri God and is held sacred.

All modern denominations of Judaism teach that the four letter name of God YHWH, is forbidden to be uttered except by the High Priest in the Temple. Since the Temple in Jerusalem no longer exists, this name is never said in religious rituals by Jews. Orthodox and Conservative Jews never pronounce it for any reason.

CHAPTER 56

JOURNEY TO EGYPT

LEADING HIS FLOCK, MOSHE SET out as dawn was breaking. The valley in which they had passed the night ran east west, and as Ra rose above the eastern horizon, shafts of light pierced the silent land casting it into sharp contrasts of brilliance and shadow. They moved west, down through the valley, moving slowly as the sheep cropped the fresh grass along the way. By noon they had reached another of the desert wells and Moshe drew water for the animals and himself. Here they rested in the scant shade as Ra reached his zenith and started to sink towards the west. They moved on, continuing west, finally reaching the safety of the shepherds' corral on the coastal path as dusk settled over the mountains. The place was deserted, but firewood lay stacked ready for use beside the ashes of the last fire. Here they would spend the night and tomorrow they would return to Maqna.

Moshe hardly thought of the soldiers. YHWH had given him a commission and would take charge of the soldiers. But he would not court trouble. When he left Midian to return to Egypt, he would not take the northern route through Ezion Geber. He would return this way, cross this gulf of water by boat, then follow the camel trail across the Mafkat. But his first duty was to speak to Jethro.

The dust thrown up by the hurrying flock as they neared their familiar home, attracted the attention of the villagers and Moshe was treated to an excited welcome on arrival. Hobab, his brother-in-law was delighted to see the size and health of the flock. Moshe had been his pupil. He had paid close attention to the training Hobab had given him. And here was the evidence. He was now a skilled shepherd. Even Zipporah offered him her smiles and his daughters welcomed him warmly. His boys, Gershon and Eliezer were full of boisterous excitement. The behaviour of children at the sudden return of the father they loved.

Moshe knew his news would be unwelcome, and delayed speaking of it until he was alone with Jethro.

"I have news for you, Sir, that will be unwelcome I fear," he said as they sat alone after eating their meal together. Jethro was silent, watching this man who had become a true son to him. But Moshe continued.

"You taught me of your God, and I have made him my God. But I never imagined that he would speak to me. That he would commission me to help his people."

Slowly a smile spread over the face of the old man.

"I have long expected it," he said. "YHWH has been training you for a great work. Your life has been uniquely planned to fit you for this enormous task."

"Enormous, or seeming impossible it may be, but I must attempt it or die trying."

"It would be impossible. But with YHWH it will be possible. He has done the impossible in the past and can do it again," said Jethro and paused. There was more he must say. There was news from Egypt which Moshe would not have heard.

"While you have been absent news has come from Egypt about this new Pharaoh, the son of Tutmose. He is building the army to be even greater than in his father's time. The news is that he is adding to the workload of the slaves making their lives unbearable. They have tolerated years of slavery, accepting their lot. But it has become unbearable. Now they may listen to you as their only hope."

Moshe listened. But he needed more than news from Jethro. He needed his approval.

"So I go with your blessing Sir?"

"You go with my blessing," said the old man smiling.

"And taking your daughter and grandsons with me?"

"You take them with my blessing."

But now the old man was silent. His weather worn face was deep in thought. Something troubled him, and Moshe read it in his face.

"Something concerns you Sir?" he asked.

Jethro hesitated.

"I fear there is something you must do that will anger my daughter," said the old man.

Moshe was silent. He too knew of this thing. And until it was done, he remained unfit to lead the people YHWH had chosen. He had failed to keep the sacred covenant. He had failed to circumcise his sons.

"I will speak with Zipporah," said Moshe quietly. "Perhaps she will think again and allow our sons to be circumcised."

But Zipporah's mind was unchanged. Her sons were now part grown. This barbaric ritual was cruel enough when performed at birth, but her boys were older and would suffer conscious shock and pain if it were done now. No! Her sons would never be subjected to this mutilation. And so it remained.

But the news that Moshe and his family were leaving, brought sadness to the village. Families never left their community. And this man had been a blessing to them. But with Jethro's leadership it was accepted, and the little family, taking with them just one donkey, prepared to leave.

They would travel light. Zipporah had a woman's mind for detail and prepared well for the journey. Moshe could leave the preparations to her. He would find game for food, but Zipporah brought flour and oil to make flat bread until they reached the next human settlement. He saddled the donkey for his wife and taking his staff they set out. The boys ran on ahead down the coastal path. This was an adventure. Going to Egypt! The centre of the world.

As dusk settled over the landscape, they chose a campsite. A cold wind was blowing from the north, but an outcrop of rocks would protect them. Moshe set about collecting wood and Zipporah started a fire and quickly made bread. She had brought a goats' cheese also so to the hungry boys it seemed like a feast. They ate, then the tired children settled in the ley of the rocks beside the fire to sleep. It was cold, and Moshe must part with his cloak for his boys' comfort Soon they slept while their parents added wood to the dying fire.

Suddenly in the darkness, Moshe and Zipporah became aware of a presence. Their first thought was danger – an animal – a loin or jackal. Moshe grasped a lighted faggot from the fire to drive it away, but the presence was silent, unmoving. The fire blazed up with warm light, but the stranger had a light of his own. An unearthly light. Then a voice! Like the voice Moshe had heard before, when the bush blazed without burning. But this time the words brought more than fear. They were a sentence of death.

"You have shown yourself unfit for the work you were given."

"You have broken the covenant."

You will die here."

Suddenly despite the cold Moshe could feel himself burning with fever. He could feel the sweat breaking out all over his body. His pulse pounded in his head drowning all thought. He lay back and closed his eyes as the agony of the fever took over his mind.

For a moment Zipporah watched him. She little cared for his suffering. But to be a widow was a fate no woman would want. And she knew the reason for this death sentence. She leapt to her feet and grabbed at the saddlebag, shouting at her husband.

"A husband! Is that what you are? A husband of blood!" [301]

But Moshe did not respond. Vaguely he was aware of her movements as she seized her sleeping sons. With the knife in her hand, she slashed at Gershon's foreskin. The boy was hardly awake when it was done, and she had turned to his brother to complete her gory task.

Taking the foreskins, she held them up, shouting at the watching spirit, then threw them at her husband's prostrate form.

"It is done!"

"Your covenant stands!"

Now all was silent except for the whimpering of the children. The wind had dropped and the eery presence had gone with it. Zipporah stood over her husband as he stirred as if out of a dream.

"I will travel no further with you. Husband of blood! I want no part in you or your God."

Dawn was breaking as Zipporah roused herself. She built up the fire, heated water and warmed bread which she gave to her sons. They had slept soundly and with bread in their bellies, hardly remembered the ordeal of the previous night. Moshe watched his wife as she gathered together her few belongings. He did not need her to repeat her words. Her intention was clear. She would return to her father, taking their sons with her. He must go forward alone.

---

[301] Book of Exodus 4 v 24

CHAPTER 57

MOSHE FINDS HIS BROTHER

MOSHE SET OUT ALONG THE familiar path following the coastline that ran south from Maqna. He knew the path well. He had taken the sheep this way many times, but never alone. Further along after a few hours walking, it would fork, the left branch leading to the shepherds' corral and the mountains beyond, the other negotiating a rough descent down to the beach. It was still early. Ra had just burst above the mountains to his left. There would be a few hours before the heat became intense, forcing him to find shelter. He covered the ground quickly. Without the flock he could move at speed. Well before noon he reached the fork and took the less trodden track leading down to the beach. Here there was shelter from Ra's glare, and the walk was pleasant. Physically it was no challenge for him. Despite his eighty years, his active life gave him the agility of a much younger man.

As he descended the path Moshe could see the features of the cove below, with its covering of sand, suitable for beaching boats. This was the place to wait. Above the beach a bank of trees had taken root, away from the salt water but benefiting from the runoff of infrequent rain from the steep hillside and mountains above. It was a place to rest. A place to wait for a boat to cross over from the other side. Noon was approaching and he had walked all morning. He settled himself in the secluded shade and closed his eyes. Still in his mind was the scene of the previous night. Would he ever see his wife and sons again? Or Jethro who had been like a father to him? He dozed, and his thoughts returned to Egypt and his childhood. Forty years had passed since he had fled that land which he had ruled in all but name, during Hatshepsut's reign. Would there be anyone who still knew him? His thoughts turned to Nepherure. What had become of her? But he must put these thoughts out of his mind. He was a different man from the one she had loved. And he was returning to champion the slaves, not to take up his old life.

Moshe opened his eyes. The silence had been broken by voices. He had slept deeply and could not at first remember where he was. But the reflection of moving light on the rippling water, reminded him. A boat was approaching with two men: the boatman and one passenger. He thought it odd that a passenger would cross to this wild land alone. And the man was old. His beard was white, but he was dressed as a working man, with a grey robe and a Kefir[302] protecting his head from the fierce heat. Moshe waited. The small craft came on, heading for the cove. As the water grew shallow the boatman shipped his oars and plunged into the sea to pull his boat ashore. They were now only a few paces away, and in the silence of the deserted beach, Moshe could hear their short exchange as the boatman took his fee. It was a long time since Moshe had heard the Egyptian tongue spoken. But even in that short exchange, he recognised more than the words. He recognised the voice! It was the voice of his brother, Amenemhat.

Now he rose from his resting place. Hadn't YHWH told him that his brother would come to meet him? Had he indeed come? In his shock and surprise Moshe was oblivious of the departing boatman, and the boat for which he had been waiting. His whole attention was on this new arrival. He stepped forward, fixing his eyes on the familiar face, and spoke his name.

"Amenemhat!" It is you? he asked, knowing beforehand the answer. His brother turned. Each had come in search of the other and their search was over.

IT WAS THE ACT OF finding his brother, sitting with him, and speaking the language of Egypt that finally turned Moshe's mind towards the future and his new task. He was leaving Midian and everything that had been his life for the past 40 years. Midian had given him a very different training from that of Egypt. He had discovered his true history and his God. He had learned the ways of the desert and living in tents. Now he was returning, but not to the Egypt he had known. His adoptive mother, Hatshepsut, was long dead

Tutmose and his righthand man, Menkheperreseneb, the High Priest of Amun who had hounded him from Egypt were also dead. Tutmose's son Amenhotep, whom he himself had never known, now ruled Egypt, making his capital not at Waset but in the north. Moshe had heard of the destruction wrought at Waset. That beautiful city that had been his home, had been ravaged then abandoned by this new pharaoh.[303] But Moshe would not see the carnage. He would remain in the north, where the slaves were. Where Amenhotep now ruled from his capital city, Avaris.

Unlike his father, Amenhotep intended to make Avaris fully his capital. To spend all his time there, when not on campaign. The large military base for the Northern Army was there with easy access to Canaan and the north. The military road, the Horus Road, which ran from the first fortress at Tharu, lay just northeast of Avaris. From Tharu, all along the Horus Road, lay a line of fortresses, each a day's march from the last, where his army could be reprovisioned. All the way to the El Arish River at the border. From there, crossing into Canaan, the wide coast road, suitable for marching troops and chariots, ran on to Sharuhen[304], Egypt's first military base in Canaan, then Gaza, reached from Tharu in ten days.

All the king's energy was focused on war and the Hebrew slaves were a vital part of his war machine, even more than they had been for his father Tutmose. And this was the challenge facing these two old men. Their commission to bring the sons of Israel out of slavery flew in the face of Amenhotep's ambitions. To free the slaves would bring an end to his dreams of glory. His dreams of conquering Naharin. Of finishing the work never fully completed by his father. To extend Egypt's Empire to the Euphrates River. Taking full control of all Syria as the great pharaohs of previous generations had taken control of Kush and Nubia. What would Egypt have been without the resources of Nubia and Kush? The wealth of those nations had filled Egypt's coffers enabling her to build huge temples to the glory of the gods. Who or what could withstand her if she now gained full control of the rich lands of Canaan and Syria? But Moshe knew he must set these thoughts out of his mind. His instructions were simple. He was not coming to negotiate but to give YHWH's commands to this proud young pharaoh.

THE INTERVENING YEARS SINCE THEY had last met, had brought great changes to the lives of the two men. Moshe, as Senenmut, had ruled Egypt under his mother Hatshepsut, but had long since set aside that famous name and become a humble shepherd. Amenemhat had risen in the world. From the back street foundry in the small town south of Waset, he had moved to Avaris and become a master chariot builder. An expert in metal work.[305] He had recovered his true identity as a member of the free Habiri community, even returning to his childhood name of Aaron. But the thing that brought them together, was a desperate longing to help their downtrodden people. YHWH had read their hearts and commissioned them both for this seeming impossible task.

It could be many days before another boat would cross this body of water separating Moshe and Aaron from the vast beach and the mountain passes of the Mafkat opposite. But there were fishermen working off the coast of Midian, who after a successful catch, would row the one schoenus[306] across to the far side to sell their fish. The huge beach opposite and the mountain passes it protected, were a significant entry point into Egypt and must be continually guarded. For this purpose, a troop of soldiers were billeted there in a substantial fortress, the 'Migdol,' and provided a ready market for the catch. They were always glad to exchange fresh fish for a sack of grain, the mainstay of their rations, to bring variety to their monotonous diet. Thus, the brothers had only a short time to wait for their crossing.

As the small craft moved out into deep water, Moshe looked back at the looming presence of the great mountain of Sinai, the place of his encounter with YHWH, receding away from them. It was a sobering sight. But with the work of two fishermen at their oars, in less than three hours, Moshe had returned to Egypt after an exile of 40 years.

They reached the beach opposite and now the mountains of the Mafkat loomed overhead. Centuries of wind and rain had cut deep wadies between these monoliths, providing passes between them, and moving vast quantities of debris to form a delta of sand reaching far out into the sea. This beach and the wadies beyond, would lead them northwest to Egypt itself. But stepping ashore on that beach brought back an appalling memory to Moshe. The scene of carnage that he had witnessed there as an adolescent on his first foray with the army. Shocking scenes. Soldiers wiping out an entire Shasu tribe[307] who had made themselves a nuisance. Who had fallen foul of Egypt's limited tolerance of other races she despised.

For the two old men crossing into Egypt's territory, there was a risk that the soldiers in the fort would demand to know their business. But either their age and simplicity of dress, or the fact that they were only two in number, attracted no attention from the guards.

The deep narrow wadis that cut through the mountains, were used continually by traders. Camel and mule trains frequented these routes, carrying goods to and from Egypt. Because of these frequent travellers, a Caravanserai had been built at the entrance to the narrow pass to provided rest and safety to travellers. It was a welcome place for the two men to spend the night. Here they would wait for a mule train to carry them through these wild mountains. Their host furnished them with a modest room. Simple straw pallets covered with woven rugs and colourful cushions would be their bed. Bread and beer with a slab of salted goats' cheese was also provided for a small fee.

They talked long into the night in the privacy of their room. Aaron had much to tell. Egypt was alive with the fear of Moshe's return. Would he come to seize control? Would the slaves rise to support him? His great age, far greater than the average Egyptian, added to the mystery surrounding him. Was he a god? He had trained as a priest of Ra, the highest education in the land and as such was imbued with the wisdom of the gods. Tutmose's spies had searched but failed to find him. Now Tutmose was dead while Moshe himself still lived. But he had no wish for fame. He knew the instructions YHWH had given him.

"We are commanded to speak to Pharaoh," he said. "To tell him to let our people go," he told his brother.

"So you will go to the court at Avaris?" Aaron asked. "The Pharaoh is away at war," he added. "He left in the spring, travelling overland. He longs to prove himself as great a general as his father."

"When he hears of my coming, he will return," said Moshe. When we reach the free Hebrew community the news will spread."

Aaron was astonished at his brother's calm but said nothing as Moshe continued.

"I will tell pharaoh to let the slaves go into the wilderness to worship," he paused. "This he will understand but he will not obey," he added.

They had spent but one day at the caravanserai when a mule train arrived from the south carrying woven textiles and spices. It was a modest affair and would only stay overnight, then move on. But it had beasts enough to hire out to the two travellers, and shortly after sunrise the following day, they entered the labyrinth of wadis that would lead to the first settlement at Etham. The mountains soared above them, casting deep shadows and giving protection from the heat of Ra. On the third day they reached the settlement at Etham. Moshe remembered it well. It was larger now and had also gained a Caravanserai. They stayed one night only as the muleteers were keen to move on and despite the tiredness of the animals, set off the following day. The fort of Tharu, within the borders of Egypt would be their next stop.

As each day brought him nearer to Egypt, Moshe felt its looming power oppressing his mind. This was not the Egypt he had known. The Egypt he had known under Hatshepsut was far from perfect, but she had not added to its cruelty. It had been cruel, even then. But since he had fled, all through Tutmose's years, Egypt had grown in power and cruelty towards her slaves. Now this proud young pharaoh was creating a brutal regime.

On the third day out of Etham, as noon passed and the day cooled, the huge bulk of the Tharu fortress loomed into view. There was power in its physical presence. Huge double walls, towering upwards, enclosing an area the size of a substantial town,[308] and controlled the crossing over a deep canal which ran north south joining the Great Sea[309] to the north, with the Red Sea to the south. This canal formed the border into Egypt proper, separating it from the Mafkat which it had controlled for millennia but did not acknowledge as fully Egypt. Soldiers checked each trader's right of entry, along with his men and his goods and fees were levied. As a trader himself, Aaron had the necessary documents, and with payment of the required fees, the two men were admitted. The fortress housed 1,000 solders, and as they entered the open courtyard inside its inner wall, to their right they saw huge grain silos ranged along the northern wall. Food for this army of men.[310] Convicts were working around the silos, men whose noses had been cut from their faces. But this punishment of deformity and banishment to Tharu was familiar to Moshe and Aaron. Egypt was cruel to those who broke the law.

Away from the soldiers' quarters, an area was set aside for merchants, wh paid a fee for the safety offered by the fort. To this area the muleteer led his beasts. He had fulfilled his bargain with the travellers and took his payment. They would travel on without him from here but would take time while here to plan their onward journey.

As Ra moved towards the west, Moshe took his brother up to the battlements. From here the vast expanse of the delta spread out before them as far as the eye could see. It was late in the season of inundation, but channels of water still spread from the main 'arteries' of the river, reflecting the glow of the setting sun and shining like burnished bronze. Small settlements huddled on the higher ground, marooned until the water subsided, and in the far distance, built on higher ground they could make out the city of Avaris above the flood plain. Central to it all was the palace where they would meet the young pharaoh when he returned from war. Surrounding the high ground which formed the centre of Avaris, the river, when in flood, divided into many channels, separating other areas of high ground from the central island. Here small satellite settlements lay marooned until the water fell. One of these was the free Habiri community, where Aaron had his foundry and his family home. This was their next destination. But the free Habiri community was not the focus of their thoughts at this moment. Looking north of Avaris, where the huge store cities of Ramesses and Pithom lay, they thought of their enslaved people. The store cites were being extended again, to hold yet more grain and support a bigger army. And here the slaves worked while the fields, the place of their usual labours, remained flooded.

---

[302] An Arab style head dress

[303] Waset was described many years later by Heriodius as the 12 gated Thebes. A magnificent city.

[304] Article 'Architecture of Imperialism'; Ellen Morris

[305] Aaron must have understood metal working as he later fashioned the golden calf.

[306] One Shonus, an Ancient Egyptian measurement, of distance of about 10.5km

[307] Nomads who wandered the Mafkat with their herds.

[308] The fortress covered more than 120,000 sq m

[309] The Mediterranean

[310] Article 'Architecture of Imperialism'; Ellen Morris

CHAPTER 58

MOSHE AND AARON MEET THE HABIRI LEADERS

THE NEXT STEP IN THEIR plan must be to meet the leaders of the Habiri slaves living near Ramesses, north of Avaris. Aaron, as part of the free community knew the names of the Habiri foremen and where they lived. He had visited them before. But as no branch of the river flowed between Tharu and Avaris, they must continue their journey by mule. And as it was as cheap to buy mules, as to hire them as part of a mule train, and as the roads within Egypt were safer than outside her borders, it seemed a good economy. Besides, they had much to discuss and could only do so with privacy, as they travelled alone.

Setting off before sunrise, they hoped to rest through the fierce heat of noon and reach Avaris at twilight. The road from Tharu to Avaris was raised above the level of the surrounding flood plain and bordered with large trees on either side providing welcome shade. Troops of soldiers and occasionally cohorts of charioteers overtook them, leaving them in a cloud of dust, but there was many a laden donkey and cart which they overtook on their way. As far as the eye could see, the cultivated land lay in every direction. But the season of inundation was passing. The fields had drunk in the flood water which was now receding as the river fell. Soon the fields would be sown again, repeating the never-ending cycle of inundation, growth and harvest.

After a brief rest at noon they set out again, and before nightfall, had reached the lanes and houses by the river where Aaron had his foundry and family home. Moshe felt strange in this Habiri community. But he was warmly welcomed and found himself harbouring feeling of nostalgia for a life he had never known. But clear in his mind came the thought that the families in this pleasant community, along with every slave family, would be leaving their homes and Egypt itself, when the day for departure arrived.

The next evening, they set out on a short boat ride which would take them upstream to the place from which they could continue on foot to the store cities. Even from a distance, Moshe recognised the store city of Ramesses, a place seared on his memory. The place that had fixed his destiny. Where he had seen for the first time the pointless cruelty of an Egyptian slave master against a slave, an old man beaten almost to death. It was one of many needless cruelties but had awoken in him such a red fury that he had murdered the Egyptian perpetrator. He forced his mind to turn from the memory. They would deal with no Egyptians here today in the Habiri settlement outside Ramesses. Here there were only slaves, and the families that shared their hovels. The vision shocked him. And yet was not this his own place of origin? His own place of birth? The place from which his mother had taken him, in a fragile basket, to hide him among the river reeds. To keep him from harm. The place where Hatshepsut had found him? But there was no time to think of the past. They must think of the future. They must rouse the hopes of these exhausted men enough to believe that change could come. That there would be an end to their torment.

As the short twilight faded into night, a group of men gathered around them. The tribal leaders and the men appointed by the Egyptian taskmasters to implement their orders. All had worked from sunrise until noon to get the bulk of their work done before the real heat of the day began. Then after a short break, had worked until twilight. While the river was high and the fields flooded as at present, the men were making bricks. The king wanted space for more grain to be stored. The more grain the Habiri grew and stored, the greater the number of Egyptian peasant farmers who could be released to train as soldiers. From all over Egypt they came. Young men glad to escape the drudgery of farming. Excited to be taken into the king's army. To go north. To see Canaan and Syria. To fight and maybe acquire a slave of their own.

So while the river was high, the Habiri made bricks. Millions of them. A mix of wet mud and a little straw, pressed into wooden moulds, then set out to dry in the sun. Row after row of them, laid out in a square for easy counting.

In the 12 hours of daylight, with a short break at noon, every man must make 500 bricks each day. Twenty rows of twenty-five bricks. Each tribal leader was responsible to know the total number for his tribe and used young men without families to assist in counting them. Finally, one tribal leader, at present it was Nahshon, tribal leader of Judah, gathered the grand total and reported to the Egyptians.

All knew Aaron, but the great Senenmut was legendary. They watched him in silence but without hope. When all the elders were gathered, and finally Nahshon and his assistant Joshua joined them, Aaron addressed the company.

"Brothers the time has come for Israel to take back her freedom," he said.

"YHWH has spoken to my brother Moshe and commanded us to speak to you," he paused.

All eyes were fixed on him.

"YHWH has spoken. He has seen what you suffer. He has heard your cries because of your taskmasters.[311] He has sent us to deliver you out of the hand of the Egyptians. To bring you to a good and large land. A land flowing with milk and honey. The land of the Canaanites, The Hittites, the Amorites, the Perizzites, the Girgashites, the Hivites and the Jebusites. The land he promised to your forefathers, Abraham, Isaac and Jacob."

Aaron watched as the people remained silent in disbelief. These men had been so crushed that they could no longer raise their thoughts to freedom. In their minds there could be no freedom. Even the great Senenmut could not give them freedom. Hadn't he himself been forced to flee Egypt? The gods and Pharaohs of Egypt were too powerful for any man. They crushed people wherever they chose. There would be no escape. What power did Aaron and Senenmut have but words?

Perceiving their thoughts Moshe instructed his brother to perform the sign that God had commanded them. Raising his staff Aaron threw it on the ground and immediately, before their eyes it became a cobra, which reared up ready to strike! As the men ran from it in shock, Aaron seized it by the tail and immediately it was his staff again. The men looked on in silent astonishment They needed no more convincing. With words of hope on their lips they fell on their knees and worshipped the name of YHWH who had come to rescue them.

Now the news of Moshe's return exploded across the city. The Egyptians were in uproar. The king must be told. Fast horses and riders were despatched to inform Amenhotep who was still at Gaza consulting with the Lords of the Philistines. The messengers arrived and were brought before the king.

"My Lord, the man Senenmut has returned! He is even using the name Hatshepsut gave him, calling himself her son, 'Moshe' again."

Amenhotep stood rooted to the ground with shock, staring at the messenger. He had left Egypt open with no army to defend her against an uprising of the slaves! Suddenly all thoughts of crushing the north were forgotten. He must return at once, taking the army with him, to combat this threat looming over Egypt. He could only hope he would be in time! Everything balanced on a knife edge. Speed was essential to save his dynasty from the claims of Hatshepsut's line. He had wiped out the physical record of her reign, but it lived on still, in the form of her adopted son Senenmut. And Senenmut himself was still held in high esteem in the minds of all Egyptians.[312]

"Tell the generals to ready their troops," he said. "We leave tomorrow at dawn."

Fear and astonishment swept through the camp. The generals themselves were thrown into confusion. But no one dared question the king's decision. There was little chance for sleep that night as the army prepared for departure at dawn. They would reach Sharuhen by nightfall. But the king's mind had two concerns. Looming large was the arrival of Moshe. But to leave Gaza was to leave Canaan unguarded. The Philistines were still arriving in large numbers. He must leave a sizable garrison of infantry at Gaza with instructions to contain the Philistines to the towns and villages of the coast. They must not be allowed to gain control of the coastal highway running north, essential for use by Egypt's army going north, and for control of the trade routes.

In ten days Amenhotep and his army reached Tharu. Here he left the remaining infantry troops. They could not march at the speed of the chariots, but they were left on high alert. They may be needed as reinforcements in either Avaris or Gaza. Then he took his bodyguard of charioteers 600 strong, and all the other chariots of the northern army and set out for Avaris. He must make a show of strength on reaching the city.

They left Tharu at sunrise and reached Avaris before the heat of the day had settled over the city. The sight and splendour of the chariot stallions wearing their battle plumes; the sound of the chariots as they roared into Avaris; the colour and pomp of the Pharaoh himself driving his golden chariot drew everyone out on to the streets. All wanted to see the spectacle and welcome their king to save them from the slaves and the old prophet who had come to champion them. But when he arrived in all his pomp at the palace, Amenhotep found his adversary was not there cowering with fear. Indeed, he was not there at all. Instead he had accepted the hospitality of the slaves, sharing their meagre repast and talking with them in their pathetic surroundings, the hovels they called home.

---

[311] Exodus 3 v 7
[312] Exodus 11 v 3; Moshe was still held in high esteem among the Egyptians.

CHAPTER 59

MOSHE COMES TO THE PALACE

THE NEXT MORNING MOSHE AND Aaron set out at sunrise. They would travel by boat to one of the trading harbours in the central island of Avaris itself, above the flood plain. Moshe looked out across the landscape of the delta, this scene long since captured in his memory. So different from every other land he knew. Ruled by the river, which rose and fell regardless of human intervention. He remembered the palace, although it was much bigger now, built on a high platform well above the highest reach of the inundation, which every year surged through the landscape, removing anything in its path that was not on high ground. The deep gorges which held and largely confined the river further south, here divided into many channels that wove their way north. Indeed, each time the river returned, its great force could cut new channels, ignoring older ones which had served their time, becoming slowed with the debris of human life.

North of Avaris rose the high walls of the store cities Ramesses and Pithom, far larger now than he remembered. But new to his eyes was the great compound enclosing the army base, built as a fort, like the huge fortress of Buhen[313] on the border of Nubia, where two thousand troops and one thousand support staff could be housed.

They reached the palace and entered unmolested. There, waiting for them was the young king, seated on his throne raised on a dais above the court. On his right sat his firstborn son, his heir. There was no throne to his left. Amenhotep allowed no woman to hold the office of Great Royal Wife. He tolerated the high standing of his mother, Meryet, at court, but would raise no other woman to a position of power. He had heard enough of the folly of Hatshepsut ever to allow women to hold power.

Amenhotep watched in silence as the two elderly Habiri entered the audience chamber and approached the dais. Never before had men entered his presence without bowing and prostrating themselves before him. His eyes followed Senenmut, mesmerised. The man showed neither fear nor pride. He entered the chamber with no outward awareness of the fact that he stood before the most powerful king in the world. The two men came to a halt in front of the king. For all their age, they showed no sign of physical weakness. Senenmut carried a staff, but they walked without faltering, and came to stand straight and at ease before him. Amenhotep waited for Moshe to speak but it was his brother who addressed him.

"The Lord, the God of the Hebrews has sent us to you saying, '

'Israel is my firstborn son. Let my son go that he may worship me, or I will kill your firstborn son.'

Hardly waiting for pause, the pharaoh answered,

"Who is this Lord that I should heed him and let Israel go? I do not know this Lord and I will not let Israel go." [314]

At this, Aaron repeated the demand.

"The God of the Hebrews has revealed himself to us. Let us go three days journey into the wilderness to sacrifice to the Lord or he may do us harm."

But pharaoh would not listen. These men had no power. Why should he waste time with them? Fury rose in his mind.

"Moshe and Aaron, why are you taking the people away from their work? They are so numerous, yet you want them to stop working. Get them back to work!" he shouted.

In a rage, the king leapt to his feet and left the chamber with his son. Then calling his servants, he turned on them shouting,

"Those Habiri slaves are idle! Make them work harder! Do not provide them with straw to strengthen their bricks. Let them find their own straw, but on no account are they allowed to make fewer bricks! I want these store cities enlarged to hold more grain - now!

The king's words were told to the waiting elders. They were astonished an horrified. Until now, their task was hard. Now it was impossible. How could they fulfil their brick quota if days must be spent gathering straw? They tried but failed. And when they failed, they were brutally beaten. In desperation the leaders went to speak to Pharaoh.

"Great king, we are given an impossible task. How are we to do it? No straw is given to us. We must gather it ourselves, but still we must fulfil our quota of bricks!"

But no pity was to be found in this young king.

"You are lazy! That is why you ask to go into the wilderness to worship your God. You will not go, and you will be given no straw! Get back to work!"

Hearing this reply, all the hope that had revived in the hearts of the slaves, was lost. They had no fight left in them. They knew their doom was sealed.

"You have given pharaoh a weapon with which to kill us," they said to Moshe and Aaron as they turned away in despair, to return to their work.

But the story of the old prophet and the king spread far and wide throughout Egypt. No soldier had touched him! Did even pharaoh not dare to arrest him? The prophet had performed magic signs before the king, but the king's own magicians did the same with their dark powers. Who would win this trial of strength? But for Moshe himself, the pain he had added to the affliction of the slaves bore down on him. He could not return to the slave community. He could not face them after increasing their misery. Instead, he returned to Aaron's village, and spent the night out under the stars, pouring out his agony to YHWH.

"You sent me to rescue these people. I told you I could not do it. Now their situation is worse than before." Then into his agonised mind came a clear reply.

"Pharaoh was given a chance to change, but he would not. Now you will see what I will do to him until he is desperate enough to drive the people from Egypt. Until he sees that he and all the gods of Egypt can have no power against my will."

Then Moshe was given fresh instructions.

"Go to pharaoh tomorrow as he goes to the river to bathe. Take Aaron with you and take your shepherd's staff. I have made you like a god to pharaoh and

Aaron will speak as your prophet. Stand by the river where pharaoh goes to bathe. Strike the river in front of you and it will turn to blood. It will be undrinkable. All the fish will die, and it will stink. Now I will begin my assault on Egypt until Pharaoh will obey me."

---

[313] Most northerly of the huge fortresses along the Nile, this one at the 2nd cataract.
[314] EXODUS 5 from v 2

CHAPTER 60

NEPHERURE

EVEN IN THE SECLUSION OF Mi-wer, the Lady Nepherure heard the rumours that Senenmut still lived. She heard but said nothing. She heard the gossip from the servants as they spoke to Jala, and she listened. She had never forgotten the words Hathor spoke to her by Oracle in her mother's shrine at Djeser Djesere[315]

"Your life will be long. At its end your eyes will see your heart's desire."

Were the rumours true? Could it be possible that he was still alive? Could he ever return? He was a hunted man. Would he be brought back a prisoner? She said nothing but she listened. Then when the world was in uproar at Senenmut's return, she heard that news also. This time she too questioned the servants. And as she listened the facts confirmed her own conviction. Senenmut had returned. He had come freely into the lion's den, to do for the slaves what he had failed to do in his former life before he fled Egypt.

Now a transformation took place in this ageing woman who had spent her life hiding away from the world at Mi-wer. Jala could not believe what she witnessed. Gone was the woman frightened of shadows. It was as if the very source of Nepherure's life grew out of contact with this man she had loved. As if finding that he had returned, restored her to life. Now, with total clarity of mind and will, without wavering, she knew what she must do.

"Jala, my dear friend, I am to leave you for a time," she said.

"I must travel to Avaris. Senenmut has returned, as Hathor told me he would, and I will see him this last time," she said.

She spoke without fear or hesitation and Jala was at first speechless with astonishment. But she could not allow Nepherure to undertake such a journey! She had not left Mi-wer for nearly 40 years. She had neither the physical strength nor the strength of mind to cope with the rigours of such a journey. And worse than that. The river itself would prevent their going.

"My Lady! You cannot do this thing! You are not strong. And have you not seen? The river is diseased! It is cursed! You cannot undertake a journey at this time."

But Nepherure hardly listened.

"My dear friend, I must go. You shall not prevent me," she said. And seeing her implacable determination, Jala changed her argument. If Nepherure could not be dissuaded, she herself must accompany her.

"My Lady, I cannot let you undertake this journey alone. If you are determined to go, then I must go with you."

And so it was. A royal barge was prepared to travel the waterways of Egypt when few other crafts would dare to venture forth. The river was blood red and stank of rottenness, but at the Nepherure's command, they set out for the north.

Throughout the journey, Nepherure rested but could not sleep. She lay on the couch in her cabin consumed by the hope of seeing the man she loved, for this last time. All along the riverbank, men and women were digging to find water. Water untainted by blood and the stench of decay. Jala used her anxiety as a goad to concentrate on the decisions that must be made. The Princess ate and drank when required, giving no resistance. Simply waiting, as the days passed. Her focus was entirely on seeing Senenmut.

Throughout the journey the river remained blood red and stank. Of necessity, other crafts started to go about their business, as slowly the journey and the days passed away. They reached Avaris and moored at the royal dock. They would attend court the following day.

THE COURT HAD GATHERED. AMENY and the High Priest of Ra among them. The pharaoh was seated on his throne, and before him stood the old prophet and his brother. Suddenly the doors of the audience chamber opened, and all eyes turned to see an old woman enter. She was wearing a gold circlet, bearing the royal cobra on her forehead, and leaned heavily on the arm of a slender Nubian woman. A gasp echoed through the chamber as the councillors, nobles and priests stepped out of her path, with something between fear and astonishment. But she ignored them all, her eyes fixed on the two strangers standing before the king. A whisper swept the chamber.

"The royal heiress! The Princess Nepherure!"

But she did not waver, nor did her gaze move as she crossed the sacred space in front of the king, without even acknowledging his presence, as he also watched this apparition, sitting in silence, with fear creeping into his face.

Then in the silence, Nepherure spoke.

"You have returned at last brother," she said. The voice he knew so well tore at his heart. He froze, while shocked silence filled the court. All eyes were fixed on Nepherure, but Moshe could not look at her. It would be his undoing. The agony of their parting returned, assailing him. He marvelled at the strength of resolve he must have found to leave Egypt all those years ago. To leave the girl who was part of his soul. The strength of the young must be greater than that of the old! But she was speaking again.

"I have wept and prayed for you in Hathor's shrine every day since you left," she said. "But to see your face again is repayment for my tears. Hathor has preserved your life." She paused watching him.

"I know now that our mother was right. She saw it at the end. You have a destiny which none of us could foresee. Even the gods did not see it, or they could not have opposed you."

Moshe had turned from the king, an act worthy of death! His eyes were drawn to her face. But no emotion was visible there. Just resolution. Nothing and no-one in this great assembly held any interest for her. Only this man. Again, she spoke, but to him alone, clearly distinctly. Each word expressed as if she were spending her life force.

"My name and our mother's name may be lost for eternity, but your star will shine more brightly even than that of our brother Tutmose, who usurped you, and this son of his who will die unknown."

No one stirred. Moshe stood as one rooted to the ground as she scanned his face, searching his eyes. But he could find no words for her. Her spell engulfed them all. The wrongs she had suffered at the hands of all the royal house, the priests and even he whom she had loved, gave her the right to speak and be heard. But her words were not for herself, but for him.

"You are Egypt's nemesis. The fate she deserves for the wrong she did you." She moved a little closer, staring into his eyes.

"Age has been kind to you brother, but you have yet a lifetime to live! To do the work allotted to you." She paused.

"You have married?" she asked suddenly.

"Yes."

"You have sons?"

"Yes."

"They should have been mine!" she said and paused. "What sons I would have borne you! Sons worthy of Egypt as you were. But Egypt was unworthy of you. Our sons would not have brought Egypt to her destruction as will this arrogant youth," she said, glancing at the pharaoh.

She turned now, and for the first time looked the king full in the face, a thing forbidden! Then raising her unencumbered hand, she pointed at him, her voice rising as she pronounced his doom.

"His pride will destroy Egypt and bring his own destruction!"

She turned again to the man beside her.

"I have seen your face again, brother and can now die in peace. I knew in my soul that you lived still and would return. I have waited for you but need wait no longer. Your name will never be forgotten while men live on the earth. It will grow in greatness as the name of Egypt fades, becoming a graveyard of the past."

For a moment there was almost a smile flickering on her face and her eyes shone. She reached out her hand and touched his own, then lowered her gaze.

"Farewell brother," she said. "Farewell from the one who loved you most in all the world."

---

[315] Deir-el- Bahri

CHAPTER 61

NEPHERURE TELLS HER SON THE TRUTH OF HIS BIRTH

AMENY STOOD SPELL BOUND, WATCHING, and listening as his mother entered the King's court and spoke to the old prophet. Now, as she slowly left the chamber on the arm of Jala, his heart went out to her. Never before had he seen the depths of his mother's heart and mind, expressed with such power and resolution. Hearing her words, he realised that the woman he had known was just a shadow of what she truly was. Of what she had once been, and could have remained, if her dreams had not been destroyed. Without a second thought he followed and took her arm. She had always been precious to him. Now he understood a little of her true worth. She was a princess of the 'Great House'. A royal lady who had taken him to her heart. Perhaps her own loss had taught her to pity him, a motherless child. But she had been good to him, rearing him as her own and giving him her name.

The three figures left the audience chamber of the king in silence as every eye followed them. Ameny longed to be present to hear the old prophet. But he did not waver. His mother was exhausted and needed his care. They returned to the royal barge which was lying ready for them and set sail south on the falling river. Each day of the journey, Ra's heat grew more intense. As they journeyed south, the river lost its blood red colour but instead a new horror emerged. The water teemed with frogs. Frogs in their millions! But the frogs did not behave normally, enjoying the coolness of the water. Instead, they fought desperately to leave the river, as if they could not tolerate the feel of the water on their skin. Leaving the river they spread across the land in every direction, and in the villages and town along the water's edge, they swarmed in plague like proportions into the houses. There they died in the heat as the days passed and the peasants swept the decaying corpses into heaps.

How they endured the journey south to Mi-wer, Ameny could not later recall. The heat and stench continued as the slaves struggled to row against the northward flow of the river, with no wind to fill the sails and take them south. By the time they reached the Fayum and the harem, both Ameny and Jala feared for the princess's life. But she herself remained calm and returned to the familiarity of her imprisonment, unconcerned. She was very weak and could not walk unaided but smiled with gratitude on all who helped her.

Delighted as she was to have the company of her son, still she could eat nothing, and in a matter of days could not leave her couch as her mind started to wander. Nepherure was dying. At no time was she left alone. Jala and Ameny sat with her and slept in turns, but she was fading. A week after their return, after a short sleep, Ameny returned to his mother to find her awake and lucid. His heart rose. Was she improving? But this hope was soon dispelled as she spoke.

"My dear Ameny. There is something that I must tell you. I am soon to die and can defer it no longer." She looked at him now with fear in her eyes as she forced herself to speak.

"I have deceived you all your life. Your father allowed the deception because he loved me, but he was not to blame." She paused. Ameny was stunned. She was fully lucid. There was no doubt of that.

"When your father died, he gave you a message intended for me. He sent me his love, but you did not understand that he spoke of me. 'Tell your mother I love her. The only woman I have ever loved," was what he said.

"I have kept the truth of your birth hidden, out of fear. Fear of losing you. Fear of you becoming a soldier. Fear of you becoming Pharaoh." She paused as she looked at him.

"And because of this, I have been the cause of all Egypt's wrongs. Tha youth who holds the throne, who holds Egypt in his thrall, is not the true hei of your father." Again she paused, but could no longer hold his gaze.

"For a short time I was Tutmose's wife. I bore him a son who should nov hold the throne. A child born of the Solar Blood. A true king of Egypt."

At this Ameny leapt to his feet.

"Mother you are raving. You adopted me out of kindness. Everyone knows the truth of it. I was born of the king's mistress, Betamun, who died."

"Everyone believes that story except the High Priest of Ra at Iunu, the keeper of the royal records. Speak to him. He will tell you." She paused again. "And Jala knows the truth. She was party to the deception."

As she spoke, the door of the chamber quietly closed, and both realised that Jala had entered. Ameny turned and looked at her as she stood solemn and mute before them.

"Tell my son what he must know," said Nepherure to her friend. "I must be at rest in my mind before I die. If he can forgive me, I will enter the afterlife in peace."

Jala could hardly hold his gaze as she answered the question in Ameny's eyes.

"You did not want the throne dear Ameny!" she whispered looking imploringly into his eyes.

"And it was feared that Meryet would harm you if you stood in the way of her ambition for her sons. It was done for the best!" She paused as she covered her face with her hands.

"But Egypt has paid a terrible price! And may have yet more to pay," she finished with a sob.

She could not look at him. To be betrayed and lied to by those he trusted most was astounding to him. He looked again at his mother's face.

"May the gods forgive me," she whispered. But her eyes were glazed. She was fading!

Falling on his knees beside her couch, Ameny took her in his arms as a cry burst from him.

"I forgive you! I forgive you mother!"

Her hand touched his face then fell to the couch. She had gone beyond his reach.

THE SEVENTY DAYS OF MUMMIFICATION and burial of his mother passed as a blur for Ameny. Jala too was a changed woman. She who had been his mother's strength, now had no strength for herself. She clung to Ameny as the

only certainty of her life. Nothing now held her at Mi-wer. She dreade
staying on in the harem alone and Ameny knew he could not leave her. Wit
his mother buried he must return north to try to control the follies of hi
brother. But still others were depending on him. With Egypt in turmoi
Hekareshu[316] had closed the school at Mut's temple in Waset, and personall
brought Ameny's two sons to him at Mi-wer. If it was possible, they woul
return north together.

Along the river, the corpses of the frogs had dried in the sun, giving respit
from the stench. Now was their chance to travel. So taking Jala and his son
Ameny used the last of the high water to travel north to Avaris. And there wa
another thing he must settle. He would delay their journey for a few days at th
great temple of Ra in Iunu to search the records. His mother's words ha
opened a wound in his heart, and to find healing, he must first be certain of th
truth. Only in the temple of Ra at Iunu would he find the truth. The High Pries
himself may still be with the court in Avaris, but he could search the record
alone. Time was short. The battle was still raging between the old prophet an
the king, and he must reach Avaris before the river was impassable. But h
must know the truth of his birth.

They reached Iunu in only three days. It seemed that the plagues on th
river were over. The water had returned to its usual dull brown colour, heav
with silt washed downstream from Kush, and the stench of the dead frogs wa
gone. As they approached the harbour, Ameny looked west, out across th
broad stretch of the River to the plains beyond, as so many good memorie
flooded into his mind. Times he had spent with his father hunting on the we
bank where the great pyramids of Giza stood, guarded by the Sphinx. Giganti
mysterious. Gazing out towards the stars over long millennia. The area wa
sacred ground, forbidden to the general populace, so no villages or towns ha
grown up there. And hunting was now a sport. The preserve of the royal hous
and those in favour with the pharaoh. This meant that game came freely to th
area, after the high river had watered the land, causing the dry ground to bur
into life.

Ameny knew he would be occupied at the temple. He could not involve h
sons in his search until he knew the truth of his parentage. And he could n
take time to go hunting with them. But there were always hunters ready to tak

the favoured few to the hunting grounds of Giza. He would set it in motion. Give them some relief from the tensions of the present chaos. He would arrange it. So while Ameny was busy at the temple, Webensenu and Tutmose could enjoy some hunting. Practice the skill of driving a chariot. Improve their ability to hit a target with a well-aimed arrow and maybe bring down a buck.

They reached Iunu and moored beside the great temple of Ra. It was the largest temple in all Egypt. A city in itself. Dwarfing even the huge complex of Ipet[317] in Waset. The palace welcomed them and Ameny arranged for hunters to take his sons to Giza the following day and spend as much time there as they chose. When they had gone, he dressed himself in his official robes, and set off for the temple. He approached the great gate, trusting that his status as High Priest of the principal Temple of Ptah would gain him access. He was welcomed without question and given free access to the vast library, famous as the greatest centre of knowledge in the known world[318].

But with such a huge collection of scrolls, Ameny needed the help of a Sem priest.

"I wish to check the details of my son's birth," he lied. "If you will direct me to the relevant scrolls, I shall not detain you."

The Sem priest was pleased to oblige. Ameny found the records for his sons, Webensenu and Tutmose, then working back, found the record of his own birth. There it was, endorsed by the name of the High Priest himself.

'Amenemhat, child of the third Tutmose and his Great Royal Wife.' There was her name, 'Nepherure, daughter of the second Tutmose and his Great Royal Wife Hatshepsut.'

Ameny was stunned. A strange feeling filled his mind as he read it. So he was born of the Solar Blood. It was true! Through his mother's line, the line through which the Solar Blood was reckoned. He was of the line of the great kings going back to the beginning if this dynasty. The dynasty set up by Ahmose when he defeated the Hyksos invaders. The line that came to him through his grandmother Hatshepsut[319]

'A true son', it said. 'Born of Nepherure. Child of her body. Born of the third Tutmose. Child of his body.'

There it was. But of what use could it be to either himself or Egypt now? Amenhotep had been on the throne for seven years. If these facts became known, or if he challenged the king, even if he wished to, it would only threaten his own life and that of his sons. He was glad he had sent his sons away. He needed time to think and maybe to mourn what might have been. He had never wanted to be pharaoh and did not want it now! But he would not have done the things that Amenhotep had done. He would not have destroyed Hatshepsut's legacy. And surely it was possible to find an answer to the problem of the slaves. If Egypt stopped her wars, she could take the heavy yoke off the slaves and make their lives bearable.

While Ameny was learning the truth of his parentage, Webensenu and Tutmose were enjoying a taste of freedom. It took them a day to reach Giza by barge and the light was fading as the hunters set up camp on the riverbank, and set a watch. There would be lions out there, and darkness would soon be upon them. Looking west, as Ra was falling below the horizon, Tutmose could see the outline of the pyramids rising out of the flat plain. He loved being out under the stars, and as darkness fell, the sky was entirely spangled with them. Dinner of roast goat was cooked over the open fire, and by the time it was cooked Tutmose was famished. But he hid his discomfort. The hunters would only make sport of his grumblings, expecting him to be a man. After they had eaten, they lay on the sand with simple rugs under and over them. The night would be cold under the open sky. Everyone else was soon fast asleep, but Tutmose lay, staring up at the stars. He knew them all. Every constellation. Astronomy was a fascination to him. But could the stars speak as the priests claimed? Could they tell your destiny? Eventually he slept, but dawn was soon upon them, and his brother was eager to drive out to the pyramids and find game before the hot noon sun brought an end to the day's hunting.

They drove west, with the sun rising behind them shining in full strength on the face of the pyramids as they approached. An extraordinary sight and growing more and more enormous as they approached. At the foot of the sphinx, they left their chariots so they could move silently on foot to approach their quarry. The two princes tried their luck with the first herd of Ibex the discovered, feeding on the fresh grass. Throughout the morning they came upon small herds and solitary Ibex, in and around the pyramids, but no matter how much he tried, Tutmose's shots fell short again and again, while Webensenu's first shot took down a small Ibex. His success fired h enthusiasm to continue, but Tutmose, both discouraged and tired from his poor sleep wanted to rest. He returned to the sphinx, with a servant, to rest in its shade, leaving his brother to continue the chase.

Tutmose was soon asleep. The sun was hot now but he had the shade of the sphinx to protect him, and he slept deeply. But it was not a dreamless sleep. It seemed as if the question he had asked of the stars the previous night was returning. Was it possible to know the future? And now it seemed as if the sphinx itself was speaking.

"Listen Tutmose. I can control your destiny. If you will care for my monument and removed the desert sand that encumbers me, I will take care of you and make you pharaoh."

Tutmose woke with a start, with the words of the sphinx ringing in his ears. How could this be possible? He was a second son of a man who was not even pharaoh - not even the heir to the pharaoh. But it was only a dream[320].

---

[316] Hekareshu was the Nubian of high birth who ran a school at Mut's temple in Karnak. History tells us Tutmose, later Tutmose lV attended that school, and Arielle Kosloff, in her book on Amenhotep lll suggests that this may be where Tutmose (lV) met Mutemwia, who was later his queen.

[317] Karnak

[318] It seems to me that much of the knowledge available at the great Library in Alexandria, that we attribute to the Greeks, came from the ancient collection housed at the temple of Ra at Heliopolis. It was Alexander the Great who built the library at Alexandria, closing the Temple of Ra at Heliopolis and taking the contents of this library to Alexandria.

[319] This is a connection I have made using the limited facts we have. It is known that Tutmose lll had a number of sons, one named 'Amenemhat' whose mother is not proven but could be the child of Nepherure. It is thought Tutmose lll may have married Neferure before she disappeared from the record. It is on that basis that I have written this part of the story.

[320] This incident is recorded in Egyptian history. The sphinx is said to have offered the throne to Tutmose, even though he was not in line for the throne.

CHAPTER 62

SHOWDOWN

AMENY AND HIS FAMILY, REACHED Avaris as dusk was falling. They made their way to the modest Temple of Ptah in the city and were welcomed by the Sem priests to their apartments. An eerie silence hung over the city, as if it were holding its breath. How many had died in this city due to the curses on the river, Ameny had no idea. And who could know what would follow? 'Hapi'[321], the river god had been powerless against the curses of YHWH. 'Heqet', the frog goddess, widely loved and trusted as one of the goddesses of childbirth, had been unable to remove the plague of frogs. It seemed that the priests of Hapi and Heqet had been able to copy the actions of YHWH but had no power against it. Nevertheless, Amenhotep was determined to pay no regard to the old prophet. He felt inadequate, and he knew he must appear strong in front of his court and the friends from his youth whom he had appointed to high office. He wanted to believe that as his priests could copy the plagues with their dark arts. That YHWH was no more powerful than the gods of Egypt. So he refused to listen.

By early morning the next day the king's audience chamber was packed with priests, councillors and nobles, and the guards would allow no one else to enter. They had stood for an hour in the heat and crowd before finally the pharaoh arrived with his heir and took his seat. After weeks of chaos, with the river, the life blood of Egypt, undrinkable, and the land inundated with frogs pharaoh had relented and asked the old prophet to remove the frogs. They had died in their millions, creating such a stench that the whole land was nauseated by them. But the pharaoh would not learn. Again he refused the slaves the right to go and worship. Now the court had gathered, the pharaoh with them, but the old prophet had not come. Suddenly a young priest burst into the assembly, screaming!

"Another plague is upon us! We are doomed!"

Even as he spoke, dark clouds of biting insects poured into the chamber through the doors and windows. The pharaoh leapt to his feet.

"Get to work you priests and magicians! Deal with this menace or I will deal with you!"

So saying, Amenhotep escaped to the depths of the palace taking his son with him. But the magicians must face the new challenge. Could they, with their magic spells perform the same feat? For days they tried, making offerings to the goddess 'Uatchit', the goddess of swamps and swarming insects. But all their offerings and incantations failed. The country was in a state of exhaustion. In desperation they sent messages to pharaoh as all the lector priests[322] and high priests in the delta gathered to plead with the king, Ameny was there. The High Priest of Ra was there, the most revered man in the land under the king. Surely Amenhotep would listen to him.

As the king entered and seated himself, the old priest of Ra stepped forward to speak.

"My lord, we are powerless against this plague. We have petitioned the 'Lady of the Marshes' but this magic is too strong for her. It is a magic unknown to us," he paused, as the king said nothing, simply staring at the old priest before him. But it was too much for Ameny. If his brother would not take the advice of his senior priests, what hope was there? On an impulse he stepped forward himself.

"My lord, none of your priests or magicians have any power over this torment!" Then as the pharaoh sat, unmoving as stone, Ameny spoke the words of doom.

"My lord, this is the finger of God!"[323]

Without a word the king leapt to his feet and strode from the chamber. He would hide away in the depths of the palace. There he would escape most of the torment. But there was no repentance. Outside the palace the horror continued. It seemed like an eternity, as days of torment for man and beast followed each other in relentless succession. But one thing was starkly different. This plague of biting insects was entirely absent from the homes and workplaces of the Habiri slaves in Goshen, where they lived out their meagre lives. They had torment enough it could be said. But in this plague, and all that followed, YHWH would show a distinction between the Egyptians and the Habiri.

Finally, the torment of biting insects subsided. Pharaoh had not relented, but again YHWH told Moshe to meet the king as he went to bathe.

"Speak to him. If he still refuses me, warn him that I will punish him again."

Moshe and Aaron did as instructed. They met the king as he went to bathe and warned him that he must let the Habiri go to worship their God or worse would come. But he refused to listen. The next day at sunrise, swarms of dog flies appeared everywhere[324] No food was free of them. Nothing was safe from their contamination. The slave girls in the palace kitchen could not make bread that contained no flies. The couches of high and low alike were smeared with their crushed bodies. But no flies troubled the slaves in Goshen. Finally, the king could bear no more. He summoned Moshe and Aaron.

"Pray to the Lord to remove the dog flies! I will allow the slaves to go and worship," Pharaoh said. "But they cannot leave Egypt. They must make their sacrifices here!"

But this did not fulfil the conditions demanded by YHWH.

"We cannot sacrifice here in Egypt!" Moshe said. "Your people would stone us. We must sacrifice rams and bulls to the Lord, and these are sacred to the Egyptians. They would kill us."[325].

"We must go three days journey into the Mafkat, away from the Egyptians," said Moshe.

"You may go a short distance only!" shouted the pharaoh. "You may not go far!"

Moshe agreed. He would petition YHWH the next day to remove the flies But as soon as the flies were gone, pharaoh broke his promise and refused to let the people go.

[321] One of the gods of the Nile.

[322] A lector priest was a well-educated senior priest responsible for reciting spells and hymns during temple rituals and official ceremonies.

[323] The book of Exodus 8 v19

[324] The Septuagint (LXX) uses the Greek word 'kunomuia' which is interpreted as 'dog fly', a particularly nasty biting insect. Today it is known most commonly as the 'stable fly', and may mean 'horse fly'. The translators of the LXX lived in Egypt and would have known this insect and named it accordingly.

[325] Bulls and rams were sacrificed in Egypt under certain rules, but in general the ram represented the god Amun and was held sacred. The Apis bull represented Ptah and Mnervis bulls were sacred to the sun god Ra. Perhaps it was the idea of slaves sacrificing these animals that would have caused a backlash.

CHAPTER 63

PLAGUES

YHWH SAID TO MOSHE, "GO to Pharaoh and say to him, 'This is what the God of the Habiri says, "Let my people go so they may worship me. If you refuse, tomorrow I will bring a plague upon your livestock in the fields, on your horses, donkeys, camels, cattle, sheep and goats. But I will make a distinction between you and the Habiri. Not one of their animals will die."

The next day the Lord did as he had said. All through Egypt the cattle, sheep, goats, and donkeys out in the fields, died in their thousands. But in Goshen not one animal was found dead. Egypt was devastated. 'Hathor', the great mother goddess, herself a cow, was unable to protect her kind.

As the shock of the plague spread through the city, Ameny went urgently to meet his old friend, the High Priest of Ra. They sat together in silence in the old priest's private chambers. But what could be done? What could they do? Suddenly a commotion was heard in the anti-chamber of the old priest and a young Sem priest burst in, his face white with shock.

"My Lord! Dreadful news. The sacred bull of Ra has been found dead in his enclosure! Smitten by the plague! He had hardly finished speaking when another interrupted them, this time with a message for Ameny.

"My Lord, word has come from Men-nepher. The great Apis[326] is dead Killed by the plague. The two men looked at each other in silence. This was no longer simply clever magic. This was an assault on the gods of Egypt! How could Ptah, the oldest god of Egypt, the builder of the world, allow his avatar the sacred Apis to die like this? And the Mnevis bull, the representative of Ra on earth, dead! Was it true of Amun also? Could none of them defend the animals of Egypt? The loss of their livestock would bring hunger to the people. And how could the pharaoh pay his troops their promised rations of beef? Egypt had no ancient god to protect her horses, but the chariot horses were kept in stables, and these were not destroyed. Only the breeding mares, out in the fields with their colts, were lost.

But while the country suffered terribly, the king would not concede defeat. His chariot horses, the creatures he valued above all things, had escaped, and he ignored the words of YHWH. He would not let the Habiri go. How could he continue his dream to subjugate Syria without slaves to do the work of Egypt's farmers? Where could he find enough soldiers for his army without the peasant farmers he and his father had trained? But YHWH had not finished with Egypt and her king.

"Go again to Pharaoh", God said to Moshe. "Take with you a handful of ash. When you meet the king, throw the dust into the air and it will become festering boils on man and beast throughout the land."

Moshe did so. All the members of Pharaoh's court were afflicted terribly with boils. Everyone from peasant to noble suffered the plague. The priests were so afflicted by the sores on their feet that they could not stand before the king. But still Amenhotep would not give way. He could not let go of his dreams of empire. And to show contempt for Moshe and Aaron, he did not even alter his daily routine to avoid them. Moshe found him again in the morning as he went to bathe. But this time the warning was not of pain or loss. His words warned of disaster as he addressed the pharaoh.

"By now YHWH could have wiped you from the face of the earth", said Moshe. "And because of your stubborn refusal, you will now feel the real weight of YHWH's hand upon Egypt. You are a fool. You are dealing with the living God! And he is in deadly earnest. But he has raised you to the throne for this very purpose. To show his power. Egypt has known greatness, but the name of YHWH and his power will be spoken of far above the name of Egypt, for all time, by all men. This time tomorrow YHWH will send the greatest hailstorm that Egypt has ever known from the time the pyramids were built, until now. If you value your livestock and slaves, bring them in from the fields or the storm will destroy everything."

Moshe turned from the king in fury, and as he did so he heard again the voice of command.

"Stretch your hand, Moshe, towards the sky and hail will fall all over Egypt."

The nobles who feared YHWH brought their animals and servants into safety but the proud, who would not listen, left them in the fields. When Moshe stretched his staff towards heaven a storm, the like of which had never been seen, broke over Egypt. Hailstones like boulders fell. Everything in the fields was destroyed. The barley and flax which were coming into leaf were utterly crushed. The hail stones were of such a size that every animal and servant left in the fields, died. Even the trees were destroyed. It was utter devastation. Nothing like it had been seen since the 'Two Lands' were joined as one.[327] Only in Goshen was there no storm and no hail.

But the storm terrified the pharaoh. He sent for Moshe and Aaron.

"This time YHWH is right," he said. "I and my people are in the wrong. Pray to the Lord for us to stop the hail. You may go and worship. I will allow the slaves to go with you."

Moshe was angry at the devastation pharaoh had brought on his own people. He must do as pharaoh pleaded, but he knew that the king would not keep his word.

"I will go out of the city and pray for you. But I know that you and your officials still do not fear YHWH," he said as he turned and left the king.

As soon as the hail stopped, the king and his friends, the young generals whom he had appointed to high rank in the army, changed their minds and refused permission for the slaves to go. But YHWH was waiting for them.

"Go to pharaoh again. I have been patient, but this folly of his will never be forgotten. A history to tell your children and grandchildren. Speak to pharaoh and warn him that I will send locusts to destroy all that the hail has left behind They will cover the face of the ground so it cannot be seen. They will fill al the houses of Egypt as never before."

Moshe did as the Lord instructed him. The king, his young friends and hi older councillors listened, the older men with fear. Locusts were a terror to an nation. When Moshe had gone the young friends of the king made light of th threat.

"Why do you allow this fellow to come here like this?" they asked. But the older priests and councillors pleaded with the king.

"Majesty, do you not see, the land is ruined! Egypt is destroyed"[328].

For once Pharaoh listened to his older advisers and called for Moshe and Aaron to be brought back to court.

"Go and worship your god," he said, but tell me, who will be going?"

"We will all go," Moshe replied. "Our young and old. Our sons and daughters. Our flocks and herds so we can celebrate to the Lord."

At this pharaoh leapt to his feet.

"I said nothing of your women and children! Clearly you are bent on evil! Only the men may go as that is what you have been asking for!"

At that, Moshe and Aaron were driven out of pharaoh's presence. As they left the palace, Moshe heard God's command in his mind,

"Stretch out your staff over Egypt to summon the locusts."

All that day and the following night, a strong east wind blew, and in the morning, the locusts came. They invaded all of Egypt and settled down in every area of farmland in great numbers. They covered the ground until it was black. They devoured all that was left after the hail. Everything growing in the fields and the fruit on the trees. Nothing green remained on tree or plant in all of Egypt. And as if the earth itself could feel the torment, the very ground was shaken. When he saw the locusts and felt the earth trembling, pharaoh summoned Moshe again.

"I have sinned against the Lord your God and against you. Now forgive my sin once more and pray to the Lord your God to take this deadly plague away from me!" he begged.

Moshe left pharaoh's presence and prayed to the Lord, and the wind turned, becoming a powerful west wind. It picked up the locusts and carried them into the Red Sea. Not a locust was left anywhere in Egypt. But as God knew he would, pharaoh changed his mind and would not let Israel go!

Then God said to Moshe, "Stretch out your hand towards the sky and darkness will descend on the land. Ra will be hidden from view. This god whom they trust to rule their lives. Who rises each morning and returns each night to the body of Nut.[329]

"They will see that I am more powerful even than Ra."

~ 331 ~

Moshe lifted his hand to the sky and before his eyes, darkness descended over the land at noon. It was darkness that could be felt. No one could see the hand in front of his face. The terrified Egyptians took to their beds and did not rise for three days. Yet the Israelites had light in Goshen. Pharaoh could not bear the darkness. It felt like an impending doom. He sent urgently to Moshe.

"Go and worship your God. You may take your women and children but not your animals. Your livestock must not go with you."

But Moses said to pharaoh,

"Our livestock must go with us. Not a hoof is to be left behind. We must use some of them in sacrifice to the Lord and we will not know what he wants until he tells us."

But God hardened pharaoh's heart. He was furious at Moshe's words.

"Get out of my sight!" he shouted, leaping to his feet. "Make sure you do not appear before me again! The day you see my face you will die!"

"Just as you say," Moshe replied. "I will never appear before you again!"

---

[326] The Apis was the bull sacred to the god Ptah and kept in an enclosure at his temple in Men-nepher, the ancient name for Memphis

[327] Egypt was known as the 'Two Lands', Upper and Lower Egypt based on the upper and lower reaches of the Nile. The pharaoh Narmer of the first dynasty around 3,000 BC, brought them together under his rule.

[328] Exodus 10 v 7

[329] The mythology was that Ra, the sun god was swallowed every night by the 'Nut' the goddess of the night. Through the hours of darkness Ra passed through her body, emerging again at dawn.

CHAPTER 64

PASSOVER

AS HE LEFT THE COURT, Moshe heard in his mind YHWH's last words concerning Egypt.

"I will bring one more plague on pharaoh, and all Egypt. After that he will drive you out!"

Moshe heard it and his blood ran cold. But his own anger against this pharaoh had grown to such a pitch that he knew that the punishment would be just. He listened again as the message continued.

Now came the words of doom.

"At midnight, on the day I have chosen, I will pass through the land of Egypt and every firstborn son in Egypt will die[330]. From the firstborn son of pharaoh who sits on his throne, to that of the slave girl who is at her hand mill. And all the firstborn of the animals also. There will be terrible wailing in Egypt, worse than has ever been or will be again. But among the Israelites, not even a dog will bark. So you will know that I make a distinction between Egypt and Israel."

Moshe heard the words and deep sadness crept into his mind. Families he had known and loved would be devastated by this plague! But still the words continued.

"Then all the officials of Egypt will come to you. They will bow down and beg you to take the Habiri and leave!"[331]

As the words of YHWH sounded in his mind, Moshe turned back to the young man seated on the throne.

"I have one last message to give you. YHWH warned you at the beginning to let his people go. He warns you again. The last plague will take the life of your firstborn son and that of every firstborn of Egypt. Take warning. Listen and act wisely."

But the pharaoh sat unmoved. He would not turn from his fixed opposition to Moshe and his God. He did not believe that anyone could enter his palace and kill his son. He would not give way.

Moshe turned away and left the pharaoh's presence, furious and yet heartbroken at the callous behaviour of the king towards his own land and people.

But now YHWH was giving him fresh instructions.

"From now on, this shall be the first month of your year because it marks the beginning of your new life. Tell the people, that from now on, on the tenth day of this month, the month of Abib, every man must set aside a lamb for his household. If his household is too small to eat a whole lamb, let him join with another household. The lamb must be without defect. It must be perfect. A male in its first year. It can be from the sheep or the goats."

The words kept coming and fastened themselves in Moshe's mind.

"The lambs must be kept ready until the fourteenth day, when all these sacrificial lambs are to be killed in the evening. Then the man of the house, where the lamb is to be eaten, must take some of its blood and smear it around the entrance door of the house. On the lintel above the door and on the door posts on either side. The lamb must be roasted whole that night, and eaten that night, with unleavened bread – flat bread made without yeast, and eaten with bitter herbs. It must not be eaten raw or boiled. It must be roasted whole, with its head and legs. And none of its bones are to be broken. You shall leave none of its meat uneaten. Anything left over must be burnt."

All these words seared themselves on Moshe's mind. But there was more.

"When you eat the lamb, you must be dressed for a journey. Ready to leave the house immediately, wearing your coat and shoes with your staff in your hand. This feast is to be called the 'Passover', for on this night I will pass through Egypt, and kill every firstborn in every house. But where I see the blood smeared on the door posts and lintels of your house, I will pass over the house and not destroy the firstborn son of that family. This is the night judgement on Egypt when I will kill every firstborn male of man and beast. When I show my power over every god of Egypt. And you are to keep this for a memorial forever, through all your generations. The night you were released from slavery. When I brought your armies out of Egypt. Out of the 'iron smelting furnace' of Egypt,[332] where you were slaves."

With YHWH's words fresh in his mind, Moshe returned to the Habiri leaders.

"I have been given the final instructions for you. But first, you are to tell the people in secret, every man and woman alike, that they are to ask the Egyptians living near them, for articles of silver, gold and clothing. When the moment comes to leave Egypt, they are to hang the jewellery round their children's necks to be carried out of Egypt." Moshe paused as he got ready to give the final, detailed instructions to the leaders. Details that would save the lives of their precious sons and the moment of escape for the whole nation.

At Moshe's command, every family chose a lamb for their household and set it aside for the sacrifice. Then they approached their Egyptian neighbours and asked them for jewellery and clothing. By now the Egyptians were so terrified of the Habiri that they gave them anything they asked for. So they would take it and go!

Then on the fourteenth day of Abib[333] every man killed his lamb in the evening and catching some of the blood in a basin, smeared it on the doorposts and lintel of his house. As the sun set, everyone congregated inside their home as the lamb was roasted and everyone from the children to the elderly dressed themselves for their journey. They put on their sandals and coats and watched as the women and girls roasted the lamb. The smell of the roasting meat was tantalising, and the children could not restrain their whimpering. Rarely did they eat meat! Fish could be had from the river, but their diet was largely of the vegetables they grew in the rich soil of the delta. Meat was for the rich. For the Egyptians.

The evening wore on. The herbs were prepared. Each family prepared large quantities of bread dough, enough for seven days, which was wrapped in cloths, ready to cook over the fire. At last, the meat was cut and distributed. So much meat! All could eat their fill! Even the children. Nothing must be left.

They ate almost in silence. The silence of hunger. Hunger that was a constant companion, yet still they were required to work hard without energy, without stamina. But not tonight. This meal would give them stamina! And seizing their freedom would require stamina. To walk all night. To escape. The children and elderly would travel in carts, but not the men and women, especially the men. They must walk and walk for long hours.

At midnight a terrible wailing was heard across the land. In every house, the firstborn son was found dead! From the palace of the Pharaoh to the prisoner in the dungeon. Every firstborn son was dead. From the first born of Pharaoh who sat on his throne, to the child of the slave girl, all died. Pharaoh rose in the night, he and all is servants, and all the Egyptians. There was a terrible cry throughout the land for no household was without death. Ameny was in a deep sleep, but Jala had heard the warnings and knew instinctively, when the cry went up that YHWH had done as he promised. Rousing herself she dashed into the room shared by Webensenu and Tutmose. As she passed Tutmose, he turned in his sleep. She came to Webensenu's couch and saw him lying peacefully on his back. But as she drew closer, the paleness of his skin, his total stillness terrified her. She reached out and touched him, this young man she had known and loved all his life, but his body was cold! In her terror she ran from the room to raise Ameny.

The same terrible scenario played out in the palace. The pharaoh, summoned by his servants, came in haste to the bedside of his son. The bed that had become his bier. Already the healthy glow of living flesh was slipping away, as greyness took its place. There was no doubting it. His son was dead. The son he had raised to fill his throne. He turned and rushed from the room.

"Summon the prophet of YHWH!"

Men scattered to do his bidding and soon the old mystic stood before him.

"Go! Take the slaves and go! Worship your God. Get out of my land! You and all your people. All your flocks! Go! But pray for me!"

His words ended in a wail as his head sank into his hands. His desire for glory, the glory of devouring Naharin. Of being greater than his father, had cost him his son. Uncontrollable sobs shook his frame.

Moshe departed. The time had come. Freedom for the slaves.

THE WHOLE COUNTRY WAS IN a state of terror.

"Get the Habiri out of Egypt or we are all dead men!" they said.

The fleeing Habiri took their kneading troughs strapped to their backs. They had no possessions. Nothing of value. Only the silver and gold jewellery they had taken from the Egyptian's willing hands which they now put round their children's necks. Small payment for their years of servitude.

The people gathered to Moshe at Ramesses. It was the month of new grain[334] and they had stored a huge harvest. But they passed it by, intent only on liberty. As they arrived in their thousands, Moshe organised them into companies and sent them off to the border fort at Tharu. It was a year since Moshe had arrived in Egypt and now the river was at its lowest and the land was dry. The easiest time of year to travel across the delta.

And still they kept coming. Families, animals, wagons pulled by oxen. They reached Avaris where all around the Egyptians were burying their dead, hardly aware of the tramping feet, the rattle of carts and the lowing of oxen as the Habiri entered the city following the only proper road leading to Tharu. A road for their carts full of those too old or too young to walk. On and on they came. Hundreds of thousands. Some of the women entered the houses, emboldened in the moment, to demand gifts. Jewellery; gold and silver; lapis lazuli. Things they had never owned. The terrified Egyptians thrust their treasures at them. Anything to be rid of them. The slaves left with their treasures but knew that in the rush of escape they could not carry jewels in their hands. Then they remembered Moshe's words.

"Put them round the necks of your children to be carried out of Egypt."

Wealthy Egyptian ladies watched as their priceless jewels were hung around the necks of skinny dirty children sitting in rough carts, who entertained themselves by showing off their baubles to their siblings as they would have done with any paltry toy.

Single men were organised into troops to lead the way, marching with their fists in the air[335] as night turned to day and the Egyptians started burying their dead.[336] No one resisted the escaping Habiri. Other slaves, seeing their chance of escape, joined them, swelling the numbers further.

Jala watched from the apartment in Ptah's temple where Ameny and his sons had lodgings. Behind her, in the centre of the room was the body of Webensenu, wrapped in a shroud. Ameny had gone at midnight after finding his son dead. Gone as other officials had gone, to find the old prophet and beg him to take the slaves and leave Egypt. Tutmose had gone with his father, terrified to let him out of his sight. The only remaining security of his life.

Jala watched the teeming hordes in the street outside. This was the culmination of the past year of horror and death. But where could all these people go? Could they really find a home in Canaan? Desperate to leave Egypt and trusting in their leader, they followed the crowd mindlessly. Egypt held nothing for them now. Cruelty beyond human endurance had become their lot. Moshe offered hope. Promises. In the normal way of life as slaves, at least they could exist. But this pharaoh had made their lives impossible. Beatings and cruelty were now imposed as a matter of course. Many had died. Any weakness was a death sentence. The promise of escape held at least a hope for the future. Moshe told them of the promise YHWH had made, to give them Canaan as their home. And Moshe had proved something. He had proved that YHWH had the power to make it happen.

Jala continued to stand gazing out into the street, watching the Habiri slaves pour through the city. Among them were many who were not Habiri. Nubian and Kushite slaves were there among them, seizing the chance of escape. She was too numb to think of the future. But here, in the company of death, the hope in the faces of the escaping slaves spoke to her. What was the difference between herself and these slaves? She had lost everything. Nepherure was gone. The companion of her life. This boy she had loved was gone. Ameny was a man obsessed. Fighting against his brother, the pharaoh who had utterly destroyed his own land. But these slaves had a leader who could be trusted. In a moment of sheer folly, Jala knew what she must do. Taking nothing with her, as if departing to meet her death, she left the apartment. In a few moments she was part of the crowd, walking, walking, walking. Still wearing her embroidered sandals, she walked on until the delicate fabric broke and she was forced to discard them. The sun was now high in the sky and she had no parasol, no water. She tramped on knowing she was falling behind. How far could she hope to go? She refused to think. The noise and dust broke in on her reverie. The noise of carts and lowing oxen pressed close to her in the escaping throng. Suddenly a voice at her side caught her attention.

"Old lady. You will not get far like that. Take a place in the cart. There is shade and the children will give you water."

Jala turned. Before her was a dark tanned face. The man reined his oxen to a halt.

"Get in, old lady," he said kindly.

Without reply she took his offered hand and with his help, climbed into the cart and under the canopy. The smell of dirty children was rank, but she closed her eyes in relief. She would not think of the future. She would go wherever it was this man and his family were going.

---

[330] Exodus 11 v 4
[331] Exodus 11 v 3
[332] Deuteronomy 4 v 20
[333] Exodus 13. Later during the Babylonian exile the name of the month was changed to Nisan.
[334] The Septuagint states this in Exodus 13 v 4
[335] The book of Numbers 33 v 3
[336] Numbers 33 v 4

CHAPTER 65

ESCAPE

THE SOLDIERS AT THARU, GUARDING the fort, brutal in their control of the border crossing, saw the vast rabble approaching with fists in the air and simply fled. On through the fort the people surged. Over the bridge crossing the canal, the border between Egypt and the Mafkat. Out into the vast marshalling yard beyond, where in normal times the pharaoh mustered his armies, in their tens of thousands, ready to go north to war.

But never before had so much humanity gathered there. As more and more arrived, hundreds of thousands of them spilled far beyond the marshalling yard, and out into the wilderness. Here in the darkness, while they waited, they lit fires and cooked the bread dough they had brought, listening all the while for orders to march.

Dawn would soon be breaking, but in the half light, far out into the Mafkat, beyond the fort, ten thousand campfires lit up the scrubland. The people had settled to rest after their first night of marching. They had bread dough for seven days and water in skins to sustain them. They would travel mainly by night and rest and sleep during the hottest part of each day. Moshe had organised scouts to pass messages throughout the camp, telling the people to listen for the trumpet blast, the sign to move on.

The gathering continued and the place beyond the fortress continued to fi as morning passed. The company of young men who had arrived first, grew impatient. They had received no orders, but they knew that the Horus Way, the military road that started at Tharu, was the direct route to Canaan. At

Canaan was no great distance from Tharu. Anyone who had listened to soldiers talking knew that only 10 days of marching would take men from Tharu to Gaza. So without further instructions the first company set off. They expected that the soldiers in the next fortress would run away as those at Tharu had done. The feeling of freedom was intoxicating. Nothing seemed impossible. In this moment of euphoria, even the Canaanites and Philistines held no fear for them.

But even with the chaos and noise around him, Moshe heard clearly in his mind the words of YHWH.

"Tell the people to turn back. They must not take the Horus Way. That road leads to Philistine territory and if they are faced with war so soon, panic will drive them back to Egypt.[338] Instead, take the road to the southeast, to Etham. The desert road. The camel trail used by the traders. Immediately Moshe sent scouts to round up the first company that had followed the Horus Way. Noon was now long past. The entire company of slaves had reached Tharu and crossed into the Mafkat. The sun was sinking towards the western horizon, and a brief twilight spread across the vast wilderness, when in the sky, a light appeared ahead of them.

"We follow that light," said Moshe as the people turned to see a light hovering ahead of them in the sky to the southeast.

Darkness fell and the light became a flaming torch, shining on the ground, lighting the way. The camel trail showed as a narrow track but with the light to guide them, the people spread out in their tens of thousands across the wide expanse of the Mafkat, moving forward, following the light. From time to time, the ground under their feet trembled, echoing their own sense of trepidation, and the smell of sulphur that wafted through the desert air added to the strangeness of their journey.

The real journey had begun. The journey out of Egypt. The people travelled almost free of belongings. Apart from the unleavened dough that would last them seven days, and their skins of water, they had no provisions for the journey.[339] They had been in Egypt for over 200 years[340]. Five generations[341] had passed since Jacob and his family had arrived in Egypt. And counting back, it was 430 years since YHWH had first promised the land of Canaan to Abraham.[342] Now they were leaving Egypt, having in that time grown from a family of seventy men to a nation numbering hundreds of thousands of men, plus their families. And as Joseph had made them promise on his death bed, they were taking his bones with them to be buried in Canaan.[343]

Now the strength of the people was put to the test, and the hard years of slavery gave them the endurance they would so greatly need. Men and women on foot. Young and old travelling in ox carts. The hours passed and they continued throughout the night. The people trusted their leader and followed the direction he chose, even though it took them to the southeast, when Canaan, they knew, was to the north. All night they marched. Some of the women changing places to drive the carts and walk in turns. Twenty miles. Drinking as they needed while walking. Thirty miles.[344] Now the sun had risen to his hottest. Time to stop and sleep. They were used to the heat, and working in the sun, and with a cloak as protection from the sun, even the noonday heat could not keep them from sleep. Those who could, climbed under the carts to find shade. Fires were lit. Bread dough cooked. Children fed. Most of the exhausted adults slept on. Finally, as the sun moved to the west, a trumpet was sounded. They woke. Drank their fill of the tepid water in the goats' skins and ate their bread. The trumpet sounded again. They set out. Another night of walking lay ahead. Another 30 miles covered. Rest at noon and grateful sleep. Egypt now lay far behind. One more day of marching and they would reach Etham. The people steeled themselves. It was within their grasp.

Four days since leaving Ramesses they reached Etham on the border of the mountains. Here the Arish river flowed past the town, rushing on its way north to the Great Sea[345] where it marked Egypt's border with Canaan. There was water enough for all to drink their fill and replenish their water skins. And here they slept again through the heat of the day, finding shade where they could.

---

337 The Horus Way was the military road that followed the coast between the fort of Tharu and the crossing into Canaan at the Arish river.
338 Exodus 13 v 18
339 Exodus 12 v 39
340 See article in the introduction on the 'Dating of the Exodus'.
341 Exodus 13 v 18
342 Exodus 12 v 40
343 Exodus 13 v 19

[344] A group of my friends, more used to office life than the outdoors, walked 33 miles in a day during the 'Thames Path Challenge' a few years ago when a few of them were well over 60 years old. See the Appendix article 'the Route of the Exodus and the naming of Sinai'.

[345] Mediterranean Sea

CHAPTER 66

TERROR BY NIGHT

HARDLY HAD THE SLAVES CROSSED the canal at Tharu and entered the Mafkat when Amenhotep had a change of mind. All around was the silence of inactivity. On every side was an absence of work. An absence of workers. The fact of work left undone forced itself on the mind of every Egyptian.

"What have we done!" they said to each other in horror. "Even our house slaves have gone."

But for the pharaoh it confirmed his greatest fears. Without slaves there would be no food grown in the delta. Without slaves to farm the delta he could not keep his army in training and ready for war. His soldiers must return to their fields or Egypt would starve.

The pharaoh had promised the slaves a 3-day journey into the wilderness to sacrifice. But he did not keep his word. At Etham, YHWH spoke again, and Moshe listened.

"Tell the people to turn back, to the southeast, and enter the wadis between the mountains leading to the Edomite Sea[346]. Camp on the beach around the Egyptian fort,[347] across the sea from the mountains of Midian. The soldiers in the fort will send signals back to Avaris. The pharaoh will think the people are trapped in the wilderness and will pursue you. I will harden Amenhotep' heart, so he comes after you."

The people did as Moshe instructed. Those in front led the way, entering the narrow wadis leading to the Red Sea.[348] The others followed. The mountains soared skyward hemming them in, directing them relentless towards the vast beach known as Nuweiba.[349] On they marched hour after hour. Night faded, and the sixth day since they left Ramesses dawned. At noon they ate and slept again, then continued their journey as the day faded to night.

BACK IN AVARIS AMENHOTEP SUMMONED his commanders. Most had been replaced with younger blood, his friends. These young leaders wanted to punish the slaves. To go after them and bring them back by force. But at a moment like this, Amenhotep wanted the advice of his few remaining older, generals. He singled out Djehuty. The king did not want his advice but feared to neglect it. The wisdom of experience. He needed it and this made him angry.

"I have retained you as commander of my army, but I do not like you!" he shouted.

"Then my lord must find a man who pleases him," Djehuty replied.

"You are clever, or I would be free of you! I hate your loyalty to my father and his old ways. His mind was contaminated by that usurping woman and that slave Moshe she brought into the royal house! They are the ones who have destroyed Egypt," he ranted.

"If I can serve you my Lord I will. But the slaves are gone. Why concern yourself with them? Leave them to the wilderness. Take other slaves to rebuild Egypt."

But Amenhotep was not listening. He was pacing the floor, driven by his own thoughts.

"Never again will I allow women to have power and breed rebellion in the palace![350] That woman Hatshepsut is the cause of all this trouble. Never again s a woman to receive temple revenues as she did. Wealth gave her the independence and power to harm Egypt!

"Yes, my Lord. You are wise.

"And I will make my own decisions!" he shouted turning his fury on Djehuty.

"We will follow these slaves and bring them back! The guards at the forts ave sent word that they are wandering in the wilderness, heading south. They re trapped. There is no escape."

Djehuty knew he was playing with fire to speak again, but he must.

"My Lord, they have the help of their God who is hostile to Egypt. He has taken his people away. We are free of them and of their curse on us!"

But the pharaoh was like one possessed.

"How can defenceless slaves stand against the might of my army? We will pursue them and bring them back. Every last man of them!" He turned to his guards.

"Prepare my chariot! Summon my bodyguard. We will take the whole army, all of Egypt's chariots with us.[351]

ALL NIGHT THE PEOPLE ENTERED the wadis, but the way was narrow and slow. As morning broke a cry of terror rang out from those last to enter. Far in the distance the pounding of horses' hooves could be heard, and the rattle of chariot wheels came to them across the stillness of the morning. Moshe knew that sound, the sound of a well-trained army. A sound he had loved. But no longer. It pounded in his head and in his heart and even in the ground beneath his feet. To their right and left the mountains of the Mafkat towered overhead leading relentlessly forward. Moshe listened. And beside the noise around him and the sound of the approaching army there was something more. The ground itself was murmuring, stirring from a cause of its own making.[352] But the clamour of the terrified people screaming their fear at him put out of his mind all other sounds, while his own heart started to pour out its supplication to YHWH.

Hours passed. Hours of strenuous walking, as Moshe hurried the people forward. Suddenly the towering walls on either side of the wadi opened, and before them spread the vast beach of Nuweiba. He stared out at the grey light over the Midianite shore. But between himself and that shoreline lay the smooth waters of the Red Sea. And suddenly Moshe remembered another scene he had witnessed in this very place - years before - as a lad. The massacre of the Shasu[353]. On this very beach! By Egyptian soldiers.

The rhythm of galloping horses pounded in his head, running out of control. Fear seized his mind! But he must not give in to fear! As dawn approached the full number of the people surged out of the wadi on to the wide beach. But ahead blocking their escape was the sea. In panic they searched the perimeter of the beach to no avail. They turned on Moshe surrounding him. Savage words were thrown at him by terrified men, but it was the women who framed the most brutal accusation.

"Were there no graves in Egypt that you must bring us here to die?"[354]

BY NOW THE BEAUTY AND elegance that had been the island of Thera, was black and broken. She had become a witches' cauldron of heat and violence. The final fury. This island, that had threatened her inhabitants and driven them away, again and again over centuries, was preparing for her death. The deep substance of the earth, hidden in normal times, when she was at peace, now burst forth, sending high into the air molten rock and searing gas, the very substance of Thera herself. Then with one gargantuan explosion that shook the whole world around her, she was gone[355] Where once there had been proud land, now a circle of islands[356], framing a cauldron of boiling water, was all that remained. But in her death, she would bring death to others. The fury of her eruption sent out gigantic waves in every direction. With her death she would bring an end to the civilisation that had made famous, her proud sister Crete, scouring her surface clean of all life[357].

A huge wave tore across the island of Crete and continued south. The harbour at Per-nepher was struck, destroying buildings and ships that were being prepared for the pharaoh's next assault on the north. The harbour would not rise again for many years. But still Thera would not die quietly. The waves travelling to the east and southeast, lifted the heavy Byblos boats plying their trade far out on the Great Sea[358], which were picked up like playthings, high into the air and brought down safely, as the wave rushed on. But as they approached land, the waves mounted higher and higher, becoming monsters from the deep, gaining speed as they hit the shore with terrible force ploughing far inland.[359] The coastland of Canaan where the Philistines had made their home was struck and ravaged by the waves. But still they rushed on, crossing these lowlands until brought to heel by the higher land to the east.

But the explosion of Thera caused more than towering waves of the sea. The force of her eruption sent shock waves travelling through the earth itself causing the junctions between the great land masses to move. The great rock masses that came together in the Jordan valley[360] and down into the Edomite Sea[361], ground against each other as whole continents slid, one side to the north and the other towards the south with sheering forces of such power that the Edomite Sea itself became unstable.

WITH THE SEA IN FRONT and the mountains running down to meet it on both sides, the wadi that Moshe and the people had just passed through was the only entrance or exit from the beach. They were trapped! All eyes turned back, fixing their gaze on the opening from the wadi. How long would it be before their pursuers emerged? Suddenly Ra burst from behind the mountains of Midian, shining with all his strength across the water behind them. The people turned to see brilliant shafts of light break over the horizon. But Moshe saw more than they. There before him, on the far side of the water, framed by the rays of the sun, stood Horeb - the blackened summit - the mountain of God. The place of his own epiphany. Where the God of his fathers had spoken to him!

"Take off your sandals Moshe, you stand on holy ground."

Standing there with the terror and panic of the people around him, he lived it again. Then other words he had heard, bore into his mind.

"When you have brought my people out of Egypt you will again worship me on this mountain." The mountain now divided from him by the deep water of the Edomite Sea. Was this mockery? Cruel mockery? He was reeling from exhaustion and the terrifying thought that all hope would die with him that day. But as he stumbled, steadying himself, he heard that voice again. As clearly as he had ever heard it.

"Stretch out your staff Moshe, over the sea. The sea will divide for you and the people to cross."

The words seemed to shake the very air and the ground itself. Mechanically he obeyed, and as he watched, the water itself was divided. The floor of the sea seemed to heave and lift, throwing off its watery mantle which fled to the north and south expanding the beach out ahead of him, creating a wide thoroughfare of land far into the distance to the shore of Midian, with the water forming a defence[362], an edge to the pathway, far to the right and left

The people stared in wonder, silenced by the vision before their eyes. But who would trust himself and his precious children to such a pathway? Only those who must, who had no choice. The choice before them was the uncertain hope of a path through the sea or certain death at the hands of an implacable pharaoh. There was no choice. In an instant the crowd made their decision, rushing forward as one body, spreading out along the length of the beach, and moving forward in their thousands. Moshe stood transfixed, the only man not racing to leave the beach as the vast company surged past him. An hour passed and still they came on, desperate to put distance between themselves and the approaching army. The sun was setting now, and darkness would soon be upon them.

By the time all the people had entered the sea, the day was gone, but the light that had shone ahead of them, returned to light their way. All night a hot desert wind blew, drying the ground they must cross with their flocks and herds, carts, and dependants. Truly it felt as if they were entering a grave as down and down the path led, in places only just passing above the line of the water. All night they travelled, their animals too, feeling the strangeness of their journey and hurrying to reach the high ground ahead on the shore of Midian.

Moshe surveyed the beach around him, which earlier that day had been crammed with people. Now it was empty and silent, churned by a hundred thousand feet and strewn with the detritus of the fleeing crowd. He looked back at the ravines behind the beach, but all was thick darkness. Dense cloud covered the wadi. Black as midnight with no moon. He looked forward across the expanse where the sea had been. Here the night was mellow allowing easy passage. He could hear the hubbub of the people. He must follow. There were no stragglers now to detain him. He set out, striding across the dry path ahead of him. Even at a good pace he only slowly gained ground on the fleeing people. For hours he walked, all the while aware, in the east - the outline of the great mountain ahead.

He was well past the lowest point of the seafloor and was climbing steadily up towards the far shore when a new sound came to him on the air. Horses, chariots, the shouts of soldiers, as like a hive of angry bees, whose exit has been blocked for too long, Amenhotep and his army burst out of the enclosing wadi and on to the beach behind him. Even in the dimness, Moshe could see the proud banner flying from Amenhotep's chariot. But the pharaoh and his army found the beach abandoned. How was this possible? His scouts had assured him there was no escape from the beach. A dull light hid from view their fleeing quarry. They approached where the edge of the beach had been, which now continued out in a great expanse across to Midian. But Djehuty knew this beach. He did not trust what he saw. Why had it changed?

"My Lord it is a trap. Let the slaves go. Pursuit could cost us our lives."

But the madness that had seized the king had only grown in intensity. He would follow these slaves. In his fury he admitted no thought of bowing to the power of this Habiri God. He himself was a god, like every pharaoh before him. A son of Ra!

The pharaoh was the first to enter the sea, and where the Pharaoh went, his bodyguard, the 'Braves of the King', would follow. Six hundred of Egypt's finest chariots and charioteers. Then all her other horsemen, each a trained Captain, entered on to the seabed. Djehuty watched, expecting to see hesitation, at least, on the part of these beautiful stallions whose animal instincts were strong. But all instinct of self-preservation, even in these creatures was gone. A hundred men were all that remained, before Djehuty and his bodyguard must start to cross.

MOSHE HAD NEARLY REACHED THE far bank when the earth beneath his feet shuddered violently. As he looked back, he saw Amenhotep and his men preparing to surge onto the pathway across the seabed, five abreast. The distance was only about one schoenus³⁶³. How soon would this army be upon them! A cry went up from the terrified slaves who had already reached Midian and turned to see this new horror. Some fled for their lives to hide among the rocks. Others stood frozen to the spot as their doom approached. Ahead of him Moshe could see the last wave of the Habiri gaining the shore in their thousands along the Midianite coast. It had been a hard march, but he was not far behind them. He ran for what had been the shoreline of Midian, conscious now of the sound of the approaching army behind him in the morning air.

He reached the rocky shore above the beach and turned. Before him the pharaoh and his warriors were racing across the dry bed of the sea. He could see the colourful plumes on the horses' heads. Beautiful creatures! The sound of chariot wheels rang on the dry rocks. What a sight. Power, magnificence, beauty. The flower of Egypt. The best that wealth and power could create. Young men whose fathers he had trained. Men whom he had loved and admired.

But the voice spoke in his head,

"Raise your staff over the sea, Moshe, and it will return."

How could he destroy such beauty and strength? It was fortunate that the decision did not lie with him because it was beyond him. A wisdom greater than his own was at work here. To compromise with evil, to allow it to fulfil its plan, would bring a greater destruction. Engulfing far more than these helpless slaves. Here the wisdom of God was at work. The judge of all the earth must judge. Only he understood the power and corruption of evil. Evil that masqueraded as beauty, as goodness, when in truth it was forged in a craven soul without pity, without love.

IT WAS THE SOUND THAT first caught Djehuty's attention, in the silence around him. He had watched anxiously, after the last of the horsemen started out across the sea floor. And as the light of Ra rose higher over the eastern horizon, he heard it. The sound of rocks moving on the seafloor. But what could move rocks on the seabed? Surely only water! The sea! The sea was returning!

For the charioteers, driving out across the open seafloor, their first warning was the labouring of their chariots, as soft mud started to clog their wheels. Then ripples of water, the herald of the sea's return. But it was the sound that stopped them in their tracks. They turned, transfixed, listening, following the direction of the sound. Faint at first, in the distance, but quickly it built to a deafening roar, as rocks carried by a huge wave, surging towards them, faster than a horse could gallop. In terror they gazed back at the shoreline they had left in their folly an hour before. Why had they ever entered on this quest? It was a death trap. The Habiri God was fighting against them. But for Amenhotep, the realisation had come too late. And as he turned to see his approaching doom, he realised at last, his folly. He was not a god. He was a mere mortal. And he would die a mortal's death.

[346] The part of the Red Sea known now as the Gulf of Aqaba.

[347] The bible uses the word 'Migdol' which means 'fort'.

[348] The Gulf of Aqaba is one arm of the Red Sea.

[349] Nuweba is the name of a huge beach on the west bank of the Gulf of Aqaba formed by sediment washed down from the wadis of the Mafkat over centuries.

[350] Amenhotep ll reflected the anti-women rhetoric of Amenemhat 1 from the Middle Kingdom quoted in the text of 'Mistress of the House Mistress of Heaven Women in Ancient Egypt' pg 34, that women should never be given power.

[351] Exodus 14 v 6

[352] The Exodus story has many elements that sound like seismic activity. See the article on the 'Route of the Exodus' in the Appendix. The plague of darkness was perhaps an ash cloud from the active volcano on the island of Thera, north of Crete. And it is probable that the dividing of the Red Sea was due to Seismic activity, as two tectonic plates meet at the Gulf of Aqaba. It is known that the island of Thera had been an active volcano for centuries, causing her people, the Philistines to leave in waves as it became more unstable. When it exploded for the last time is not known but could have coincided with the crossing of the Red Sea.

When Thera finally exploded, it would have de-stabilised the earth's crust in the whole area, especially where the tectonic plates met, as they did along the Gulf of Aqaba, causing the sea to move back then return as a tsunami.

[353] Shasu were nomads who wandered the Mafkat with their herds and were considered a nuisance by Egypt.

[354] Exodus 14 v 11

[355] It is thought by some that Thera is the Atlantis spoken of by Plato.

[356] Santorini

[357] The civilisation on Crete was destroyed when Thera erupted.

[358] The Mediterranean Sea.

[359] Proof that the Red Sea incident could have been caused by seismic activity along the Dead Sea rift, and possibly related to the demise of Thera can be seen in this article in the publication Science Daily
www.sciencedaily.com/releases/2019/06/190612141418.htm)

[360] The junction between the earth's tectonic plates of Africa and Asia lies along the Jordan Valley, down the length of the Gulf of Aqaba and forms the Great Rift Valley of east Africa.

[361] Gulf of Aqaba

[362] Halley, in his 'Handbook of the Bible' interprets the word 'wall' as used of the water dividing in the story of the Exodus, instead as the word 'defence'. So it would read 'the water formed a defence on either side'.

[363] A shonus was a measure of distance equalling 10.5 miles. The Gulf of Aqaba varies. but is about 11 miles across.

EGYPTIAN DYNASTY 18

AHMOSE I	1576-1551
AMENHOTEP I	1551-1530
THUTMOSIS I	1530-1517
THUTMOSIS II	1517-1504
HATSHEPSUT	1504-1483
THUTMOSIS III	1504-1450
AMENHOTEP II	1452-1417
THUTMOSIS IV	1417-1390
AMENHOTEP III	1390-1352
AKHENATON	1352-1336
SMENKHKARE	1338-1336
TUTANKHAMON	1136-1327
AYE	1327-1323
HOREMHAB	1323-1295

Conventional 18th dynasty family tree
Pharonic names shown in boxes

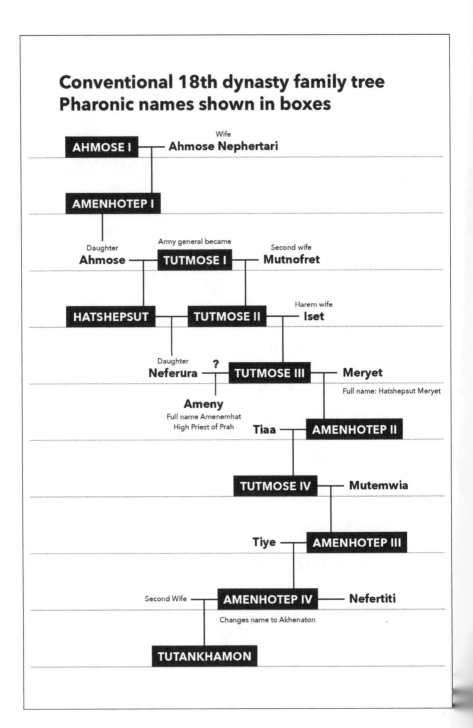

Wife
AHMOSE I —— **Ahmose Nephertari**

AMENHOTEP I

Daughter   Army general became   Second wife
Ahmose —— **TUTMOSE I** —— **Mutnofret**

                                    Harem wife
HATSHEPSUT —— **TUTMOSE II** —— **Iset**

Daughter   **?**
Neferura —— **TUTMOSE III** —— **Meryet**
                                    Full name: Hatshepsut Meryet
Ameny
Full name Amenemhat
High Priest of Prah   **Tiaa** —— **AMENHOTEP II**

TUTMOSE IV —— **Mutemwia**

Tiye —— **AMENHOTEP III**

Second Wife —— **AMENHOTEP IV** —— **Nefertiti**

Changes name to Akhenaton

TUTANKHAMON

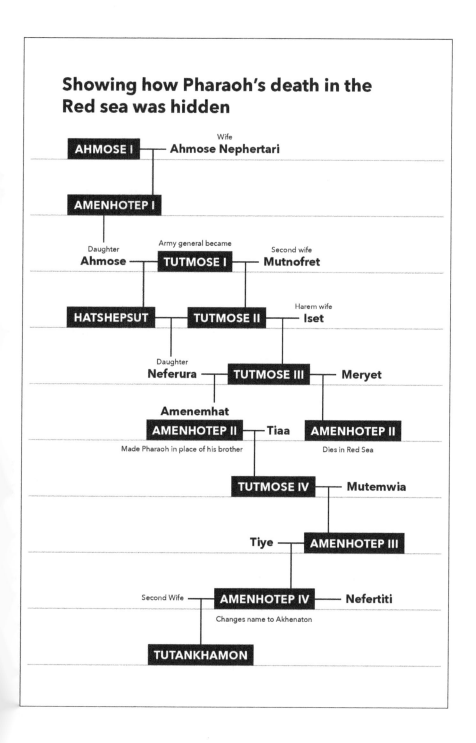

Showing how Pharaoh's death in the Red sea was hidden

AHMOSE I — Wife **Ahmose Nephertari**

AMENHOTEP I

Daughter **Ahmose** — Army general became **TUTMOSE I** — Second wife **Mutnofret**

HATSHEPSUT — **TUTMOSE II** — Harem wife **Iset**

Daughter **Neferura** — **TUTMOSE III** — **Meryet**

Amenemhat
AMENHOTEP II — **Tiaa** **AMENHOTEP II**
Made Pharaoh in place of his brother   Dies in Red Sea

TUTMOSE IV — **Mutemwia**

Tiye — **AMENHOTEP III**

Second Wife — **AMENHOTEP IV** — **Nefertiti**
Changes name to Akhenaton

TUTANKHAMON

Appendix

The High chronology of Egyptian dates fits with the Biblical facts

The date of the Exodus in 1446 BC, fits most closely with the reign of Amenhotep ll. His father Tutmose lll, (who died in 1450 in line with the High Chronology), was one of the longest reigning Pharaohs and during his reign, Moses hides in Midian for 40 years. Then Exodus 2 v 23, says "After a long time the King of Egypt died." Not many Pharaohs reigned for 'a long time' like Tutmose lll, so this gives another confirmation that we have identified the correct period of history for the Exodus.

Store cites of Ramesses and Pithom

Store cities built in the Delta for the storage of grain, as opposed to Capital city of Pi-Ramesses which was built in same area but in a later reign, ie 200 years later in the time of Ramesses ll.

Recognising the effect that the Hebrew slaves had Tutmose lll's ability to go to war

The story of the Hebrew people in Egypt and their Exodus is universall: denied among secular Egyptologists. Even among those who accept th biblical record, their dating of the Exodus is rarely in line with the dating give in the bible; (see article on Dating the Exodus in Appendix.)

More recently some archaeologists have come to accept the biblical datin which lines up with an Exodus around 1446, but I have never read anywhere recognition of the profound effect that the slavery of the Hebrews had c Egypt's history, because they were a vital part of Egypt's war machine.

The wars of Tutmose lll

To provide Tutmose lll with large numbers of trained soldiers, the peasant farmers who became his full-time troops had to have their farm work done by others. This was the great advantage that the slaves provided for Tutmose.

The slaves could grow vast quantities of food to feed the country, freeing the Egyptian peasant farmers to train as crack troops in Tutmose's' army.

Tutmose could campaign year after year, going to war 17 times in 20 years against Canaan and Syria and leaving garrisons in each defeated town to maintain control. In this way, each campaign built on the previous year's work, as he slowly gained control of Canaan then Syria.

He could not have done this without his large slave population, who were "doing all kinds of field work"; (Exodus 1 v 11-14). Raising livestock. Growing and storing grain in the store cities of Ramesses and Pithom which they had built. "They (the Egyptians) made their (the Hebrews') lives bitter in hard labour with brick and mortar and with all kinds of work in the fields."

With the Exodus, when the slaves left, in the time of Tutmose's son Amenhotep ll, Egypt's war machine was broken and this powerful Empire was forced to make peace with her sworn enemy, Naharin / Mitanni.

But it does not stop there. In later books I will be telling the story of how the Exodus caused Egypt to lose much of her revenue, first from Syria in the reign of Amenhotep ll and Tutmose lV, and how the Hebrew entry into Canaan caused the loss of revenues from Canaan during the reigns of Amenhotep lll and Amenhotep lV. This last-named Pharaoh turned so vehemently against Amun, the pre-eminent god of Egypt at the time of the Exodus, that he closed the great Temple of Amun at Karnak. He was so angry with Amun for his impotence in the face of the Hebrew God Yahweh, that he forbade the use of the word 'Amun' in anyone's name and even removed it from his own name Amenhotep. He changed his own name from Amenhotep ɔ Akhenaten to remove the name of Amun from his name and replace it with ιe ancient god, the Aten.

Moses the Exodus and a family feud Brilliant article on dating Exodus

https://www.academia.edu/s/a9024dea3e?source=ai_email

Some of the characters encountered in this story

Tutmose lll son of Tutmose ll reigned for 54 years from !504 – 1450 BC

Menkheperreseneb the High Priest of Amun under Tutmose lll. Incidentally his name means—'Tutmose is healthy', suggesting that this was in question.

Nepherure daughter of Hatshepsut and Tutmose ll

Jala There is an unnamed Cushite woman in the biblical record whom Moses marries after the Exodus. There is only one brief reference to her with no details of her life. I have created a story around her and named her Jala.

Amenemhat is a key player. He is Habiri, but before the Exodus would have used an Egyptian name, so I have called him Amenemhat. He is Moses' brother and after the Exodus reverts to his Habiri name, Aaron. I have created the story around him as the bible gives us very few facts about Aaron before the exodus

Senenmut/Moshe See the note in the introduction.

Jethro. In the biblical record Jethro is Moses' Midianite father -in- law, sometimes called Reuel.

Zipporah. In the biblical record Zipporah is Moses' Midianite wife.

Hobab. In the biblical record Hobab is Moses' Midianite brother-in-law.

Languages and scrips used by the Hebrews

I found this interesting article on a site www.chabad.org but it is no longe there. This is a precis of that article.

Language and writing

Since the beginning of the Hebrew nation, they have used 2 differei languages and 2 different scripts.

a) Scripts;

i)   The Alphabet used by the Phoenicians called the Paleo or Ear Hebrew script and

ii) The Assyrian script used in the time of Ezra, in Babylon, which loo like the modern Hebrew alphabet.

b) **Languages;** 2 different languages were used at different times.

i) The sacred Hebrew language spoken from the beginning

ii) The Aramaic language of Babylon spoken since the Exile; the language spoken by Jesus.

c) **Present day Israel has chosen one of each**

Israel has adopted the ancient Hebrew language but writes it in the Assyrian script which was adopted during the time of Ezra and the exile.

Dating of the Exodus How did two different dates arise?

In 1822, Jean-Francois Champollion, the French Egyptologist and linguist achieved his first true breakthrough in the translation of Egyptian hieroglyphics, with the decipherment of the two Pharaonic names, 'Ramesses' and 'Tutmose'. This must have caused great excitement throughout the world of biblical scholarship, because the Bible had always retained the name 'Ramesses' in the opening chapter of the book of Exodus. 'Ramesses' was a store city, built for the storage of grain and it was built by the Hebrew slaves.

From there it was a logical step to equate the name of that store city, 'Ramesses', with the most famous of the Ramesside kings Ramesses ll, and the famous Capital City he built, Pi-Ramesses, equating the two cities as one, and connecting Ramesses ll with the date of the Exodus. But these were major mistakes, which set biblical scholars on a false trail, culminating in the erroneous theory we now have of an Exodus in the time of Ramesses ll's son Merneptah, the theory of 'the late date Exodus'. This is exactly what we find in the writings of Amelia Edwards in her book 'A thousand miles up the Nile' She visited Egypt in 1873-4 and wrote of it, including a chapter on Ramesses ll whom she describes as the persecutor of the Hebrews with his son Mernepta as the Pharaoh of the Exodus.

But the huge Capital city of Pi-Ramesses became a source confusion for another reason. The search was now on to find the site of Pi-Ramesses and when in the 1930s Pierre Montet found statues of Ramesses ll at Tanis appeared that the site had been found. Those who understood that the store city of Ramesses was distinct from the capital city of Pi- Ramesses, and built earlier, still expected that the two cities were built on the same site. However, it was found that the statues and buildings of Pi-Ramesses, found by Pierre Montet stood on virgin land, with no older buildings on the site. It therefore had to be assumed that Ramesses the store city and Pi-Ramesses the Capital city were built at the same time, in the time of Ramesses ll.

Slowly, as the new science of Egyptology made discoveries and the world of the Pharaohs was uncovered, it became clear that the Biblical dates given for the Exodus did not match with the time of the Ramesside kings. But the evidence at Tanis still stood, and so a division occurred between archaeology and the Bible. Archaeologists who still believed in an Exodus started looking for an Exodus in the 1300s or 1200s BC, the time of Ramesses ll and his son Merneptah.

Then in the 1960s, Manfred Bietak's painstaking work led to an extraordinary breakthrough. Bietak realised that the city of Pi-Ramesses had been positioned on the easternmost branch of the Nile, the Pelusiac branch. This branch had become blocked over time by silt, but he was able to follow its course, and discovered the bases of huge statues, cut off at the ankles in present day Quantir. He then realised that the entire city, instead of being abandoned, had been transported 30 miles northeast to Tanis where statues without their bases were found. This gave an understanding that the original site of Pi-Ramesses was at Quantir, and this site was much older than Tanis. So it was clear that the store city built by the slaves could well have predated the time of Ramesses ll and the building of Pi-Ramesses, in line with the biblical dating of the Exodus. But by now much work had already been done to find evidence of an Exodus in the time of Ramesses ll and his son Merneptah and so the late date Exodus had become established.

In fact, the Bible has many texts dating the Exodus, but none of them point to the time of the Ramesside kings and their heirs who came too late on the scene to be involved. Instead, the bible clearly points to an Exodus in 1446 BC which in the High Egyptian Chronology is in the reign of Amenhotep ll,) as I explain below. It is a remarkable record.

I Kings 6 v 1 states that Solomon started building the Temple in the 4th year of his reign, 480 years since the Exodus. We know that Solomon's 4th year was 966 BC, thus fixing the Exodus in 1446 BC.

In Judges 9 v 11 Jethro states that by his day, 300 years had passed since the Hebrews entered Canaan. Jethro was one of the last judges of the pre-monarchy. He lived around 1100 BC, before both Saul and David. (David's date is around 1000 BC). Adding 300 years to the 1100 date gives us 1400 BC, the correct period of the Hebrews entry into Canaan.

Now let's look at the promises to Abraham
God's first promise to Abraham is in Genesis 12 v 2&3 when he is about 70 years old. We know this is 430 years before the Exodus because Paul tells us in Galatians 3.

In Galatians 3, Paul gives us a time span of 430 years, from the first promise to Abraham to the Exodus when Moses was given the Law.

He says that the law was given (by Moses) 430 years after God made his promise to Abraham. So the 430 years covers Abraham's years from the time the first promise was given, all of Isaac's life and Jacob's time in Canaan before he went to Egypt, plus the time the Hebrews were in Egypt. This makes it clear that the Hebrews were not in Egypt for the whole 430 years.

The next time God makes a promise to Abraham is 30 years later.

In Genesis 15, God says "for four hundred years your descendants will be strangers in a land not their own."

The text also states that they will be 'enslaved'. Isaac and Jacob lived in Canaan for 190 years, from the birth of Isaac until Jacob went to Egypt. They were not enslaved but were "strangers in a land not their own," and oppressed by the Canaanites. Then Jacob went with his family to Egypt to join Joseph and there, later, they were enslaved.

This promise to Abraham in Genesis 15 is the hardest to decipher.

It covers a lot of ground and is confusing. I have found a paper by Moshe Anbar of Tel Aviv university who suggests that Genesis 15 is a combination of two separate narratives.

But the text of Exodus 12.v 40 in the Samaritan Pentateuch version helps clarify the meaning of Genesis 15 as it covers the same ground; it is as follows—

"Now the sojourning of the children of Israel AND THE FATHERS OF THEM WHO DWELT IN CANAAN AND EGYPT, was four hundred and thirty years.

So the 430 years includes the time of Abraham Isaac and Jacob in Canaan before the family went to Egypt, as well as the years in Egypt.

As it is 30 years longer it must include the period of Abrahams life when he was in Canaan before Isaac's birth.

Adding up the dates

1   Paul tells us that there were 430 years from God's first promise to Abraham and the giving of the Law to Moses just after the Exodus. So from the first promise given to Abraham, 430 years pass before the Exodus.

2   God's first promise to Abraham Genesis 12 v 2&3 when he is about 70 years old.

"I will make you a great nation"

3   30 years pass until the birth of Isaac, (when Abraham was 100 years old).

4   Genesis 25 v 26 states that Isaac is 60 years old when Jacob was born.

5   Genesis 47 v 8 states that Jacob is 130 years old when he goes to Egypt.

TOTAL 220 years

5   The remainder of the 430 years, another 210 years, the Hebrews are in Egypt, first under the Hyksos kings who welcomed them, then under the New Kingdom Pharaohs who forced them into slavery for around 80 years.

All the above point to an Exodus around 1446 and must be explained away if the Exodus is to be dated after 1300 BC.

My understanding of the names Senenmut and Mose/ Moses / Moshe

The evidence we have from Egypt and the bible suggests that the man known in Egypt as Senenmut was the adopted son of the Pharaoh's daughter, Hatshepsut, an infant she found abandoned when she herself was very young, living at the Harem in Men-nepher.[364]

In my first book, 'The King and her children', Hatshepsut names her adopted son, 'Men-messes', meaning 'my son'. '**Messes**' means 'son' as in 'Ra**messes**', son of 'Ra', the sun god, and is the same word as '**mose**', as in 'Tut**mose**', son of 'Thoth' the god of wisdom. Remember that vowels are not indicated in hieroglyphs and have to be assumed.

During Mose's childhood, there was no son born to Pharaoh Tutmose ll and his wife Hatshepsut, only one daughter, Nepherure. But Hatshepsut hoped her adopted son would be accepted as a future pharaoh. And if he was given a wife, the royal heiress, Nepherure, her daughter, his kingship would have been confirmed. But when Mose was 16 years of age, a son was born to Tutmose ll by a harem woman, and on his father death, two years later, this child became Pharaoh Tutmose lll.

Now Hatshepsut's plans were thwarted, preventing her from making her adopted son king. She was made Regent for the new child pharaoh, but he was not strong and may die, giving her a second chance to put Senenmut on the throne. Hatshepsut also realised, that as Regent she could not pass the throne to Senenmut, but if she made herself Pharaoh, she would have more chance doing so.

It was an acceptable practice to have two pharaohs when one was old and may not live, so why not when one was young and may not live? So Hatshepsut had an excuse to make herself Pharaoh, which she did.

But now Mose saw the temptation that his mother faced, to help nature along and make sure the young Tutmose did not live. Realising this, 'when he came of age', probably around the age of 17, we are told (in the book of Hebrews) that 'Moses refused to be called the Son of Pharaoh's daughter,'[365] removing himself as a possible rival to Tutmose, because he knew his mother's ambition could lead to murder. She did not want her dead husband's child to rule Egypt. She wanted her adopted son to rule.

So Mose deliberately stepped back from his high position. He changed his name, removing the name 'son' and instead creates a name making himself Hatshepsut's brother. 'Senenmut' means 'mother's brother'. They were close in age, with less than 10 years between them so this was a logical conclusion that retained the kinship.

As Senenmut, Hatshepsut's right-hand man, Mose achieved great fame both in Egypt and beyond. Joyce Tyldesley, the well-known Egyptologists in her book 'Hatshepsut', writes a chapter entirely about him, entitled—

'The Greatest of the Great'.

But when his enemies, the supporters of Tutmose, force him to flee Egypt, Senenmut must 'disappear', and to do so he must get rid of his name. But what name should he use? He returns to the childhood name his mother gave him when she adopted him, Mose, known to us as 'Moses'.

In this second book, 'The Napoleon of Egypt' I have used the name Moshe instead of Mose as it is in more common use today.

---

[64] Men-nepher was the ancient name for Memphis
[65] The bible, book of Hebrews 11 v24

The route of the Exodus and the naming of Sinai

There are many aspects of the Exodus that are uncertain, and I am endeavouring to examine these in a series of articles and suggest the most logical scenario.

In this article I do not wish to negate the miraculous way God intervened in the story of the Exodus. But God often uses natural phenomena in an extreme way to bring about his plans, such as the plagues of frogs and gnats, boils and hail. The miracle is in the exaggeration of natural things and events, and their timing. So now let us look at the title and contents of this article.

'The route of the Exodus and the naming of Sinai', under numbered headings.

1)   The name and correct location of Sinai

As far as we know, the words 'Sinai' and 'Horeb' are unknown in Egyptian records. The peninsula between the present-day Suez Canal, and the ancient border of Egypt at the El Arish River, was known in Egyptian history as 'the Mafkat', meaning the 'land of turquoise'. because this valuable stone had been mined there since the dawn of history.

In the bible, Sinai was the mountain where, after the Exodus, Moses was given the Law by God. Because this mountain was presumed to be in the peninsula east of Egypt, the peninsula was also given the name Sinai, but this is almost certainly a mistake.

The first reference we have to the mountain we call 'Sinai' is recorded

Exodus 3 and is the story of Moses and the burning bush. There is no doubt that this event took place in Midian, which lay on the east coast of the Gulf of Aqaba, nowhere near the peninsula called Sinai. Moses is attending to his father-in-law's sheep and takes them to the 'far side of the mountains, to the wilderness'. The mountain is named here in the text as 'Horeb', but the 'Illustrated Bible dictionary published by Tyndale, identifies Horeb and Sinai as one and the same. Could it be that 'Horeb' is the Midianite name and 'Sinai' the later Hebrew name. We do not know. It is also possible that the name 'Sinai' has come from the name of the moon god 'Sin', but if this god once had a connection with this area, this information has been lost.

At the burning bush, God directs Moses to go to Egypt. He tells Moses that when he has brought the Hebrews out of Egypt, he, Moses will bring them to worship God on this mountain. This is the occasion when Moses is given the first part of the Law, by God, and we know that this occurred at 'Mount Sinai'.

So we can conclude that 'Mount Sinai' is in Midian. This is confirmed by St Paul in his letter to the Galatians, 4 v 25, where he states that Hagar represents 'Sinai',' **in Arabia'**, where God gave the Law to Moses, confirming the geographical position of this mountain. It also has had periods in the past when it was volcanic which fits the story of the giving of the Law in Exodus 19 v 18.

Ancient Midian is now largely in Saudi Arabia, with a small area in Jordan. There is an Arab tradition that 'Mount Sinai', the mountain where God gave Moses the Law, is the same mountain as the one known today as 'Jebel Larz.' It is in Saudi Arabia, and the Arabs consider their land to be a 'holy land' because of the presence of this holy mountain.

Again, the Illustrated Bible Dictionary p 1460 says that Sinai used to be thought to be in Midian but is now uncertain.

But if Mount Sinai is in ancient Midian, who decided that it was in the peninsula east of Egypt? It is generally believed that it was Helena, mother of the first Emperor Constantine, who was herself a Christian and was very interested in identifying biblical sites. She thought she had identified the mountain of the 'Burning Bush' and set up a religious house at its base, that was later developed by the emperor Justinian into the well-known St

Catherine's monastery on the same site. The naming of the mountain as Sinai led to the naming of the peninsula as Sinai.

2) 'You will never see the Egyptians again'

Exodus 14 v 13. During the Exodus, the Hebrews realise they are being pursued by the Egyptians and they are terrified. God says to Moses, tell the people that 'the Egyptians who you see today, you will never see again, for ever.'

This promise is pretty clear. So after the Exodus it will not be possible for the Egyptians to harass the Hebrews any more. They will never see them again. Where could the Hebrews go where they would never see Egyptians again?

Looking at a map we see that the peninsula known as Sinai is adjacent to Egypt. In fact Egypt had controlled, and continued to control this peninsula, all through history. Its mountains towards the southeast had been mined by Egypt for copper and turquoise for millennia, and they continued to do so. The Egyptian army travelled across the peninsula constantly on route to Canaan which was subject to Egyptian rule. The Hebrews were wandering for 40 years, and they were a vast company of people, so if they were never to meet Egyptians, they could not have been living in this area.

On the other hand, if we follow the thinking that the people crossed into Midian which lies on the eastern shore of the Gulf of Aqaba, as the Illustrated Bible Dictionary says was previously believed, they would not be exposed to any contact with the Egyptians.

3) Water

The peninsula called Sinai had very limited access to water with only seasonal rain filling its few transient rivers. We know that God provided water miraculously twice, in emergencies during the Exodus period, but this does not seem to be a repeated pattern, and they moved around what was called 'the wilderness', many times in the long period of the 'wanderings'. They were huge company of people, with their flocks and herds, living for 40 years in hot wilderness. So there must have been a supply of water that we are not told about.

If we look at the present-day deserts of Jordan and Saudi Arabi, which cover ancient Midian, it does not seem any more promising. But this is not the case. In fact, there are huge underground aquafers of fresh water, under these deserts even to this day. The city of Aqaba uses this as its water supply still, and Saudi Arabia uses it to grow vegetables in the desert. The water has come from snow melt from the mountains to the north and gathered in the rock layers over millennia. It is probable that the water table was also much nearer the surface in ancient times when it had not been tapped by large thirsty cities as it is now. This body of water was and is still, vast, and would have been available for the people to access from wells. Any number of wells. Easily supplying their needs for 40 years.

4)   Could the slaves have reached the west coast of the Gulf of Aqaba (one branch of the Red Sea) before being overtaken by the Egyptians?

We know from the Exodus record that they had carts with them with which to carry the young and old. The adults were strong. Very strong. They had been slaves, required to do very hard unrelenting work. Any weak among them would not have survived. I think we can assume that God chose a time of year when there would not have been vulnerable young animals in the herds. They left Egypt after gathering at Succoth, believed to be the fort of Tharu, as this was the only substantial bridge crossing the canal forming the border into Egypt proper, at its junction with the peninsula called Sinai. This was where the army crossed when entering the peninsula. The distance from here to the Nuweiba beach on the coast of the Gulf of Aqaba, is 167 miles. There is a record of Moshe Dyan, the Israeli military General, in the late 1900s, making a similar crossing on foot, in the other direction, with his men in 6 days. I know relatively sedentary men, in their sixties, who have walked 33 miles in a day in 'Thames Path Challenge'. And the Hebrews had every motivation to cross this terrain. They were escaping from slavery. With all things considered, this doable in my opinion.

The text of Exodus 12 is informative. It is the story of the first Passover which was to last 7 days and during this time all their bread was to be leavened bread only. On the night they left Egypt, the slaves had just eaten a nourishing meal of roast lamb, as much as they wanted to eat. Now they were told to leave immediately. It was night. Verse 34 says they took their dough before it could rise. Enough for 7 days. These were the rules of the Passover in order that they would remember this night and this journey. Roast lamb, then 7 days of unleavened bread; chapter 12 v 15. It is a picture of this Exodus. They were escaping. It took 7 days until they had crossed the Red Sea. So this is the time scale I have used in my story. They travelled at night, guided by the 'pillar of fire' God provided. They ate and slept during the hottest part of the day then continued their walk as evening fell. They crossed the Gulf of Aqaba on the seventh night and reached the shore of Midian as dawn was breaking.

5) How could the Gulf of Aqaba be the place of the Red Sea crossing?

The Gulf of Aqaba is about 11 miles across. There is a huge beach on the Egyptian side called 'Nuweiba' where the people gathered after coming through the narrow passes between the huge mountains of the peninsular of Sinai.

More interesting and relevant, is the fact that the Gulf of Aqaba is part of the junction between the earth's Asian and African continental plates. This junction runs south from the Jordan valley, down the Gulf of Aqaba, continuing as the Great Rift Valley of east Africa. So we might logically expect seismic movement to occur here. It occurs to this day.

The story of the Exodus suggests seismic activity in other places. The plague of darkness 'that could be felt' could well have been caused by ash from volcanic activity on the Island of 'Thera' north of Egypt in the Mediterranean Sea. There had been minor eruptions on Thera for centuries causing the population of Thera and Crete, the Philistines, to leave these dangerous islands and settle elsewhere. And it is possible that the last great explosion of the Island of Thera happened when the Hebrews were about to cross the Red Sea in 1446 BC. It would have destabilised the whole region. And where the continental plates met, was the most likely point of movement. One of these junctions was the Gulf of Aqaba.

The return of the sea which took out the Pharaoh and his army, sounds very like a Tsunami. And I found an article recently describing a 4-meter-high tsunami that took place in the Gulf of Aqaba in the 1990s damaging the village at Nuweiba beach. The article, in the scientific publication, 'Science Daily' went on to give warning that industries around the coast of the Gulf of Aqaba must make contingency plans for future tsunamis that could be damaging to their infrastructure.

About the author

ANNETTE WAS BORN IN SYDNEY Australia, spent some formative years in Central Africa, but was largely schooled in the UK. Her first profession was physiotherapy followed by motherhood, then beekeeping.

A visit to Egypt in 2010 alerted her to the mysteries surrounding the royal heiress, Hatshepsut, the subject of her first book, 'The King and her children'. Why, after leading Egypt as pharaoh for 22 successful years, was all record of Hatshepsut's reign, wiped out by those who followed? What had she done? Egyptologists have no real answer. But there is one.

With a fair knowledge of the biblical record, Annette saw that this period of Egypt's 'New Kingdom' history, coincided with that of the Hebrew slavery. So how did Egypt benefit from this nation of slaves?

It is after Hatshepsut's death that the facts emerge, as Egypt enters her great Empire building stage, under Tutmose lll Hatshepsut's successor. Tutmose had the manpower to wage war on the Levant and Syria continuously for 20 years without impoverishing Egypt. But how? He uses the slaves to grow all the country's food, so freeing vast numbers of Egyptian peasant farmers to train as his permanent army. As a result, Tutmose never loses a battle.

So, with her knowledge of biblical history and her research into Egyptology, Annette's second novel. *'The Napoleon of Egypt'*, uncovers proof of the Hebrew slavery in Egypt, so long denied.

Bibliography

The Complete Royal Families of Ancient Egypt, *Aidan Dobson / Dyan Hilton*

Ancient Records of Egypt Vol 2, Eighteenth Dynasty, *James Henry Breasted*

War in Ancient Egypt, *Anthony J. Spalinger*

The Monuments of Senenmut, *Peter Dorman*

Mistress of the House, Mistress of Heaven, Women in Ancient Egypt, essays *edited by Markoe/Capel*

Amenhotep lll *by Arielle P. Kozloff*

The Armana Letters, *Moran*

A Commentary on the Exodus *by Duane A. Garrett.*

The Bible

The Septuagint

Milton Keynes UK
Ingram Content Group UK Ltd.
UKHW012024170823
427054UK00001B/144